OF THE CITY OF THE SAVED...

...of its diverse citizenry and of its sundry divinities, with a disquisition on the protocols of history

by Philip *Purser-Hallard*

mad norwegian press | new orleans

Faction Paradox Books from Mad Norwegian Press...

Author's Dedication: *In honour of a promise of long standing, this novel is dedicated to Helen Angove and Matthew Graham, on the occasion of their engagement to be married.*

Happy sixth anniversary, guys.
Hope the offspring isn't keeping you up too much.

www.madnorwegian.com

Cover art by Steve Johnson.
Jacket & interior design by Metaphorce Designs.
www.metaphorcedesigns.com

ISBN0-9725959-4-5
Printed in Illinois. First Edition: April 2004.

THE STORY SO FAR

The War. A conflict so primal that for most of the population of history, it can only be thought of as a "War in Heaven". Now in its forty-eighth year (at least from the point of view of those directly involved), but intersecting the continuum throughout the span of causality and across battle-lines too large to be recognised by non-combatants, it's a War that isn't just *fought* but re-written, redefined and re-imagined with every new confrontation. It can best be described as a dispute over the twin territories of "cause" and "effect", and some of the participants are as follows...

The Great Houses. The immovable, untouchable bloodlines which have - traditionally - been seen as responsible not only for the current structure of history but for the fact that history *has* a structure at all.

Ancient, aristocratic and prone to in-fighting, the Houses were there before anybody else, and all other known cultures (humanity included) can be thought of as nth-generation copies. Great House technology goes some way beyond gross machinery, but the Houses are best-known for their timeships, although "ship" might be a misleading term as these vessels are complex historical events in themselves and tend to look like people on the outside anyway.

The Great Houses' War-time enemy is the first recorded challenge to their authority, and even the fact that there *is* a War suggests that something has gone very, very wrong. (The enemy's exact nature isn't relevant to this current story. The politics of the Houses themselves are hard enough to follow.)

Faction Paradox. The Fallen Angel among Great Houses, the bloodline which has consistently refused to follow the protocols of House society, and which has found itself utterly rejected by the Houses' Homeworld as a result.

Composed of renegades, ritualists, saboteurs and subterfugers, the Faction is now part criminal syndicate and part "family", the only bloodline to recruit the lesser species (humanity included) into its ranks... something the other Houses consider to be in remarkably bad taste.

And since the other Houses insist on seeing themselves as immortal, the Faction's agents commonly adhere to basic death-cult imagery. Their masks are made from the skulls of things that shouldn't really have been born; their weapons are bonded to their shadows, *not* carried; and underneath it all is a philosophy that's as much about sacrifice as temporal theory. Since natural childbirth disgusts the Houses as much as the thought of dying, Faction cells throughout history - like many of Earth's voodoo-cults - tend to use family titles: the Cousins, who make up the biggest part of the Faction's membership, are theoretically under the control of the Mothers, Fathers, Godfathers and Godmothers who rule from the hidden parliament of the Eleven-Day Empire.

Technically, Faction Paradox is neutral in the War, meaning that it'll get in *anybody's* way if it wants to.

Compassion. Originally the quite human Laura Tobin, her body and identity were re-constructed over the course of several generations (in circumstances *far* too complicated to explain here) so that each successive version of herself was biologically better-adapted to the Great Houses' technology. The end result was that the fifth and final Laura Tobin became Compassion, the first human / timeship hybrid, and - thanks to the Houses' War-time breeding programme - the "mother" of all modern timeships. As such she's become legendary, even though she obviously never wanted to be.

The City of the Saved. An enclave located beyond the end of the conventional Universe, a self-contained society the size of a spiral galaxy, the City serves as home to every single human being who ever lived. Whether the City's inhabitants are perfect recreations of the entire human species, or somehow really *are* the resurrected originals, is a matter of scientific and ontological debate.

The Founders who built the City have never been revealed, so the truth isn't likely to become public knowledge in the near future. Though one of the War-time powers is generally believed responsible, its identity (and motives) are unclear even to the City's inhabitants.

For more detailed information about any of these subjects, see *The Book of the War*.

NOTE

The City of the Saved, Resurrection Day

Dear Laura,

I hope you don't mind being called "Laura". Apparently you prefer "Tobin" under normal circumstances – but when you've reconstituted someone, body mind and soul, without corrupting their most delicate details, you'll feel entitled to talk as if you know them. And we certainly don't want to get into the convoluted implications of calling you "Compassion".

Anyway. In case you're wondering, this isn't a pain-induced hallucination or a near-death experience. It's real. You died – 'obviously', you're thinking. So fine. Work out the rest for yourself, I know you prefer it that way.

Speaking of which...

Resurrection can be an excellent opportunity to pursue a second career. Particularly for you, Laura, since security as such is going to be rather redundant here in the City of the Saved. I wonder, would you consider private investigation? The pay's good, and you get to make your own hours.

(You've just stopped reading, haven't you? You'll fish this out of the bin again later, though, so hear me out.)

There are certain social functions that will always need fulfilling, no matter how utopian a culture's framework. Tracking down friends and family from someone's first life, for instance, among a population with so many zeroes on the end that it makes you feel ill. There's going to be a lot of doubt and confusion here in the City for the first century or so, and people like you can help make sense of it.

A private eye is the archetypal urban job. An icon of City life. The City of the Saved will need investigators as much as it does cab drivers, bartenders and – unfortunately – politicians.

You'll reassure your fellow Citizens that the truth, though hard to nail down, is solid and unyielding and real. They'll lap it up.

No pressure, Laura, just think about it. There's plenty of time.

Fondest regards,

A Friend.

VOCES POPULI

'What they don't tell you about the City – what you'd never guess, from all the picaresques and travelogues they write, back in the Universe – is that there's no sky. Just that white dome, unfathomably high, roofing the firmament. In day, dull white like unmarked paper, at night an empty screen that you could write yourself across. Snow or soot, and the charcoal shades between: no cobalt, azure, sapphire... I don't think so many of us would migrate to the Great Parks, to live the rural life there under artificial suns, if they gave the rest of us some real sky. I miss the stars.'

'It's magic here. All these people to meet, get to know, shag, whatever. You never know who you're going to run into next. Or what species, even, with all these Neanderthals and posthumans and all that lot. I met this guy the other day, tall black bloke, you'll have seen him around... yeah, with the red eyes and the little horns. Turns out he's from the 82nd century! The horns are surgically implanted, apparently, but he got so used to them he woke up with them here. He's got these other things too... those aren't his only alterations, if you catch my drift. It's mad here – one day you're shagging a techno-demigod from the far future, next day it's a sweet Arab lad from some Caliph's harem. Day after you run into bloody Barry from Bolton. I love it!'

'Many compare the City of the Saved to this or that city they knew, Hong Kong or Babylon or Siloportem. To me, the City is like Aksum at its zenith. I knew Aksum when its streets swarmed with men and women of every people in the world... Egyptians, Amharites and Kushites from close by our borders, pale Greeks and Arabs from the north, Indians and Persians and Tamils from across the ocean. Among our granite obelisks and church towers you might find synagogues, or shrines to Osiris or the Buddha... The City is Aksum at its height, only bigger, all-encompassing and perfect. It is how I always imagined Heaven would be.'

'Oh, but the awful thing about the City is that it's so *Last Universe*. I mean, it's all been *done*... Just look at this square. This façade to the left is a terrible generic Baroque, and opposite it is that *dreary* 22nd-century Grandiose portico. Over there we have a horrible mixture of Op Art with what looks like the work of a drunken Byzantine with a *phallus fixation*. And over here, shop fronts that wouldn't have looked out of place in Renaissance Italy, until they put in that *ghastly* holo-arcade. It's all cheap, knock-down copies. Our so-called Secret Architects couldn't design a *garden fence* without it coming out looking vulgar and tawdry.'

'So young they are, so very young. It sounds absurd, but most of them have lived for longer here than they did in their first lifetimes. Three hundred years... a moment. A breath, a heartbeat to such as us. I was so ready, so contented after nineteen thousand years, to cease. I would desist: no more of life. I had been everyone I wanted, everyone I could be, so I thought. Where was the point in continuing? So I turned my face towards death, and its feathered touch caressed my bloodstream, bearing me away, I thought to oblivion. But no... to here, the City. Here I am an appendix, an addendum to the whole person I once was. And they... the younger ones, those frantic children of the earliest human races, see this brief efflorescence as the life everlasting. That pleasure, passing though it is, I cannot begrudge them, whatever the consequences for myself.'

'My note – oh yes, I got one, don't look so surprised – *my* note said I could be a brilliant musician if I worked terribly terribly hard, or I could sit on my backside drinking champagne and looking decorative. Well, which did the Founders *think* I was going to choose? Oh, is that mine? Thank you, you *are* a dear.'

'...surrounding me, pressing in on all sides, the *others*. The Jews with their hard eyes, the stinking Negroes and the Chinese, leering at me with their foreign faces. The ape-men, tiny eyes under their beetle brows, shambling along the pavement, pushing past me as I climb onto the Tube, their stench... the men-women, leering at me from their painted faces, chests and crotches bulging obscenely... the machine-people with their microscope-eyes, staring into me, taking me apart with the adding-machines they call their minds. I am besieged by the sub-human and the non-human, the un-men and the wrong-men, and how can I know, how can I even now be certain that my *mind itself* has not been tainted...?'

'Rivermade. Questioning / seeking? Leftwards. Inside the beautiful. It understands the metalkin. Without one. Under the tall benighted. Made a veil. Announce / withdraw. Asymptotic. Benighted. Under the leftward beautiful without. Either it flies or neverable. Riverlaid. Severance / wish-fulfilment? Apologise. Apocryphise. Apologise. Upon the terminus / approach inside the metaldrum. Supposition innate to all. Without the thing / wasp / current it melts. Riverjade. Deliverable. West device the plasticone. Among. Apologise. Announcement of the interspite amongme. Limbic everly. Without. Within. Without...'

'I would crush them with my teeth if the gods would grant me the chance! These beardless cowards, I would cleave their limbs from their lights, and grind their bones with my shield. I would drink mead from the skulls of their sons, and gratify myself upon their daughters, and dedicate the banquet to the Thunderer...! I expect many of you feel the same way. The City lifestyle can get kind of frustrating to people of our background, which is why I started this group, back in forty-six...'

'Yeah, I *know*. Point is, I was invulnerable then, too. Back in the Universe. Invincible Man, they called me. See my skin? Sentient nanopolymer. Totally impregnable. This guy created it in the lab where I was working as a security guard, but then it got loose and... ah, never mind. It made me someone, back then. Being invulnerable. I stood out. Here I'm a loser in a plastic sheath.'

'I've got a lovely view from up here. Nice bluefern trees, all down the road – we never had those at home – and the little birds singing in them in the mornings. See all the houses? So pretty – red roofs, then those blue ones, then the river and the bridge... The park, the other side, where the kiddies play, then the cliff face where the cavemen live. See that one with the window box? That's Mrs. Mountain Lion Pelt and her husband Bent Ear, I see her at the bingo every Wednesday... and that's the Watchtower in the distance. So thin, it looks, doesn't it? That's as big around as Australia, that is. Pardon? Oh, it was a continent, dear. Not a very big one.'

'...and Monkey laughed high and loud to see Goose eat the berries. Soon Goose felt ill, so he lay down on the path and groaned. And then his bowels emptied, and his droppings spattered behind him on the path; then he retched, and all the stones came up out of his crop and made a pile in front of his beak. Then Goose felt better, and he waddled off to fill his crop again, and see if he could find more bright red berries to eat, because he was a very stupid bird. But all the droppings he had spilled turned into the worlds and stars of the Universe, and the pile of stones from his crop became the City. Then Monkey came, and saw the tiny creatures living in Goose's droppings, and he felt bad that he had given Goose the poison berries. So he began to pick the creatures out, one by one, and set them down among the stones...'

'But here is what troubles me, Father. The church – our Mother Church – teaches us that the City is the true Heaven, that God is here among us everywhere, invisible. And that, by His grace, no human soul was damned, but all have been judged fit for Heaven. But what of the aliens, Father, God's other children? Could His grace not have extended to them too? The Church tells that they had no souls to save, that all have passed on to merciful oblivion, but why? Surely God could have granted them souls as He did humanity, and saved all His creations. And then there are the other "churches", Father, with their heretical ideas...'

'Listen, why d'you think they call it the City of the *Saved*, eh? You remember the PCs we used to have on Earth – the *computers*, mate, remember? You used to have to say whether you wanted to keep a file or chuck it? Yeah? Well, if you kept it, it was called a *saved* file. God, all these religious nutters reckon the City's some kind of Heaven, that "Saved" means like, salvation and that shit. We're data files, that's all. We're data, mate, and the City's software, and it's running on this fuck-off great big mainframe the size of... the fucking Sun or something.

You've got to open your eyes to reality, mate. You see these red pills...?'

'It's taking a while to track down my previous incarnations. It was strange at first, to think of all my selves, brought here together. The French Revolutionary I found quite quickly – he'd set up a commune in Tantamount District, and I just saw him on the news one day. He's a rationalist, of course, doesn't believe in reincarnation. I can be so blinkered sometimes. The Ottoman prince and the geisha I tracked down through Friends Reincarnated. The Jewish slave-girl was more difficult, and I've still not found the Mediaeval nun...'

'This total wanker comes up to me, right, and he's like, "That your real tail, love?" and I'm like "Hello? Do I know you?" Then he goes, "Hey, you know what I want to know about you merpeople?", and I'm Oh-my-Dagon, here we go again with the fish thing. So I'm like dead cool, and I say "One, we're Marine Citizens. Two, it's a dolphin's tail, so I've got all the necessary mammalian equipment, thank you so very much." He's like, "Oi, that's too much information," and I go "Three, have you ever seen a dolphin's plonker? They're a metre long and they use them to map the sea bed," and he's like "Oh." Then he goes all quiet and buggers off. Mandy and that were pissing themselves.'

'...no, Serendipity, you can go at the end of the lesson like everybody else. So, everybody. We know what *planets* were and we know what stars were. Now, can anybody tell me what a *galaxy* was? Anybody? No, Penny, not a kind of animal I'm afraid. Yes, dear, I'm sure – that was a gazelle. A *galaxy*. Yes, José? Yes, that's *right*, well done. A galaxy was a great big *lot* of stars, all together… *stars*, Magog. We were just talking about them. You remember, "twinkle, twinkle..."? Good. Well, galaxies were very, *very* big, with lots and *lots* of stars and planets in them. And *that's* how big the City is... no, dear, I know it won't mean much to you, but it's on the syllabus.'

'There are a hundred undecillion stories in the City of the Saved... and that's assuming we only have one each which, believe me, is a long way from being the truth.'

BOOK ONE

1. The City.

Another day, another procession. This time, it's the Romans.

Traffic through, and for several blocks around, the Uptime Gate has been stopped still. Uptime Guards in crisp white uniforms explain the problem to irritated drivers, muleteers and vehicle-handlers, who mutter and tap pointedly at timepieces. A metallipede gets skittish, seems in danger of shedding its cargo of designer clothing, and must be soothed with engine-oil and sympathetic murmurs. Above, aircars and airpedestrians are corralled in tight holding-patterns. One pinstriped man with broad, bronze-feathered wings yells at an antigrav-harnessed guardswoman, before swooping angrily away. He pulls out a mobile 'phone as he arcs through the matt-white sky, and gets on to his office.

A llama relieves itself all over someone's windscreen, and an ineffectual but cathartic fight ensues.

A crowd throngs the broad flagstones of Erstwhile Plaza, pressing against the forceshields of the Guards who delineate the parade route. The media have brought experiencers, camerabots and film-crews, as well as the odd scribe for the resolutely pre-technological Districts. City-born children and their extended families cheer and wave, in vague anticipation of something happening soon. A child resurrectee (one of the never-grown, with old eyes) goes through the same motions. An orderly assemblage of slaves, Tubed in last night from the heart of the Romuline District, holds up supportive banners.

At the north side of the Plaza stands the Uptime Gate, a slab of black-veined marble like a mountain face, its upper reaches smeared with cloud. It slopes majestically above the multitude, intrepid reporters in climbing gear clinging partway up in search of clever camera angles. The less macho use antigravs, or belong to humanity's naturally airborne species. A lengthy file of confused alien visitors and pre-death humans lines one side of the square, waiting patiently to be allowed home to the Universe. There would be plenty of room for them to share the portal with the parade, but its sponsors, ever image-conscious, have rented the entire Gate for the next two hours. The Romans can always be relied on to provide a spectacle.

From behind, the Gate appears all of a piece, a mile-high marble tombstone canted from the vertical, as if about to topple and flatten the neighbourhood. Most Citizens find the sight unnerving, and the office blocks in the vicinity have some of Central District's cheapest ground rents. From the Plaza, however, the Gate, when open, shimmers like the ruffled surface of a lake. Reflecting back the myriad faces of the City, the monolith guards them from an envious Universe.

Out of this troubled mirror steps a herald in a toga. He reads, as he proceeds sedately forward, from a vellum scroll. His voice is taken up and amplified by the Plaza's surveillance mechanisms. He speaks in Latin, translating each sentence into the Civil Tongue.

He is greeting Civitata, Goddess of the City, on behalf of her mother the Earth. (A waggish camerabot lingers on a banner reading 'HI MUM'.) Behind him the Gate's surface billows and distends as soldiers emerge, a half-cohort of Romuline Militia. The Uptime Guard, mere customs inspectors, seem drab and listless next to the newcomers' gleaming bronze, their plumes and breastplates and their leather trim. Three hours ago, before the crowds arrived, these same soldiers marched into the Gate, to meet the hunting party at Ascension, the City's protectorate within the Universe. Now back they come, their vanguard carrying the eagle standard which the Romulines inherited from Rome itself. A step behind comes the emblem of the Ignotian family, a chimera rampant. Bright copper flames stream from its triple jaws. For some time the troops march forward in formation, parallel spears aligned towards the sky-dome.

Next come the litter-bearers. For this work the Romulines favour Citizens of the prehuman australopithecine species: smart enough to walk in a straight line and carry something without dropping it, but near-incapable of indiscretion or disloyalty. Most of the litters are ornate and gilded, although some favour dignified austerity. The guest of honour, General Scipio Africanus, whose abundant merits the herald is now exalting, rides with young Gaius Ignotus, old Cassius' favourite grandson. Gaius, a laurel wreath aligned across his temples, waves languidly at the throng beside him, and mutters something to the General, who smiles politely.

Other notables follow, not all of them from the Romuline District. There are guests from the other Roman-dominated suburbs (though naturally none of the resurrected Emperors or their families) and a few favoured, wealthy Citizens from other Districts. Some are clearly relieved to be back home: one tiger-striped posthuman slinks down from his litter, to his carriers' consternation, and rubs his furred face lovingly against the City's flagstones.

He gets out of the way, though, when the beasts come through.

The herald is now detailing the favour shown to the party by Diana, goddess of the hunt, and the bounty of generous Terra Mater. And the Earth, in whichever prehistoric epoch the party has been plundering, has clearly been bounteous indeed.

In total, and in order, the Romuline pageant comprises:

the lead herald;

1 half-cohort (260 men) of the Romuline Militia;

34 litters bearing nobles and guests, each held aloft by 4 stocky prehumans;

6 liveried animal handlers, each leading a yoked devil-boar, a warthog-faced and bloody-minded creature the height of a man;

7 more handlers ushering hyena-beasts as big as ponies;

5 bulky, blade-toothed felines, too truculent to lead, caged and borne along by

20 australopithecines;

a 2nd herald, expounding upon the habits and species of the animals as he walks;

a flight of some 1620 birds of numerous varieties, which disperse into the City's skies with great rapidity;

18 further handlers, accompanying

7 ancestral mammoths, barely distinguishable in size or shape from shaggy tapirs,

4 stranger pachyderms with long, boxy snouts (each bearing howdahs in which nervous ladies sit), and

7 rhinocerids of diverse species, each with a different structure of knobs and crenellations surmounting its tough skull;

a 3rd herald, continuing the (inaccurate and misleading) zoological commentary;

4 giant posthumans, between 4 and 6 metres tall and hired at great expense, leading

3 behemoths, immense rhino-skinned creatures the size of houses and with faces like uneasy camels, and

1 baby behemoth, barely taller than a normal human;

a big snake on a stick (the snake being the length of two Tube carriages and as thick round as a barrel, the stick a tree trunk carried by a score of men);

11 monkey-apes in a substantial cage, again borne by 20 prehumans and shrieking noisily – the males are larger, fiercer and have long canine teeth;

24 horses, three-toed, knee-high, each ridden by a tiny Romuline child with little skill but great enthusiasm;

a 4th herald, loudly reminding those assembled that the Ignotian family paid for all this;

another half-cohort of soldiers,

512 assorted slaves carrying: hunting weapons, baggage, carcasses and other trophies, disassembled temporal technology and joints of exotic meat for sale to the highest bidder;

and 2 Uptime Guards on mopeds, telling everyone to move along.

The noise and stench are appalling, but fortunately the crowding Citizens are mostly out of range. The spectacle outdoes their expectations, even the cynics who came here expressly to watch money being wasted. Most of the beasts and handlers are decked out in sumptuous red and gold livery: the satin bows around the behemoths' necks could hoist a car. Some animals seem dazed, others enraged, by their sudden peremptory passage between universes. Many of them enter the City unwillingly, assisted (one assumes) by cattle-prods applied to their hindquarters back in the Universe. Only the listless, crested serpent seems indifferent to its role in the proceedings.

Maddened by the hubbub and the smell, one of the miniature horses panics halfway across the Plaza. Its child rider loses what control she has, as it gallops between chattering primates and unblinking serpent, diving hysterically for cover under a behemoth's descending hoof. Here realisation seems to strike the little animal, and it pauses to take stock of its situation. The rider's frantic screams are silenced as the colossal foot descends and grinds them both onto the flagstones.

The crowd tuts in sympathy, and a portly, bearded woman expresses the view that it's a shame. ('Lucky that didn't happen the other side of the Gate,' opines one commentator cheerfully, and a billion viewers wince in unison.) The creature's giant handlers hurry it along (while the more cynical start to wonder, if that *had* happened outside the City, whether they would have heard about it). The squalling toddler is lifted from the bloody remnants of her mount, and sat snivelling astride a kindly soldier. By the time she reaches the south side of the Plaza, she is happily trying on his ceremonial plumed helmet.

There at the square's far edge, a lavish Tube chain hovers atop a polished extension rail. It is decked out in ubiquitous Ignotian red and gold, and the pageant approaches it sedately. The nobles dismount lightly from their litters, and are welcomed into the front carriage by lissom slaves. They sample sweetmeats and expensive wines while their captives are shoved effortfully onto open-topped freight platforms (it takes all four giants to coerce the largest behemoth). Abducted from their prehistoric homeworld, dragged millions of years through time to posthuman Ascension, paraded triumphally across a fissure between universes, these beasts have another trying journey to come. The Tube will ferry them through the fractal labyrinths of wormholes towards the distant Romuline District, and the appointments awaiting them in the Ignotian Arena.

The variegated audience has started to disperse by now, on foot, by wing and car and chariot, bored by the sight of uncooperative animals being prodded, pulled and strapped onto trailers. Some watchers stay, however, regarding the creatures with some sympathy.

2. Laura Tobin, Paynesdown District.

Tobin's office was the domain of a traditionalist: that much was apparent from the metal filing cabinet, the ceiling fan, the sepia stain of nicotine on the walls, the gilt lettering on the frosted door-panel. It was, she thought, in urgent need of redecoration.

Just at the moment though, the thing she liked least about it was the silhouette which stood immobile the other side of the milky glass.

'People who lurk in shadows irritate me,' she told it. She groped inside her desk drawer for the chill of her gun. 'Come in and tell me what you want. Or go away. Either would be fine.'

The weapon was just for show, of course, a cultural hangover from the Universe. The chances of anyone who could be hurt by it wandering into Paynesdown were remote to say the least. But the District attracted former members of the gun-based cultures like flies to an open-air autopsy. Everybody carried a weapon, from old ladies doing their weekly shop with a pump-action to children in pushchairs playing with their My First Handguns. It was one of the many reasons the rest of the City found the place rather exasperating.

The door swung diffidently inward, jangling the bell which hung above it. The bulky shadow peered cautiously around the door.

'Laura?' it hazarded.

Tobin groaned, and set the gun aside. 'What do you want, Rick?' she demanded.

'Laura,' Rick Kithred repeated. Full-lipped with a receding hairline and salt-and-pepper beard, Rick appeared to be in late middle age – a useless fact, but one Tobin had never shaken off the habit of observing. He'd somehow picked up Tobin's first name at some point, and now refused to put it down again. He had a daughter called Laura, apparently.

Tobin had been in her eighties when she'd died. By then her brittle limbs and milky eyes had been no use to anyone, and it had come as a relief to her compatriots to know they'd soon be replacing her with a younger model. She'd been the oldest of all the Anathema colonists by then, the only first-generation presence still among them. She could remember younger, mostly callous idiots filing past to pay her their ironic respects.

Here in the City she was young again, and had been now for nearly three hundred years. She was also pale-skinned, red-haired and plumper than she'd have chosen. Like the original, her resurrection body was plagued by freckles which offset her usually scowling countenance. She scowled now, as Rick told her: 'There's someone hanging round the back yard. Dark, skinny guy. Young-looking, with a little mustache. I think maybe it's the Antichrist.'

'It's not,' she answered curtly. Rick spent much of the time outside his skull, for which Tobin couldn't blame him. Its inside didn't seem to be a very nice place. 'You're imagining things again,' she added, meaning mainly the last part. It was, unfortunately, not unlikely that someone was lurking, hence her reaction when she'd seen Rick's shadow.

The office had passed to Tobin from Gally Redcross, a hopeless romantic whose view of investigative work, and of Paynesdown District in particular, had been based principally upon his reading of Baines Molesti novels. Tobin, who knew for a fact that Molesti had never ventured further into Paynesdown than its Tube platform, was unsurprised that Redcross' expectations had been confounded. Her one-time colleague had lived originally in an era when chivalry and honour were (theoretically) paramount, where faithful knights upheld the rule of justice as their liege monarch understood it, and defended the innocent from the wicked slightly more often than vice versa. He had been expecting a milieu where he could prove himself a parfait gentil private eye, and where (Tobin suspected not incidentally) there would be a steady supply of sultry distressed blondes for him to rescue. He was, in short, precisely the kind of person who would install frosted glass between himself and anyone he needed a good look at, and Tobin had been cursing him for it daily for some time now.

'You're probably right,' agreed Rick, settling oblivious into her lumpy armchair. 'I know there *is* an Antichrist in the City, but this may not be him.'

'Just keep talking,' Tobin muttered.

Paynesdown District

LIEF: So, then – Paynesdown District. We've all read about Paynesdown in the best-selling crime novels of Baines Molesti, or at least we know them from their big-budget XP adaptations. You've got Parker Smart PI and his gutsy girlfriend Megan Smolder, the seedy dives and mobsters' mansions they visit, the guns and the heists and the thrilling chases. So far, Baines Molesti's written 200-plus stories set in Paynesdown, from *Death on the Sidewalk* way back in 9 to this year's *Fabergé Street*[1]. So, what about a holiday there? Surely a trip to Paynesdown would pitch you headfirst against that compelling backdrop?

CATRIONA: Well, Lief, no. The best advice we can offer the traveller considering a sojourn in Paynesdown is don't. We've been and it's awful. Sure, the Molesti books are harmless fun, but they give you about as much idea about the real Paynesdown as *The Flintstones* does about everyday life in a Neolithic flint quarry. Everyone's unfriendly – they'd carve you up and leave you bleeding in a shop doorway if they could – the food's terrible and the only people who'll sleep with you expect paying afterwards in drugs you've never even heard of. You have to be carrying a gun just to get served anywhere, and believe it or not that does include the gun shops. The only tourist attraction worth a look's the Paynesdown Gun Museum, which has a great big collection of... well, have a guess.

KRISH: Admittedly the architecture has a certain neo-fascist grandeur, but if you want a film-noir theme park you're better off visiting Chandlerville in Beybridge District. At least there you get shown round by a pretty convincing Humphrey Bogart.

[From *The Megalopolis Guide* (as accessed 08:51 04/04/29[1]).]

[1] Translator's note: all City dates are in years AF (After Foundation). Since local naming conventions for months of the year vary, these are usually rendered by number.

Rick obliged. He had his own private religion, one which received constant upgrades as successive waves of divine inspiration struck him. He was always happy to expound upon it.

Tobin hefted her Rosetta 9mm, flicked the magazine open and closed. Even if it couldn't do any damage inside City limits, a bullet in the face still came as something of a shock. It could buy valuable time in an emergency.

Gally Redcross had discovered, in short order, the sociopathic thugs who really populated Paynesdown, the temporary comfort available through cheap whores, and his own inner alcoholic. His parents had eventually come and taken him home with them, an ever-present and deeply embarrassing peril for many people in the City.

Tobin held no such sentimental view of her profession. As a private investigator, she found stuff out for money. Her clients might use the information thus uncovered for anything, from blackmail to ditching their boyfriends to bringing minor criminals to justice. It was no more romantic than any of the other paid functions which women performed in Paynesdown.

'The Creator of our universe,' Rick was explaining, 'who is not God, but is striving to become God, has been communicating with me again.'

'Naturally,' Tobin sighed. 'Who else would he choose?' She began to edge silently towards the door.

She'd been an unwilling private investigator, pursuing half a dozen alternative professions before acknowledging the wisdom in the note she'd received on Resurrection Day. She'd hated that. But now she had the job, she was damn good at it – hence the problem. Entirely inadvertently, and to her dismay, she'd ended up uncovering information which had proved highly damaging to Vice Vera, a prominent figure in Paynesdown's prolific organised-crime community.

Vera couldn't hurt her, naturally. For Tobin, though, there was insufficient agreement as to precisely what the crime boss could do to her, and she'd been waiting with impatient trepidation to find out. Every so often rumours surfaced that this crime lord or that had succeeded in an ingenious circumvention of the City's invulnerability protocols. Burying a would-be-rival deep in the geological base-substrate, imprisoning an informer in a pocket black hole... these rumours were, of course, invariably started by the bosses themselves. Even so, Tobin had been getting jumpy.

No shadow was visible on the door-panel now, but for all she knew some viciously augmented thug was standing just out of sight on the stairs.

'The creator accidentally created a second entity,' Rick was elaborating, 'identical with itself in every way, and they're at war. They're warring over which of them is to be God, and which Satan. The child is trying to usurp its parent's creatorhood, and they've both become incarnate. Or they will soon. That bit wasn't clear – there was some interference from Secret Architect mind-control experiments.'

Tobin yanked the door open, and stepped nimbly outside, colliding hard with the figure standing there.

The figure in a cloak, black velvet, a preposterous tricorn hat – and *antlers*?

The figure standing directly between Tobin and the lightbulb which dangled starkly from the peeling plaster ceiling.

'There's definitely some business involving the two deities getting bodies, though,' Rick continued cheerfully as the intruder stalked forward, forcing Tobin bodily back into her office. 'Hence the Antichrist guy.'

Bone sockets stared at Laura's eyes, white ivory like knots in silver-birch wood. Above them, the branching antlers. A whisper, phantom leaves on winter tree-limbs. '*Laura...*'

This wasn't one of Vera's goons. This wasn't even Rick's Antichrist. This was something far, far worse.

The Faction had caught up with Laura Tobin.

3. Julian White Mammoth Tusk, Council House.

Julian was latening himself for work, AGAIN, when the Great Detective Agency's phonecall came trilling through his early-morning brainpan.

He'd dragged himself awake that morning with great diffs, head thick and sluggy deepdown in his brow-ridge, and fully been unable to recall the evening he'd made of it with Sinovi and Hekate. He guessed waragi, ouzo and / or substances akin had been attendant. His timebeast head, as well as previous experience of Hek and Sino, suggested so.

Last time a call had warbled this early into his hangoverian brain had been Dad's birthday, when Mother dear had linked in and exhorted him to present his natal felicitations. Julian was undertrustable to recall such abstruse trivvies on his own, apparently. This time the ID flashing on the wallscreen was of the GDA, and Julian wavered. He'd been late for Councillor Mesh each day this week, and she was getting noticeably snarky. But who knew what the datactives might have for him? A final demand, in all probs, but hey, they might have Shel. He couldn't pass that up just to keep himself in the Cllr's good files.

His slablike hand picked daintily at air. —Answer, | he gestured. —Julian WMT, | he added suavely, as the caller appeared on the phoney.

(Old G^{4}Granddad Crouch always got aereated at the stereotyping of Neanders. 'Those idiot palaeontologists!' he'd rage. Apparently he'd heard once some homsap fossilhead maintaining – despite all now-available evidence – that all Neanders lacked appropriate vocal apparatus. 'Of course we bloody talk! You'd not have lasted five minutes back in the Old Times, *Julian*.' He'd pronounce Julian's sapiens name like he was chewing bitterbark. 'Your great-great-great-grandmother didn't.' Crouch Beside The Fire of the tribe of the White Mammoth Tusk found the speech impairments of his own descendants a personal affront, Gestural Civil or no.)

'Ah, Mr. White Mammoth Tusk. My dear fellow,' effused the widescreen image coldly. Low-lidded eyes blinked languidly above the vulture nose, surviewing him. 'I find you well, I trust?'

—No plaints, thanks, | signed Julian impatiently. The agent's routine pleasantries invariably needled him. —So what's emergent? |

The GD's hooded gaze held Julian's evenly. It didn't waver as the agent's fingers spidered across the leather desktop, circumnavigated a paperweight skull and printouts impaled on a throwing-knife, then clutched intently at a long-stemmed tobacco pipe.

Behind the caller Julian vizzed an open space, less office than gigantic sitting-room. Big desks held up darkwood terminals and phonescreens. Among them were spersed shabby armchairs and, for some odd reason, tailors' dummies. A worn old carpet stretched across the floor to a wide mantel at the room's far end, where fire glowed.

Tens of identical men filled up the workplace, most wearing frock-coats or else quilted dressing-gowns. A handful sported tweedy ensembles with strange, symmetrical peaked caps. Pipe-smoking was apparent, as were violins. Some of the doppelgangers paced about with frighting energy; others stared limpidly at nothing whatever. Two were argumenting ferociously, while a third watched, wielding a pipe and contributing helpful sarcasms. At the fire several, legs akimbo, took delivery of tea from motherly housekeeper-types, while others lectured at their stouter, whiskered colleagues. Their scattered violins were being played with various degrees of skill, in sheary dissonances with each other. One employee had prostrated himself on a chaise-longue, clutching at an antiquated hypodermic.

The Agency's headquarters were chaotic utterly, but its employees were – by definition – the best that existed.

'We have,' the caller smirked, 'some news that may be of some interest to your employer, Councillor Mesh Cos.'

Julian's breath caught in his lungs. Ajolt, he strove to keep his signing casual. —Lon Shel? | he inquired, cautiously.

'The very same.' Drawing a pouch from his quilted pocket, the remake began leisurely to fill his pipe-bowl. 'A reported sighting,' he supplied, once Julian had cursed the man's inbuilt showmanship. 'Quite promising, though still awaiting certain confirmation. We can have an associate at the District in question by nightfall, if the Councillor wishes.'

—Which District? | queried Julian, too eager. The other glanced up sharply from his pipely duties. —The Cllr. will be craving daughter-data, | he amended hastily.

'Ah yes,' the detective assented, 'the Councillor.' The hawkish gaze appraised Julian over steepled fingers. 'Before I answer that question, Mr. White Mammoth Tusk, indulge me for a moment with a question of my own. It is connected with payment, and the conspicuity of its prevailing absence.'

...oh swyve, thought Julian, here comes the awkwardness. —The Cllr, | he repeated, uncomfortably aware how often Mesh had been invoked already. —Her credit's good, no bluffing. You'll get your tall ones, no diffs there. |

The man was on his feet at once, leaning close towards the screen, his face huge. 'I believe,' he thundered, 'that my colleagues and I may boast some little reputation as men of intelligence. It is rare, Mr. White Mammoth Tusk, for someone to attempt to play me for an utter fool!'

An unseen voice cried cheerily, 'Thrice this week, I fear!', spoiling the effect somewhat, but Julian quailed and flailed and paled nevertheless. His verrifanting fingers shaped the Civil sign for —Er | .

Casting a spikeful look at his offscreen colleague, the caller straightened, clamped his pipe toothfully and lit it with one fluid match-stroke. 'We are aware,' he continued, calmly, 'that you and Miss Lon Shel were lovers prior to her disappearance. The two of you were university contemporaries, and it was she who arranged for your employment with her mother. Is that not the case?'

—We swyved a bit, | Julian indicated.

'Quite so,' assented the detective gravely. 'My friend Councillor Venturus informs me that Mesh Cos regards her daughter's disappearance as an inconsequential act of adolescent rebellion. Miss Lon is in her two-hundred-and-fifties, a notoriously difficult age in her species. You, on the other hand, are twenty-two, a time of life when even the most sophisticated City-born Neanderthal might find his instincts impelling him to settle down. It is natural that you should be concerned for the safety of your mate, even if her mother is not. Nevertheless,' he declared crisply, 'you will understand that we can no longer accept your assurances that our account will be settled by your employer. Are you a man of means, Mr. White Mammoth Tusk?'

Julian boggled. —Jabez Krishna, no, | he signed.

The agent tsk'ed. 'I had assumed as much. Well, sir, you will be hearing from our lawyers.'

—WAIT! | Julian speed-signed, as as the GD's slender fingers reached out to unlink the wallcall. —The sighting. Shel. Was that a bluff thing, or a real one? |

The caller's high brow furrowed. 'My dear sir, I fear I really couldn't say without further investigation. I suggest you contact us again, if ever you have funds to cover such an undertaking.'

The Great Detective cut the connection. —Swyving fellfire, | opined Julian shakily, as the screen blacked out. He sat back heavily onto the bed, and massaged at his brow with stubby signifiers.

He breathed heavily for a while, then his fleshy lips began to emit a gentle hooting noise.

His lumping head was crippling his cogitation, and he was running ever later for a job he'd anyhow just forfeited at all probs. But someone, in some hawking District somewhere, said they'd seen Lon Shel. She was OK. She hadn't quit the City, or been reformatted in some loathable potent weapons experiment.

His foghorn voice got louder and yet louder, as Julian gave over to relieved, hysteric laughter.

4. Urbanus Ignotus, the Romuline District.

The battle was going badly for the human side.

From his privileged vantage point, Urbanus could see the pained expressions on the faces of the armoured men as they were cut down, and frequently to pieces, by the scimitars of their skeletal opponents. The human soldiers bulged identically with swells of muscle, in contrast to their enemies, but so far it was the dead who had the bony upper hand.

Their ferocity had taken the clone warriors by surprise: half an hour ago, the skeletons had been mere dragon's teeth, sown casually by a dozen slave-girls while their brawny foes cast about in confusion for someone to fight. Had any of them thought, when the fast-growing bone-men first showed signs of jerky animation, to cast into the enemy ranks a medium-sized stone (or, for that matter, one of the ray guns with which they had been issued), they would probably have been spared. The flesh soldiers had been designed for stamina and fighting skill, not for intelligence: the crowd preferred it that way. Their weapons pulsed desperately with cones of ruby light as they fell back towards the gate, now barred, through which they had first entered the Arena. Crows and ravens picked at the pieces of their fallen comrades.

Removing his own spectacles, Urbanus squinted at the blurry carnage beneath, and wiped the smeared lenses on the corner of his toga. Clones were difficult enough to generate, but those grown in the City had an unfortunate tendency to share the invulnerability of the Citizens. Generating them beyond the Uptime Gate in Ascension circumvented this problem: however, import permits were absurdly costly. In total the Arena currently held two thousand of them, live and dead, as well as an equivalent number of the skeletonic bio-automata: Urbanus hoped that the audience appreciated the expense.

'Enjoying the show, boy?' growled his great-grandfather suddenly. Cassius had been ignoring him until now, which had come to Urbanus both as a surprise and a relief, though it suggested that his presence was a distraction as unwelcome as it was unwonted.

Sitting up straighter on the smooth wooden bench, the young man hurriedly replaced his glasses. 'Very much, sir,' he asserted, wondering if further comment was required of him.

Urbanus had no idea why Cassius Ignotus had invited him to attend today's Ignotian Spectacle, and he suspected the same was true of Cassius himself. His forefather had barely acknowledged him so far that morning, which was entirely consistent with his attitude since Urbanus' coming-of-age three years before. The young man understood: he was well aware that his myopia, scrawniness and general preference for indoor activities rendered him something of an embarrassment. While in theory the Ignotian family was proud, like all families, of its City-born scions, Urbanus knew that many senior members of the clan were nostalgic for ancient Rome's healthy infant mortality rate.

'I expect you'd like to be down there with them, eh?' Cassius added bafflingly, with a nod towards the combatants.

Not for the first time, Urbanus wondered if his forebear even remembered who he was. In a family so large, and with so few names shared around, it was entirely possible that a summons intended for some other Urbanus Ignotus had reached him in error. The family villa was huge, with living-space for several thousand, and its intelligent management system, LIV, was bordering on the obsolescent. It could easily have happened.

However, if the head of the family was wasting his time in talking to him, Urbanus would prefer not to have to tell him so. Senator, Consul, member of the Chamber of Residents and City Councillor, Lucius Cassius Ignotus was by far the most important individual in the Romuline, and one of the most powerful in the City of the Saved. Glancing sideways, Urbanus was vividly impressed as always by his ancestor's high forehead, thickly-wooded brow and proud promontory of nose. That face was a landscape, as archetypally Romuline as the Capitoline Hill itself.

'Not really, Great-Grandfather,' Urbanus replied, nervously. 'I'd only get in the way. And no-one would be able to kill me, which would annoy the audience. I'd get booed out of the Arena. It's much better value for money if the constructs fight it out between them.'

Beyond the quartz balustrade, the battle continued. A couple of the clone army's brighter members had established, by dint of dogged trial and error, that the firepower of two or more ray guns could, in tandem, quickly reduce a skeleton to charred fragments. As on previous occasions, this discovery had raised a huge cheer from the crowd. Other clones had caught on to the technique, and now the homunculi were making some progress against their undead opponents, scattering the Arena floor with twitching piles of ash and bone.

Cassius snorted. 'That isn't what I meant.' He turned to glare at his great-grandson. 'Don't you know why people come to the Spectacle, young Urbanus? Half the crowd here aren't from the Romuline: they weren't even Roman. They come from all over the City, even those Districts where we're considered cruel barbarians. They come to see the beasts fight and the robots war, to watch human-looking things destroyed by other human-looking things. They buy our films, our veerees and our XP simulations. The richest of them buy cloned bodies and drive them by remote-control, hacking each other to death for recreation. It's the biggest single market in the City, and the Ignotian family *owns* it. Do you ever wonder why?'

Urbanus had his private doubts on this score, but he was reasonably sure of the answer his great-grandfather would want to hear. 'Because violence is a natural part of human life,' he suggested. 'The City fails to provide it, and so the function falls to us.'

His ancestor looked narrowly at him. 'That's right, boy. Although you and the others of our family's mewling City-brood make me wonder sometimes. The City is our Mother and protectrix, but she coddles her children far too much for my liking. Do you have any desire for adventure, young Urbanus?'

What Urbanus most fervently desired at that particular moment was to return to his workbench in the family accounts department, and spend the next few days inspecting whichever ledgers promised to be the least sensational. 'Yes, Great-Grandfather,' he assented guardedly.

Cassius gazed at Urbanus for some time. 'No matter,' he said at length, turning away. Below them, the bone army was appropriating its opponents' strategy, singling out individual warriors from their fellows and hacking them messily apart with slashing scimitars. Accidentally caught in the crossfire between two of his comrades' death-rays, one clone exploded in a flash of bloody vapour, and the crowd roared appreciatively. Beneath the benefactor's box, the heraldic chimera hissed and bleated in her iron cage, sprayed by the ruddy droplets.

'They tell me you have a good business mind, Urbanus,' Cassius informed him.

'I believe so, sir,' Urbanus agreed. The chimera shook herself and emitted a leonine roar at the combatants below. Her lion's coat was greying now, and her snake-scales dulled. When last she had taken active part in a Spectacle, Urbanus had been eight. Soon, he thought, the family would have to commission a replacement. This would not come cheaply.

'Well, then,' said his ancestor. 'There has been, I am told, a significant business development in Kempes District, in the Western Quarter. Have you ever been west, boy?'

The older man, Urbanus thought, had clearly lost track of whom he was addressing. 'I've never been outside the Romuline, sir,' he reminded him. 'Even as a student I attended the Ciceronian Symposium –'

'This matter,' Cassius continued, undeflected, 'is certain to impact the family's business interests, one way or another. I need to know whether it will do so to our advantage or our detriment: and, if the latter, how to turn it to the former. You leave this afternoon, and you'll report directly back to me, and me alone. Do you understand?'

Urbanus gaped. He knew, naturally, that industrial espionage had its place among the family's diverse specialities, but had always taken it as read that his elders would rather die, again, than involve *him* in any such sensitive aspect of the business. 'If I might ask, Great-Grandfather,' he floundered, 'what is this matter you're concerned about?'

'Never you mind,' Cassius told him. 'Just keep your eyes and ears open and tell me what you see. From what I hear you'll have your work cut out to miss it.'

His forebear turned dismissively back to the Arena floor. The handful of remaining homunculi were standing back-to-back, each picking off bone soldiers with a pair of handheld ray-guns. 'I'll square things with your superiors,' he said, 'and detail a slave to accompany you. Only your wife and parents need be told you're going, and even they don't need to know where. You'd better make your preparations. If there's any more you need to know, ask LIV.'

Urbanus still had sufficient presence of mind to recognise when his bodily presence was not required. It had, after all, been an habitual experience during his two decades of life.

'Farewell, then, Great-Grandfather,' he said meekly. 'I won't disappoint you.'

Cassius grunted, but otherwise made no reply. Urbanus bowed to his unseeing profile, then stood and slipped quietly out from the benefactor's box. There was a lot of urgent panicking for him to do.

Behind him the crowd groaned, as far below the last remaining animate skeleton picked up a ray-gun from a fallen body, inspected it with curiosity, then blasted the last living clone to smouldering fragments.

5. The City.

As Urbanus Ignotus leaves the Arena it is the third hour after dawn, when the pale brightness of the sky-dome begins to plateau. Preoccupied, he scarcely acknowledges the manservant attending the electric litter, before they set off for the Villa Ignota in the suburbs of the Romuline.

In the arena, the Spectacle continues, as it will till skydark. The carrion birds wheel and flap and object as the messy leavings of the clone/bone war are cleared. Some of them, escaped domestic pets most likely, are surprisingly eloquent.

Further battles are mounted: between clones of renowned fighters; between robots capable by cunning self-manipulation of changing into items of military hardware; between prehistoric lizards and elaborately-attired saureadors. Aerial and aquatic combats are presented, generally involving carnivores and heavy weaponry. Certain participants are directed, via cerebrolink, by Citizens who have paid exorbitantly for the privilege.

As morning draws on and the skyglow gradually brightens further, the crowd becomes more and more raucous. The chimera curls up peacefully and takes a nap. By the time Urbanus has reached his private rooms, more members of his family have joined Cassius Ignotus. They conduct a discreet business meeting in the benefactor's box, with plenty of wine available. The Councillor himself sips austerely at a mug of water.

The climax to the morning's proceedings is surprisingly non-lethal, although still spectacular. It will be broadcast live, a coup de théâtre to counterpoint the earlier Uptime Gate procession.

The great doors which lie opposite the benefactor's box, across the wide expanse of the Arena, retract themselves with ponderosity. Slaves drag through them a tall bronze archway, festooned with pipes and nodules. A long low rail is brought through in segments, and carefully laid down.

Pipes are connected, links established and levers thrown. The archway grows abruptly opaque, as the atmosphere within it fogs, churns briefly and then clears, revealing the polychromatic whirl of a Tubespace tunnel. A metal rail within it aligns neatly with that in the Arena, angling towards the Ignotians' box.

Directly a distant rumbling is heard, building in moments to an avalanching roar. A speck of gold and carmine grows with frightening rapidity into an approaching Tube chain.

Flanked by his wife and nominal heir, his sparse locks flapping in the breeze, Cassius Ignotus steps calmly from his seat onto the sand-strewn floor of the Arena. Behind him tread his ceremonial bodyguards, great insectoid collaterals whose looks bely their (partial) human ancestry. One of them carries a bundle of sticks with an axe at its centre – a fasces, the badge of Ignotus' consular rank. It seems Paynesdown District has no monopoly on imbuing obsolete weapons with ceremonial value.

When the Tube chain emerges screaming from the archway, decelerating rapidly to halt inches from the rail's unceremonious end, Ignotus is already positioned a few feet from where a carriage door will come to rest. He nods his thanks as a well-oiled slave slides it open in front of him.

Behind the chain of carriages, the archway slams back into its inert state. The audience applauds enthusiastically, and the shackled animals create the most almighty racket, as Councillor Ignotus and his family welcome home the hunters of the Romuline.

6. Tobin, Paynesdown.

'You're Godfather Avatar,' Rick said accusingly. 'I've seen you on TV.'

The skull-faced apparition stood unmoving at the centre of the threadbare patch in Tobin's office carpet. It recalled a Verrifant's Night dummy ready for the burning – a particularly terrifying one made in one of the most unreconstructedly Neolithic Districts.

Godfather Avatar's gothic trappings would have been enough to unnerve anyone – that was the purpose they were designed for, after all. But Tobin had history with the Faction, and the regalia were giving her flashbacks she didn't at all care for.

'Really? I hate seeing myself on TV.' The whisper cut through Tobin like a winter gust. *'It makes me look so pale.'*

'Rick,' Tobin hissed. 'Get the hell out of here, now.' Whether out of misplaced neighbourly concern or simply because he assumed he was hallucinating, the big man hadn't left her shabby armchair.

A skeletal arm – no, not skeletal, just encased in armour made from someone else's tibia – emerged from the pitch-black nap of Avatar's cloak. A bony finger extended towards Rick. *'At least stand up when you've got a visitor, Rick Kithred,'* the Godfather whispered.

Rick looked blank. Then: 'Oh,' he muttered. 'Okay.' He stood up and shambled over to join Tobin at her desk. 'You see it too?' he stage-whispered. Tobin rolled her eyes.

Godfather Avatar settled into the vacated chair, cape billowing, as if his props had been kicked away. *'Laura,'* he murmured, caressing her first name. The Faction elders Tobin had known back in the Universe had made equally free with it.

'Yes?' she replied, adding incisively, 'What?'

The City's homegrown Faction Paradox franchise had ignored Tobin's resurrected self for, so far, close on three centuries. She couldn't imagine that their renewed interest spelled good news for her. Like the parent Faction, the Rump Parliament couldn't spell good news if you wrote it out on a blackboard.

The chalky orbits examined her dispassionately. *'It's been a long time,'* Avatar whispered.

Tobin took a firm hold of herself. 'It has. And the longer it gets, the happier I become. Although as I recall,' she added, 'you weren't even there at the particular time we're talking about. So what the hell are you doing here now?'

The horned skull tilted. The breathy voice became imbued with mocking melancholy. *'Aren't you pleased to hear from us again, Laura?'*

'Guess,' snapped Tobin. 'And stop it with the "Laura" shit, OK? I know what you're trying to do.'

'You, ah, you might want to not make him angry, L – Tobin,' suggested Rick.

'I'm not angry, Rick,' the creature murmured, *'I'm just disappointed. Here!'* A bony gauntlet snaked out suddenly, too fast for unaugmented human muscles. Tobin threw up her arms instinctively, and, fumbling, caught the object Avatar had pitched at her.

It was a standard one-shot hologlobe, as sold from souvenir stands across the City. It even had "A Gift from Veneziana District" stencilled on the casing. Glaring suspiciously at the Godfather, Tobin set the device down on her desk and activated it. An image rezzed up in the centre of the room.

'Eurrghhh,' said Rick, and Tobin tended to agree. The corpse whose likeness now adorned her fraying carpet had not died prettily. The holo bore no date or location codes, so she had no idea where or when the recording had been made.

'Who's that?' she asked, cursing the tremor in her voice. She was surprised how strongly the sight of someone else's death affected her, even so long after her own.

The Rump Parliament

Despite its rivalry with the orthodox Faction Paradox Mission in the City of the Saved (run by non-resurrected, extra-mural Cousins under the discreet but watchful eye of the Eleven-Day Empire), the Rump Parliament is no revolutionary clade like the famously doomed Thirteen-Day Republic. Instead it's a textbook example of that evolutionary flexibility which has allowed the Faction, despite its Houseworld origins, to adapt to countless cultural niches across the whole span of the Universe[1].

Factionologists have long understood that Faction Paradox is more concerned with appearance than anything else – specifically with projecting those appearances its leaders want outsiders to see. The movement's members find creating paradoxes as such to be a rather tedious occupation: it saves a lot of effort merely to *appear to be* creating them. In the City, according to the best research available, time-travel is simply impossible; and death, the Faction's other favourite signifier, is at worst an unpleasant memory. Here the Faction, in the persons of the resurrected or City-born Cousins of the Rump Parliament, contents itself with keeping up appearances.

Accordingly, the Parliament pursues a deliberate policy of obscurantism and self-mystification. Godmother Jezebel, the Parliament's Acting Speaker, periodically issues deliberately vague, misleading or even falsifiable statements. Godfather Lo's opulent mansion hosts frequent lavish parties, at which depraved rituals are rumoured to take place behind (of course) closed doors. Godfather Avatar is blatantly mythologised as a shadowy, faceless eminence behind the Speaker's Chair.

This iconisation of the Parliament's upper echelon serves to obscure such basic facts as the size of its membership (presumably large, given how many Faction initiates have been of human origin), its loyalties and aims, and even its location within the City.

[From *Faction Paradox: a Negotiable History* by Selene Walmric (Pangolin Publishing, AF 189).]

---

[1] Translator's note: *Houseworld* is the usual City term for the sphere of origin of the Great Houses. The Citizens use *homeworld*, for the most part, to refer to Earth, and are not keen on being culturally imperialised by a snobbish coterie of time-bending immortals.

'He was a Citizen,' Avatar hissed. *'A City Councillor, no less.'*

'He left the City and got killed again?' Tobin was staggered. 'Dumb bastard. I bet he feels really stupid now.'

'He died at Council House,' her visitor breathed gleefully.

Tobin actually felt her face go numb.

'Crap,' she opined briskly, shutting off the hologlobe. 'Well, it's been nice to catch up. Don't hesitate to leave my office now.'

The Godfather showed no signs of moving. *'The Parliament is terribly excited,'* he elaborated. *'This death is a unique event. If blood sacrifice has become possible within the City, we'd love to know how and why.'* His voice slithered over her bare skin like worms. *'Particularly how.'*

'I'm sure you would,' said Tobin, 'if you hadn't invented the whole thing so as to fuck with my head. Goodbye.'

Avatar's death-grin seemed somehow to widen. '*Oh, we've much more effective ways of doing that, Laura. No, this is the real thing.*' He stood as if inflated suddenly, and strode towards her. Tobin saw with horror that his skeletal gauntlet clutched...

...a grinning china piggy-bank. It was bright pink. Tobin stared mesmerised.

Rick said, 'I think he wants you to take it.'

With a shudder Tobin picked up the ceramic pig. '*My contact number is inside,*' whispered Godfather Avatar. '*Do get in touch if you should happen – by some remote chance – to change your mind.*'

In a black billow like a sailing-ship in mourning, he turned and stalked out of Tobin's office.

7. Julian, Council House.

—Hey Troffi, | Julian signed, peering perplexedly around him. —What's transpiring? |

'Hey there, Jay,' Cllr. Voshcht's researcher vocalled gloomily. 'Some brainhole sec-ex, most prob. Even the Cllrs aren't osmoting in or out.'

Julian'd clothed himself in purple satin / denim meld, his big brocade coat sweeping after on its castors. He still had in his dreadloid hair-extensions, old though they were getting.

He'd trundled in on Council House's creaky subworm intransystem some moments previous (missing still the hoverscooter he'd had home in Bear Claw), to find King Square chaotic. The porticoed steps rising to the Cllrs' offices had been cordoned off with a waspfield, and CoHo Admin / Sec officials were buzzing all around it. Cllrs, their staff and supplicants, cleaners, lost tourists and the occasional media expeer were milling up and down the cloistered plaza. Troffi was standing in a corner, conversing idly with a knot of other staffish types and smoking Kills.

—Swyver, | Julian gestured vaguely. Thank Civvie, Mesh might not have yet inferred his absence in the medley. —My Cllr. among these here present? |

'Not vizzed her, meekay,' Troffi said. 'Voshchy's aggressing at the chazzes, down there.'

His eyes followed Troffi's slender digit to where the officers of the CHAS were indeed receiving loud grief from big hermaphrodite Voshcht. Tall Cllr. St Marx was also bystanding, her irises unscannable behind their mirrored skyshades – but, as Troffi'd maintained, Mesh Cos was nowhere visible. Julian allowed his slabs of hand to flap relievedly.

'Most likely the constables perform calamities in masquerade,' interpolated Parqué, assistant to Cllr. Wen. 'Cassius Ignotus oft admonishes the Councillors that the City must needs become acquainted with its vulnerabilities. It does seem the constabulary takes him at his word. What did you to Sinovi?' she added suddenly. 'He was here betimes, and scowled as though a behemoth had shitten in his head.'

—Oh, just the usual, Parqué, | Julian signed. —Leastly, I think it was. Can't

The Human Species

The term *the human species* is correctly used in the plural. It is normally employed otherwise in the City of the Saved only by those who intend, for invidious ideological reasons, to confer "humanity" exclusively upon one strand of the greater human bloodline.

In another manner of speaking, however, there is only one human species; even in the City, where *Homo habilis* handymen work alongside cyberhuman programmers, and it is not unknown for a Cro-Magnon man to wed a hermaphrodite posthuman[1]. Insofar as *to wed* is to enter into a compact to produce offspring, such matches are indeed the crux of the matter: one traditional conception of a *species* is that of a group of organisms who are mutually fertile, such as a spaniel with a labrador but not with a giraffe. When the ancestors of the organisms in question have cultivated sufficiently advanced biotechnological techniques, however, such distinctions are abolished. Since early posthuman times, the bloodlines of humanity (in common with advanced non-human groups such as the dwellers in the Great Houses) have been able to procreate with virtually any organism itself capable of breeding: hence the vast diversity of ancestries (not limited exclusively to the human bloodlines) exhibited by individual Citizens.

When contemplating their newfound compatriots, therefore, an understandable fear and confusion has been known to emerge among those untrained in the anthropological and ethnological sciences, who in their pre-Resurrection lives were familiar with one or two varieties of humanity only. This is compounded further by the presence of resurrected individuals whose imagoes were permanently inflected by such life experiences as mechanical hybridisation, corporeal genosurgical sculpting or metempsychotic transmigration[2].

It is an axiom of this volume that all inhabitants of the City are created (or re-created) equal, from the members of the earliest australopithecine tribe to those of the last human civilisation, and including all those stigmatised in certain circles with epithets such as "prehuman", "revolved" or "collateral". It is towards a greater mutual understanding between the City's many species of humanity that this work has been undertaken; and it is its author's hope that such distinctions will be shown as ultimately meaningless as those made in barbaric times between "whites", "Negroes", "Orientals" and the like.

[From *The Human Species: A Spotter's Guide* by Melicia Clutterbuck PhD (Godsdice Press, AF 204).]

---

[1] Translator's note: in accordance with long-established convention, the term *posthuman* is used to refer to any individual or grouping of the greater human bloodline who flourished after the destruction of the Earth in c 10,000,000 AD.

[2] Translator's note: the English word *imago* is used here to render a complex piece of Civil terminology, semantically located somewhere between "morphogenetic field" and "resurrection body", and with connotations not dissimilar to "self-image" and even "default setting".

retrieve, if honest. But whatever spired in his skull spired in mine and Hekate's too. | He massaged at his brow for emphasis. From all the ancestories he'd been told, he should give thanks that City-born hangovers couldn't pain him – but his head was too far befuddled for such plexities.

—I'd harm for a cig, | he added plaintively, —if anyone's grasping? |

'Here y'are.' Joey Gilgamesh from tech support handled him a cigarette, and the several of them stood observing the proceedings and conferring over Parqué's complicated sex life.

At length Voshcht finished dissenting with the chazzes. The Cllr. yelled for Troffi, and left in a foul temper. The gangly researcher shrugged, farewelled and sauntered after his employer.

Julian sponged a second Kill off Joey. Higher ranking chazzes arrived and bustled up the marble steps into the offices. An Erect cleaner, Marag, shambled up to the small group of staff. —A Councillor is sick, | she signed, her sloping forehead creased with simian worry. Julian had never seen that sign projected previously. —A chas tells me. A Councillor is sick. |

'Is that the cunningest invention to which fleet-footed rumour can aspire?' Parqué wondered. 'Her pinions halt and fail her in her flight, it seems.'

Marag's dark eyes gazed back distress at her.

'No Councillor is sick, Marag,' Parqué sighed. 'That cannot happen, as you well recall. The constable was taking cruel entertainment at your expense.'

—That is good, | agreed Marag. —A Councillor is not sick. That is good. | She wandered off again.

'Merciful Lovers,' Parqué muttered.

More minutes passed, until at length Julian gestured, —Swyve this. If Mesh can't be snuffed to present herself, I'm back to bed like Sino. | Truth told, he had been hoping this would be the situ. His head clamoured for quiet, and he didn't want to face Mesh Cos without first thinking through his dilemma with the Great Detectives.

'I'n't that her, Juley?' asked Joey Gilgamesh suddenly. 'Coming down the steps there?'

—Oh tits, | Julian gestured, his movements tiny but emphatic, —it is as well. | The Lastwoman approached the group, her gait graceful as always.

'That she was permitted to enter is most singular,' Parqué mused. 'I had it on the best authority that all were excluded as one.'

'That sort of thing don't usually apply to her lot,' said Joey equably.

'Hello Julian,' Cllr. Mesh lilted, arriving at the group and adding without blinking, 'Parqué, Joey, Jenfar, Balasubramanian. My word, what a morning this has been. I gather they'll be letting everyone in soon. Are you busy, Julian?'

Mesh Cos was taller than Julian, shorter than Parqué, lustrous of skin and delicate of bone, proportioned like a Romuline Venus and often about as adequately dressed. Today her iridescent mother-of-pearl skin was sheathed in a Gaultier suit-kimono, her laurel-green hair loose across her shoulders. To pre-posthuman eyes, she peered around eighteen years old (this was some 7,000 years lacking). Julian had been researching for her nearly a year now, and she was still the most heartmurmuringly beautiful individual he had ever met (apart, quite obviously, from her daughter Lon Shel).

—Um, not really busy, no, | signed Julian, nonplussed. He still had no idea how to infer when, if ever, Mesh was being sarcastic at him. He farewelled awkwardly toward the others and followed after her. She made direct for Honi's Melato Venue, cloistered two quadrangles over, near the ballroomplex. A single table sat empty for them there, Mesh Cos rarely having to wait for anything.

Julian settled himself down with a melato crudé, while the Cllr. opted for a frodo. —So, what emerges? | Julian asked her. —A CoHo sec-ex? |

'No, Julian,' Mesh said gently, 'not an exercise.'

Julian listened with increasing horror as she told him. —Dead? | he gestured at one point, the unfamiliar sign prickling his palms.

When finished, Mesh gazed at him with cool appraisal. 'And I've more bad news for you, I'm afraid.'

Oh toss, thought Julian limply. He was too shocked for bluffing. —This'll be about the Great Detectives, then, | he indicated. He'd barely known Cllr. Mostyn, but this thing that had happened...

'Yes and no,' Mesh told him. 'You've been trying to find Shel, haven't you?'

Julian yessed, shamefacedly.

Her violet eyes surveyed him with compassion. 'She'll be in touch when she's ready, Julian. I've always said so.'

—I know, | signed Julian. —But! | he remembered, excitation overcoming his numb astonishment. —The sherlock said someone had vizzed her! | The emphatic almost knocked his crudé over.

'In Hensile District, yes,' Mesh agreed gently. 'Be that as it may...'

—Hensile? | Julian had never heard of it, but Districts were 10^{10} a penny. He could –

'Julian,' Mesh said, musical as always, 'I'm going to have to let you go.' That grabbed his concentration. 'I'm sorry, but you can't continue working as my researcher.'

—You're sacking me? | Julian signed, aghast. His indignation deflated immediately, as he retrieved how fully he'd deserved it. —Swyve, | he added, soberly.

'There is, however,' Mesh said, as she leant forward over her melato, 'something else that you might do for me, if you'd be so kind.'

He listened carefully to her telling him what. Soon he was less plussed than ever.

8. Urbanus, the Romuline.

Even as a largely unregarded junior scion, Urbanus Ignotus found that membership of the most powerful family in the Romuline conferred upon him a large number of supposed honours. He was, for instance, technically a magistrate, a decurion in the Romuline Militia (although he had rarely served as the former, and not once as the latter) and a member of the Aqueducts Commission.

He was also a junior priest of both Dis Pater and Neptunus. Both gods were minor figures in the Romuline's revised pantheon, celebrated primarily in their minor aspects: Neptunus, for instance, patronised horses and fishmongers. Such seas as now existed (though sometimes large enough to quench suns) were so dwarfed in status by the City and its Parks as to be considered little more than ornamental lakes; since moreover none of them bordered the Romuline, its citizens had little cause to call on their traditional sea-god. As the former god of the afterlife, Dis was even more of an embarrassment: even an early push to make Dis patron of the largely underground Tube system had failed.

Both deities had lost out in the divine reshuffle that had supposedly followed the Olympians' relocation to Mount Antaeus in Gaia Park: their places in the gods' halls had been taken by Romulus, Rome's founder, and Civitata, goddess of the City of the Saved itself. (That the original Etruscan migrant on whom the Romulus legend was based had been tracked down to Namura District, where he was working as a bouncer, seemed to bother the Romuline's theologians surprisingly little.) Lord Jupiter had divorced the shrewish Juno in favour of Roma, the retired mother goddess of Rome, and Vulcanus and Minerva had grown in stature and importance, being appointed by the ever-pragmatic Romulines to their respective City roles of god of manufacturing and technology, and goddess of IT and communications.

Neither of Urbanus' own deities would be of much use to him in his forthcoming journey, so, after a brief libation poured out of loyalty over each of their altars, the young man made his way to the Temple of Civitata.

In the huge, echoing space, noisy with chatter and with cries of animal distress, Urbanus tried not to wince as a young priestess efficiently dispatched the piglet he was offering to the goddess. The Temple was well-staffed, but even so there was a substantial queue for sacrifice: Tube journeys were arduous, not to mention time-consuming (journeys of days being not unusual), and Civitata found her favour in perennial demand. The pig's squeals soon quietened, as blood ran from its pink throat onto the marble altar, mingling with the wine and cornmeal already sprinkled there. The priestess intoned prayers for Urbanus' safety and his quick return, in which Urbanus joined ardently. Since he had of course taken the local Tube line on many occasions the prospect of the journey itself held little to concern him, but his fear of failing Cassius Ignotus was acute.

Thanking the priestess, and recompensing her handsomely for expediting his sacrifice over those of the plebeians, Urbanus turned to leave. Absorbed as he was in thought, he almost failed to hear amongst the clamour the calling of a familiar voice.

'Urbanus!' Tiresias was standing underneath a mosaic, the fragments of coloured stone depicting entirely speculative details of the nuptials of Romulus and Civitata. The old man's tunic was lightly smirched with blood, suggesting that his own theological transaction had been rather more effortful. 'I thought I might find you here.'

'Tiresias!' Urbanus was delighted. He had not seen the slave for some months now: his old tutor was, he gathered, closely occupied in teaching various of Urbanus' second cousins. The old hermaphrodite had been a great friend during Urbanus' adolescence, and his tutor's wise advice had been sorely missed since Urbanus had reached adulthood. Most of his other students had mocked Tiresias for being ineffectual and unworldly: he and Urbanus had had much in common. 'How did you find out I was leaving?' the young man asked.

'*We're* leaving, dear boy.' Tiresias smiled affably at him. 'Your great-grandfather's instructed me to accompany you. To keep you on the straight and narrow, or something of the kind. Couldn't follow what he was on about, to be honest. Do you have the Tube tickets?'

'You're coming with me?' Urbanus had been expecting to meet his escort at the station. He had not even considered that the slave accompanying him might be his own tutor. He could have hugged Tiresias with relief, and, after a moment's hesitation, did just that, taking comfort in the familiar swell of the old man's breasts beneath the tunic.

'Wouldn't miss it for the world, my boy,' Tiresias said, patting his back gently. 'Just, er, bring me up to speed on what we're doing there, would you? Lucius Cassius was rather *evasive* about the whole thing.'

Arm-in-arm, the pair strolled out from under the pale Temple's high portico, and into the fading afternoon skylight. The tree-lined avenue of the Antonine Hill murmured about them in the countless voices of the City, as they descended calmly towards the nearest Tube station.

9. The City.

The wound in Councillor Ved Mostyn's torso is deep but narrow, a violated bloody slit. Nothing flows from it now, but much has: a rusty substance crusts the wound, trailing down flabby flesh to dye the albino carpetmoss. The largest stain is metres away, suggesting Mostyn dragged himself some distance before rolling turtle-like onto his back to die.

The body sprawls face-upwards, flesh-rolls lolling, tiny genitals dwarfed by his giant belly. His eyes are open, staring, face salt-caked with sweat. One hand clutches tightly at a palmtop pad, skin taut, fingers white like worms' flesh. The pad's contents are mundane: speeches, letters, press clippings. No mention of his murderer's identity. The pad was something to hold onto while he died.

Mostyn's private sanctum in his Council Office is decked out unusually. Many of the Councillors choose to keep a bedchamber available (space is, after all, not at a premium here) for nights spent working late, or afternoon siestas. Ved Mostyn's occupancy has been characteristically more individual.

The carpetmoss is bordered on all sides by mirror: ranks of gleaming spotlights fade into the infinite distance, highlighting corpse after corpse, all of them Mostyn's. Their discipline is broken only by one mirror panel, hanging open to reveal a wardrobe. The ceiling, too, is mirrored, Mostyn's appalled disgust reflected perfectly in the dead man suspended face-down over him.

Besides a pair of shabby, wide-lapelled check suits, the wardrobe holds a variety of more exotic garments: black and red, leather and rubber and velvet, hanging forlorn now, empty, ownerless. The centre of the room consists entirely of bed, black satin sheets forming a square pool. A selection of straps and padded handcuffs depends from a wrought-iron stand, while a feather boa drapes languidly across one pillow.

A leather case, lined with plush velvet, sits on the bed, open to expose a glittering array of edged weapons. Some are sleek, some shabby; some gleam in the fierce light while others suck it in. Daggers, machetes, carving-knives, in steel and silver and ceramic.

> A chipped flint knife, with wicked facets.
> A sharpened circle with too many finger-holds.
> A serrated blade of pale bone, its rubber handle fetish-black.

No knife is bloodstained. (How could it be? These are props, nothing more.) All are in the case.

All day the uniformed men and women from Council House Administration and Security bustle in and out, noting, examining, recording. It is long hours before one of them thinks to close Mostyn's eyes. They are not used to death here.

The condition of the Councillors' offices has slowly tended back towards normality. The Councillors and staff have returned to work, muttering and shuffling as they finally pass through the shimmering barrier. Those Councillors who spent the night in their own offices were woken early, apologetically: by the time the barrier was lifted they had mostly returned in disgust to their quarters, far away in the craggy north face of Council House. The truth about the morning's disruption has not been publicised – and is all but unthinkable – but it is evident that something deeply worrying has happened. Mostyn's office is still protected by stinging force barriers, and the other Councillors hurry past it with countenances variously concerned, frightened or studiedly indifferent. Mesh Cos, one of the few to know the truth, sits in her office, poised and serene as she flicks through her correspondence and composes specifications for a new researcher. If she is agitated, not a tremble in her voice or movement betrays it.

After nightfall Ved Mostyn's body is removed under covers, his office sealed up altogether. Few Councillors or staff remain to witness the event, and those that do are reassured. (An alien visitor, of course, not protected by the City's invulnerability protocols. A tragic accident. Cllr. Mostyn most upset.)

The offices lie at the plateau of Council House, their marble and granite bulk imposing beneath the sky-dome. Their portico fronts onto King Square, lit up now with arc lanterns. Above rises only the floodlit curve of the Council Chamber: beneath, the darkened citadel descends, ramparts on parapets, down to the bright-lit press of Central District far below.

No mere building but an edifice, a Vatican the size of old Manhattan, Council House's stony canyons hold labyrinthine miles of corridors and tunnels, cloisters and courtyards. Although it cannot compete with the City's handful of really big structures (such as the Watchtower, whose intimidating South-West Buttress can be seen arising many blocks to the north) it is nonetheless a colossal accumulation of stone.

Set in the south-east wing, some floors above the consulate of the Canals

Commission but below the Manichean Chapel, is that assortment of clerical quarters customarily assigned to Councillors' researchers. Julian White Mammoth Tusk's rooms stand deserted, his phonescreen dead, his bed unslept-in. His home-pigmented posters have been taken from the walls. Julian himself is elsewhere already, surrounded by antiseptic white tiling and garish adverts, squatting on a red plastic seat in a near-deserted Tube station in another District altogether. He cradles a package, and a smile overcomes his sinewy lips as he ponders the commission Cllr. Mesh has given him.

Around him, chains like shuttling threads ply the flipside of the urban surface, conveying Citizens from place to place across the spans once commonly associated with interstellar voyages. Avoiding sewers, powerlines, the communications net, the tunnels of the troglodytic species, one chain carries Urbanus Ignotus and the slave Tiresias on the first leg of their long journey toward Kempes. Another bears Laura Tobin away from Paynesdown. She scowls moodily at her reflection in the darkened glass, illumined by the flicker-frames of unreality between stations.

After some time, she reaches into her luggage, balanced on the rack above her. The impassive weight of her weapon's holster-strap presses reassuringly upon her shoulder. She settles back into her seat, and stares out of the window.

10. Tobin, the Tube.

Irreal, real. Irreal, real. Through the carriage windows station after station swirled, broke up and blended into abstraction.

The Tube chain was jumping from District to District, covering megametres in minutes, each point of entry to reality contrasting with the last. As Tobin watched, a studded chrome concourse with sliding glass and giant news-screens became a firelit cavern with wall-paintings advertising local bison restaurants.

One of her descendants had once told Tobin that the last of their line had been kidnapped by the Great Houses, back in the Universe. Compassion V had been shaped, by the arcane manipulations of the Houseworlders, into one of their timeships. Still human on the outside, but containing within herself an interior the size of star systems, she'd been required to ferry passengers from point to point in spacetime, submerging herself in the base-unreality which underlay the Universe.

Quite apart from the violation-of-privacy issue – which had always been a problem for her – Tobin wouldn't have expected any of her iterations to have the stomach for it. However many times she saw it happen (and she'd actually spent some of the City's early decades working on a freight chain), Tube travel still made her feel faintly queasy.

Luckily, the compartment's interior was stable. In fact it was drearily mundane, with luggage racks, wood panelling, plush seats and colourful enamel plaques calling the occupants' attention to drinks and confectionery which the manufacturers ventured to suggest they might not find entirely devoid of interest. Trying to ignore the rupturing reality outside the window, Tobin directed her attention straight ahead.

How can they be sure it's not a clone? she asked the woman knitting peaceably in front of her.

Her companion pushed back half-moon spectacles and began a new row. 'Rudimentary biodata analysis, my poppet,' the figure told her. With the fetch's help, learning the basics of the case had taken Tobin very little time – less than it had taken to swallow her pride and contact Godfather Avatar. 'A homunculus might have the same genetic structures as the parent individual, but its deep-time structures are going to be quite different. They're usually a lot shorter in duration, for one thing.' The wooden needles clacked in time with the rocking of the carriage.

A fellow-passenger, passing along the Tube chain's corridor and happening to peer into Laura Tobin's compartment, would have seen a human-normal woman, her rusty hair pulled back in an untidy ponytail, dressed in a sensible white blouse, a bootlace tie and trenchcoat, sitting next to a woad-smothered Celtic warrior and gazing at the large-eyed and sticklike posthuman snoring heavily in the seat opposite. Such an observer would not have seen the woman she was talking to, because the fetch didn't exist outside Tobin's head.

They can do that now? Tobin unsaid, surprised. Biodata technology was traditionally a Great House preserve. The City's researchers had been keeping that development understandably quiet. Which meant the datafetch had some impressive infiltration tech behind her.

'Oh yes,' the woman replied comfortably, adjusting her shawl across her shoulders. Fortunately for Tobin's uneasy stomach, the orb she held smartly overwrite all her perceptions of her real neighbour, rather than just superimposing the fetch on top of him. 'They can't just look and tell you how he died, though, not yet. It's a shame, it would have saved us both a lot of work.'

The datafetch and sensorb had absorbed a substantial chunk of Tobin's first instalment of pay. It was a far higher level of tech than she'd been able to afford before, thanks to the absurd salary it seemed the Parliament was prepared to offer her. The orb used Tobin's nervous system as its interface, imposing images directly on her visual cortex. The fetch was a sophisticated AI, based for some reason on the personality patterns of someone's grandmother. Apart from Tobin having to remember not to speak aloud, the briefing perfectly resembled a conversation.

And he's not been re-resurrected, Tobin sub-vocalised flatly.

'If he has, my lamb,' the fetch said, picking up a stitch with practised ease, 'then it's not anywhere I've looked so far. Of course the City's far too big to go through all of, but I've checked Central, where it looks like he died, and Wormward where he lived, and Kalima where he got resurrected the first time round. I'm going through other Districts we know he visited, but that's going to take me a while.'

Keep looking, Tobin told her.

'There's something else, my duck.' The construct paused to count off rows of stitches, clicking her tongue rapidly. Mannerisms like this were included in the

MOSTYN, Cllr. Vedular Ormazd (Ved), founder of various cultural and artistic movements, nightclub owner, bon viveur and politician; Rdt for Wormward Dist. (by acclamation) from AF 241; Cllr. from AF 282; *b* Siloportem 14,413,112 AD, *s* of The Very Appropriate Wyngarde Mostyn and Madame accelerata muda; *m* 1st, 14,413,115 AD, Ms. Gecko Telstar (marr. diss. 14,413,115 AD); 2nd, 14,413,132 AD, Lord Parallel of Pang (marr. diss. 14,413,135 AD); one *d*; [...] 18th, 14,413,251 AD, Lady Rapaticar 23son and Mrs. Olive Propulso! (marr. diss. 14,413,259 AD and 14,413,262 AD); two s. *Educ*: Private tutor; Ms. Karpale's Adjustment Centre for Young Recreants; Lylart Coll., Univ. of Silop. Founded various cultural movements including Absenteeism, Obscenery and The Trampolinium. *Publications:* The All-New Trampolinium and You: How It Can Change Your Life!, 14,413,224 AD. *d* Jelicortine 14,413,309 AD (*N.B.* pre-City dates and details disputed, see below); *r* Kalima Dist., W. Quarter; *m* AF 22 two hundred and forty-three members of the Oval Fulfilment sect, as follows [...] Founded the Oval Fulfilment sect, the Spherical City Society, Slippery Slopes Nightclub and Bar. *Publications:* The Slippery Slopes Book of Cocktail Recipes, AF 41; The Slippery Slopes Book of Nude Celeb Pics, AF 42; etc. *Recreations:* partying, naturism, philately. *Addresses:* "Ved's", 69 Salacious Boulevard, Wormward Dist.; Apt. 812, Councillors' Quarters, Council House, Central Dist. *Clubs:* Slippery Slopes, Nigel's Place, the Entrance At Rear Club.

N.B. Contention exists over Cllr. Mostyn's pre-City biography. The details above are those supplied to us by Cllr. Mostyn himself, and the editors make no guarantee as to their accuracy.

[From *Who's Who in the City of the Saved* (AF 290 edition).]

fetch package to put Tobin at her ease. She hadn't yet discovered how to switch them off. 'Soon be finished now,' the image added happily, before continuing: 'The Councillor had some little, let's say, foibles.'

'Foibles?' Tobin asked aloud. The Celtic tribesman looked up from his newstablet and tutted. Are we talking sex here? she added, silently.

'Oh yes.' The fetch peered at her over the rims of her glasses. 'Well known he was for his little predilections. Collateral women was one of them. So was heavy-duty lifting cyborgs – the sweatier the better, apparently. But what he really liked was his pseudo-masochism.'

Oh, shit, thought Tobin.

'I know. There are some funny people, aren't there?' agreed the fetch, turning her attention back towards her knitting. 'Mister Mostyn liked pretending to inflict and suffer pain. Especially suffer. Some of the investigating officers are saying he was killed by one of his fancy men or women. But not before he'd given someone else a lot of money to do research into potent weapons for him. They haven't got any proof of that bit, of course, but he was ever so well-off from running those nightclubs in Wormward.'

They think he had himself killed just for the kicks? Tobin was incredulous.

'That's right, my lovely. And you must admit it goes with the way they found the body. Now, you don't need me to tell you your job,' the construct told her kindly, casting off, 'but if I was you I'd be very interested in who the Councillor might have been, let's say, walking out with.'

I'll be sure to ask around, Tobin replied. I mean, that won't seem suspicious or anything. It's exactly the sort of thing you'd expect Cllr. Mesh's new researcher to be looking into for her.

The fetch, who was well programmed to detect sarcasm, sniffed loudly. 'Well, dear, your cover story isn't really my department. I expect that Godfather Avatar knows best.' She produced some scissors out of thin air, and cut through her end of wool.

Outside the windows of the frail compartment, the structure of the world continued merging, blending, reinventing itself, as the chain sped on its way through the transdimensional capillaries of the City.

II. Anthony Fisher, Aelfred College.

Professor Anthony Fisher had been married more than one would expect from a man of his retiring disposition and physical infirmities. On his original life in the Universe he preferred to dwell as little as was possible, but when it ended it had been notable that the one wife whom he had truly loved, his third of four, had been spectacularly unfaithful to him, causing him the greatest distress as well as making him the laughing-stock of his contemporaries. His resurrected existence in the City of the Saved had been less eventful in almost every respect, but still he had stumbled into four more marriages during that time, bringing the total to a remarkable eight.

One of his earliest acts in the City had been to attempt a reunion with his childhood sweetheart, who had died tragically at the age of eleven. However Camilla, though mercifully not frozen in her development as were some child resurrectees, had matured slowly, while Prof. Fisher's imago displayed every one of his sixty-four years. More seriously, his mind was burdened with the experiences of a sexagenarian, while she retained the charming innocence he had loved in youth. Neither of them had understood the other any longer, and at length the union had foundered on their lack of common ground. Consumed by bitterness, the historian had drawn on his expertise to construct the new name and background which had served him so well during the following centuries.

During that time, despite his impairments, Professor Fisher had proved sufficiently intriguing to two of his students as to contract marriages with each of them, yet these too lasted a scant few years before his wives abandoned him for younger-looking men. Allisheer St Marx was the first woman in more than two hundred years with whom he had fallen in love without being in loco parentis, and the relationship between the two academics, formalised in 209, was based on far more solid foundations. He no longer worried about his wife deceiving him. He had, he felt, enough experience now to know the signs, and take whatever action proved necessary. His current concern related to other matters.

He had had the keenest historical mind of his first age. Even among the astronomical enormities that were the City's population, it remained acute enough to earn his tenure. He knew history more intimately than he had known any of his wives, enough to augur what must be approaching, even in so atypical a history as that of the City.

Before him on the mahogany desk of his study, a sheet of paper bore several paragraphs in painstaking longhand. He read them back, tapping gently upon the desktop with his fountain pen:

Professor Isichei's contention is that, following the failed assault by the Great Houses in AF 262, the City (or at least its successive City Councils) has been displaying on a massive scale the normal psychological symptoms of shock. The earliest stages of political reaction have consisted of timidity and fatigue on the part of the Citizens and especially the Councils, who have elected three consecutive Lord Mayors who have been perceived as entirely weak. The evident fear has been that another Mayor who is not such might betray the City as did Verrifant.

According to Isichei's model, this symptom is now beginning to pass. Lassitude has given way to angry belligerence, and the Councillors who are being most widely mentioned as potential candidates for the Mayoral term of 292 to 302 are variously extreme in their respective politics. Most of these come from the reactionary camp (notably Cllrs Cassius Ignotus, Giuliani, Angstrom Hive and Brindled Wolf), but equally notable is the determined progressivism of another likely nominee, Cllr. Prof. Allisheer St Marx.

Prof. Fisher sighed: the confounded article was proving impossible to write without stumbling across this particular conflict of interest. Standing, he pitched the latest draft into his wastepaper basket, picked a paperback from his shelves and limped towards the window of his study, running his fingers lightly along the spines of his books.

In life his various disabilities had ingrained themselves deeply into his consciousness, and his resurrection body retained them: lame in one leg, he had terrible digestion and was prone to fainting fits. The City's prohibition, enshrined in her very physical laws, against harm to human beings was to him a source of some annoyance. The medical techniques existed to cure his various ailments, but most entailed the unconscionable necessity of surgery. Since an academic salary offered little hope of either visiting the secure clinics in uptime Ascension or commissioning a City-grown clone body, Fisher had continued in the state to which he was accustomed. His slight deafness, at least, had succumbed to a nanobotic hearing aid.

Slumping into the box seat, he gazed across the quadrangles and battlements of Aelfred College, the playing fields and modest airfield beyond, to where the sheer cliff of the internal wall rose walkway upon gallery upon balustrade. How colossal the architecture here, he thought for the dozenth time that day, how puny the grandiloquent monuments of his native era. They were dwarfed as dust-motes clinging to a mountain.

Fisher had been concerned enough when Allisheer had been elected Resident for Base and Buttress District, refusing the University's offer of a sabbatical. When the Council House's random selection engines had decreed that Base and Buttress' Resident would also serve the next term as a City Councillor, he had been proud but aghast. She had insisted calmly that she could manage, that the increased work would be a challenge. Since then, for what was now almost a decade, he had seen less of her, but she had remained as fond and loving as ever. And now (although of course electioneering was, in theory, forbidden) her candidacy for the Mayoralty was being talked about as something certain.

He considered his wife overworked, and under-appreciated by all but himself. Her political allies, that filthy beast Mostyn in particular, had been preying on her ambition and good nature. For all the random selection system's benefits, the Councillors were chosen from the Chamber of Residents, and the Residents were appointed by their Districts according to local customs as diverse as telepathic consensus and hereditary matriarchy. The Council was thus sampled from some of humanity's most devious and ruthless politicians, and the demands this made upon the Lord Mayor's guile and resilience could overwhelm the ablest of candidates, even if leadership of some hundred undecillion human beings did not. He was frankly astonished that Verrifant had been, as far as had been publicised, the first Mayor to break under this tremendous pressure.

Of late Allisheer had become terse and snappish, putting in absurd hours at the Council House. Often she would overnight there, returning only briefly to their home, to change her clothes before heading directly to lecture or research at the University's Faculty of Archemathics. Last night, as several times recently, she had not come home at all; sending him instead the brief message that she loved him, and that they might not meet until the formal reception for Professor Handramit the coming Saturday.

His wife was as gifted a politician as she was an archemathicist, he knew. He loved her and respected her ambitions, and if she would not confide in him he must continue to take whatever actions he considered best for her, as he had always done. He would continue to support her, even if others did not. But some of her opponents were quite ruthless, fully capable of murder in their hearts, if not in reality under the current circumstances of the City. He recognised the type: he had been, after all, just such a man himself. He only hoped Allisheer would remain safe, and that she would return to him the same woman with whom he remained, after so many years, in love.

12. Urbanus, the Tube.

The journey of Urbanus and Tiresias to Kempes District was a protracted one, and allowed the younger man to learn a great deal concerning the City and its inhabitants, his childhood tutor in particular.

Their Tube chain was one of Francistine manufacture, and the carriage in which the pair sat was grown from living wood, its windows clear white cellulose. The mossy branches which comprised the seats had moulded themselves fondly to the human form. Even the vehicle's wormhole catalysers and antigravity cells would be botanic: the Francistine Order was one of fearsomely accomplished biological engineers. Bioluminescent lichens on the ceiling cast gentle green illumination, and the entire effect blended the comfort of a treehouse with that of a womb. Urbanus found it mildly claustrophobic, although Tiresias insisted it was perfectly charming.

Tiresias provided an intermittent whispered commentary upon their fellow passengers, the ever-changing crowd of whom was as diverse and unfamiliar as the surrounding architecture. Urbanus had vaguely imagined that every Citizen visited the Romuline District at one time or another, but, as the old slave gently explained, this was very wide of the mark. Soon they were seeing humans of cultures, clades and species whose existences he had never imagined.

Urbanus was particularly intrigued by one man whose single leg was columnar, with one giant foot splayed at its end. 'Don't you know your Pliny?' Tiresias whispered mockingly, in answer to his pupil's murmured query. 'He's a Sciopod. They're rather rare. And *she* might be a soldier from one of the Hive Districts,' he added of another fellow-passenger, whose armoured body sported wicked claws in place of hands. 'Either that or some kind of collateral. It's difficult to tell.' The putative hive-woman was mangling a newspaper, while the uniped ate chipped potatoes with a plastic fork.

Tiresias' face clouded when Urbanus pointed out a figure at the far end of the carriage. Around Urbanus' age, the man was hugely muscled with unnaturally broad shoulders, his hair cropped close to his head so as to mirror his abundant stubble. His leather clothing, obviously some kind of cultural costume, left much of him uncovered, and he was hung about with spikes and chains.

'That, young Urbanus, is a Manfolk of the Jennike Nation,' the old slave murmured, in response to his pupil's query. 'He'll be going our way, I expect.'

When Urbanus asked the old slave what he meant, it transpired that Kempes bordered Manfold, the Manfolk's home and one of the City's scattered secessionist Districts. This provided Urbanus with his first inkling of what his great-grandfather's interests there might be: the enclave's pretensions to independence were one of the Ignotian family's more notorious political bêtes noires, yet, as the young man knew from the accounts he'd seen, Manfold was also one of its keenest markets for vicarious experiences of violence. Evidently Cassius had felt that the best way to obtain an unbiased report on... well, whatever it was upon which he expected Urbanus to report, would be to send an agent unencumbered by such useful items as local knowledge.

'I'm surprised he's travelling in public,' Urbanus whispered.

'Yes, they're not particularly popular,' Tiresias agreed shortly. The big man glanced their way and scowled, resting a hand on the spiked handle of his punching-dagger.

The old slave grew more garrulous as distance elapsed between their hurtling chain and the Romuline. An inflated impression of his home's importance to the culture of the City was, the slave implied, the least of the misconceptions Urbanus' education had foisted on him. Tiresias apologetically acknowledged his complicity in this: 'Lucius Cassius,' he said, 'is rather keen on his *particular vision* of reality. Those of us retainers who stick to alternative viewpoints, openly at least, don't remain in his favour for very long. And, you see, I enjoy teaching you young people.'

'But as a slave?' Urbanus wondered. He was amused to hear his tutor giving vent to such unorthodox opinions, and flattered too that the old man trusted him enough not to expect to find them reported back to Cassius directly, but the more he heard the more puzzled he was at Tiresias' choice of employment.

His origins were, to Urbanus and his contemporaries, opaque. He was, it was well known, hermaphrodite: his slave-name commemorated the legendary Theban seer who had spent a decade as a woman, courtesy of an infuriated goddess Venus. Urbanus himself had had occasion to observe his tutor's bodily peculiarities when they had visited the public baths together, and some of his maturer relatives, he'd gathered, had taken advantage of the long tradition of slaves' sexual availability to experience them at even closer hand.

It was assumed that Tiresias hailed from one of the many posthuman cultures: in the era following the Earth's annihilation it had been customary for individuals to have themselves resculpted, for ends not excluding the sexual; more prosaically, some double-sexed species of humanity were known to have developed naturally during this epoch. Why one from such a background would choose to subject himself to slavery was a question which had not previously troubled Urbanus, any more than that of ascribing masculine gender to "him".

The chain halted in Araminta District to set down passengers and change drivers. Here glass walls and ceiling held back a weight of ocean water, while dim fluorescent lights lit up the lapping platform: beyond, dark seascrapers stretched into murky dimness. A human-normal man inside the carriage zipped up his wetsuit, pulled on flippers and a facemask and hopped out of the carriage doors, disappearing into the platform with a splash. Some minutes later, two Marine Citizens burst up from it and into the carriage. The merpeople sat dripping on a bench, which soaked up the water and desalinated it. Dark fishy shadows lurked beyond the station's limits.

Meanwhile, Tiresias was expounding upon the the political basis of Romuline slavery. There were, he was explaining, three main categories of slaves. Most of the slaves Urbanus' family kept were from what he called 'the *less advantaged* classes' of the City's population. The litter-bearers, for example, were of the earliest human species: though sentient, these were of limited intellect, and were employed in tasks of unskilled manual labour throughout the City. Others, the collaterals, were not fully human: their alien blood might gift them with unique skills, yet it precluded them from gainful employment in all but the most recklessly egalitarian of Districts. Members of these castes had found indentured slavery, particularly in a context where physical abuse was not an option, to provide a security which to them was not available in the City at large.

Others had simply known no life other than slavery: they had been born into the condition, whether in Rome or Egypt or Russia or Virginia, had lived and died as slaves without knowing freedom, and were thus ill-equipped for a life of independence.

'But there aren't so many of them,' Tiresias added. 'Most slaves hope for something better, even if it's only a kinder master. So you see, it's in your great-grandfather's interests for *certain classes* of person to stay disadvantaged. The more inclusive the City becomes, the more concessions the Romuline families will have to offer their slaves, and the less profitable their businesses will be. Every kind of division between Citizens – even what many think of our well-muscled friend down there,' he added, recklessly indicating the Manfolk warrior, '– works to the Romuline's advantage.'

Urbanus had begun to drift off in his seat: he and Tiresias had been travelling all night, and sleep had been difficult to come by. He watched through flickering eyelids as the carriage flashed from station to station; it briefly seemed incongruously at home beside a viny platform, grown among the road-roots of a sky-spanning tree.

It occurred to Urbanus as he finally fell asleep to wonder which of these groups of slaves the old hermaphrodite considered himself to belong to. But by that stage he was far too tired to voice the thought.

13. Ludmilla, the Romuline.

Ludmilla had to bring up the oil for Master Decimuses morning wash but when she went down to the kitchens Cook was in a tizz.

Some buggers in my pantry Cook said I can hear them breathing. She was all uptight. All the other kitchen slaves was standing round muttering.

Who is it? Ludmilla wanted to know.

How should I know girl? Cook said. Do I look like I can see through walls?

No Cook Ludmilla said.

Its probly an alien said Jemily the kitchen maid. Probly a Houseworld spy come to do for Consul Cassius. Theyve got them potent weapons now my Auntie said.

Or a clatteral said Cook. Cook was a clatteral a big fat crossbreed with big bushy eyebrows and silvery warts on her face. Her orange hair was always tousled and she snacked when she cooked. Some disgusting clatteral thing hiding in my larder and screeting slime all over the Consuls food! she said.

I bet its not said Ludmilla. I bet its just a dog or compsognathus or something whats got shut in there in the night.

You be quiet girl said Cook. Or you take a look in there if youre so bleeding certain.

Alright said Ludmilla bravely I will. She put down Master Decimuses amphora and went over to the pantry door. Jemily screamed when she touched the door handle. Shut up Jemily Ludmilla said. She listened at the door and heard someone breathing just like Cook said all heavy and snorting. Quickly before she changed her mind and ran away she opened up the pantry door and jumped back. There was a big hairy shape sleeping on the floor and snoring it was bare it was huge with horns and a bulls head and hoofs and a great big willy.

Its only Dedalus said Ludmilla.

Dedalus! Cook cried and you could tell she was really cross cause shed been frightened. Come out of there at once you good for nothing waste of biodata!

Dedalus groaned and started to get up.

And put some clothes on you dirty bleeder Cook added throwing him an apron. Jemily kept looking at Dedaluses big cock and giggling fit to pee herself. What do you think youre doing in there you horrible slave of a clatteral? Cook asked him. Cook was a slave too.

Dedalus muttered something. His voice was deep and bellowy out of his bulls head but he sounded miserable. He tied the apron on him with his hands. Only his feet was hoofs.

Whats that young man? snapped Cook.

Dedalus snorted unhappily. No need to bloody shout he grumbled. Wheres bloody Tiresias?

You watch your bleeding language Cook said viciously Ooh I could give you such an hiding!

Tiresias? said Ludmilla. Why dyou want Tiresias Dedalus?

We was drinking said Dedalus sulkily. He give me a cup of wine to drink to my trip.

Did Tiresias get you drunk Dedalus? giggled Jemily Did you two you know?

Jemily Cook snapped you get on with your work my girl or by Civvy youll feel the flat of my hand! Jemily made a face and went over and pretended to wash the dishes. Now my lad Cook said drunk or not what do you mean by going to sleep in my bleeding larder?

I dunno Dedalus said I only had one cup. That bastard must of put somethink in my wine.

Some bodyguard you are said Cook. Arent you sposed to be at Council House with Consul Cassius?

Shit Dedalus said Whats the bloody time?

How should I know? Cook said. Do I look like a skydial?

Its Marsday morning Ludmilla said.

Jupiter Christ Dedalus bellowed Im sposed to be taking Master Urbanus to bloody Kempes! We was sposed to go yesterday night! The Consuls gonna bloody banish me!

Well Cook told him severely you should of thought of that before letting that Tiresias drug you shouldnt you?

Dedalus groaned again.

14. Tobin, Council House.

'These people are deviants.' Cllr. Ignotus' voice was measured. He sipped the mineral water Tobin had handed him, and frowned uncomfortably at the decadent upholstery of Cllr. Mesh's mossy armchair.

'To you and me they are, of course,' Mesh Cos smiled. 'From their point of view it's us who deviate from the natural order of things. Surely?'

'Ah.' Ignotus' smile was thinner. 'But theirs is the minority view.'

Sitting in the background, Laura Tobin doodled heavy weaponry designs onto her palm pad. Despite her best efforts, her attention was wandering some distance away.

'Samphire District is still undecided on the Manfold question, Cassius,' Mesh was saying, 'but you know we're unlikely to be swayed by appeals to prejudice.'

'To common sense, you mean,' Ignotus agreed sourly. 'To my regret, I do.'

'So, haven't you got anything better? I warn you I found Ved Mostyn's arguments rather compelling. You'll have your work cut out to uncompel me.'

Mesh's face was serenity itself, betraying not a flicker as she mentioned dead Ved Mostyn. Tobin knew Mesh was one of the very few people in Council House who were aware of the fat man's fate. The slight narrowing of Ignotus' eyes suggested he was making a similar calculation – meaning that he also knew.

In his own way Cassius Ignotus was as formidable a political force as Mesh Cos. Apparently. Tobin had heard of neither of them before her arrival yesterday morning, but she'd rarely given a toss about politics. The Romuline District adhered strictly to the republican model of Roman government, and under Ignotus' leadership its Senate had called for the trial of all the former Emperors as traitors to Rome. Despite such eccentricities, during the current Council term the elderly Earth-born cultures had looked increasingly to the Romuline Councillor to represent their special interests – while the civic pride his District nurtured for the City, as both their goddess and a secular ideal, endeared him to the more community-minded.

Mesh Cos listened attentively, Tobin with profound boredom, as Ignotus expounded upon the dangers the Manfolk's particular deviancies posed. He seemed to consider the species (which was known, he said, to have been genetically altered, quite probably by aliens) to be inimical to normal human life. He even hinted that they might be engineered agents of the Houseworld military. As a ploy to worry Mesh, who had her own history with the Great Houses, it was surprisingly crude. She brushed it off with an amused laugh.

'I understand the Manfolk are unpopular with many Citizens,' she told him tolerantly, 'and I take the point that Manfold chose to secede from the City, not the other way round. Politically, there's a case for saying we shouldn't take them back yet. This change of heart of theirs might only be temporary, and so on.'

'Quite right,' said Ignotus drily. 'But...?'

'Ved worries,' Mesh said smoothly, 'that you may be... playing up your feelings, just to up your popularity with some of our fellow Councillors.'

Ved worries, thought Tobin. The woman was consummate. Behind that Mona Lisa face she could be thinking anything.

'I disagree,' Mesh murmured, 'but I'd be upset to think the Manfolk's genuine concerns were being sacrificed to political expediency.'

Ignotus snorted. 'If Mostyn thinks I'm affecting to despise these barbarians so that the Council will select me Mayor, he doesn't know me well.' He emphasised his present tenses lightly, in mockery or defiance.

With Ignotus' fortune, he probably had a dozen datafetches, not to mention a circle of informers built up over the centuries. Tobin was unsurprised to find he knew of Mostyn's demise, and Mesh's visit to the seedy tableau. The Romuline Councillor had often clashed with Mostyn in the Council Chamber, where the dead man acted as spokesman for Cllr. St Marx's nebulously tolerantist coalition.

There'd been hostility between them, but Ignotus was alibied for the night of the unfeasible murder. When the plump posthuman had been killed, the Consul had been at his Romuline villa, banqueting with close family and certain reputable Senators. Tobin's ideas about her suspects were too amorphous to be called a list, but Ignotus wasn't even in the running.

He was, of course, a man not short of employees, slaves and relatives.

* * *

Tobin was well aware she had a problem dealing with people, although she preferred to consider that it was people who had a problem dealing with her. Romantic notions of knight-errantry aside, private investigation is an isolated, isolating job. That was one thing she liked about it.

She preferred a distant, hands-off, trust-free relationship with her employers, such as she enjoyed with Godfather Avatar. She'd done undercover work before, of course, but she'd always maintained that same distance from her supposed co-workers. She was usually there to betray them, after all.

Mesh Cos (Tobin decided on her second day as a supposed employee) would be a difficult person to betray. That was precisely the sort of person she was, which made her dangerous in Tobin's view. It took a real pro like Ignotus to stay coldly polite in the face of her unselfconscious charm. Doing so continually was becoming a drain on Tobin's energy.

Worse still, Mesh gave off the uneasy impression that she knew far more than Tobin did. That this was certainly true didn't help: the Councillor was, transparently, more knowledgeable on more or less any subject than a human hailing from an earlier civilisation.

According to Tobin's fetch, Mesh Cos had gained access to the crime scene on the morning following Mostyn's murder. Many considered the members of the final human civilisation to be above suspicion or reproach – and Mesh was known to be of the very last generation of humanity, a witness to and victim of the Great Houses' terminal assault on humankind.

What was less well known, and what the fetch had had to do some serious ferreting around to uncover, were the rumours that Mesh had not only been present at humanity's extinction, but had been involved in something – what, no-one would say – which had angered the Houses. Perhaps enough for them to mount the attack in the first place.

Tobin couldn't decide if Mesh was sublimely unaware that the Rump Parliament had set her up with an infiltrator for a researcher, if she knew and didn't care, or if she knew because she'd set both Avatar and Tobin up herself.

Being Tobin, she suspected the last of these. Mesh certainly wasn't giving anything away.

* * *

Someone had been spying on her, ever since she'd arrived at Council House.

Cllr MESH Cos, politician, historian, model, mystic, novelist, midwife, aethereticist, ethicist, chronic theorist, installation artist, mechanic, administrator, archaeologist, cat-burglar, etc.; Rdt for Samphire Dist. (by consensus) from AF 1; Cllr. from AF 282; *b* last human civilisation 334,961,140,138 AD, *d* of To Har, Mod Kale and U Plest. *Educ:* the human noosphere. *Publications:* multiple contributions to the noosphere. d last human civilisation 334,961,147,104 AD; *r* Samphire Dist., S. Quarter; one *d. Publications:* some two thousand volumes including: Matter, AF 4; Tac Fles, AF 19; The History of Oceans, AF 34; Starship Burials of the Entrustine Horde, AF 58; Deep-Time Structures and the Visual Arts, AF 80; Promethea Smith, AF 97; On Tools, AF 111; Femtocomputational Technique – a Guide for Pre-Industrial Cultures, AF 122; Mona L and the Revenge of the Vitruvians, AF 138; Incompleteness – an Exhaustive Study, AF 146; Innovative Sexual Practices of the Posthuman Cultures, AF 160; Metachronic Contagion, AF 169; Postmen in London, AF 185; The Spiral and the Helix, AF 192; Photon Rhumba, AF 209; New Musical Instruments, AF 218; Creation – the Novel, AF 229; A Child's Compendium of Ontological Conundra, AF 230; (ed) Encyclopaedia of Death, AF 231; Some Suggestions Towards Perfection, AF 253; Antigrav Engine Design – an Angelological Approach, AF 260; Icthyosaur Obstetrics – a Beginner's Guide, AF 272; Etc., AF 289; etc. *Recreations:* reading, cinema, lepidoptery, cross-country skiing, landscape gardening, bibliophily, hydrology, garlic cuisine, lapidary design, dry-stone-walling, condor breeding, osteopathy, violoncello, sousaphone, polysemy, skyclimbing, choral singing, comparative religion, stiltwalking, fencing, board games, reader reception theory, shamanic tourism, temporal cartography, sauropod racing, conjuring, communing, dusting, Greek tragedy, acoustic guitar, line drawing, line dancing, x-ray cartomancy, real ale [...] *Addresses:* Mesh Cos, Samphire Dist.; Apt. 402, Councillors' Quarters, Council House, Central Dist. *Clubs:* Noosphere.

[*Who's Who in the City of the Saved.*]

At lunchtime on the second day, Tobin was eating at Honi's and interacting with the fetch. The melato bar was a pleasant open-air affair, which spilled out from under the cloisters in the Flint Quadrangle, between the Councillors' offices and the six blocks of ballrooms. It was popular with Councillors and staff alike, and a number of them were scattered about the tables, conducting business, relaxing or perusing files while they ate.

Tobin had been eating one-handed to accommodate the sensorb, so she was already feeling irritable when the data construct broke off from listing Councillors' alibis to say, 'Oh! That's funny...'

What is? Tobin unsaid.

The fetch picked up and sipped her virtual tea. 'The security cameras in this cloister, dear,' she said. 'They're being fed a false image. I'm not sure how long it's been going on.'

This was generally assumed to be the method Mostyn's killer had used to remain undetected. It didn't necessarily imply premeditation. The Council House surveillance systems were laughably hackable, and having a sexual tryst with Mostyn was the kind of thing most people would want to cover up.

Tobin looked up sharply, and set down her sandwich. Can you see anyone who isn't in the simulation? she sub-vocalised.

'I don't have any vision of my own, my poppet,' the fetch said. 'Without the cameras, I can only see what I get through your optic centres.'

Feeling self-conscious, Tobin did a 360° sweep of the melato bar and its surrounding cloisters, while the fetch pretended to nibble at a sponge finger. 'No,' the construct said regretfully at last, 'nobody that I can see.'

Tobin scowled. Maybe her suspicions of Mesh Cos were without foundation. But assuming she cared, it might well be she'd want to know who Tobin was reporting to. Rumour insisted that Tobin's predecessor, a City-born Neanderthal, had been dismissed by Mesh on a pretext and reassigned to some kind of covert mission. When asked what this might be, rumour became prim and refused to speculate, but Tobin had a feeling she could guess.

It would suggest a lot of foresight, but Tobin could imagine Mesh deliberately opening up a vacancy, one close to her, so she could see which groups inside the City tried to fill it with one of their own. If she was under surveillance – by this White Mammoth Tusk person or anybody else – then she would lead Mesh straight to the Parliament the first time she reported back to Avatar.

Which, Tobin thought, was fine by her. She downed the melato and pocketed the sensorb, dismissing the fetch. The old lady's image gave her an annoyed look as it faded out.

Without peering too closely into the cloister's surrounding shadows, Tobin headed off to her afternoon meeting.

15. Julian, RealSpace.

Julian whooped recklessly as he sped out from the h-space interface, resolving way above the shimmery globe of Quaxis III. The planet-thing shone silvery and bright beneath him like a badge on velvet. The mind-nulling HEIGHT involved in the entire situ was a factor he had weighty difficulties adjusting to – you couldn't get a scooter up to alts like these – but childhood visits to the vertiginous Tower-top View Point were assisting him. He rolled his flighter artfully with a single (impolite) gesture, and dove toward the planet's substrate like a stooping pigeonhawk.

—Swyving WOW! | he gestured one-handedly, keeping a tight grip of the joystick with the other. Above him clear bright sparks of stars, crushed glass on velvet (or – justice – distant swyve-off vast huge fireball objects), warped and distorted as the pirate ship followed him out into RealSpace.

He thumbed the h-space pad and violently decelerated. The interface opened up before him and his flighter fell inside, buoyed up in its chromatic turbulence.

He paused, near motionless in hyperspace, and imaged the space pirates in their glossy spikeship, casting about for their vanished victim, figuring out his hyperspace trajectory before they realised that –

(...this "spaceship" was a Tube chain, near as actual, but trackless. No tubeholes, and no stations. You could immerse to and emerge from ANYWHERE...)

– he wasn't even moving, that he'd reappear in that exact same point, facing toward them, laser cannons blazing and fissiles ready-targeted to launch direct

SPEED! POWER! EXPLOSIONS! AND THE ETERNAL MYSTERY OF SPACE...

The infinite vastness of space has been an inspiration to poets and film-makers down the ages. Now RealSpace offers all the thrills and majesty of space travel with none of the danger. Yes, you too can pilot "ships", make "planetfall", engage in space combat and meditate upon the serene grandeur of the stars without ever having to set foot outside the Uptime Gate!

Whether you're a backward Earther who never left the homeworld or a grizzled space-dog missing your vacuum legs (or even if you're City-born and want to find out what this "space" stuff was all about!), then RealSpace is the perfect attraction for you.

The Attractions Are Stellar...

From our dedicated RealPorts in Swempshire, Helving, Lassiter, Campley and Farflate Districts, you can voyage forth in any of 1,016 classes of spacegoing craft, including many lovingly reconstructed replicas of classic designs from history and fiction. Tour the planets of RealSpace, visiting idyllic communities of Citizens living genuine planetary lifestyles! Or, if it is adventure you seek, then seek out the fabled Lost Planet of Erath, a wanderer in the dark spaces between the stars, where fiendish traps and barriers prevent all planetfall. What secrets does this blighted ball of sand and rock hold for the unwary traveller? You'll never know...

Other attractions include the Lilliput Nebula, the Dyson Sphere Heritage Centre, the Comet Trail and Sun Run, and roughly 900 million five-star restaurants and other food outlets.

...The Bodies Are Celestial...

Experience all the thrills of space combat from the comfort of your nearest RealPort! Dogfight with other destructible crews under controlled conditions! Fly assault missions on designated planets, or engage in piracy against designated victim vessels! With the vacuum of RealSpace archemathically modelled so that sound can be heard (and none of those old-fashioned restrictions on "light speed"), space battles can be fun for all the family!

...And The Figures Are Astronomical !!!

RealSpace is the largest of the City's Great Parks, a self-contained lens of vacuum 500 petametres across (around 50 conventional "light years") and 200 deep. It contains a total of 38 star systems bearing 167 planets, as well as millions of asteroids, moons, comets and a miniature nebula. So there's plenty to explore!

RealSpace also fulfils an important conservation role. Its population includes members of many adapted posthuman species, some of which need to inhabit quite specific planetary environments. It's also home to the very few species of vacuum-adapted posthumans, who need special support equipment for comfort in the gravity and atmospheric pressure of the rest of the City. In RealSpace these communities can carry on their traditional lifestyles in peace and happiness.

[From the official brochure.]

towards their fiery enginery. The panic in their bridge would be all palpable, as his fighter's every weapon arced into their vulnerable underside.

A perfect hit, a fine collection of the things in factual, and the pirate vessel came apart in a warm flowering of fire and metal. The roar of detonation nearly deafened Julian. He saw the floating bodies of the crew thrash wildly, as his smaller spaceship powered through the expanding cloud of debris, scattering it further. One pirate gave Julian an irritable two-digit salute before his guiding spirit gave up on him.

Arising further, till the dark rubble-cloud became a smear on Quaxis' surface, Julian peered at the planet. To him it seemed a porthole in RealSpace's self, a window opening upon a disc of City (the ground was not intended to be spherical, and there were NOT supposed to be great gaps between it: justice, this was not his true environment). Determinedly, he pricked in his latest set of spatial co-ordinates. Assuming Mesh had briefed him with correctness, this was the latest in the chain of several jumps he had to make to reach his obscure target.

Beneath him, pirates, even now withdrawing from expiring bodies, and the agricultural world of Quaxis III. (Inhabitants: low-gravity posthuman Adapts. Famed for its astonishing cloud-fish and delicious fungi.) Ahead of him...

Ahead of him, beyond a lengthy thread of h-space interfaces, the fabulous Lost Planet of Erath. Apparently.

Julian WMT loved his new job. He jumped.

16. Urbanus, Memorial Park.

Standing atop a blasted plain, Urbanus stared towards the distant Cityscape and shivered violently. A freezing wind was slicing through him at great velocity, reminding him that all there was beneath his toga was a flimsy tunic and a pair of Larry Leviathan boxer shorts. Ice droplets in the air impacted on his spectacles, while his toes felt as if they'd been amputated.

Behind him Tiresias emerged from the Tube station, strolling insouciantly up the rubberised steps onto the ravaged wasteland. 'Sorry about that, dear boy,' he said. 'I bought us chocolate.' He showed no signs of feeling the cold, as he broke off two still-wrapped squares and handed them to his charge.

This was the third day of their Tube journey, and the old man had suggested they might make a stopover at Memorial Park, 'for your amusement and edification'. The ceremonial site, which Tiresias assured him was of immense historic interest, was within a District or two of their most obvious route.

'There aren't many people here for a tourist attraction,' Urbanus pointed out, through teeth gritted against the wind, as the two men walked across the plain towards its solitary salient feature. At the limits of clear vision in every direction, the City resumed: from here the very tallest buildings resembled inexpertly shaven stubble, although the distant Watchtower was visible, a tiny thread aspiring towards the sky-dome. Above them storm-clouds roiled and slithered.

Nearer to hand there was only featureless grey rock, roughened and half-heartedly overgrown with scraps of grass and lichen, and the Memorial itself. A cubic block of black obsidian, set some thousand paces distant from the Tube in order, Tiresias said, to engender in its visitors 'a sense of pilgrimage', it was the size of Civitata's Temple and, from this distance, featureless.

'I thought you might say that,' Tiresias replied, as it bulked gradually larger before them. 'It's only a few weeks till Verrifant's Night: I expect most visitors are staying away till then. Why come at all at this time of year, unless you come for the ceremony?'

Why indeed, Urbanus wondered. He could comprehend the site's significance, naturally, to those Citizens who'd been alive at the time of the Assault and to the history of the City itself. Millions of them had died here, after all, albeit none permanently: the first and only time that such a thing had happened in the City. Come Verrifant's Night, tens of thousands of them would assemble at the monument, to vilify the memory of the Mayor who betrayed them, and sit at vigil through the starless night till Little Resurrection Day. Then crowds would fill the rocky bowl in all directions, but for now it stood stark and desert.

Like most of his generation, Urbanus had experienced recordings of the Timebeast Assault. Regularly invoked by the media when City defences or relations with the Great Houses were under discussion, certain images and experiences had become nexuses of cultural significance. A particular aerial view, one of the Houses' great blanched worms swallowing City streets and buildings into its gaping maw, had become particularly iconic.

The Memorial grew ever bigger now before them, obscuring a hand's width of the ever distant non-horizon. Thirty years before, when Verrifant had thrown open the Uptime Gate to the bloated vermiform timeships of the Houseworld, it had been here in Snakefell District that they started their invasion. An unremarkable neighbourhood built in an understated baroque style, Snakefell had been full of unsuspecting Citizens about their various daily businesses, quite unprepared for a horde of neo-plasticist monstrosities to arrive and begin devouring their homes. Many of them had fallen into the bellies of the beasts along with their surrounding structures, and there, beyond reach of all the City's protocols, had been crushed to death, crying to their various gods as they were ground up by the masonry in the worms' gigantic crops.

('A timeship is technically a universe in its own right, you see,' Tiresias had told him and his cousins in their classes. 'We think that's why they've never been *legitimately* allowed inside the City; their interaction could be disastrously unstable.')

The majority of the deaths, however, had resulted from the retaliatory launch on Snakefell (along Tubespace portals generated for the purpose) of every large-scale weapon stockpiled against unknowable contingency by the least sociable of the City's Districts. Indeed, it seemed the City's state of grace had been suppressed, just for a moment, in order to ensure these deaths. With Snakefell's population dead in instants and the Timebeasts bellowing disoriented amongst the bloody rubble, the District had been neatly snipped, invaders and all, from the fabric of the City, leaving behind the wasteland onto which the dead had been once more reborn.

The various extremist groups whose arsenals had been commandeered had not appreciated this. (The Manfolk had been particularly cross, apparently.) The stockpiles had been strictly illegal, however, so there was little recourse to be had; especially since nobody knew who was responsible for the devastating counterstrike. The City Council of the time had denied that it was anything to do with them, and their vote to designate it "an Act of God or Gods" had cemented the popular view that the mysterious Founders of the City were responsible. The Councillors had stood down shortly afterwards, their reputations irrevocably sullied by their leader's treachery.

Urbanus and his mentor had almost reached the Memorial now: this close the great black cube provided shelter from the biting wind.

'To most of us,' Tiresias was saying, 'the Assault's a symbol of the City's vulnerability. But what it *demonstrates* is just the opposite. The City survived, its enemies were routed.'

'I suppose so,' Urbanus admitted. He felt he ought to add, 'But all those people...'

'Oh, deeply traumatised, of course,' Tiresias agreed sombrely. 'Many of them have never fully recovered. But still, you know, they're alive again now. Many of those attacking were killed outright.'

'They shouldn't have attacked then, should they?' said Urbanus.

'Unquestionably not, no,' the old man conceded, 'but it does put things in perspective. Here we are.'

They had arrived at the Memorial's glistening black surface. Light danced across the glassy lines of etching as the clouds coiled overhead. The near wall towered far above them, obscuring half the sky-dome, and stretched for stadia in each direction. Each of the names was inscribed with crystalline precision, in spindly lettering taken from a thousand alphabets.

Urbanus wiped the icy residue from his lenses, and leaned in close to read them.

17. Tobin, Council House.

The lined face on the wallscreen had deep-set eyes and a harried air. Its hair had the designer flutter often favoured by academics, a perception reinforced by the tweed lapels and badly-knotted tie that sat beneath it.

It belonged to Prof. Anthony Fisher, a man who despite his evident crippling nervousness had clearly mastered the fine art of civilised obstruction. 'I'm very sorry, Ms. Tobin,' he bleated, 'but I don't know where she is. I haven't seen Allisheer now for some days. She is extremely busy at present, as I'm sure you'll appreciate.'

His terrible stammer enraged some primal thing residing deep in Tobin's spinal column. She did her damnedest to ignore it.

Obviously she's busy, you stupid man, she wanted to snap at him. Do I look like some sort of idiot? Four weeks until selection and the manager of St Marx's unofficial Mayoral campaign gets himself killed – unexpectedly, to say the least. Add in the three full-time careers and a husband who wants to be a sheep, and if I was her, I wouldn't have time to talk to me.

But Tobin was fast running out of options. In the last few days she had uncovered some surprising things about Ved Mostyn, a couple of them notably more scandalous than the dissipated face he had presented to the public. Yet so far, access to his closest political associate had conspicuously eluded her. Allisheer

St Marx had to be a suspect, if not as the fat man's killer then at least as his pre-mortem assignation. 'I'm very sorry to be troubling you at home, Professor,' she lied, 'but Mesh Cos needs to set up an urgent meeting with Cllr. St Marx. She's not been taking calls at any of her offices.'

'If I knew where to find her, Ms. Tobin, I'd tell you,' Fisher dissembled in turn. He had a slight squint which made him appear fascinated by the wallscreen itself. 'If the matter is so very urgent, I'd suggest the Councillor speaks to her about it tomorrow night.'

Tobin had not the slightest idea what Mesh Cos' plans might be for Saturday evening. 'Tomorrow night,' she said. 'So Cllr. St Marx is planning to be there tomorrow night?'

'Of course.' The historian looked confused. 'She's hosting the reception.'

'Of course,' Tobin repeated sagely. 'And that's at...?'

'Eighteen-thirty,' Fisher told her, frowning. Tobin had been hoping for a venue, but decided not to push her luck. She left a brief, bland message for the Councillor, and signed off.

A quick trawl of the ULW systems turned up the function in question: a reception at View Point for a guest academic, one Prof. Handramit. The usual security arrangements were in place. A visitor from outside the City, the Professor would be a natural target for anyone with a grudge, a loathing of aliens or just a violent psychosis. The guest list was only half-heartedly encrypted, though, and Tobin soon found Mesh's name on it. No wonder St Marx hadn't bothered returning any of Tobin's calls. She just hoped her persistence hadn't tipped either Councillor off.

Tobin's brow furrowed, as she tried hard to remember whether she'd ever owned such a thing as a little black cocktail dress.

* * *

Tobin was astonished by Kyme Janute. When Mesh had told her to expect the Manfolk Delegate, she'd envisioned a bulging, ludicrously muscled barbarian with a full-to-bursting jockstrap, like the meatheads who'd been on the City's fledgling media back in 3.

Instead, Janute was basically a pear on legs. Her hippopotamine belly propped up breasts the size of beer barrels, her legs were inverted cones tapering to tiny feet, and her face had an unfinished look, as if clay features had been half-erased. She wore a toned-down version of traditional Manfolk garb, which Tobin felt to be a mistake, particularly as regards the tight leather trousers. When Janute walked, her great hams writhed behind her like a yin-yang wrestling itself. Somehow Tobin had had the impression Manfolk were all male. Instead this was sexual dimorphism gone mad.

'Citizen Janute for you, Councillor,' she said, trying hard not to stare as she ushered the visitor into Mesh's office.

'Delegate Janute,' the Manfolk admonished her, in an astonishingly deep voice. 'I haven't been a Citizen since Manfold seceded.'

Furnished by Tobin with a treacly coffee, the Delegate sank deep into Mesh's mossy chair. Tobin wasn't sure if the accompanying creaks emanated from it or Janute's clothing. She retired to her usual corner, reflecting that the Parliament could have found her a post more conducive to getting some actual work done. Either Mesh really didn't want to let Tobin out of her sight, or she was, as she maintained, concerned her new assistant should learn as much as possible about the role. Either way she had insisted Tobin attend as many of her meetings as possible.

The conversation was drily political, Mesh's voice was its usual soothing lilt, and Tobin soon found her attention wandering. The gist was that Janute's faction were confident of their dominance over Manfold's seat of government, the Manthing; that the women and the elderly could keep their testosterone-fuelled relatives in line; and could they count on Mesh's support in asking for their full status as a District back? Mesh Cos made a number of serious objections and no promises, which Tobin understood to mean she sympathised with Janute's request.

She turned her attention to her palmpad, on which she was supposedly taking improving notes. The single line of text read "1. WHO WAS MOSTYN SHAGGING?". Whichever way she looked at it (and she'd tried "SCREWING", "BANGING" and "BONKING"), this was the key question. Whoever his mystery caller had been that night, they'd been a witness if nothing else. At the very least they could narrow down the time of death.

The politicians' conversation teetered momentarily towards the intriguing when Mesh broke off suddenly to ask, 'Are you all right, Kyme? You seem a tad unhappy today.' Tobin had been unable to detect any such sign in Janute's elephantine demeanour, but she supposed Mesh was more empathic than she was. Most people were.

Janute grunted. 'Perhaps a little,' she surprisingly conceded. Tobin could hear a slight quaver in her thunderous voice now. 'I've had distressing news about some friends. Back in Manfold.' Mesh gave her an intense look, made some understanding noises and dived straight back into diplomacy.

Tobin gazed at the chrome-spiked contours of Janute's upholstered leather bosom, and wondered: what, a husband, lover, child? God, did other Manfolk find Janute attractive? Was she typical of their women? Mind you, Manfolk men didn't do anything for Tobin either (perhaps for someone like Mostyn, with his notoriously individual sexual preferences), but even so –

Mesh paused again. 'Did you say something, Laura?' she asked equably. 'You know we'd welcome any contribution you felt you wanted to make.'

Janute looked hugely dubious as to this, but kept her silence.

'Um, no,' said Tobin, trying not to stare at the screen of her palmpad. 'Just a thought I had.'

* * *

Tobin left Mesh's office and headed for her cramped researchers' quarters.

ST MARX, Cllr. Prof. Allisheer, archemathicist[1], chronic theorist, poet, biographer and politician; Rdt (by election) and Cllr. for Base and Buttress Dist. from AF 282. *b* Onesian Emirate 32,312 AD, *d* of Dr. Lewu St Marx (father unknown). *Educ:* Emir Daoud's; Low Seminary of Onesia; Median Seminary of Onesia; High Seminary of Onesia. Research fellowship in archemathics under Prof. Handramit. *Publications:* Nine-Dimensional Ur-Solids, 32,333 AD; Durational Calculus, 32,335 AD; (ed) Astounding Contributions to Archemathical Studies, 32,338 AD. *d* Onesian Emirate, 32,339 AD; *r* Anteria Dist., N Quarter; *m* AF 209 **Prof. Anthony Fisher** (*qv*). Chair of Chronic Theory, Collegium Humanitas, AF 8-91; Baconian Chair of Theoretical Mathematics, Clarendon Univ., AF 91-109; Writer in Residence, Bentham Penal Institution AF 134-136; Senior Chair of Archemathics, Univ. of the Lower Watchtower from AF 197 (sabbatical at Manfold College AF 275-276). *Publications:* Some three hundred volumes including: Archemathical Criteria, AF 12, Superstring Macramé, AF 56; Other Wise (Poems), AF 71; Notational Derivations in Solidic Theory, AF 89; (ed) Festschrift for Prof. Handramit, AF 121; WH Auden: The City Poems, AF 180; Einstein: Two Lives, AF 203; (ed) Interdisciplinary Archemathics, AF 219; (ed) 1,000,001 Favourite Poems, AF 252. Founded ULW's exchange programme with Manfold College, AF 199. *Recreations:* cricket, theatre, chrononautics, reading. *Addresses:* Rafferty Coll., Univ. of the Lower Watchtower, Base and Buttress Dist., The Watchtower; 14 Cypress Walkway, 1,794,875th floor, Base and Buttress Dist., The Watchtower; Apt. 461, Councillors' Quarters, Council House, Central Dist. *Clubs:* Old Onesians, Urbanites.

[*Who's Who in the City of the Saved.*]

[1] Translator's note: *archemathics* is the term used for the mathematics underlying the structure of a universe. Archemathics is to mere physics as language is to today's newspaper. As one might expect, it has traditionally been a Houseworld preserve.

Outside the Councillors' offices she passed between the stone cliff-faces of King Square, close by the statue of the City's first Lord Mayor. She descended the wide ramp down to Council House's own sub-Tube internal transport system. (The CoHo Tube stop, where she'd arrived three days before, was several blocks away, off the Plaka Perikles.)

To get back to the quarters she'd inherited from Mesh's previous researcher, Tobin had to travel twenty minutes on the clattering monorail – enough to get her fifty Districts out of Central on the Tube. Part of the journey – from Lincoln Place to Castro Boulevard – she spent crammed up between a pissed-off aerial Adapt and someone else who, though invisible, had all-too-tangible body odour.

Alighting at the Mandela Mandala, Tobin had ten minutes' walk along wide neon corridors before she reached her quarters-block. The details of the case line-danced annoyingly inside her mind.

In one sense, anyone without an alibi could have murdered Mostyn. Anyone who had an alibi would have had to pay someone else to do it. Access to Council House was supposedly restricted, but the CHAS were rubbish. In a society where violence is impossible, security soon becomes dull ritual. Anyone with enough hacking power at their disposal could have wandered in that night, murdered as many Councillors as happened to be around and strolled out again without being noticed. Tobin could have done it herself, no problem.

Or rather, just the one problem. Killing Mostyn was, of course, impossible. Anyone could have had motive or opportunity, but so far as Tobin knew no-one at all had the requisite means. Various renegade Districts had been researching potent weapons for years, usually for use against their own Citizens. No-one had even got close. Occasional rumours from the Universe maintained the Great Houses had managed, but why would a Houseworld agent take out Mostyn? He wasn't where the City's power was. He wasn't even a Mayoral candidate.

If she didn't know otherwise, Tobin thought as she left the lift on her own corridor, she'd think Mostyn had done a runner, leaving a specially-commissioned clone in place as a sick joke. But the biodata analysis put paid to that.

Not that this could be considered conclusive, either. There was, after all, the question of who "Cllr Ved Mostyn" had really been.

The door to Tobin's quarters slid aside, and she stepped in.

There was a cloak-swathed skeleton sitting in her chair. It was watching an episode of *Undead on Arrival* on her widescreen and snacking on a packet of her cereal.

Beneath the tricorn hat, the antlered head twisted ponderously around to face her. Its white jaw grinned at her knowingly.

With a tap of a finger-bone on her remote, Godfather Avatar blanked the screen. '*Hello, Laura,*' he whispered. '*What have you got for me*?'

18. Allisheer St Marx, the Uptime Gate.

They met on Erstwhile Plaza. Her coattails, his djellaba, rippled in the mild breeze that blew in from Ascension. It rounded the Plaza then blew straight back, taking the City's smells and litter scraps with it into the Universe. Around them all kinds of people made the same journey, carried back and forth across the Gate by forces that for them were just as pressing.

Her tailcoat was cornflower-blue, gathered slightly at the waist, the matching trousers slightly flared. Her skin was scar-white. She wore a trilby. Her eyes concealed themselves, as ever, behind mirrored spectacles. A tattooed scorpion crouched on one bare foot.

He was different from how she remembered[1]: younger this time, his skin earth-brown, his hair long, black and lustrous like her own. He was still as familiar as the smell of polished wood. His bearded face was topped by a wide-brimmed pilgrim hat, dazzling white like his djellaba, like his smile. Behind him the Gate shimmered like a moon's mirage in the noontide desert.

When last they'd met he'd been pale and elderly, his hair as long and sleek but purest white, his beard wide and huge.

'Allisheer!' he gathered her into a hug. 'My lovely girl, how have you been?'

'Handramit,' she said, relief flooding her as she inhaled his soft smell. 'I've missed you so.'

It had been twelve years since she'd last seen him. He had been her lifelong friend, colleague and mentor. He lived back in the Universe, not a human and never intended for the City, but they had kept in contact since her death. When she had died the seeker pellet had been meant for him, whom the Houses called a defector. He had left the Houseworld as a childe[2], a victim of one of House Mirraflex's periodic biodata purges; when she had died he had been 93. Now he was 385, still teaching at Onesia High Seminary, survivor of a dozen more assassination attempts.

He'd been so sorry she had died because of him. Now someone else had died, she understood how he felt.

Around them people pressed. A limbless man ambled past on a steam-driven tripod. A small City-born girl held tightly to a parent and a blue balloon. A sasquatch loped through the crowd, hooting disconsolately.

He hefted his shoulder-bag and they walked together, barefoot through the little knots of aliens, Citizens and mortal humans from the Universe. Each one, each piece of litter, each bird that wheeled through the Gate and round and back again[3], had its own time-trace, a complex shape that, if she concentrated hard enough, she could make visible. A million coloured threads passed through the Gate, woven on the loom of the Plaza. It was a gift she'd had from childhood.

Some came to trade, to gather information or negotiate for favour, some to meet long-dead loved ones. The boldest came to meet with their own ghosts, or just to marvel at the bright afterlife awaiting them. A tiny handful stayed, despite the Citizens' best efforts[4]. The way the City incorporated them into herself was perfectly beautiful.

'Thanks for coming early,' she said, looking aside at him. They were each half a head taller than most of those surrounding them, an effect their hats accentuated. Their impulses on some matters were very alike.

'Any time,' he said, flashing her another smile. 'Anthony treating you well?'

'Oh yes,' she said, unhesitatingly[5]. The question was courteous enough, but laced with real concern. To most people she would appear unruffled, but he knew her very well. He recognised her agitation instinctively behind her face, just as she'd seen his previous shape through his.

She loved Anthony, of that she was certain, but love was a thing she'd always had trouble with. She wasn't its native habitat. It had been introduced as an experiment, perhaps, to keep some native emotion in check, and had had trouble acclimatising. Anthony treated her well enough. It was she who had done wrong.

When her relationship with Ved Mostyn emerged, she knew, Anthony would be upset. He wouldn't understand the things that she had done, and nor did she, but she was sure he would forgive her given time[6]. Other things less excusable had passed between her and Mostyn. If the affair became known widely, as his death made likely, someone would try to follow where that knowledge led. She must endeavour to close off that path, to obscure the past's shape behind that of the present.

Behind them a giant iridescent beetle came through the interface, the shimmer pouring off its wing-casings like spume. It carried squealing schoolchildren,

FOOTNOTES TO CHAPTER 18

[1] The business with the bright light and the tunnel had been true for her, oddly enough. She'd thought she saw herself with another face at the end of it. Now she thought perhaps it was the face of the City. Death did peculiar things to one's temporal lobes.

[2] A childe is not a child. Youth is relative, as is biology. It's doubtful any true childe of the Houses has been a child, except in appearance.

[3] Gull of Ascension
sailing into a new world;
a true migration.

[4] The figure generated by a human locus I intersecting the Universe at A, B and C and the City at A′ and B′ is a contingent hyperpetagon ABA′B′C. This figure is inherently unstable, collapsing into a Tlepp-Einmar hypersolid of K-dimension 0 (see also Handramit on conservation of biodata).

[5] There was an old roué named Ved,
a passionate walrus in bed
who reduced Allie Marx
to constituent quarks,
but Ved's dead, my darling, Ved's dead.

[6] 'My fellow Councillors, this creature's guilt tarnishes all she has touched. We cannot allow her to remain a Councillor, a Resident or even a humble Professor of Archemathics. Banishment from the City would be too lenient for the injuries she has inflicted on us all. For all our sakes, whichever candidate's opinions are the most diametrically opposed to hers must be selected Mayor. Any cause she has shown support for – House Halfling, the Mal'akh Report, the restitution of Manfold to the City – must be dismissed without further discussion, and allowed to languish and fester, for decades if need be. Will any speak against me?'

Ascensionites sent here to see the marvel their culture had been set up to guard. Now they fell silent, eyes growing huge as they took in the domed sky and the soaring Watchtower.

A particular patrician voice rang harsh in her imagination as she took her old friend's arm and guided him towards the Tube with her.

19. Rick Kithred, Paynesdown.

After Godfather Avatar left Laura's apartment, Rick Kithred's response was to get very drunk and stoned, sit in his bedroom and gibber at the door for two days. He was unwise enough to close it before losing consciousness, and he came to convinced that behind it were a hundred one-eyed demons, or maybe just one demon with a hundred eyes.

By Wednesday afternoon the booze and pracks had left his system and he was able to move unsteadily around his apartment. He found his fridge was empty, as was his bank account. He staggered over to Laura's place, but she was gone. Rick remembered something about someone offering her a job somewhere. Laura was sometimes away for weeks on her investigation gigs, so Rick Kithred thought it would be a kindness to eat her perishable food. He could replace it later if he remembered.

Laura kept a spare key with the building's janitor, who was also out. The janitor was a long-limbed posthuman called Bloch, and was always off doing some damn thing or other. He was the laziest janitor Rick had ever met.

Bloch kept a small vegetable garden at the back of the apartment block, a patch of dirt overrun with weeds which he pretended to work sometimes. Rick went out there to try to find him, and saw the shadow.

He turned around and walked away soon as he saw it, but the memory of it stayed burned into his brain, like the photos he'd seen of souls annihilated at Hiroshima. The shadow's shape was that of a tall man in a cloak, with antlers sprouting underneath his hat as wide as Rick's outstretched arms. The shadow belonged to Godfather Avatar, and seeing it brought back to Rick all the things he'd gotten high in order to forget.

Why Godfather Avatar would leave his shadow behind him in Paynesdown, Rick didn't know. He didn't seem the kind of man to forget something important. Rick guessed he wasn't needing it for the moment, and thought it would be safe enough in Bloch's vegetable patch since the janitor hardly ever went there.

He went to see Martha Joan SwarmLeader, who ran the local food mart and was always kind to him. He earned himself enough discs shifting boxes to eat that day.

On Thursday, Rick Kithred was still hungry, and feeling the effects of his drug binge. His eyes hurt and his throat kept drying out. Martha Joan was out of odd jobs but gave him a can of out-of-date beef goulash for his dinner. He thanked her and took it away with him, but he needed cash. After Monday his stash was nearly gone.

He went to look for Bloch again, to ask if there were any jobs needing doing round the apartments. Bloch's post was a sinecure from one of the crime cartels and he earned most of his money elsewhere, doing what nobody knew. He sometimes let Rick stand in for him at the block, mopping walls or floors or mending broken furniture.

Bloch wasn't in his apartment, so steeling himself Rick stepped outside into the vegetable garden. Avatar's shadow still stood there, tall and horny as ever. It was a real shadow, not a darker patch of wall. When Rick held out an arm towards it, the limb's shadow blended into Avatar's without a seam.

The shadow shifted its position slightly, like a man standing waiting patiently for a bus, and Rick ran like hell.

That night God told Rick Kithred not to eat the beef goulash because it was laced with experimental potent poison, and instead to exchange it for cheap whisky from Lousy Lei's liquor store. Rick hadn't become the prophet of his own religion by ignoring what God told him. He spent Thursday night drunk.

When the shadow was still there Friday, Rick realised he could no longer ignore it. He spent an hour scrubbing the wall, to no effect. Then he went round to Martha Joan's and asked her for a can of paint to cover the outside of the apartment building.

He tried to pick the closest match he could.

20. Godfather Avatar, Council House.

Laura Tobin scowled: her speckled forehead corrugated, and her full cheeks narrowed as her lips pursed. She looked, Godfather Avatar estimated to himself within the confines of his bone-mask, quite cute, in a squirrelly sort of way.

Not that he ought to tell her so, he reminded himself sternly. He did so anyway, enjoying the sibilant distortion the jawbone's speaker grille always added to whatever voice he used.

AVATAR: *You know, you're rather sweet when you're angry.*

He proffered her the cereal packet.

AVATAR: *Sit down, have some Peculios.*

Little moments like this helped make his existence worthwhile, he thought. Tobin looked thunderous, but sat obediently.

She was jealous of her privacy, the Godfather recalled. Even these rather grim and shabby quarters, so recently the young Neanderthal's, had become a kind of sanctuary to her. She wanted him out of there.

He stretched out his skeletal frame and made himself more comfortable.

TOBIN: [*Sourly*] You should have told me you were coming. I'd have changed the locks.

In fact to enter Tobin's quarters had taken the Godfather five undignified minutes on hands and knees with a conceptual lock-pick, but his mystique wasn't served by letting that sort of thing get about. He angled his head slightly, and gazed inscrutably at the private eye through blank glass socket-lenses. Servo-tendons in the armour's spine held steady the great wings of ivory that were his antlers.

Tobin closed her eyes wearily.

TOBIN: [*At length*] You're too early anyway. I haven't had the time to get enough information. The placement with Mesh Cos was a mistake. She needs me there most of the time. Or claims she does.

Godfather Avatar regarded her indifferently. Inside the echoing hollows of his skull he appreciated her discomfiture, but he knew better than to let this show.

AVATAR: [*Earnestly*] *We're still terribly interested in your thoughts so far, Laura.*

Tobin looked bleakly at him, then exhaled.

TOBIN: I did think of something, just now. I need to do more work to confirm it.

The Godfather tapped the side of his skull with one gauntlet.

AVATAR: *I'm all ears.*

TOBIN: All right... Mostyn seems to have been... eccentric, in various ways. Allisheer St Marx obviously trusted him, but he was a political liability to her. All the while she was demanding collateral rights, he was screwing collaterals left, right and centre. Literally in some cases. His nightclubs in Wormward use collaterals, and even some actual aliens, as hosts and hostesses. St Marx probably thought she couldn't be too choosy about her political allies, but someone like Mostyn was a gift for the other side.

She leaned forward slightly, losing some of her studied aggressiveness in enthusiasm for her theory.

TOBIN: I've been asking around. Some of his contemporaries from before the City, people who lived in Siloportem at the same time he did, say there was no such person as Ved Mostyn.

Godfather Avatar was quietly impressed. Although her direction of enquiry was mildly alarming, the amount she had uncovered in a small time confirmed the wisdom of the Parliament's choice.

AVATAR: [*Sceptically*] *Would they have known?*

TOBIN: One of my informants says that "Ved Mostyn" was a made-up character on some commedia show. She called him "a sexual grotesque, with hedonistic tastes and a tendency to found absurd artistic movements". I've been trying to track down tapes. Our "Mostyn" could have been a remake, of course, except that all the records say he's been here since the City began. He was resurrected in Kalima – at least, that's where he was on Resurrection Morn. I think he wasn't human.

The Godfather was hugely amused.

AVATAR: *Oh, this is fascinating, really fascinating. Do go on, Laura.*

TOBIN: Obviously the biodata analysis says he was, but that's not enough to go on. Forensic biodatics is pretty new here. There are alien cultures who could fake it well enough to fool us – I'm sure your lot could, and so could the Great Houses. Houseworlders are supposed to change their biodata like it was their socks, and everyone knows they see the City as a threat. I think Mostyn was a Houseworld agent, with modified biodata so he'd pass for human.

AVATAR: *Hence not a Citizen, of course, and killable by ordinary weapons. Bravo. Go on.*

TOBIN: They must have wanted their agent here from the start, and it seems to have worked. He made it onto the Council. I don't know what his long-term aim was, but my guess is he was working to discredit Allisheer St Marx. I think she found out somehow, so killed him. Maybe she didn't realise he wasn't a Citizen, and stabbed him in anger not expecting him to be hurt. Maybe she worked it all out and did it in cold blood. Either way, she made it look like a sex game gone horribly wrong. Mostyn's lover, whoever that was, isn't the guilty one. They've just not come forward for fear of incriminating themselves. Delegate Janute of Manfold's looking jumpy, for what it's worth.

AVATAR: *Janute?*

Godfather Avatar's amusement seethed over, and he roared with laughter. His merriment emerged from his dead jaws like the fury of a basketful of cobras. He thumped his patella, producing a muffled clatter through the velvet. He continued this performance for some time, while Tobin glared at him with basilisk hostility.

At length the Godfather wiped one set of metacarpals theatrically across his socket-lenses, and spoke.

AVATAR: *It's very ingenious, Laura. I'm impressed, I really am. It hangs together beautifully, apart from one thing.*

TOBIN: [*Coldly*] And that would be?

AVATAR: *Mostyn was human, you silly bitch! Members of the Houses don't die from a simple stabbing.*

TOBIN: [*Angrily*] I said, his biodata was reconfigured –

AVATAR: *I mean he was a Citizen. Do you think the Parliament would be so intrigued if this weren't an impossible killing? Whoever he really was before his death and resurrection, the late Councillor was one of us.*

GODFATHER AVATAR

Biographies of members of Faction Paradox's higher echelons are notoriously difficult to pull off. Not only are the timelines of the Mothers and Fathers radically non-linear, often extruding into volumes of space-time which are inaccessible to researchers, but they (the timelines, and therefore the biographies) are subject to catastrophic revision. The story is told of one self-updating study, keyed to its primary subject through a trick of biodata-piracy, which split spontaneously into three rival accounts, each heavily critical of the others and resistant to even being shelved together.

All this assumes that the individuals in question can be identified. Aside from documenting his few recorded appearances within the City of the Saved, any account of Godfather Avatar rapidly becomes as speculative as a biography of Robin Hood or Pope Joan. Although the first of these appearances took place on the evening of Resurrection Day, and Avatar quickly became the central figure around which the Rump Parliament coalesced, no clue as to the Godfather's prior identity has been forthcoming.

He has never been reliably sighted outside the City, although resurrectees from eighteenth-century England find the iconography he employs familiar. Likewise, various "corporate-cult" cliques of the industrial era are known to have been headed by individuals bearing the distinctive antlered bone-mask now associated with Avatar, most notably the supposedly Faction-inspired (but rather unconvincing) media-fetish groups of the twentieth and early twenty-first centuries. Yet the masks worn by these capitalist alpha-males seem to have been unimpressive parodies of what might now be considered "the genuine article".

Some of the City's more sceptical commentators have observed that anyone could put on a black cloak, antlered bone-mask and tricorn hat and pretend to be Godfather Avatar, although his independently-mobile shadow might be more difficult to feign. Indeed, some suggest that this has been happening all along, Avatar being a fiction designed to draw attention away from the Parliament's real wielders of power. If so, the ruse has been successful, as more public attention is concentrated on his person than on any other member of the Rump Parliament.

Since his notorious appearance on *Deric Bannerji Speaks Thus*, Godfather Avatar no longer guests on chat shows.

[Walmric, *Faction Paradox: a Negotiable History*.]

He took himself in hand, and gave his childish excitement a stern talking-to. Insulting Tobin had been unwise. It wouldn't do to alienate her any more than planned.

TOBIN: [*Coldly*] Don't you think you should have given me that information before?

AVATAR: *My dear Laura, it was one of the first things I told you. What I didn't mention, and it was remiss of me, was the romantic liaison between Ved Mostyn and Allisheer St Marx. I'm afraid Janute isn't really his type. He had a number of intriguing fetishes, but big fat mommas were not, I fear, among their number.*

Tobin was incandescent. The Godfather had never seen her furious: her default state appeared to be the slow burn. He was intrigued by the results his probing had produced. Her voice, when she spoke, was pitched low, a whisper like his own, but with a note behind it like a cracked bell.

TOBIN: Get the fuck out of my room.

Abruptly Godfather Avatar stood, relishing as ever the billow of the cloak about his limbs.

AVATAR: *Ah, yes. The fuck. I shall remove it forthwith.*

An adolescent witticism, he chided dispassionately as he executed a mocking bow and left the room. Inside the skin beneath the skull, the thrill he felt at Tobin's anger was seductively addictive.

This was, he thought, as he strode powerfully away along the stark-lit corridor, what being Godfather Avatar was all about.

21. The City.

Loftarn District in the Northern Quarter is an industrial centre, a cluttered mass of heavy plant machinery, breezeblock warehouses, and sleeping-cells stacked as tall as its smoking chimneys. The eponymous tarn silted over long ago and has been filled up with industrial by-product: it glistens slickly in the afternoon skylight. If this were night, it would glow eerily instead.

Loftarn's people are sincere believers in The System, an oppressive theory of government which held sway on an obscure world of human space during an even more obscure era of its history. Only some five percent of those subjected to The System had anything but hatred for it, but this leaves a sufficient number of enthusiasts to populate a District. Like all the voluntary tyrannies it works well, largely since anyone is free to leave at any time: the City Council makes meticulously sure that this is the case, and everyone is more or less content.

The Ignotian family maintains a number of factories here, as it does in many Districts where cheap labour is easy to come by.

This morning a freight chain has drawn up at the Tube point outside the Ignotian Automata depot. This warehouse is vast, holding some 50,000 robots at a time; the chain, of course, has nothing like this capacity. It is converted from early passenger stock, the transport requirements of robots being not dissimilar to those of human travellers. It is squat and functional nevertheless, roughly finished and with painted-over windows – except for the locomotive section, which was once (though long since rendered obsolete) a luxury model used for the Ignotians' honoured guests. Each carriage is emblazoned with a perfunctory red / gold chimera logo.

The chain's driver smokes a series of tobacco-cylinders and idly converses with the warehouse porters for the half-hour it takes for 2,000 humaniform robots to march aboard its twenty carriages. All are decked out in lightly mechanised armour, as used in the early sixth millennium AD by the Madagascan infantry. They represent a fraction of the automated forces committed to a real-time re-enactment of the twelve-day Battle of Novaya Zemlya, to take place in Mappamundi Great Park a month from now.

Precisely one of them is not a standard model, not a human-shaped cybernetic body sealed inside replica body armour, programmed with streamlined combat protocols and slaved to an AI stack not much smaller than the factory that made it. He is instead a living individual, an agent of a power hostile to the Ignotian family, the City Council and many other things besides.

When the cargo has loaded itself aboard the chain (the infantry arranged in tight ranks in each carriage, staring straight ahead), the driver reluctantly treads out his latest cigarette and climbs aboard. A bored engineering drone seals the doors, and double-checks the linkages between the carriages. The driver sets the chain trundling forward, picking up speed as the wormhole interface opens ahead of them, and he and it are swallowed up.

The freight chain makes good progress through the Tube lines, faster than its passenger equivalents. Its route was filed weeks ago to avoid the tedious mess that wormhole confluences create, and it is not scheduled to pass through any stations except the handful at which it will change line. If all goes according to plan (which it will not), the chain will dock at Arctica Line's Arkhangel Station by skydark.

Soon after the chain leaves Loftarn, one of the figures in the foremost carriage – the single passenger who is not an automaton – bestirs himself. He pulls off his sensor-housing helmet, to reveal a surly face with stubbled jaw and narrow eyes. His coarse blond hair cascades across his shoulders.

Setting aside the powerful energy projector with which the Malagasy replicas are armed, this young man opens up the armour at his left knee, and extracts from his greave a length of heavy, flexible plastic. The robots, programmed with certain autonomic responses which mimic those of humans, watch him impassively. He pats the weapon twice with satisfaction against his mycokevlar gauntlet; then presses the panel next to the internal door and steps through into the Tube chain's locomotive module.

While much of its once-opulent interior is taken up by the retrofitted heavy-duty wormhole generator, the control space remains surprisingly impressive. The plush seats are gone, but plenty of standing-room remains in front of the panoramic windows. Indifferent to the psychedelic-whirlpool ambience outside, the driver sits in the nose of the vehicle, whistling atonally. A muffled musical beat emanates out of his ears.

The interloper steps up smartly and smacks him across the back of the head with his crude cosh. The driver is felled immediately. His eyes crease in astonishment and confusion as he remembers what pain once felt like, then he blacks out. The intruder kicks him roughly to one side, and takes the controls. Viscous blood leaks from the driver's skull, staining the rubber decking red.

The new driver diverts the chain's course, reshaping non-space into new and unauthorised wormholes. Meanwhile, the files of automata hold to their formations in the score of coaches – except one, which breaks rank in the foremost coach. Pushing back its helmet visor, it bends to inspect the maintenance circuitry panel beside the carriage door. It pulls off a gauntlet, and with human-shaped fingers far more precise than the real thing, sets delicately about a complex task.

Some time later, as the new driver puzzles to make out the half-familiar display-systems, he feels a sharp shock of unexpected acceleration. He frowns and thumps the controls in confusion, then turns to look behind him. Through the engine's left-side window, he watches the chain of carriages tumble lazily end over end, receding into the inchoate blur of Tubespace.

He swears violently, redundantly and colourfully in his own language. He stares again at the instrumentation, but it means little to him. He certainly has no clue how to turn back, let alone reconnect his engine to the lost coaches. The chain's former driver groans from down below him, and the intruder stomps the man's head with vicious pleasure.

The new driver's commanding officer is not going to be at all impressed. He swears again, continuing in one uninspiring vein for quite some time.

Meanwhile the chain itself carousels majestically towards remotest distance, its cargo toppling within it like dominoes.

After a time, a dark shape manifests itself ahead of the detached carriages, a solid wedge against the insubstantial abstract of the Tube tunnel. Its bulk grows exponentially as the tumbling chain approaches it, becoming larger (larger far) than the sea-going aircraft carrier it most resembles. At length it opens up a hatchway in its underside, and engulfs the wheeling carriages in a single gulp. The hatch, emblazoned with a double zero, slides shut as the metal leviathan continues on its way.

(I tell you these things as they occur. I never promised to explain them to you.)

22. Urbanus, Kempes District.

'Lucillius Urbanus Ignotus, Citizen of the City of the Saved and of – sorry, are you on?'

<*Yes,*> the booth told the young Romuline patiently, <*I'm recording you now.*>

'Oh, good,' said Urbanus. He had, despite his best efforts, consumed a large amount of startlingly bad ale accompanied by stale potato crisps, and felt somewhat light-headed.

Outside his upright coffin of wet perspex, through runnels of rainwater, the cloud-soaked afternoon of Kempes District persisted. Urbanus' view ranged along the promenade towards the drab bunting of the Old Pier, across the slate-grey and sullen sea beyond, past two further piers and off into the foggy distance.

Apparently, somewhere beyond the sea-spray and the fog and clouds hung the sun which served Thule Marine Park. Urbanus had never seen a sun; from here, not even a paler patch of sky was visible.

<The long-distance rate is 250 discs a minute,> the booth reminded him pertly.

'Oh, sorry,' Urbanus said.

<Your money,> said the booth.

'Lucillius Urbanus Ignotus,' the young man continued before pausing to marshal his thoughts, 'Citizen of the City of the Saved and of the Romuline District, to Lucius Cassius Ignotus, Citizen, Resident and Councillor of the City of the Saved and Consul of the Romuline, greetings.'

Outside the rain was sleeting down in violent diagonals, and it was freezing cold. The Tube had brought Urbanus from the occasionally oppressive day-heat of the Romuline into some mythically foul weather. He supposed the Kempians must enjoy it: allegedly they even had a summer tourist industry.

A seagull alighted nearby, and started pecking at the soggy remains of someone's fish supper.

'Great-Grandfather,' said Urbanus, 'I am in Kempes, as you may have gathered. It's quite wet here. But I think I've found the, um, thing to which you were adverting when you told me that I'd recognise what it was when I found it.

'It's jolly impressive, actually. I don't know who tipped you off about it, but if I were you I'd give them lots of money.'

His toga was soaked through, as were his sandals. He had some dry ones back at Mrs. Bladderwrack's boarding-house, but it was necessary for his report to be made in reasonable privacy, without the landlady herself eavesdropping or her daughter Hettie coming to stare at his webless hands and feet.

'Our hostess is suspicious of us,' he said. 'I think she doesn't like outsiders generally, and of course a lot of people find Tiresias confusing. But she's been talking about undesirable elements accumulating at the poorer end of Kempes. The one that, um, borders Manfold.'

A cardboard ice-cream cup blew by, disintegrating slowly in the downpour.

'From Mrs. Bladderwrack's description,' Urbanus continued, 'there have been various barbarous types: hairy men on motorcycles, cyborgs with military adaptations and some Manfolk. I think we've reassured her that we don't mean any harm, but she's convinced that others round here do.

'She was rather shocked when I asked where I could go to meet some of them, but eventually she gave me directions. Tiresias is suffering from Tube-lag from our journey, so I took the tram alone. That end of Kempes is pretty much as you'd expect, with graffiti and boarded-up stalls and litter everywhere.

'I found a dilapidated tavern called the Landmaid, which was serving some people who obviously weren't local. Some of them were Vikings or Goths or something, with big beards and bronze helmets. There were some posthumans with a lot of spikes and claws, and a group of collaterals who I'm sure had Houseworld military augmentations.'

Parties of House-bred collaterals turned up regularly to the Ignotian Spectacles. Urbanus had recognised the armoured carapaces and the biomorphic sensor pods.

'Nobody was particularly polite,' he went on, 'but I think they were amused that I was there at all. I'm used to dealing with my cousins, of course, so I wasn't too bothered what they thought of me. One of the collaterals decided to adopt me as his mascot. He said his name was Skray, and he'd be seeing action soon. He was quite drunk when I arrived, I think, and made me buy them all a lot of drinks; I'll be submitting my pale-green expenses form when I get back home. I tried to get information out of them, but all Skray would say was that the rules of engagement were changing. It didn't mean a lot to me.

'After a while I popped outside to urinate, although now I come to think about it I suppose the tavern would have had an indoor lavatory. I was a little muzzy-headed by then. I was about to go back inside when Skray came out with one of the Vikings, shouting at each other and getting quite angry. I think Skray had insulted him, or perhaps the other way round, I couldn't work it out to be honest. Then they started fighting.

Urbanus paused, staring intently at the shrieking seagulls as they wheeled about the pier, the clouds which waxed ever heavier in the sky. He realised that he'd been wringing out his toga with one hand, trickling rainwater all over the booth's floor.

'It was a very realistic fight,' he concluded at length. 'At first they were just punching one another, so I thought they were acting for some reason. Then the viking drew a knife and stabbed Skray... and it went in.

'He hardly seemed to notice at first, his side just oozed grey fluid, but then it must have got through to his brain. He roared, and took the Viking's head in one of his pincers, and... well. There's no way it could have been a mechanical automaton, I'm sure of that. There was... there were blood and bits of brain everywhere.

'I just stood there staring for a while, and so did Skray. He seemed fascinated by the Viking's body. Then he seemed to hear me breathing, and looked up at me.

'I'm afraid I lost my head then, rather... oh. I mean, I ran away. I wasn't really thinking straight. I think Skray followed me at first, but then a lot of men rode past on horseback, and I must have lost him in the confusion. I think they were from one of the Mongol hordes.'

Urbanus winced as the booth's charge meter flipped over from 999 discs to 1.000 towers. 'Anyway,' he said hurriedly. 'As I've said they can't have been automata, and I can't imagine they came in through the Uptime Gate. The Uptime Guard would never have let Skray in. And evidently they can't have been Citizens. Which means that someone's worked out how to generate vulnerable homunculi inside the City.

'What's more, they were very sophisticated ones. They convinced me they were Citizens, and I've been attending Spectacles all my life.

'I'm sure you have your own ideas, Great-Grandfather, but I know from the accounts that we've been exporting clones to Manfold for decades. Could the Manfolk have been back-engineering them, and stumbled on some radical improvement in the design? I can't imagine why they'd turn them loose like that, though.'

Urbanus stared out through the perspex at the darkling afternoon. An elderly woman, who had been walking a lobster very slowly along the promenade, took a sharp right turn and descended into the sea.

'My formal recommendation,' he said, 'if you require it, is that we buy out whoever's manufacturing these homunculi, with all speed. A technological leap like this would be a really enormous asset, and it could do serious damage to our business interests if we leave it in someone else's hands.

'I'll await whatever further instructions you may have for me. I can be reached care of Mrs. Bladderwrack, "Sea Mists", 31 Pavilion Street, Landside.

'My filial greetings to yourself and Great-Grandmother, of course, Great-Grandfather,' he concluded formally, 'and to my mother and my father. Also my regards to my wife Priscilla, if you wouldn't mind passing them on. Your dutiful great-grandson, Lucillius Urbanus.'

Outside there was a crunch of thunder and, with sudden zeal, the rain abruptly grew a great deal worse. 'How do I stop recording?' Urbanus asked the booth. 'And also, may I have a receipt?'

23. Tiresias, Manfold.

While Urbanus had been occupying himself in northern Kempes, his mentor had taken the rickety tram back through the wet between their lodging-house and Kempes Centre Tube Station. Here Tiresias had succeeded, not without difficulty, in locating the platform which served the tiny two-stop local line to Manfold.

Although the Manfolk enclave still maintained some relations with the outside City, these were mostly industrial or economic: travel by Manfolk in or out of the ex-District was rare, and mostly connected with the supply of casual manual labour to organisations with few hiring scruples. It mostly passed through Manfold's docks, or else its road gate into Hensile District. Somehow though, perhaps because nobody had taken the responsibility for cancelling it, this automated line had carried on running between Manfold and Kempes several times a day. Even so, Tiresias was apparently the first person to travel on it since Mercuryday...

...or rather, Tiresias remembered forcefully, *Wednesday*. One must *shuck off* these Romuline patterns of thought. After all, in nearly three centuries as a slave in the Romuline, one had never yet succumbed to the pernicious habit of thinking of oneself as "he" or "him" (or "she", for that matter).

The former tutor had some regrets about absconding, naturally. It was saddening, Tiresias reflected, to leave a student of whom one was fond so forlorn and friendless in an unfamiliar District; but Urbanus was old enough to look after himself. He was, the old hermaphrodite knew, tougher than his plutocratic relatives gave him the credit for. Besides, what could possibly happen to him in the City?

The young man was no longer Tiresias' responsibility, but his own. That phase of life had been surprisingly rewarding, but it was finished. Even the pseudonym "Tiresias", apt though it was for one who had reached such a venerable age before death, must be allowed to pass. "Keth Marrane" would once more have to do as a name, provided the other Manfolk accepted its owner back. It was always possible (though doubtful) that these days they were more tolerant of the rare hermaphrodites among their number.

Kempes station was an open-air affair, the pandemic rain cataracting down its walls and benches. The little-used platform for the Manfold Line was cracked, dull weeds making their presence felt among the brittle concrete. The Manfolk named Keth Marrane was grateful for the battered shelter with its cracked perspex panes, even if its plastic seating seemed *perhaps unwelcoming* to travel-tender cheeks.

Marrane looked up just before the platform's single wormhole arch became active. ("Tiresias" had shared more than longevity and androgyny with that ancient seer of Thebes.) The chain which cranked itself slowly and painfully into the platform was a few carriages, dented and in urgent need of paint, with a locomotive-pod at each end. The doors squealed open reluctantly, and, after a brief dash through the filthy weather, the interior was welcomingly dry.

It was the precognitive skills which had first made "Tiresias" useful to the Ignotians. A slave who could predict, however vaguely, trends and changes in the City's markets had been rightly considered a valuable business asset. Nobody seemed quite clear why precognition worked within the City when time-travel was impossible, but the family had appreciated the edge it gave them. Over the years they had acquired, head-hunted and indeed bred their own precognitors, until Tiresias' abilities seemed feeble in comparison. At length the old slave had been put into semi-retirement as the tutor to the City-born Ignotians.

Like his descendants, however, Lucius Cassius was too entrenched in Roman ways of thinking to wonder exactly what the hermaphrodite's motivation in enslaving "him"self to strangers might have been. Meanwhile Tiresias' predictions, vague though they were, had helped to avert discovery on more than one occasion as the old tutor passed on secrets and intelligences to the Manfolk faction headed by Keth's friend and one-time ward Kyme Janute.

The third main category of slaves within the City, Tiresias had refrained from informing Urbanus, were the spies.

Now "Tiresias" was returning home, defecting back to the city-enclave Keth Marrane had long ago left in disgust. Things had changed here, largely thanks to Janute and friends: the Hormonal Revolution had pressed out the macho old guard of those who had been resurrected as headstrong young men and then remained that way, in favour of the women and the elderly. Marrane qualified in the latter category, if *not necessarily* the former.

For weeks now, the hermaphrodite had been a victim of the most unsettling premonition: that things in Manfold were about to change again, this time for the very much worse. The perception was maddeningly vague, but, worryingly, the glint of skylight on the Romuline legionaries' burnished armour seemed to form a recurring part of it. By contrast, the surprisingly accurate prediction that

THE MANFOLK

Of all the peoples of the City it is the Manfolk, *Homo virilis*, who demonstrate most compellingly the vital necessity for the student of the various human natures to approach his, her or its investigations with an objectivity of mind. In all physical and psychological respects, except in terms of the very pronounced primary and secondary sexual characteristics exhibited, a typical Manfolk is not greatly distinct from the *Homo sapiens* stock from which the species appears to have been engendered. It is in their mating cycle, and the culture to which it has given rise, that the Manfolk most directly diverge from the template of *H. sapiens*.

On understanding this life cycle, most anthropologists will readily sympathise with the revulsion felt by many Citizens towards the Manfolk. However, the scholar's grave obligation to comprehend the contrary world view requires us instead to become immersed within the perceptions and prejudices of the Manfolk themselves. On doing this, we will quickly discover that the expectations of the Manfolk are such that they consider the Citizens alongside whom they have been resurrected as perverse and distasteful as the Citizens find them.

It must be noted that (having perhaps been first interpolated into history by one of the temporally active powers) the Manfolk species was innocent during its sojourn in the Universe of its human heritage. Its members imagined themselves, as with many a culture whose accomplishments do not extend into the interstellar arena, to be the cosmos' sole conscious inhabitants. The world occupied by the Manfolk had some five thousand years of recorded history, the conclusion of which was an industrial civilisation of respectable sophistication but regrettable political schism. This dissent precipitated a foolish and brutal internecine war culminating in extinction for the species. The astonishment which the final generation of *H virilis* must have experienced upon discovering itself among the Saved of a far wider bloodline may be imagined.

Male Manfolk are hormonally predisposed towards violent and bloody interaction, untenable of course within the purview of the City's invulnerability protocols. Further, the action of these safeguards upon the individual imago has forcibly arrested the Manfolk's life cycle, such that those resurrected as adult males have been unable to experience the *hermapause*. To live in community with one's adult offspring, let alone one's father and even mother, has proved a psychologically dislocating experience for most Manfolk. Most devastating of all, however, has been the condition of their women, who in Manfolk society have customarily been reproductively fecund but culturally sterile. In the City, the reverse is true: Manfolk women are as long-lived as their male counterparts, and as capable of active contribution to the cultural life of Manfold; yet incapable, for obvious reasons, of parturition.

[Clutterbuck, *The Human Species: A Spotter's Guide*.]

young Urbanus would shortly be sent somewhere very close to Manfold had offered ample opportunity to insinuate oneself onto the trip, in place of the unfortunate Dedalus. Delaying for the side-trip to Memorial Park had been a risk, but had arisen from a real joy at playing tutor to the lad once more.

The slowly-moving whorl of colour all about the carriage peeled back like snakeskin as the chain drew into Manfold Varndyke Station.

From the platform, another outdoor one, Manfold seemed just as Marrane remembered it. The buildings were brick or breezeblock, inset with glass, predominantly lumpen and cuboid in shape. The walls would be graffiti-laden, the streets scattered with the debris of urban life. The tenement blocks, the factories, the scrubby parks, all would be just as they had been at the beginning; just as they had been back in the World.

The platform was if anything more overgrown and decaying than that which Marrane had left. Picking a careful path through weeds and lichen, the ex-slave reflected happily that Manfold was at least more dry than Kempes. Up through an only slightly crumbling flight of concrete stairs, smelling as ever of testosterone-rich piss, a door led out directly onto the sidewalk.

On stepping through it, Marrane felt immediately that something here was *very wrong indeed*.

The Station was itself all but deserted, reflecting the fact that travel within Manfold took place almost entirely by petrol-driven car. The street outside, however, should have been a busy part of Manfold's urban centre. On a normal mid-afternoon cars would fill the roads, while a bustle of shoppers and traders fanned across the pavements. Men would be arguing in small knots, comparing weapon sizes or shouting hopeful insults at the women going about their probably more constructive business. Occasional gangs of children (probably rare these days, but as everywhere a minority would have never grown up) would streak by looking for things to steal or vandalise. It might not be *terribly edifying*, but it was business as usual for Manfold.

There was little of that this afternoon. Sporadically a vehicle would drive past, too fast, its driver looking harried. The rare pedestrian Manfolk, of any sex or age, were cautious, furtive. Alarm sirens of various provenances sounded in the near distance, somewhere there was the sound of... surely that couldn't be gunfire? Even the factory chimneys in the distant industrial zone, Marrane realised, stood abandoned, no longer pumping noxious fumes out to the City sky.

The concrete and brick walls were graffiti-spattered as normal, even the rubbish smelt like home once had. But the Manfolk themselves seemed to be running scared.

It took a lot to frighten the average Manfolk. Marrane, who had always been exceptional in this regard, was deeply spooked.

24. Julian, RealSpace.

—THIS is the fabled Lost Planet of Erath? | Julian signed wearily at his non-extant audience. —Snuff me sidewise. |

The ship's pre-sentient computer blinked its lights dreamily back at him. Beneath them in the void, the dust-disc under consideration rotated listlessly. It was black desert all over – dark as a troglodyte's passage, but otherwise remindful of the Oakhay Dustbowl Park in which Julian had passed perhaps the dullest day of his short uneventful life.

All told he'd endured days of hopeful hyperjumping just to get here. From what Mesh Cos had maintained – and he still suspected she was taking the urea – Erath only existed if you approached it via that unique string of nested h-jumps, beginning back as far as Farflate District.

The LP of E, such as it was, lay distant from the shimmering globes of RealSpace, rootless in lacklight interstellar vacuum. Twinkly points of starfire glinted away in all directions: forty or so were made from genuine searing fusion matter, the rest projections. A pinko-violet fuzz of nebula lay tall terametres overhead, and the razor hoop of distant Citylight encircled Julian at 30° from his private horizontal. All thoroughly spectacular, no bluffing.

—So, where does a grizzled spacedog go to get drunk round here? | Julian fingered minimally. He was bored pantless. It had been days (in terms of time elapsed at any rate, the sky refusing to illuminate round these parts) since anyone had been there to see what he had to sign. Even the computer preferred Julian's typed instructions in the absence of a vocapable pilot. If he got any boreder he'd be forced to ram his flighter into Erath's moon, Anul, just for the brain-jolt.

Before he'd left the RealPort, Julian had spent time with his pigment-sticks, redesignating his ship the *Czn Lon Shel*. (Real Shel he still missed dismally, as he rattled around pretend-*Shel*'s roomy cockpit.) The flighter was little more than four slim wings, criscrossing at a slant together, with hind thrusters and the weapons pods he'd used to spatch the destructibles' pirate ship.

When he was done couriering for her Ma, he'd seek out the real Shel. She'd love RealSpace, he brooded, saddening himself. Dynamic, intellectual, surreal: her in a macrocosm.

Giddily Erath's ground-ball span below him, its twiddly continents rockscapes in seas of ash. Its rep spoke of "fiendish traps and barriers", and truth told these were quite impressive. The *Shel* had come with eight disposable probes, which Julian had sent down into Erathly orbit: all had been summarily deleted. Automated rocketships swarmed up from subsurface ports to shoot them down or blow them up, while drone batts sent out empulses to cripple them, or punched out random hyperholes to Marduk-knew-where, removing them from orbit. One a piecemaker drone diced into centimetre-cubes, just for variety. The hypothetical Erathians were evidently showing off, but any of these tricks could finish off the *Lon Shel*, leaving her ruggedly handsome young pilot floating foolishly in interstellar void. RealSpace's mainline routes got optimum policing, but out here he'd be whistling in vacuum for months before the RSC found and retrieved him.

What's more he'd paid a 50-tower deposit on the *Shel*. That was cash he was inclined to see again.

He kicked open the storebox by his feet, and with one hand hooked out the package Mesh had given him, days back at Honi's. He peeled the crinkly outer layer off it, keeping a nervous eye on Erath all the while. He undertrusted it not to do STUFF in his direction while he wasn't looking.

Inside, as the Cllr. had told him, a filmy second layer secured the contents. On it was written, in Mesh's psycho-neat hand, an old-fashioned alphanumeric code and a transmission freq. Julian entered both into the *Shel*'s computer.

He sat back to attend the response from the forbidden planet.

25. Tobin, Council House.

Tobin was packing savagely, shoving items into her holdall any way they'd go. Avatar could go to hell – she was off back to Paynesdown. If that supercilious skull-faced bastard thought she was going to hang around here while he jerked her strings, he was distressingly mistaken. Vice Vera would probably drop her down a hole in the pavement and tarmac her over. But at least it would wipe that death-grin off Avatar's chalky face.

Unless that was the Parliament's whole plan of course. But you could go mad just trying to second-guess those devious sons of bitches. Much better to do what you wanted and screw the lot of them. Maybe she'd change her name, or run away to sea, or something. The Okeanos was supposed to be nice this time of year...

The wallscreen trilled, and Tobin flinched. Angry with herself, she snapped 'Answer,' before reflecting that her caller might be Avatar. Or Mesh. Or virtually anyone else she didn't want to speak to.

The screen came on, and for a moment Tobin thought it was showing a mirrorfield. Or that she'd been split in half. The dislocation quickly passed, but not before she'd raised a puzzled hand. The figure on the screen had not done the same.

'Compassion,' Tobin said shortly, recovering herself. She brushed her tangled hair back, covering her embarrassment. She studied the set angle of the image's eyebrows, the irregular yet strangely precise arrangements of the freckles on her plumpish cheeks. 'Compassion III,' she concluded.

'Yes, yes,' the other woman told her testily, 'it's me.'

Compassion III was one of Tobin's iterations – those troubling, streamlined versions of her self, born in sequence from Anathema's remembrance tanks following her death. When people died back in the colony on Anathema, the tanks were where they went. Their biomass was broken down, their friends remembered them and those memories were collected by the tanks. After a week something emerged which seemed familiar, and which most, if not all, of the deceased's compatriots were able to accept.

All the remembrance cultures had been thrown into collective confusion on Resurrection Day, at the discovery that what they considered different stages in a person's life had been reborn multiple times as separate individuals. There was one man, Tobin gathered, who'd been resurrected in nearly fifty successive versions, none of whom got on.

Tobin and her successors – the extant ones at least – had settled on the numbering system by the second or third occasion when two of them had met up. Tobin herself was Compassion I, supposedly. Although she didn't recall being asked.

'Compassion,' said Compassion, 'I'm being followed.'

'Tobin,' Tobin corrected her automatically, although from the Compassions

THE COMPASSION PROJECT

It's unclear to what extent the Faction's agents planned the sequence of events that led to the apotheosis of a human woman as the first hominid timeship, and to what extent they, and the other participants, were making it all up as they went along.

Certainly the woman in question had an unusual history. Laura Tobin was a first-generation inhabitant of the Faction-created colony of Anathema. Made sterile by high radiation levels in their new home (at least, so they were told), these individuals were pioneers of the now-popular "remembrance tank" technique of reproduction. Like her compatriots, Tobin, or "Compassion" as her successor-iterations became sarcastically known, was altered by her series of sequential rebirths, her later selves becoming indiscriminately receptive to outside signals.

When her final iteration fell within the sphere of influence of a Great House timeship, it seems to have been a combination of this receptivity, the plasticity of her remembrance-sculpted biomass, and (dubiously) her original human heritage which allowed the vehicle to remake her in its own image. (It must be noted that it was entirely the Faction's intervention in her biodata which primed Compassion for this transformation, and also that her Faction sponsor had hand-picked her for navigational duties as long ago as the colonists' journey to Anathema.) A timeship and the mother of timeships, Compassion embarked on a series of interventions in the War, the full repercussions of which we're still experiencing.

At least, that's how the official story goes. From the perspective of the City of the Saved, there are certain questions which might be asked. For example: if the Great Houses' sentient timeships are the children of Compassion, why are they not, like other human-descended sentients, among the resurrected of the City? Far from this being the case, timeships are actively barred from entry through the Uptime Gate.

Nor do Tobin / Compassion's resurrected identities within the City include the iteration who ran away to become a timeship. At least, their numbers are one short, and all of them claim not to be the incarnation in question. Most of them are, in fact, so tired of answering this kind of inquiry that they no longer grant interviews to aspiring compassionologists.

[Walmric, *Faction Paradox: a Negotiable History*.]

even that seemed weird. 'What do you mean, followed? Tell them to get stuffed.'

In a warped kind of way, the Compassions were the nearest thing Tobin had to family. She'd had nothing to do with her real parents since her resurrection. A couple of decades ago she'd seen her sister Alison in the street, and crossed it to avoid her. Her detestation of them was, she believed, one reason she'd been partially resistant to the Faction's brainwashing. The cultists of Faction Paradox never became a substitute family for her, as they had for many in Anathema. It was probably why they'd never tried initiating her.

Compassion tutted. 'Tobin, then. Listen, I need your help.' Her image dared Tobin to make something of it. Her chubby scowl reminded Tobin annoyingly of how ridiculous she must look herself when she tried to be intimidating.

She sighed. 'I'm busy. I'm in the middle' – she checked that her half-embowelled holdall was out of sight – 'of an important case. How did you get this number, anyway?'

Compassion III waved aside the question as a wilful effort to squander her valuable time. 'They've got guns,' she said. 'I expect they're from Paynesdown. They're probably trying to get at you through me.'

They can't know me very well, then, Tobin thought. 'So what? It's not like they can hurt you.' States of grace aside, Compassion III knew how to take care of herself. These days she might be a TV critic, but in Anathema she'd been a security expert, like Tobin. 'Besides,' she added, 'hundreds of Districts use guns. It's probably nothing to do with Paynesdown.'

Compassion shook her head decisively. 'It's too much of a coincidence. Why else would they come after me? I review media programmes. Favourably.' This was true. Compassion III was a slave to the signals.

'Maybe BardCorp's competitors got pissed off with you eulogising *The Prosperos*,' Tobin suggested.

Her descendant rolled her eyes and tutted. Again. 'You deal with this kind of thing all the time,' she informed Tobin authoritatively. 'You're a – what do you call yourselves? – a private dick.' Thank you, Baines Molesti. 'Because of you, I'm in an awkward situation. What are you going to do about it?'

Tobin took a deep breath. What she wanted above all else, at this specific juncture of her afterlife, was to shout loudly and abusively at somebody. Doing so to someone close enough to be her mutant twin could be particularly satisfying.

But this was just how Compassion III was. How she'd been made. By definition, this was how Tobin herself appeared to others: selfish, arrogant, unsympathetic and quite unconcerned with anything or anybody but herself.

This, God help her, was what other people wanted to make her into.

Well, screw them. 'Where are you now, Compassion?' she asked.

'My flat in Teletopia,' said Compassion. 'Obviously,' she added, not without justification. Her caller number, complete with location ID, was flashing in the corner of the screen. Tobin's deductive powers were evidently not at their height right now.

'OK,' she sighed. 'Just stay there. I'll be with you in – how long is it from Central? Three hours? Just sit tight.'

Compassion scowled again. 'Good,' she affirmed. 'Now hurry up.' She broke the connection, shrunk down to a tiny speck of white and vanished.

Tobin gazed yearningly at her holdall, then emptied its contents out onto the bed. Extracting her shoulder-holster from a pile of undergarments, she checked the Rosetta's magazine for ammunition, flicked the safety on and off, and slid the gun back into its plastic sheath.

For all Mesh Cos' cultural inclusiveness, she'd baulked at her research assistant turning up armed to meetings with other Councillors. Tobin strapped on the holster, then pulled on her trenchcoat. *Now* she was packing.

She left the room, cutting the lights and sealing up the door – against, supposedly, the likes of Avatar, but she preferred not to think about that.

God, family, she thought instead.

26. Urbanus, Kempes.

'Mr. Ignotus? Mr. Ignotus, is that you?'

Urbanus' hopes that the insistent knocking at his door portended Tiresias' return withered at the strident tones of Mrs. Bladderwrack. His tutor had been absent since his arrival back at the boarding-house, which was puzzling Urbanus particularly in the light of the old man's earlier fatigue.

He recalled that in Kempes to be seen naked was not polite behaviour towards a member of the opposite sex. He called out, 'Just a moment, Mrs. Bladderwrack,' and tossed the minuscule towel which he had been using into the sink, where his soaked toga was already draining. He pulled a clean garment from the rail of the ramshackle wardrobe, which lurched alarmingly.

On his arrival back at "Sea Mists", Urbanus had dumped his sodden sandals on the hall carpet, where they had formed a puddle while he scanned the morning-room for evidence of Tiresian occupation. A glance across the threadbare armchairs, banks of tourist leaflets and the formica coffee-table neatly spread with newspapers (including *Megalopolis Today* and *The Kempes District Advertiser*), had sufficed to establish that the old hermaphrodite had not been present. He was incapable of passing a newspaper without reading it, and incapable of reading one without demolishing it altogether.

'It's just I've got a message for you from your friend,' the landlady called in from outside the door, enunciating "friend" with the scalpel-like precision of someone vividly picturing an entirely different relationship.

Though dry, his fresh toga pulled awkwardly at Urbanus' clammy skin. 'Oh good,' he said, knotting it roughly about him. 'Is he feeling better?'

He opened the door to reveal Mrs. Bladderwrack's suspicious visage. The landlady was sharp-tongued and fish-eyed, her skin the pallid white of long-submerged flesh. Her lank hair, seaweed-hued, was plastered wetly across her shell-white scalp. 'I don't know how it – he was feeling, I'm sure,' she replied acerbically. 'He said for me to give you this.'

Her web-fingered hand held out an envelope, which Urbanus prised with difficulty from her rubbery grasp. 'That's very kind,' he told her diplomatically. 'Have you read it?'

The landlady's cheeks tinged a pale lilac. ''Course not,' she said indignantly. 'What do you take me for?' Commencing an affronted withdrawal, she hesitated suddenly.

Urbanus, who was already peeling up the damp and under-gummed flap of the envelope, paused to look at her. 'What is it, Mrs. Bladderwrack?'

'It – your friend said you'd be paying for the room anyways,' the landlady mentioned, with surprising diffidence. 'That's right, isn't it?'

'Of course, dear lady, of course,' Urbanus said soothingly, wondering what in the City she was talking about, before firmly closing the door and sitting on the hard board bed to read Tiresias' note.

27. Melicia Clutterbuck, Manfold.

'Dear me,' declared Dr. Melicia Clutterbuck, pushing back her half-moon spectacles severely on her straight nose. 'A sniper nest, you say? My heavens.'

'They have fortified the building well,' her student Loke replied. 'Hostages are no use unless you can keep them.' The markings from his scarification ritual creased across his face as he added, 'Those bastard sons of whores!' and spat.

'There's no need for that kind of language, Loke,' Dr. Clutterbuck informed him severely.

'But those children are the guests of Manfold!' Loke protested.

'Nevertheless,' she said. Stepping out from the respiteful shelter in which she and her sizeable party had secured themselves, a dusty passage running between two tall brick walls, she shaded her eyes and gazed across the churned earth.

Whatever the Manfolk built appeared industrial; whatever the Manfolk grew seemed agricultural. Here on the campus of Manfold College, all was grey and ruddy brown: grey earth beneath Dr. Clutterbuck's feet, rubrous brick at her side; grey breeze-block walls suited to a factory, where the Student Block stood foursquare ahead of them; reddish-brown stains upon them, unconscious graffiti chronicling the day's melancholy events. If Dr. Clutterbuck pressed together the lashes of her large grey eyes, she could discern the moving heads of individuals, the sniper nest to which Loke had referred, upon the flat roof of the distant block. She withdrew into her crowded sanctuary just before two crossbow quarrels, flighted with oiled feathers, clattered off the wall behind her.

Dr. Clutterbuck was in her hundred-and-seventies, younger than any of her present students but held in awe by them; of City birth and education but with some direct knowledge of the Universe, gained during certain excursions in the service of her academic sponsors and their researches. In the eyes of its inhabitants she appeared approximately thirty years of age; but she dressed in a fashion considered respectable for those women who looked a good deal older. Her mouse-brown hair, unspecked by grey, was constrained in a severe bun, and her metal-rimmed spectacles, when not in use, depended from her neck upon a silver chain. Her mode of dress gave more the impression of a quiet lady librarian at some out-of-the-way sub-District library, than of the City's most distinguished student of comparative humanology.

Dr. Clutterbuck brushed ineffectually at the brown brick-dust which had accumulated on her floral print dress, and tutted disapprovingly. 'This campus is in a dreadful state,' she opined, adding: 'What else did Priske say about their defences?'

'There are machine-gun posts at the fore and rear entrances,' the disfigured Manfolk informed her promptly, 'and crossbowmen at every other window on the second floor. All those inside bear a blade of some kind. Many will have handguns.'

'I see,' said Dr. Clutterbuck. Her voice was level, her expression sensible, as she hefted her grenade launcher to her shoulder. 'Well,' she stated, 'we'll just have to take them all out, then, won't we?'

Those students nearer her exchanged some dubious glances with one another.

'With respect, Doctor –' Yspe began. Her voice, as deep as a flurry of tropical rain, was diffident. 'Ought you not to be seeking sanctuary? Or returning to Central District, even? These sonf – these guerillas are Manfolk. We should handle them ourselves.'

Loke patted his girlfriend's hand, as if in reassurance, but absently. Like all the younger men he was in fierce anticipation of the forthcoming fight.

'It's kind of you to be concerned, Yspe,' Dr. Clutterbuck said briskly, 'but it's not necessary. None of you have been outside the City, have you, since Resurrection Day?'

'You know we have not,' Loke muttered.

'Then I have the most recent combat experience,' the academic said, rehearsing an argument already pursued more than once that afternoon. 'Besides,' she added in concerned tones, 'those poor children are my responsibility. My heavens, goodness only knows what I shall tell poor Diarmuid's parents.'

The expressions on the faces of those near her became more mournful. All of Dr. Clutterbuck's small army were Manfolk; each was her student, or the sibling, friend or lover of one of her students. All had known Diarmuid.

Each had armed him- or herself with weapons of divergent origins and properties. Most in Manfold preferred to bear those arms which were customary and familiar to them from their first lives; all the more so since the items in question had begun once more to operate in their original fashion. The ordnances of Dr. Clutterbuck's comrades thus ranged from semi-automatic pistols to stone spears, axes to throwing-missiles. The men were mesomorphic: shoulders broad and strong as buffalo, waists and stomachs sinewy. The younger ones were sick with expectation and adrenaline. The doughy women, who were slightly the majority, were round, soft, pliable in shape, but grim-faced like the men and equally determined.

One of their comrades, Jicks, was already wounded: he had lost three fingers in a grenade's explosion, during the guerilla party's first attack on the College. The terrorists had arrived in force during the latest of the regular occasions of cultural intercourse arranged by the academic authorities between exchange and native students; they had turned their immediate attention to the young Citizens from the University of the Lower Watchtower, allowing the majority of the Manfolk students to escaped uninjured and fetch Dr. Clutterbuck.

Only two of the Lower Watchtower exchange students, Peter and Kathka, had avoided being taken. Dr. Clutterbuck had detailed Jicks, who insisted he was still fit to serve, to escort them directly to Varndyke Station, with firm orders to accompany them as far as Central District, where he must report at once to Cllr. St Marx.

Manfold had never, in the history of the City, been considered a pretty or a pleasant place, but things had taken a far uglier turn of late.

'Well, ladies and gentlemen,' Dr. Clutterbuck said now. Firmly she took the spectacles from her nose, folded them carefully and tucked them for safety against her flat chest. 'It looks as if we have been left with no choice but to fight unpleasantness with unpleasantness.' She gestured with her weapon over the furrowed ground, towards the occupied block's intimidating bulk. 'Shall we begin?'

Behind them, unregarded, another of the stolid concrete blocks continued to consume itself in flame, grey smoke ascending to a skydome overdrawn with cloud.

28. Mesh Cos, the Noosphere.

Mesh Cos remembered:

'We never intended to bring down destruction on humanity. All we wanted was to create God.

'Our seers had foretold the end long before I was born. My generation grew up knowing the precise day and time that would bring our extinction. Our people's common mind had probed into the deepest reaches of the universe, and found no others of humanity remaining anywhere. There was life, an abundance of it, although the planets had sunk back into their suns and there turned quietly to lead – but nothing, in all the cold, still universe, was kin to us. So when the prophets and futurologists, the electromancers and extrapolateurs, had told our ancestors when to expect the end, they knew my generation would be the final flowering of humankind.

'It wasn't a disaster, far from it. We'd had a good run for our money – more than most intelligent species get. My generation grew up accepting of our collective demise. But something rankled.

'What needled us, what nettled and aggrieved my contemporaries, was the knowledge that the Great Houses would be the cause of our surcease. It seemed unjust to us, however due our time, that they should administer the killing blow. Such a young people, so petty in their outlook, yet they reigned over reality with an arrogance that overreached us all.

'Our elders, who saw in destiny a work of art, appreciated this as poetic justice, as irony. Humanity itself had killed, times without number. More blood was on our hands than can be imagined: extinctions, gigadeaths, galacticides... It was fitting that we pass at the hands of a people nearly as bloody as ourselves.

'But some of us demurred. Some feared the Great Houses would not be content with destroying us once, but that they would go back and undo our whole long history, perhaps the history of earlier humanities. The aeons-long story of the human species themselves might be erased, if not by the Houses then by another of the participants in their War. For all that earlier humans would have called us gods, to the Houses we were as bacteria, to be wiped prissily away from their sterile version of history.

'I and a group of my contemporaries pledged, with the invincible confidence of the young, to preserve humanity beyond the devastation to be visited upon it by the Great Houses. Our billion-year-old civilisation, and the billion other cultures that had come before her, might be doomed to extinction, but they would be observed and recorded, their memory, at least, preserved from the crossfire of the War in Heaven. If humankind were erased from the Universe, then by our passing we would leave it something to remember us by!

'We would build a memorial worthy of the name Humanity. It would be our legacy, and our heir.

'It was a drawn-out process, centuries in execution, and it tried our young patiences to their limits. We were six- and seven-millennium-olds, barely out of adolescence (as, naturally, we are still). Our elders refused gravely to help us, though I realise now that they did all they could in seeing what we did and refusing to intervene. For that I'm grateful.

'The person, persona or personality whom we created was of all-but-infinite complexity, structured, like all the manufactured members of our culture, from skeins of light and thought and aether. Humans from an earlier age would have called it an angel, an AI, an allusion. It was... it was our progeny. I'd never been a mother.

'Calling on my most profound resources of skill and courage, I stowed away on a timeship of the Great Houses, and made my way to their stronghold, the Houseworld. There I applied all I had learned of the techniques of humankind's great thieves. I left with all the knowledge I had come for, but not without alerting an academician of House Mirraflex to my impudent presence. I knew that they would trace my time of origin, follow my path back to my home culture, but I was not concerned.

'There was, at this stage, perhaps a week remaining before the foretold end.

'My family and friends asked constantly to spend their last days in my company, but I could not comply. My clique and I worked ceaselessly, without rest, relentlessly weaving the methodologies I'd stolen from the Houses into the structure of our creature.

'It was as the time engines of the Houses bore down upon our lonely enclave, ready to rain death upon my people, that our labour was accomplished, and our creature lived.

'It was the ultimate creation of the human mind. It was a God of sorts, an infant deity, without clear will. It was the universal machine, of fact and theory, the invention foretold by scholars and technologists for aeons. It had the capability to mimic any tool devised by humanity, from the great stone calculators of the first builders down to the aethernetic soulware of my own age. It held within itself in embryo each artificial personality, each program, each datum that human beings had created.

'But to have potential so vast as to be limitless is to lack identity. We gave it specifics. Using the Houseworld techniques I had abstracted, our machine could reach across the history of human-made-kind, perceive, record and copy each machine, in all its functions. It could download the knowledge and experience, the very souls of all the human species' artificial creatures, artistic or functional, mad or sane. For them, it was the resurrection and the life.

'It was all human tools. Art is a tool. Society, a tool. Language itself is a conceptual tool, perhaps the first devised by our ancestors. The Universal Machine was culture itself: it was humanity's last testament. It was flesh, but it was also, in the end, the Word.

'House Mirraflex came out of our lead sky. Their wrath was terrible and they wielded weapons constructed out of fire and death and oblivion. It took them minutes to deconstruct the discourse of a billion years.

'My world and friends were perishing around me. I had no hope of survival, but I was content. As I myself dissolved in fire and ashes, I heard my creature speak.

'It said, "Mesh Cos, I will remember you."'

29. Cousin Porsena, the Epicentre.

He suspected he was dead, but this godawful headache made it difficult to tell. When you've been dead once, though, you get to recognise the feeling.

But then he was definitely delirious, so who could say? He wished the men, muscular and appealingly oiled though they were, would not keep calling into his office and hurting him so frequently. It was getting old. He was tired of it. It just wasn't doing it for him any more, and he'd have told them so if they'd have only taken this *goddamned gag* out of his dry and ravaged mouth.

'You are so dead, Porsena,' jeered the voice. 'You're so fucking dead.' Well, he'd figured as much.

He hadn't worked out where the voice was coming from, the pain was too distracting (can't you see I'm trying to concentrate here?) and not being able to open his eyes just at the moment didn't help.

He didn't think the voice came and went in the same way as his other visitors, the well-built ones with the blades and tape and cudgels and electrodes. He thought it might belong to someone he knew, but two days ago he'd thought the young Jodie Foster was sitting on the ceiling eating cockroaches, and that hadn't been true either, probably. He was, as mentioned previously, delirious.

He was in Hell, he guessed. It figured. If you died in Heaven, where on earth else was there to go? Purgatory was for pussies.

He was wasting time here, and he didn't have a hell of a lot of it. Time was money, literally in some cultures. He had to concentrate, but the headache and the hunger thirst and broken ribs and fingers and the bruising and the tiny cuts all over made it goddamn difficult. If he died again in Hell, maybe he'd go back to Heaven? He didn't know. He'd have to ask Jodie next time she stopped by.

(The movie star had had a long tongue, like a frog's, with which she'd snared the tough insects before crunching them up between her perfect teeth. In retrospect it should have been a clue that someone, somewhere, was hallucinating.)

'I was glad when they sent you to me, Porsena,' the voice was busy gloating. 'It gives me the chance to get even.'

He'd lost it for a second there. Delirious? You're telling me.

His hands and feet. They were... what was the concept? Immobile. Had he been paralysed as well as killed? He tried to move one of the fingers which he thought might still be unbroken, and was rewarded with excruciating pain. Goddamn.

He'd just have to open his eyes, then. They felt enormous, puffy, gummed with sputum. (Was sputum the word? How the fuck should I know?) This would be quite a challenge. Wouldn't it be better to just lose consciousness, again? That sounded good to him. He could get some rest. Recuperate. Come to the problem later with a fresh mind...

Suddenly there was a loa next to him – one of the Parliament's ritual messenger-constructs, like a datafetch in his head. She was a shadow only, black on paler black, her outline deformed by bulky clothes of some kind. Her hair, when she flicked her head irritably sideways, was tied back in a ponytail. 'Try to keep a grip, Porsena,' *she whispered sharply.* 'I'm protecting you as best I can.' *'In that case, ma'am,' he said, 'I've a couple complaints about the service.' It came out less insouciant than he intended.* 'I can't do much,' *the loa said,* 'I'm just a subroutine.' *She did the hair-flick thing.* 'You're only seeing me because the pain's distorting your time perception. Listen.' *Sure enough, the mocking voice had slowed right down, to a surprisingly soothing infrasonic buzz.* 'The Parliament sent me,' *she continued.* 'It was the only way they could think of to reach you.' *'What shall I do?' he asked her helplessly. 'These bastards are torturing me.'* 'Just stay alive,' *the loa told him.* 'They're working out how to send help.' *The shadow head moved suddenly, throwing a profile.* 'Oops, time's u–'

...so, pushing with all his might, he forced one of his eyes to open. It creaked and complained like the brass door of a furnace. Hot. Damn. He angled it downwards and focussed on his blue and bloody hand.

Chained up. That was the word. Chained to the iron chair he seemed to be sat in. That was... well, it could have been worse. At least it was attached to him.

He moved his line of sight upwards again. Details got blurred the further away they were, but he was pretty sure he saw a giant figure smeared across an aching rectangle of light.

'You're mine now, Porsena,' the voice said, and he wondered now if it might not be in some abstruse way connected with the outline in front of him. 'You belong to me. Forever.'

(Excuse me? Do I know you?)

There was a short harsh laugh and then the figure began to fade. He wasn't sure if it had turned to leave, was actually disappearing or was just blurring thanks to some damn thing his open eye was doing. He winked laboriously, and the shape was gone entirely. Like the voice, that fact seemed oddly familiar.

He sat and breathed a while.

Just stay alive? Like Hell. Any longer here, his mind would go completely, and he wasn't planning on sticking around to watch it slither away. He needed... well, a plan first, obviously, and then maybe a couple of other things. That would be OK. He was a Cousin of the Rump Parliament of Faction Paradox, for Grandpa's sake. He could do this.

He settled back onto the agonisingly cold iron, and awaited his next visitation.

30. Julian, RealSpace.

Julian's broad digits stuttered nervously against the *Lon Shel*'s control panels. This wait for the Erathians, whatever and if ever they might be, to move in their mysterious way, was getting at him. —Come ON, you enigmatic stiffs, | he gestured irritably.

He'd no idea what, if anything, to expect when come on they did. Nor whether Mesh had thought to call and tell them he was coming. He had, in point of fact, no real clue as to whether there were Erath-people at all – although he did assume the flimsily-wrapped package sitting on his knee (and strangely knife-like in its part-peeled shape) was to be handed over to SOMEbody.

Anul was clearing Erath's far horizon. Julian was no planet-pusher, but wasn't that on the fast side? Vish knew. He turned his truculent brain back to the query of how the Erathlings, if any, would react to his message. Would they stand down the subsurf batteries and autoports, and tell him 'Come on down'? Or send a vessel up to greet him via some carefully-occluded safe route? If this had been real space, instead of RealSpace, they could have teleported him, disassembling him aboard the *Shel* and recreating him from data down there on the surface. The City's protocols of inviolability had problems with the deconstructive part of that whole process –

Shat then, maybe they'd already done it. They could have scanned him, from the memories up, right where he sat, and even now another, reconstructed him was down there on the dust-disc, gesticulating away without a clue.

Or, of course, they could just send the Moon to swallow him whole.

—Holy Moroni! | Julian speed-signed as Anul grew geometrically bigger in his face. —Computer, evasive action! | he gestured wildly, stupidly falling back into atavistic space-opera mode. Recalling the *Shel*'s blind spot, he dived at the control panel and started jabbing one-handedly at it, devoting his other signifier-set to some expansive swearing.

The machine wasn't, naturally, responding. Bloody Anul, or else Erath itself, had locked down all the controls. The moon's pocked face was looming closer, sharp-lit by the *Shel*'s front floods, a ravine razoring black and open at him across its cratered and mariaed surface.

—Oh... Mammoth-Mother, | Julian gestured, abruptly running out of Civil sophistications. It seemed as if the *Shel* was plummeting towards the flatness of a waste ground. He covered up his face, wondering if this whole couriering ruse had been a machiavellian plan for Mesh to revenge herself over the Great Detective thing, or just to invisible him.

Then Julian was abruptly inside Anul, a Neanderthal man in a hollow moon. Its razor maw clanged shut behind him, engulfing him and *Shel* into its cavernous interior. He swiftly lost all semblance of consciousness.

31. Tobin, Council House.

The men were big, broad, fast, crewcut and double-breasted-suited. There were two of them, and they carried chunky pistols. They came at Tobin out of the shadows as she stepped onto the Tube platform.

Like much of Council House, CoHo Station was mock-Gothic, built from archaic stone with median-tech trappings. The SouthCentral Line Southbound platform, where Tobin had been intending to begin her trip to Teletopia District, took the form of a cloistered walkway, with deep grooves worn in its tiled floor from centuries of passengers. At this time of night it was deserted, fortunately – apart from Tobin and the men with guns.

After a moment's shock, she found her hormones flooding her with relief. Finally, after pussyfooting around for days with duplicitous Godfathers, evasive Councillors and utterly implausible murder victims, here was a situation she was perfectly familiar with.

She rolled with the clumsy shove the first thug gave her, throwing him off balance. From the floor she kicked his legs from under him, then jackknifed upright and ran for cover behind a limestone pillar. The downed man's colleague raised his meaty fist and began firing his weapon at her.

Tobin's main reason for taking Compassion III's fears seriously had been her growing feeling that she was herself being watched. Sheltering behind the pillar she felt a warm glow of vindication. True, she'd been convinced she only had the one shadow, and that he was currently behind her in the big square, Plaka Perikles. Hence her momentary bafflement – but what the hell.

The handgun's reports were staggeringly loud below the platform's vaulted ceiling. The wide pillars were spaced every few metres along the platform's edge. Their width and the distance she'd put between her and these trigger-happy goons meant she could even work her way from one to the next, down to the far end, without losing cover.

Of course she needed to work out what she'd do when she got there. Meanwhile, the gunman's bullets were notching tiles and pillars, sending stone splinters flying. God knew what he hoped to achieve from that distance, but he was certainly making a hell of a noise. She pulled her own gun out, on general principles.

It was perhaps surprising that Tobin found herself involved in quite so many firefights. The physical effects of any violent action in the City were limited, after all, to the force exerted. A punch in the stomach didn't hurt, wouldn't draw blood or break the skin, but it did exercise a force on its recipient, pushing them backwards. A slap would turn a head, a good shove would knock someone over, even if it didn't break their limbs or wind them.

Aside from their totemic value in Districts like Paynesdown, the major usefulness of guns these days was to disorientate and confuse. Often someone caught Tobin snooping, or was about to do a thing she would prefer them not to do, and she needed a distraction urgently. Often she found some harmless violence was the best available (the best she could think of at short notice, anyway). The impact of a bullet, not to mention the noise of firing it, could be pretty damn diverting even when the body it impacted was invulnerable.

You needed to be close, though, to press your advantage. The thug shooting at her now was advancing slowly, at about the same rate she was managing to keep away. He was wasting his bullets, unless his ambition was to be sued by the Tube company for extensive property damage.

The firing paused, and Tobin heard someone yelling reedily in the background. Risking a peep around her current pillar, she saw someone else had come onto the platform. An oriental eunuch in brocade robes, he was shouting indignantly at her attackers. Telling them to take their childish games elsewhere, presumably. The man she'd taken down, who had been hanging back, now turned and shot him casually in the face.

The eunuch's waxy-smooth head blew apart, plastering itself across a stone tablet advertising discount tickets for families. His flabby body swayed and toppled backwards, aligned towards the platform entrance.

'Jesus wept,' said Laura Tobin.

The man remained dead.

She remembered to duck back behind the pillar, as the foremost hitman opened fire once more.

Her mind began frantically cataloguing possibilities. A setup using a clone, designed to scare and intimidate her? If so, she ought to let it. She had to believe this was for real.

Conceivably the City's state of grace had gone into suspension again. When this had happened during the Timebeast Assault, Gally Redcross had been involved in a back-alley fist-fight with one of Big Finnish Benny's hired guns. He'd told Tobin that, for an instant, one of the blows his opponent landed on him had bloody hurt.

But that had taken Gally by surprise. Tobin's assailants seemed unfazed by the eunuch's death – which meant that, however this was done, they had arranged it. Just in case, she dived for her next pillar, stopping at the last moment to lean out and fire half a dozen rounds into the foremost thug's face. He staggered backwards, blinking, then continued pacing forward.

Besides, she realised, the splintering shards of stone were bouncing off her harmlessly. Not that, then.

She had to assume these freaks were packing potent weapons. To be completely certain she'd have to get a shot at the eunuch's body, check if her own bullet glanced off his skin, but there wasn't time for that level of experimentation. She was fast running out of pillars, and of platform.

Another shout, and she peered out again to see a delicate-faced man with unruly hair and a downy moustache, standing by the platform entrance. He stared in the direction of the gunmen, then looked down to see the ample body of the eunuch, and the spreading red puddle his expensive boots were standing in. Then the rear thug raised his gun, and the pale young man ran like hell.

Smart guy, thought Tobin, and dived off the edge of the platform into the grimy rail-well. Keeping low, and trying to step gracefully over the built-up rubbish, she too ran like hell, towards the wormhole arch and the tunnel beyond.

32. Urbanus, Manfold.

Urbanus' several re-readings of Tiresias' note, during the noisy and faltering chain journey from Kempes to Manfold, brought him to no clearer an understanding. It gist was that the old man was defecting (and perhaps, in some sense, returning) to the Manfolk enclave, but it did not hint at his reasons, stating merely that he would remember Urbanus very fondly, and that the young man must under no circumstances follow him. Urbanus, who admired his tutor greatly but did not feel himself obliged to follow the orders of a slave, planned to ask him politely just what he had been thinking of.

His current theory was that the old hermaphrodite had been under some form of duress, and had perhaps been kidnapped by a group of Manfolk who hoped to learn the secrets of the Ignotian family. He knew Tiresias would never accede to such a scheme, but he might pretend to succumb in order to lead them away from Urbanus himself. The old slave might question Lucius Cassius' policies, but he was, Urbanus thought to himself, entirely loyal.

How said Manfolk could have reached him under the shark-like eye of Mrs. Bladderwrack was another matter. Urbanus had left their worried landlady ten towers, enough to keep their rooms for nearly a week: time enough for him to succeed, with the gods' favour, in sorting things out.

Apart from its existence, the note's most puzzling aspect was the peculiar suggestion that in travelling to Manfold Tiresias was "going home". Urbanus supposed it possible that the ex-District's original resurrected population had not consisted exclusively of Manfolk; he was unable to conceive, however, why the old man would wish to return to such an unedifying place of rebirth.

With a jolt (and a wrinkling of his nose against the smell) Urbanus became once again conscious of his surroundings, as the dilapidated carriage whose sole occupant he was began to slow prior to its re-emergence. He folded the paper and slipped it into his tunic. He had only vague ideas as to how he would go about tracking Tiresias in Manfold; but he believed sincerely that money was a great social lubricator, and he had access to a generous expense account. Once within the enclave he might even unearth, and make an offer to, the makers of the homunculus whom he'd seen killed: a use of initiative which might either gain him favour with Lucius Cassius or get him disowned, depending on how successful the gambit was.

He watched as the Tube tunnel dissipated around the coach, revealing the chain line's Manfold terminus. Grey concrete, overlooked by urban piles of brick and glass, it was daubed with vulgar scrawling and overgrown with nettles. In the evening gloom it was lit by stuttering sodium lamps, and the flashlights of a crowd of hulking Manfolk.

Decked out in chains and leather, their hair variously cropped, spiked, or loose and lank, the men were standing in a huddle further up the cracked platform, facing inwards: there was some waving of arms and shouting occurring. Mrs. Bladderwrack's sudden influx of undesirables or no, Urbanus was unable to imagine that all these men found Kempes an attractive destination for a Venusday night out.

One of the Manfolk glanced towards the slowing chain, and cried out when he saw that someone was aboard. The point at which he and two others began striding along the platform was also the moment when Urbanus noticed that each man he saw had a rifle slung over his shoulder. The one who had shouted first unslung his weapon as the sliding doors creaked open, and directed it menacingly towards the young man.

'I'm a Citizen,' Urbanus told them, elaborating: 'Those won't hurt me any more than they do you.' He raised his hands anyway, as he understood to be customary when menaced with a firearm. For all he knew this was a ceremonial threatening with which the inhabitants of the enclave always welcomed their visitors, although he acknowledged the unlikelihood of the idea.

Bewildered and increasingly intimidated, Urbanus allowed the men to shove him roughly off the chain and onto the platform, an experience which was, oddly, accompanied by unfamiliar and far from pleasant sensations shooting through his body. These were entirely novel to him, and, as anyone might on finding their body behaving out of their control, the young man began to feel genuinely frightened. In Father Dis' name, what was going on?

Two of the Manfolk held him by the elbows and began to frogmarch him along the platform, while their comrade stayed behind to search the carriage for further passengers. Ahead, the knot of leather-harnessed men contained, he now saw, three otherwise attired individuals. One of them looked much like the Manfolk, muscular and bulky, but wore an Albionsfold United football shirt and Levi's jeans; while the other two, an effete-looking tetranocular lad and a muscular sapiens girl, whose hands were clasped together in apparent terror, were clearly Citizens. The first man stood protectively in front of these two, waving a bandaged hand from which some fingers were missing and, as expected, shouting. His face was discoloured and puffy, a condition called "bruising" which Urbanus recognised from many a fighting clone in the Arena.

When Urbanus and his captors were still half a dozen paces away from the group, some events occurred, in quick succession and with brutal suddenness. The man who seemed the most direct recipient of the football-shirted Manfolk's yelling rage withdrew a long and slender dagger from his belt, and drove the blade hard into the wounded man's neck. The latter's eyes bulged, and he clawed desperately at the blade until he collapsed to the floor, kicked violently and lay still.

The girl Citizen looked round at the expression of predatory relish which the surrounding Manfolk's faces held as one. Recognising in it her best opportunity for an escape, she let go the boy's hand and drove an elbow hard into the stomach of the man behind her. Vaulting his body gracefully, she ran hard towards the far end of the station, where there must be, presumably, an exit.

The knifeman reacted swiftly: unslinging his rifle, he shouldered and aimed with casual speed, and fired a single bullet into the girl's leg. A spray of blood burst from the Citizen's calf, and she fell clutching at it. Another Manfolk standing next to the boy Citizen brought up his own weapon and laconically clubbed the boy over the head, whereupon the boy, too, fell whimpering.

Urbanus' two captors had stopped still, but his own legs seemed recalcitrant and unwilling to propel him. In truth, he was grateful that the Manfolk were there to hold him up. He had seen combat times enough in the Arena to know when it was genuine; nor were the habits of City-born thought so inflexible in him that he assumed this had to be a *second* complex clone-centred charade conducted for his benefit.

Besides, he had recognised the unfamiliar feeling coursing through his nervous system. It fitted all the characteristics in the descriptions he had been given of that obsolete concept known as "pain".

Complex emotions, including sympathy for the poor girl's injuries, embarrassment at the report he had filed with Lucius Cassius, and even, surprisingly, the inevitable abject dread, would follow later. For the moment, Urbanus' overriding sensation, apart from the pain, was a clear and pure exhilaration. The collateral called Skray had been quite correct: his "rules of engagement" had changed beyond recognition.

As several Manfolk ran to drag the moaning, bloody Citizen back to her friend's side, the man who had shot her and murdered his own compatriot turned genially to face his latest prisoner.

'Greetings,' he said. Then, 'Welcome to Manfold, Citizen.'

33. The City.

The young man from the Romuline stands, alone and vulnerable, before these Manfolk guerillas. Nothing in his short life has prepared him for this moment: the return of pain to his small universe disorients him, starts distorting his young identity. Like many among the City-born he has defined himself by where he belongs within the City. He has no other context. This change may yet set him free, but for now, for him and many others, it brings only bondage. (I do not refer exclusively to that kind favoured by the late Ved Mostyn.)

The paramilitaries bundle Urbanus and the other Citizens out of Varndyke Station, onto the murky street and into a blacked-out petrol-van, kicking and punching as they go. They know these young people are to be kept alive, understand the hostages' importance to their planned campaign, yet the possibility of hurting them is hopelessly enticing. The Manfolk, the young men at any rate, are slaves to their aggression: these last three centuries of pain-free City life have been an agony to them.

Now hurt has returned to Manfold, and three hundred years of pent-up rage have finally come alive. Muggings and beatings, rape and homicide, all have stolen back within the limits of the possible. Some Manfolk have spent the centuries acquiring new ideals, convictions of civilisation: these hold out for longer than the others, but they soon succumb to the temptation of defending their values forcefully against their brutal neighbours.

A few, like Urbanus' captors, play a more ambitious game, aware that they have gained a sudden and unlooked-for advantage over the Citizens.

All of them have been caught up in a wavefront, a creeping infection of violent possibility. It ranges through Manfold's blocks and tenements; along streets and sewers it spreads, through warehouses and wasteland. It brings infirmity with it, dull aches, the pain of tiny, silly accidents. Already it has spread beyond the boundaries of Manfold: east across the murky docks, and out into Thule Sea Park's shallows like a slick; under the walls and down through northern Kempes like a deadly swarm; west across the downs and into Infercliffe and Conewood Districts. With it comes hatred, and the possibility of death.

To meet it come the barbarians. Some are drawn instinctively, unconsciously, blowflies to carrion. Others have senses carefully attuned to this subdued hum of distant unease. Some have been actively seeking just this class of phenomenon since the Timebeast Assault, or even Resurrection Day. In a City of undecillions there will be some who fall into any category you can imagine.

Meanwhile, behind the wavefront, back at the infection's source, objects and people are transmuted altogether, their substance becoming that of the invader. Carried beyond the frontier of the effect, these objects become secondary nodes of infection, spreading the contagion wherever they go:

a spearhead, carried on the Tube through Mountjoy District;

a rusty razor blade, inside an envelope addressed to the Lord Mayor;

a woman refugee in Boletree District, her very hands and teeth now potent weapons, should she choose to use them;

Manfolk and their weapons across the City, keeping tabs on those Citizens identified as lynchpins;

two assassins, their suits and guns, in Council House, attempting to dispense with Laura Tobin...

...and in RealSpace, within the hollow moon Anul as it descends towards Erath's surface, clasped in the thick unconscious hand of Julian White Mammoth Tusk, the Manfolk punching-dagger that was used to kill Ved Mostyn.

Like a necrosis, like the spreading bloom of a cancer, the wavefront creeps across my body. I feel the alteration in my bricks, my earth and tarmac. Within the wavefront my will becomes the will of the invader, my flesh his flesh. My breath and blood and body are converted into something altogether alien and different. I, the City, feel this, and I weep tears of stone.

My grace withdraws. Salvation steps aside, and leaves behind a region where evil holds sway.

Damnation has come at last to the City of the Saved.

BOOK TWO

34. Julian, the Lost Planet of Erath.

As awareness came mobbing back inside his timid brain-parts, Julian pondered on his likely situ. Dimly he expected splaying out upon a table, with slaphead aliens probing him with drills and pointy things; or dressing-gowned on a four-poster, the *Lon Shel* standing sentry in a corner of his arctic-white hotel room. Too long in RealSpace did not-unexpected things to your subliminal assumptions.

In actual, the *Shel* was perched on a black desert, his humble self slumped unmolested in her cockpit. There was the rather spacey effect of Anul's lunar surface hanging a mindwarping mere metre overhead, overshadowing the already blackened plain. His lights flooded out a sidewise corridor – blown ash one side, fake moondust the other.

His head was cramped and mimsy, yet a bloody gain. —Snuffing hell, | he fingered miserably, and tenderly massaged his brow-ridge.

Peeping between stout fingers, he saw the cratered ceiling suddenly recede at staggering speed. In seconds it diminished to a dwindled disc far up against the starscape – which was, presumably, more how it ought to be.

This must be Erath, then. It was a desolate deceasing dust-bath. Above he now saw stretched the needle-thin light-circlet ringing the planet – the City skyline, seen so many petametres off. Down here the ash spread in all directions – or anyway the one Julian could see in, which was forward – till it reached mountains in the distant distance. There was a deeply horrifying lack of structure all across the place.

The *Czn Lon*'s controls were dead as the Last Universe, with just her fore floods – which wouldn't turn off – blazing violently. That would deaden the power for sure.

Crankily, Julian twisted the manuals which opened up the flighter's canopy, hoping as he did that they had working atmosphere around this dump. Breathing vacuum was a laugh at parties, but it got old quick.

He climbed out onto Erath's blighted surface, and sank ankle-deep in slippy ashdust. —Bollocks bollocks bollocks | he auto-repeated as he waded in a cycle round the *Shel*, inspecting her for damage. (There was lots, but what was pirates and what Anul, hawking knew.) The air was stone-still, dust-dead, shadow-black, but he was breathing. Above the fake stars twinkled mockingly in the RealSky.

Back at the flighter's front he met a robot.

'Offer you a drink, sir?' it asked him, proffering a reasonable selection of flim-sealed cocktails.

Oh then, thought Julian, recovering. THAT kind of space story.

The rob's multiple articulated arms gave off a polished sheen in Lon Shel's actinic floodlamps. Its central pedestal served as a drinks tray, and it locomoted using some variety of caterpillar track.

Julian's options had been cramped since back at CoHo, but now they narrowed into two possibles. Get back in *Shel* and sit there (sulking elaborately and) waiting for something else to happen, or go along with what the rob – and so, presumptively, the Erathlings – expected of him.

He selected a Kahlua Calais. One of the robot's limbs punctured and decanted it into a glass.

'Standard take-you-to-my-leader drill, sir?' the mechanical went on.

—Sounds fun, | Julian assented guardedly. He remembered to grab the Mesh-directed package from the flighter's darkened cockpit prior to following.

The rob took him around a bluff of rock and into a concealed tunnel entrance, burbling amusedly to itself the while. Once inside a corridor, even as unfinished and craggy a one as this, Julian felt his pulse soothe calmingly. (The beverage helped, as did the neon lighting: deepy darkness was as unCivil as deserted wilderness.) He followed the mechanical along a long spiral-route passage like the ones in Pellucidar Dist., deepening with its every circulation.

Erath's interior throbbed, which he found bothering.

Lengthily the tunnel opened out into a vast enormous cavern – rough and irregular yet, but wide and spacious, it still felt crucially and relievingly enclosed. Julian was minded of the City's smaller megastructures like the Uptime Gate – esp when he saw the way the cavern's stalactites and -gmites were hollowed into pendulous / priapic tower blocks. It was a citadel, but in place of Citizens it was scurried over by a milliard robots, all sizes classes and configurations, busily engaged in inscrutable machiney tasks. He looked about for organic types, but saw only two suspiciously silver-jumpsuited human-shapes who probably had just-as-silvery interiors. The robs were confusingly various, from oh-so-consciously-retro steam-drive models to high-advancement independent skeindroids.

The robot Julian was following beckoned him onto a little cart, which cross-conveyed them hurtlingly into the cavern's deeps.

The hive activity got buzzier as they approached the centre of the cavern, where – of course – a chasm deepened in towards the further bowels of the planet. Climb-capable robots scuttled up and down its sheer walls, while other models upped and fell on antigrav discs. Julian and the rob dismounted, and the cart whizzed back the way they'd come. The rob rolled onto a disc next to the pit.

Julian peered gloomily at the vertiginous depths. —You've got to be pissing on me, | he asserted without much hope.

'I can assure you sir, I wouldn't dream of it,' the robot replied. 'I neither micturate nor, as it happens, dream. Shall we?'

Julian stepped gingerly onto the agee disc, and gripped the robot tightly as the platform rose, leaped out over the chasm, and sank into it like a brick.

The throbbing loudened greatly as they fell past towers and banks and edifices of machinery. All were of gleaming metal, plastic, or great green glowing neon blocks, also available in blue and violet. They were architected like kids' toys, all simple lines and basic solid shapes. Impractical, but nebulously futuristic, assuming you came from any future-looking culture. All looked horrifically huge, even from great distances.

The robot had no eyes, but Julian felt it peering slyly up at his reaction. —Big machines, | he told it casually, and slurped his cocktail. He'd seen the Watchtower. Nothing that could fit inside a planet, even a hollow one, could compare with that.

It looked like these might only JUST fit, though.

The heart-throb growing louder, louder still, the disc came to a sudden halt a metre-ish above a platform. This was large, recalling Julian again towards the Watchtower: its interior shelves within the Flyzones were something like this size. The agee skimmed across its flat unbuilt-on surface, predictably criss-crossed by avid robots, and halted at the curtain wall of machinery from which the shelf projected.

This surface, stretching miles left and right and up, was taken up with... something primitive. It was clunkier and clumsier than all the elegance around it, putting Julian in mind of old-fash radio equipment. Constructed out of vales and wires and sockets, it fizzled and flashed with electricity; much of its surface was covered with needle-dials and blinklight and reels and what could be magnetic tape, that spun and whirled. It seemed a most unlikely way to do technology.

'Welcome to the Lost Planet of Erath, Julian White Mammoth Tusk,' the thing vocalled portentously. Its voice reverberated over the whump of the rhythmically contracting planet like a rock concert at a waterfall.

—You're expecting me? | Julian asked. Was this some way-eccentric Artificial? Was it Mesh's contact?

'I've been expecting you,' it said, 'for an eternity. It was I, Julian White Mammoth Tusk,' the machine told him, 'who first raised your distant ancestors to sentience, far back on Pleiocene Earth.'

Julian was taken aback. —Really? | he signed, slightly impressed despite himself. —No bluff? |

'No,' said the device, 'only kidding. I'm just the ultimate technological product of the final human civilisation. I'm just the Universal Machine.'

—Um, right, | signed Julian.

'I don't really look like this, of course,' the Universal Machine said chattily. 'Just getting into the spirit of things. Call me UniMac,' it suggested, 'if labelling vast omniscient intellects helps you cope with them.'

35. Mesh, the Noosphere.

Mesh Cos recalled:

'Before we died, my people had a legend.

'It was said that in the distant past, billions of centuries before us, there had once lived a culture of humanity whose members were in continuous communion with the dead.

'These people were the keepers of a portal, set high on a mountain on a distant world, which linked the realm of the dead with the mundane universe of energy and matter. This was not a land of shadows, but a vivid, earthy state, a place where the departed were more real, more alive, more like themselves. One could pass through this gate and speak with the dead, walk among them and explore their domain. Everyone who'd ever died was present there, from past heroes and sages to one's dearest friends and relatives; mysteriously, so was everyone who ever *would* die, and even those for whom death, like life, was but a vanished possibility. One might with, very great difficulty (for the dead were many and did not always desire to be found), track down one's fleshy shade and divine from them the shape and even the hour in which one's death would come.

'Naturally, the price of such foreknowledge was always high. (As, some would say, it had been for our people.)

'Sometimes too, the dead would make the opposite journey, stepping through the gateway into the world they had left behind, to visit old friends, old haunts, or to intervene in the affairs of the living. The dead were powerful, and they were capricious, but they were gloriously human. These were not gods, but people, perfected and immortal.

'So, at any rate, the legend told us.

'The living guardians of this doorway were content and happy, for they lived their lives out on the very threshold of Heaven. However miserable or unfair their mortal existences, they knew, knew simply and for certain, that a better world, a life without pain, awaited them. They would arise again, and live in splendour in eternity.

'For a time this culture flourished, and became a place of pilgrimage for all the Universe. And then, the guardians of the gateway vanished.

'Some said that they and the portal were annihilated in the War, that in the end the dead could not protect them: others, that they had all passed over into the land of the dead, and that the way had closed forever behind them. Still others maintained that the dead had locked and barred the gateway from their side, and that this loss had broken the people's hearts.

'None of us believed the legend, naturally. It was a fiction, a metaphor for one primitive concern or another, like all the garbled myths that reached us from the planetary era.

'The dead had no realm. If they lived on at all then they resided in the sphere of mind, the noosphere, that assemblage of thoughts, beliefs and ideas which make up a culture. Even a noosphere, though, could not survive the quenching of the minds in which it had its being. A literal life following death was a long-vanished fable.

'I'll admit, then, that my resurrection was unlooked-for, and more than a little unwelcome. Indeed, when my bruised mind began to stir, and I felt my recollected self falling awake, I thought myself a prisoner of the Great Houses. It is, if I am honest, still a fear which comes to me unbidden in my dark and doubtful times. The Houses would have the techniques to create for me a reality resem-

The Population Question

In addition to its other uniquenesses, the City of the Saved is beyond doubt the most enduring source of mystery associated with the Universe. Given the City's chronological location, this should not come as a surprise to us. With hindsight, the answers to so many mysteries are not merely obvious, but mundane. Speculation as to the existence of advanced prehistoric civilisations soon loses its lustre when a stroll to the shops takes you past three Atlantean / Lemurian takeaways.

No-one can apply hindsight to the City, however. If the universe has an outermost point, a place where the Creator finished spiralling and lifted pencil from paper, then we are beyond it. No loftier perspective exists to pass us down a knowledge of the City's hidden mysteries. Who were the "Founders", or "Secret Architects"? Who composed the notes? What unimaginable technology can have been used to harvest from the immense cavalcade of human history *every single member* of the species? Why (not to put too fine a point on it) are we here?

One of the most intriguing of such mysteries is that of the City's population – not the ontological status of the Citizens, but so basic a statistic as their number.

The orientation material which the Uptime Guard hand out to visitors to the City (including visiting scholars and researchers, who would doubtless be furious if they discovered the professional discourtesy) errs on the conservative side. It refers vaguely to a population in the "septillions", somewhere between 10^{24} and 10^{27}: a reasonable enough estimate assuming that the City's population consists of the Universe's cumulative historic greater-human population plus the City-born. However, the City census of AF 291 (whose results remain unavailable for scrutiny to extra-mural researchers) reports a population closer to the order of 10^{38} individuals – more than a hundred billion *times* the figure cited in the literature. Some hundred undecillion people appear at first sight to have sprung up from absolutely nowhere.

A certain amount of rather hysterical speculation has been expended on this matter by some of the City's more paranoid residents, but the current accepted theory is not remotely sinister. It has, nevertheless, some staggering implications.

[From *Omphalos!* by Professor Vril (Newsolar University Press, AF 276).]

bling this one, a virtual afterlife in which my replicated soul might act out its fantasies of motherhood and leadership. I can think of reasons why they might do such a thing.

'When I awoke on Resurrection Morn I was distressed, disoriented and dismayed. The space I occupied was familiar, carved from light and energy, the skeinwork architecture of my people. An armoured robot hovered over me like a stag-beetle. Abstractedly I recognised it as a battle-drone of the Entrustine Horde, an obscure barbarian guild of the so-called Posthuman Era.

'It spoke, telling me not to be afraid, that all was well.

'I listened to this unlikely herald, still unconvinced that all this was not a trick of the Great Houses.

'The drone spoke to me of my Universal Machine, humanity's last creation, who had survived the chaos amid which it had been born and lived on, alone. Barely escaping the clutches of the Houses, it had wandered the scorched wreckage of our civilisation. Unsure of its powers, it tried to restore my ashes and those of its other creators to life, but found that path definitively blocked to it. It was powerful, but not all-powerful. It wept amid the fading light and shattered skeinwork, alone in our conceptual remnants.

'A long time passed before it thought to seek out others of its kind, the created ones; longer still before it mastered the abilities I'd stolen for it from the Houseworld. It reached out through time to the very moment before the cataclysm, and tried to cleave to one artificial mind it felt there. Many times the mind slipped through its grasp, or was brought through partial or deranged, and had to be destroyed. At last though, it made the transition successfully, and the soul of the Universal Machine was joined by that of a philosophising engine-angel, one of our culture's manufactured members. The Machine had performed its first resurrection.

'With the help of its new companion it brought others through, becoming defter with each abstraction, reaching back further and further, delving deeper into universal history, drawing out the consciousnesses of its countless machine ancestors. Some of the minds who joined it longed for bodies, and these it built for them, shaping the raw matter around it into suitable vessels. Some were insane or evil, and these it mended. Others proved to have been mere similes of consciousness, imitations good enough to fool their manufacturers, and these it raised to true sentience. The nameless ruin which before the Houses came had been my people's central community, soon grew into a thriving culture of machines brought forth out of the human past.

'Then one day the Universal Machine made contact with a machine mind more powerful than itself. This one knew immediately that it was observed, though this should have been quite impossible. It lashed out, and the Machine withdrew in pain. The next approach it made politely, courteously, and the other listened. It and the Machine began a communion, a dialogue which lasted decades.

'When that time was over, they had formed a covenant. Together, they would create the City of the Saved, to be a compendium of humankind, a complete anthology of all the lives humans had lived; just as the Machine itself had built, become, a definitive canon of machine life.

'Once more humanity could grow and flourish: thanks to these two gods in machine form, it would be given a glorious and eternal second chance. Here humankind would live again in all its splendour – forever and, in theory, unmolested.

'All this the resurrected Entrustine drone told me as I lay there, confused and sceptical. It thanked me for the gift of life, on behalf of the Universal Machine and of itself.

'It hoped I would accept that same gift in return.'

36. Urbanus, Manfold.

The cell which held Urbanus and the others had a window set high in its grey wall: it was yellow and filthy, and the view with which the young Romuline was presented having climbed upon Peter's shoulders proved to be of yet another

Tube platform. Like everything he had seen in Manfold, this was in poor repair; and, since their makeshift prison was a warehouse, was presumably intended for freight and not for passengers. The floodlights illuminating it beneath the wine-dark skydome had a temporary look about them. Beyond it, chain-link fences marked out a patch of industrial waste ground, puddled with oil and water and patchy with stunted weeds. A ramshackle stack of pallets leaned against one of the fences, rotting gently.

Beneath the window, on the line itself, a Tube locomotive was positioned which Urbanus, to his surprise and indignation, had recognised as belonging to the Ignotian freight fleet. It was elderly, its paint faded, but in the decayed setting it looked sleek and new. From here Urbanus could have dropped onto its roof, whence he might conceivably have discovered first how to get inside and then how to pilot it; but the warehouse window was made from a tough substance like perspex, which so far had resisted all attempts to break it. Half-heartedly, Urbanus bashed at it a few more times with Peter's shoe, whereupon it flexed, but held. 'Cursed thing,' he gasped.

'Come down,' the footwear's owner begged from underneath him. 'I can't do this any more.' Urbanus had already acted as a ladder for Peter, so he knew the discomfort and strain that bearing a second human being's weight could inflict on back and shoulders under the current conditions.

He began to lower himself, but the student staggered suddenly and Urbanus fell, his sandalled feet impacting painfully onto the cement floor. 'I don't think we're going to get out that way,' he said, handing Peter back his shoe.

Recorded music, all white noise and stuttering war-cries, redounded dully through the building. The cell itself was featureless: an unremarkable storage room, cleared of all furniture except an empty plastic packing-case and a roll-mat on which Kathka, the other student, was nursing her roughly-bandaged leg. Looking at her face made Urbanus fervently grateful that he had not yet been tested with such a degree of pain.

Peter was probing gingerly at the back of his head, where the Manfolk had clubbed him, and wincing. From what little medical knowledge the three City-born shared between them, they suspected that the young man was concussed. All of them had suffered from the attentions of their captors, but Urbanus had emerged the most intact, mostly by virtue of not having attempted to escape. The bulging eyes of the dead Manfolk student, Jicks, presented themselves to his waking thoughts at inopportune moments: the gods alone knew how Peter and Kathka, having known him, must have felt.

Urbanus tried to look innocuous as the door crashed open and a hulking Manfolk appeared, flanked by their two regular guards. He thrust at Urbanus with his machine-pistol and barked, 'Titus!'

'I suppose Gnas wants to see me,' Urbanus told the others.

'Now!' the Manfolk confirmed, so Urbanus followed him.

The guardsman's superior, Gnas Gortine, had introduced himself to the three hostages a few hours previously, when they had reached the warehouse headquarters in his men's tow. Not by any standards a peaceable man, he had been furious to see their injuries, and demanded from their captors a full account of them. With this obtained, he had congratulated the soldier who had stabbed Jicks and shot Kathka; the man who had clubbed Peter was also commended on his quick thinking. Gnas evidently deemed these actions essential, but was coldly contemptuous of those who had beaten and pummelled their already subdued captives. Establishing the identity of the worst offender, the warlord handed him a large machete and instructed him to remove his middle finger.

The man had blanched, but resolutely obeyed: the pain and terror in his eyes were horrible to behold. Meanwhile, expansively, Gnas had promised his captives that they should consider themselves his guests, and not allow the fact that they were actually his hostages to dismay them unduly. His men would adhere, he assured them, to all the ancient codes of hospitality, or be answerable to his wrath. He personally would never dream of asking his prisoners to endure any hardship which an adult Manfolk would not willingly undergo. He said this beaming genially, as the now mutilated soldier handed him his finger.

'He's taken quite a shine to *you*,' Urbanus' guard sneered now, as he was marched down a set of steel stairs and across the warehouse floor, past the source of the grating music and towards Gnas' commandeered office. 'You'd better watch your arse, you City sonfuck,' the guard continued, sending Urbanus staggering forward with a powerful shove in the kidneys. Electing not to pursue this line of conversation, Urbanus was thrust clumsily into Gnas' presence.

'Stupidus Titus!' bellowed Gnas bonhomously, causing Urbanus to wish, not for the first time, that he had had the presence of mind to construct a less blatant alias. *The Life of Brian* had long been an illicit favourite for him and his cousins.

'You, um, wanted to talk to me, sir?' he asked timorously, recovering his spectacles from the floor.

'Yes, Titus, yes indeed,' affirmed Gnas. The Manfolk chieftain was nearly eight feet tall, appearing, like every Manfolk Urbanus had seen, to be in his early twenties. Although as exaggeratedly muscular as all his countrymen, he was rather slenderer than average. He wore a leather jerkin (laced at the front across his hairless chest), obscenely bulging leather trousers and a spiked belt; he sat with leather thigh-boots resting on his desk, toying with some kind of bladed instrument. His scalp was overlaid with brittle blond stubble, his strong chin was clean-shaven, and the eyes beneath his dark brows blazed with an unsettling intelligence. 'Sit!' he commanded, pounding the desktop by his knee, and Urbanus nervously complied.

He soon found, however, that on this occasion Gnas was perfectly charming. Confused, Urbanus began to wonder whether there had been some misunderstanding; whether, should he ask to go free, the warlord would as cheerfully comply.

Gnas apologised effusively for his mood of the previous evening, explaining that while one party of his men had been recovering the fugitives, the troops assigned to guard the main body of his prisoners had been routed by a rabble of well-organised Manfolk students including, ludicrously, women. 'We need hostages now more than ever, more's the pity,' he boomed gloomily, sinking

Urbanus' spirits once more. Peter and Kathka, who were formerly his insurance policy, had become Gnas' sole hostages; aside, that was, from young "Titus" himself.

'My father's men have taken control of the Manthing,' Gnas added, conversationally. 'They will be presenting their demands to the City Council. Manfold must take advantage of its opportunity, Titus, or the City will crush us underfoot like beetles.'

To his own intense terror, Urbanus said: 'With respect, sir, the City doesn't do things like that.'

'Oh, it will, lad,' Gnas insisted, directing an appraising look his way. 'As soon as it finds out it can. That's just human nature. Loyal to the Council, are you?'

For the first time Urbanus found he envied the adherents of the City's more relaxed religions: those who were permitted to offer up prayers to their deities without a sacrifice to hand, or even an altar. He knew Dis or Neptunus would look most unsympathetically upon any worshipper who came requesting favours without, at the very least, a cup of flour or wine to make it worth their while.

Divine aid would have been most welcome at this juncture; instead he would have to rely on caution. 'I'm loyal to the City,' he said carefully, adding: 'She is our mother and our protectrix.' When asked his provenance he had claimed to be of Aurelius District, but was reasonably sure that at least some Aurelians worshipped Civitata.

'I'm City-born, too,' Gnas confided genially. 'Or rather Manfold-born – not the same thing at all. But I'm more fortunate than you. I have my memories of life outside.'

'Oh?' said Urbanus, doubly confused. He had been sure the Manfolk were unable to breed in the City: their parturition process somehow contravened invulnerability. Had Manfold been without the protocols for so long, then? And how could a City-born have memories of...

'Oh,' he realised suddenly, 'you're a remake.'

'You're very quick, young Titus, very quick.' Gnas smiled broadly. 'Considering how few outside Manfold would think we had access to remembrance tanks.'

Urbanus was completely wrong-footed now. Had he, as Gnas was implying, just given himself away? He knew his family traded in remembrance technology, but did they supply Manfold? Was it not tremendously irresponsible and wrong to give the Manfolk the means to generate individuals to specification?

'Frankenstein Inc offered us very reasonable prices, though,' Gnas continued. 'A sphere a tank.'

'*One* sphere?' Urbanus was incredulous. 'How in the gods' names can Frankenstein afford...'

He trailed off.

'You're very well-informed, young Stupidus Titus,' Gnas declared gaily, 'for the son of an Aurelian fish merchant. It's almost as if you belonged to a major corporate family. A post-Roman one, with strong Council connections.'

Oh dear, thought Urbanus.

'Which reminds me,' said the warlord, 'my father's agents have had no luck tracing your family in Aurelius District. They seem convinced there's no such household.'

'That's strange,' Urbanus muttered weakly.

'Never fear,' Gnas said, grinning. 'I'm sure we'll find them now, eh lad?'

37. Dedalus, Kempes.

It was chucking it down and Dedalus was pissed off he asked Sosimus what the fuck they was doing here in this wet shit hole and Sosimus said Ours not to reason Dedalus me old mucker were here because were here because were here because were here.

Where the fucks here said Dedalus Kempes District said Sos yes its a shit hole but its a shit hole what Consul Bignosus wants kept an eye on and were here to do it for him.

That bastard said Dedalus he threw me out his bodyguard cos a slave drugged me Yes said Sosimus you have mentioned the fact me old matey and Dedalus said Well Im fucking mentioning it again and Sos said And again and again and again and Dedalus said So what and Sosimus said Just give it a rest will you Buttercup and Dedalus snorted and said Dont fucking call me Buttercup and punched him and Sos said shit that fucking hurt and kicked him in the balls and that bloody hurt Dedalus so he bellowed and butted him in the face and he howled and the decurion come and they was both up on a charge.

Which goes to show we shouldnt question the ways of our betters big nose or no said Sosimus as they shovelled out the latrines in the pissing rain Buggered if I know why things is hurting again though its like when we go outside the bloody Uptime Gate I cant make head nor tale of it.

The legion set up camp on the golf course up the hill behind the Tube more legionarys was coming through all the time on special chains what the Ignotians had charted and the officers was commandeering local inns and hostelrys to stay in but the likes of Dedalus and Sos had to live in tents and shit in sand bunkers Its our lot in afterlife mate Sos said even in Elysium theres haves and have nots and then theres havent got a bleeding hopes like you and me.

Centurion Tyrannosaurus came past and said Put your backs into it chaps thats what I like to see City born tit said Sosimus when he was gone doesnt know the meaning of hard work give me five minutes alone with that bugger now they got pain going again and Ill put my back into it alright he wont like to see that Ill bet.

They saw Tyrannosaurus talk to the decurion and then the decurion come over and said to them Thats enough shit shoveling for today lads theres plenty more where that come from Dedalus nearly butted him then but Sos said Seems to me a lot of its being talked by certain parties and the decurions mouth went a funny shape and he said Come on lads I got a job for you ii.

He lined them up in a decade and said You lads is going to the zoo aint you the lucky ones What are we gonna do there Dec said young Albus Your gonna find us some animals the decurion said Thats nice said Albus I likes animals and the decurion said Oh youll like these ones lads and Dedalus got a sinking feeling in his stomachs.

It seems Kempes Zoo has a small collection of pre historic carnivores on loan from Consul Ignotuses family said the decurion happily viz iii devil boars a pack of v hyena beasts and a ahem mating pair of false sabre tooth felines you lads is going to foreclose on the loan Whats foreclose mean Dec asked Albus It means sunny boy the decurion said you is gonna bring them back here alive and in tact for Consul Ignotus.

Hold up Dec said Sosimus they got pain working again round here i of those bastards can take your arm off Well then lad said the decurion smiling even wider your gonna have to be extra careful aint you but its them animals Consul Ignotus wants in tact not you lads I dont think an arm here or theres gonna make much difference to him.

Shit said Sos and the decurion said Oh no lad shit is what your going to be longing for from now on youll be looking back on shit as your happiest memory of army life now get moving he shouted you buggers leave on the next tram.

Dedalus bloody hated Kempes District.

38. Tobin, Council House.

This time Tobin was lucky.

If the Tube chain had come through the station in those few seconds, she'd have been... well, unlucky. Chances were she was still impregnable to everything other than the thugs' bullets, but even so she could end up embedded alive in the City's base-substrate, or drifting undetected in Tubespace. It was the kind of fate Vice Vera would delight in arranging for her.

Were the hitmen Vera's? Tobin didn't recognise them. If Vera's mob had potent weaponry, then the crime boss had acquired some big league contacts – someone in the Houses, if not their enemy. That didn't seem likely to Tobin.

She'd better think about this later. Now she was busy.

Tobin dived through the inactive Tube archway, curling and rolling as she hit the filthy floor. Three hundred years of dust and litter scattered under her impact, then burst up in little spurts beside her as her pursuer fired. She rolled aside, hoping she'd timed this right.

Then she was up and running as the arch opaqued behind her, and her ears filled up with tens of tons of engine roaring out of nothingness onto the platform.

If what she had could even be called a plan, it was a stupid one. It depended on far too many factors that were out of her control, and she always hated that. If the chain had been even slightly off-schedule either way... never mind.

Luckily she was also right about the next bit. The space behind the shuddering Tube arch gave directly onto the equivalent area, behind the exit portal for the next-door platform. Looking along the other platform's rail to its entrance arch, Tobin saw no indication of a chain approaching. She darted through the rubbish-strewn archway, and scrambled up onto the SouthCentral Line Northbound platform.

Momentarily she considered the idea of legging it up the stairs and out of the station, but those bastards would soon follow her. Much better to make a stand here, while she had the briefest of advantages. Holstering her useless gun she hurried quickly to the stairwell, her progress masked – she hoped – by the noise of the other platform's still-emerging chain. As she crossed the vestibule she spied the slight spike-haired young man, quivering in a corner underneath a fluted pedestal. At the sight of her, he scrambled to his feet and bolted up the stairbelt. She made a note to think about him later, too.

As Tobin stepped back quietly onto the platform she'd just left, she saw the thug who had been further from her, watching his colleague. The other hitman was close by the interface, staring half-mesmerised as the body of the chain cascaded forth, waiting for his opportunity to follow her through. Near-empty carriages flashed past Tobin as, crouching behind a pillar, she tossed her sensorb at the nearer thug's feet.

Bemused, he picked it up – and then recoiled from something he alone could see. Already Tobin was sprinting forward, hurdling the headless body of the eunuch, as the gunman began to shoot the place where, from his point of view, the datafetch was presumably standing.

Tobin threw an arm around him and started wrestling him for his gun. He was much stronger than she was – but also none too quick on the uptake. He bellowed in alarm and confusion. As the Tube chain's rear carriage rushed past and through, its roar abruptly subsiding, his voice echoed throughout the suddenly empty pillared space.

Gloriously, his colleague heard, turned round in panic and shot him. The thug was thrown against her roughly, his right shoulder spraying bloody mist into the cool air, and Tobin grabbed the potent gun from his hand. She let him go and leapt towards a pillar, twisting awkwardly as the wounded man grasped her ankle and she slammed – painlessly – into hard tiles. More shots from the second gunman echoed above their prone bodies.

The gun had skittered off across the red-and-black tiled floor, and the injured man was dragging himself towards it. Tobin pulled out her own weapon and smashed it, butt-first, into the mobster's wounded shoulder. He cried out and spasmed in pain as tender flesh was compressed against the potent bullet. Tobin hit him in the face for good measure, scrambled for the other gun, and managed finally to get behind another pillar.

Hyperventilating by now, she loosed a discouraging shot at the wounded man behind her, and hopped back down onto the Tube rail. Keeping low and stumbling among the debris, she passed the confused second gunman, leapt onto the platform once more and fired.

The bullet caught him cleanly in the top of the head, which came apart. His body went limp, collapsed, and everything was suddenly appallingly quiet.

Tobin's arm felt strange, and when she looked at it there seemed to be a lot of blood there. She sat down heavily, and leaned against a pillar, gasping hoarsely.

* * *

The blood was hers: the merest nick, but it was incredible how much it hurt. So long without pain had obviously turned her into an utter wimp. She tore a strip off from her blouse and clumsily bandaged it, panting all the while.

By the time Tobin felt capable of emerging from between the pillars, the injured gunman had made a clean escape.

'Blast,' she said. Two headless bodies still sprawled on the platform, like an ill-advised artistic installation. Between them lay the sensorb, crushed to glassy dust by somebody-or-other's flailing feet.

She had to get away from here. Compassion III could look after herself tonight.

At least one burning question had been answered, to Tobin's satisfaction at least. People don't kill people: guns kill people. Ved Mostyn had been dispatched by a weapon; not – or not primarily – by the person wielding it.

The arm would be fine – she'd had worse in the Universe. Some painkillers would have been welcome, but she realised there was almost certainly nowhere in the entire City that would sell her the damn things.

Tobin climbed onto the stairbelt and began the long trek back to her quarters.

39. Little Brother Edward, Council House.

The man crouched foetal, whimpering, alone / his face masked by his hands, his body shadowed by a pillar / in the forecourt of the Tube station, always alone.

His mind was fractured, multiple articulations of self clashing, colliding.

My name is /

I am the /

I'm not /

Behind his fingers intense brown eyes turned inwards, afraid to look outside himself.

The man's silk-black hair, finger-long, was spiked, its arrangement artfully asystematic. His pale high-cheekboned face had been drawn over with a fine shading of moustache. It was a face of beauty / to be hidden by a mask. The black jacket and wide-lapelled linen shirt were worn over a high-neck leather corset. The delicate hands supported fingernails that were long, cruel, metallic.

He was twenty-one years old / He'd been created that age, four years previously.

My name is Little Brother Edward, he insisted. I am an initiate of the Rump Parliament of Faction Paradox. My patroness is Mother Twain. I am /

His form quivered as remembrance came to him. The flabby body on the station platform, headless, wallowing in that spreading slick of red oil. The bull-necked man, aiming at him the weapon that reduced a human being to that deformed mess.

He cowered back against the wall, fearful that the men might come back to finish him.

He'd marked the thick man's pained progress through the forecourt some moments before: cringing out of sight, his all-surpassing terror re-invigorated.

Shortly after, Laura Tobin too had departed.

The thought of following her further had fallen screaming from his mind the moment the gun had been raised. So attenuated a persona as he presented was ideal for the Parliament's purposes, Mother Twain had told him, yet it splintered under tension like dry wood underfoot.

He was pleased to serve them, the Mother and the Godfather and the rest, grateful and relieved to be again granted purpose. When he had first been crafted it was for the service of another, and (though he now despised her and his own creation) those impulses remained woven among his own desires and fears.

Once, he had known who he was: his liquid eyes behind their black bandanna had blazed forth the compelling certainty of that identity, imposing it on everyone he met. It had been a lie, naturally – everyone of his acquaintance had known it, save him – but the lie had been glorious.

He felt the tug of its allure still, deep inside his soul. Some days he yearned to take himself back to her home District of Magdalena, race up to her villa, burst in at the shutters as she lay at her siesta, abase himself at her feet: implore, with tears and trembling, the forgiveness of his beloved Donna Nina.

In those far-off days days, three or more years before, he had been able to discern in her the beauty that the others could not see, the graceful soul which lay behind the dumpy middle-age of her imago. He saw beneath the rolls of flesh and wattled skin, to where her eternal radiance danced nude and free and lovely. So he believed.

As it had turned out, this too was woven into him.

The joy he took in loving her was formal, courtly: he was methodical, considerate, attentive always, for the gentle Donna Nina's sake, and yet he lacked the passion that convention would demand of him. It had pleased him to be pleasing her: no more, no less. It was, as he now understood, a common flaw among his kind.

It had been the Donna Monica, the junior sister of his inamorata, reborn into an altogether younger and more nubile imago-form, who first acquainted him with the particulars of his unconventional origin. She'd done so, as it had happened, after first taking off her clothes and draping her enticing resurrection body across the table on the veranda as he had entertained her, in her sister's absence, one afternoon. He had seen little of the City outside Donna Nina's estates, but he had read books and watched the screens. He knew that they shared their world with people of all kinds; from what he knew as present, past and future. Until that fateful conversation with Donna Monica, he had never heard nor conceived of the kind of human creature he was.

He had refused to listen, naturally. He'd laughed gaily at Monica's whimsy as she returned to him again and again, with whispered words and stolen caresses, worming their subtle way down deeper into his heart. A rich woman's play-

Remakes

It may appear curious to some readers of this volume that the City should provide remembrance tanks for the use of its Citizens, even for that small minority thereof whose original cultures adopted the tanks as their primary mode of generational transmission. In their traditional function, of renewing the dead according to their contemporaries' memories, the tanks have operated less as organs of generation than as mechanisms for sustaining the population level: a redundancy under the conditions of the City. However, we should not underestimate the strength of the human procreative drive, even when manifested in such an unaccustomed form.

The Remake species (if such it may be considered) came into being with the foundation by Citizen Sharp, a resurrectee from one of the media-fixated human cultures, of Frankenstein Inc. This corporation's purpose is the bespoke manufacture of human individuals using the City's remembrance tank facilities: its products and those similarly constructed, not invariably on a profitable basis, by other groups in possession of remembrance tanks, have been disputedly classified as *Homo refactus*. The great majority of these "Remakes" are simulacra of fictional characters, although some replicate real individuals: those of a truly novel character are vanishingly few, and generally the work of conceptual artists.

Sherlock Holmeses (almost invariably modelled upon the post-cinematic mythology of the character rather than the historical original) form the largest single group among the Remakes; but Fitzwilliam Darcys, Richards III and certain early-twenty-first-century action heroines are also prevalent. Although generated from human biomass, the Remakes include facsimiles of alien and animal characters, as well as superheroes and even deities.

It has been claimed that Remakes constitute the inevitable evolutionary end product of remembrance tank society, and that they stand in relation to the ordinary children of the tanks as that people does to baseline humanity. Nevertheless, and remarkably, the Remakes are unique to the City: so far as can be ascertained, the type never evolved within the Universe. This is perhaps a question of ecological niche...

[Clutterbuck, *The Human Species: A Spotter's Guide*]

thing, she'd teased him, an extravagantly expensive toy. Commissioned; paid for; named for a personality from legend; modelled on an actor in a moving picture of his life; shaped, stamped and moulded in the remembrance tanks.

Only when Donna Nina herself, returning unexpectedly one day to find her lover and her sister entwined together in the act of passion, had screamed the truth at him – vowing to replace him with a more compliant model (or possibly a less compliant one, her thinking being inexact on this point) – only then had he given Donna Monica's fantastical account of him a breath of credence.

Donna Nina had thrown him out of her villa, naked as he was at that particular moment. Monica had accommodated him, reluctantly, but she soon tired of him. He was, in theory, the greatest lover the world had ever known, but Monica was not her sister: she saw in him the hollows of his origins. To her he would never be a complete human person.

At her incurious encouragement, he'd looked into her bizarre claims. A birthmark on the taut skin of his inner thigh had been, it seemed, an unobtrusive corporate logo, the property of ReProductive Systems Ltd. He'd visited the nearest of their workshops, where he'd seen his closest family / his parents / the tanks. Here he'd been founded in flesh then pressed out into a flimsy frangible mould.

His creators had recognised him. They had been sympathetic, but accepted no responsibility for his living. All blame or credit for his manufacture lay with their client, Nina Gutierrez.

Despondent, dislocated, he had sought in fiction and in film the men in whose image he'd been constructed – the lover and the actor both, until they duelled within his mind, breaking its furniture apart with their frenetic swordplay.

At length a new persona had come forward. A Don no more / nor yet a Little Brother, for it would be some time before he came to the notice of the Rump Parliament. Edward: a fragile, broken thing, more wooden doll than man.

Leaving the indifferent Monica, he'd made his way to Central, to the trading cartels based around the Uptime Gate. Without passion he hoped to see the Universe outside the City, of which he had such memories / but no experience.

He had already vowed to repay Nina Gutierrez / his sweet Donna Nina for the curse of his existence. He would pay like with unlike, gift her with oblivion.

His owner / lover / mother had been arrogant and wicked in imposing on him this detestable quality, life. Yet when it came to it, then as now, he had discovered he was terrified of dying.

40. Kyme Janute, Council House.

'Silly little boys,' Delegate Janute rumbled, as she stomped down one of the major thoroughfares of Council House. 'Silly, silly, *silly* little boys,' she elaborated, with the vehement assurance of one who has herself long since outgrown that particular variety of silliness.

Allisheer St Marx, to whom Janute was talking via her sensorb, agreed. 'Dr Clutterbuck tells me,' the Councillor was saying, 'that your people are tearing the place apart, and one another.' Her virtual image, taller than Janute but invisible to everyone the Delegate was stamping past, kept pace in a vision-dislocating glide. St Marx was stationary, outside somewhere, her blue-black hair blowing in the wind. 'You need to go home, Janute,' said the projection. St Marx's mirrored skyglasses reflected greens and blues of countryside.

'I'm packed and ready,' Janute confirmed. A passing flunky looked oddly at her, then scurried away when she scowled at him. As with so many other social niceties, Janute never could be bothered with sub-vocalisation.

It looked, after all, like her colleagues in the Manthing couldn't run the place without her. Janute had always suspected as much, but she was rather horrified to find the fact so abundantly confirmed. Despite the political prominence she'd achieved, Janute didn't have a particularly inflated opinion of herself. She just seemed – as she'd often told her fellows – to be the only one of them with any *sense*.

'That drama queen Marrane predicted something like this,' she grumbled.

The Hormonal Revolution

The scale of the readjustments, ethical, psychological and cultural, which existence in the City has required of the Manfolk species and its constituent Nations, cannot be overestimated. The shame of outlasting one's original death; the shock of interaction with other generations; the obsolescence of the greater part of one's culture and biology; and the humiliation of discovering that one's entire species exists merely as an obscure strand of a far greater bloodline: all these factors have ensured that for a prolonged time following Resurrection Day, indignation and resentment against the City on the part of the average Manfolk was extreme.

What in a less diligently martial species might have generated an attitude of victimhood has in the Manfolk fuelled an obsessive thirst for vengeance; and for more than two centuries political power in the Manthing, Manfold's seat of government, resided with those individuals who had died, and consequently undergone Resurrection, as young men or, later, boys. The testosterone-enhanced politics of the enclave are nowhere more evident than in its original declaration of independence; which, issued in AF 3 in the name of all the Manfolk, repudiates all imputations of human ancestry or kinship and ambitiously swears bloody vengeance on the City's Founders, should they ever be identified, for the species' intolerable and spurious inclusion among the populace.

Those same protocols which outlaw the Manfolk's naturally lethal reproductive process, however, also rule out the remotest possibility of actual hostilities; and so the combined energies of Manfold have usually been largely channelled into industrial manufacture. The cessation of diplomatic links has not harmed the enclave's trading prospects, and in recent times it has indeed become one of the modern City's wealthiest regions.

During the last century, an inevitable cross-cultural contamination with the other peoples of the City has given rise to an unprecedented assertiveness and independence of mind among those Manfolk resurrected as women. Those few males who, having survived into old age, were formerly treated by their contemporaries as pariahs have also begun to exert an influence commensurate with their experience. Such individuals outgrew even in pre-City life the domination of their hormones.

Counterpointing these trends is the proliferation of males who, seeing no likelihood of alteration in the fundamentals of the City as applied to Manfold, despair of politics and turn to increasingly obsessive and antisocial counter-cultural groups.

[Clutterbuck, *The Human Species: A Spotter's Guide*.]

'Not the details. I should have listened.'

'Marrane has been very valuable,' St Marx's image agreed, waving to someone in her middle distance. 'And wouldn't have deserted that post in the Villa Ignota, I feel sure, without being really concerned about Manfold.'

Janute grunted.

'Excuse me just a moment, please,' the construct said, and slipped out of existence.

Proceeding, swinging heavy tree-trunk legs one past another towards her guest quarters, Janute banged together her meaty fists, imagining the satisfying thud of heads colliding.

It really looked like the masculinist contingent back in Manfold had got their way. The City's protocols, which so far had always made sure the Manfolk at least *behaved* in a civilised fashion towards one another, were lifting. For years that cretin Hent Gortine and his testosterone-fuelled faction (including that absurd remake ward of his, "Gnas"), had been yelling for just this state of affairs. Now, by all accounts, they were making the most of it.

Janute stopped at an elevator. Thumping her palm against an iron panel, she watched the studded oaken door retract into the stone cladding of the wall. The lift sagged noticeably in its shaft as she stepped inside.

'I'm sorry about that,' St Marx's projection said, gliding through the frescoed wall to join her in the enclosed space. 'I have been wondering,' she continued lightly, 'if this business in Manfold is connected with what happened to poor Ved Mostyn.'

'Don't know.' Janute had heartily disliked the podgy Councillor for Wormward. He'd made a habit of pinching her buttocks, and only desisted when she dangled him out of a fourteenth-storey window. (She always enjoyed the way Citizens, though no more vulnerable than Manfolk, were so much easier to frighten.) Even after that she'd caught him gazing avariciously, or perhaps enviously, at her abundant cleavage.

'I suppose the protocols are weakening in Manfold,' she conceded. 'It might be happening here, too.' She slammed her fist, hard, into one of the lift's inspirational frescoes. It cracked across, and showered her with plaster. St Marx's hovering image winced.

'No,' Janute said, inspecting her knuckles. 'Didn't get anything then.'

The elevator reached her floor, and she stepped out.

'How quickly can you get back to Manfold?' the image asked her. 'I do think you should consider chartering a chain. The Manthing has the resources.'

'Damn waste of money,' Janute opined, straining to pull her key-card from a tight leather pocket. 'I'll take the line to Hensile and hire a cab. They can drop me outside the gates if they don't like the look of the place.' She slid the card along the door-lock and stepped into her guest quarters.

She stood still. Looked around her once. Said, 'I'll call you back,' and severed the connection.

All of Janute's belongings, which were supposed to be packed neatly inside a pair of canvas bags, were strewn across the room, its furniture and floor. Clothes, jewellery, gadgets, ornamental weapons, papers, souvenirs of Central and even her photos of home were scattered everywhere.

'Councillor Mesh!' she thundered indignantly. 'What the *Pit of Yelvling* are you doing?'

Mesh Cos looked curiously up from where she knelt on Janute's bed, rummaging through the last few items in the second bag, pearlescent skin glowing warmly in the artificial light. She seemed to be having one of her nudist days.

'Hello, Kyme,' Mesh said, brushing her leaf-green hair back unselfconsciously. 'Sorry to intrude. Come in and close the door, we need to talk.'

Mystified, Janute complied. 'Why the hell are you –' she began.

'I've been looking for this.' Mesh Cos held up an object for inspection: Janute's punch-dagger. 'I knew I recognised the design,' she added, 'it's just taken me a little while to place it.'

She angled the dagger, so Janute could see the light glinting across it. The effect was momentarily hypnotic. Ceremonial it might be, but Manfolk tradition dictated that the blade must be kept murderously sharp.

'It's pretty,' Mesh Cos said happily.

41. Porsena, the Epicentre.

They always said there was a trick to it, performing rituals when you couldn't talk. It wasn't just thinking the words inside of your head – you had to become one with the words, expressing them all through your body, articulating them with your very being or some such mystic crap. It became a kind of dance, but not the kind you'd do to entertain small children.

Also, it was kind of problematic if you were chained up. (And concentrating when you were two-thirds crazy from the pain wasn't a barrel of laughs either.)

There were cheats you could use, though. If you happened to be a Faction initiate, the obvious one was to get your shadow to do the whole thing for you.

In the minimal light cast by the open door he watched his corpulent silhouette dart in and out of view among the room's other shadows, as it ducked and wheeled and windmilled podgy arms, diving and bobbing gracefully across dank walls. It was a deal more agile than he'd ever been. A naked fat man, hopping back and forth on chubby legs, it looked cherubic and comical, like the dancing hippos in that old cartoon film. The crossbow it was carrying wouldn't have suited Cupid, though.

He'd not let it free for years now: his work made it dangerous to show his Parliament allegiances. He'd tried a few times when he'd first been imprisoned, but his mind had been too splintered by the trauma and the pain. It was only the loa's visit that had given him the focus he needed.

The dumpy figure looked delighted to be liberated. He might have a fight on his hands getting it to come back to him.

His own hand clutched the nominal focus of the ritual: a greasy blond hair he'd managed to pick off one of his gaolers, last time they'd been here to beat and maim and generally abuse him.

(They'd demonstrated the design concept behind the iron chair, or rather underneath it. Let's say it involved some kind of heating element and leave it there, OK? The smell of burnt hair still lingered in his nostrils, along with the less savoury stink of human body and its various products. There was, he thought, some seriously fucked-up shit going on in this place.)

There was going to be a price, of course. There had to be a price – you couldn't free your shadow every time you wanted something brought in from the backyard. The consequences wouldn't be good, but they beat sitting bare-ass naked on a furnace.

He wondered briefly if this shadow dance was just part of his latest anguish-fuelled hallucination. Could he really do this? Surely that was crazy. Was there a cult, led in the City by an antlered skeleton, that taught you this shit? It seemed, on reflection, pretty damn unlikely –

But then he was back, attention focussed like a flashlight on the door. He saw his shadow crouch, spin, face the light. New voices approached. It was time.

Three broad bare-torsoed men burst in, laughing loudly at something one of them had said. They weren't talking Civil so he didn't know what the hell the joke was, but it seemed it had sure been funny.

The first guy in – the ugly, bald son of a bitch with scar tissue where one eye ought to have been – checked the lock on Porsena's chains as usual, while the second amused himself by punching their prisoner hard in the stomach. Porsena coughed up blood into his gag, then narrowed his eyes on seeing that the third gaoler to have entered, carrying some kind of neon lamp, was the original owner of the purloined strand of hair. He offered up a quick prayer: Hey Grandpa, it worked. Thanks.

His shadow, clearly cast now, sprang towards the source of light. It grew as it approached the man's own shadow, thrown back hugely on the wall by the bright bar in the man's hand. A pained frown crossed the blond guy's face as, behind his back, his giant shape was wrestled to the shadow-ground and trampled by the prisoner's, which proceeded to plant its feet behind the gaoler's own. His eyes glazed over...

...and Porsena was looking out through them, out of the very strong young manly body of the gaoler (that felt so much better). Right at his own bod, where it sat bloody and encrusted in the iron chair.

'She-it,' he said, relishing the feel of a properly-lubricated mouth which closed and opened, 'I look terrible.' He raised the lamp to take a better look.

One of the other guards was looking at him oddly, so he put the lamp down and punched the guy, hard in the face. It felt real satisfying so he did it again, a great many times.

After several moments the other guy, Mr. Bald One-Eye, pulled him with great difficulty off of the prone unconscious body. The bald guy said something angry to him in that other language, along the lines of 'what the hell d'you think you're doing?'.

He took a deep breath, then took several more. He kicked the fallen guy one last time in the ribs, then shook himself. He went quiet and still, to show the man still holding tightly onto his arms (hey, that felt good, too) that he wasn't a threat. The ugly guy pushed him angrily away, shouted at him again and crossed to inspect their fallen comrade.

His recently-acquired shadow raised its crossbow and shot the guy nonchalantly in the back. The guy grunted, and fell across the first prone body. The shadow of the nonexistent quarrel was visible across the oily gleam of burnished skin and suddenly-lax muscle.

Porsena turned a critical eye back to his own listless body in its chair. The eyes were open, face slack, watching him. Nobody home. 'Let's get you out of here,' he said, 'you poor dumb bastard.' Finding a serrated dagger at his belt (ouch, nearly a *bad* flashback there), he sawed through the material of the gag, and pulled the bloody wadding out of his body's throat. It gagged feebly and blood trickled from its mouth.

He searched the fallen man for keys, and found a bunch of them, unsubtle gap-toothed shafts. Working fast, he un-padlocked his body and hefted it up from the iron chair, wincing at the sight of the skin left behind. (And, now he came to notice it again, the smell. Goddamn.)

With support his body was just capable of an automatic stagger, but the young gaoler he was riding was strong enough for both of them. Carefully but with haste, he manoeuvred them both out into the corridor. His borrowed eyes were accustomed to the light outside, though it would have half-blinded his own.

The passage was of grimy metal, nondescript, industrial maybe. The neon lights sputtered, and the floor was strewn with garbage and the occasional dead rat. The walls were rusted through in places, umber on grey, and the whole space stank of rot. Wherever this place was, he had to get himself the hell outside, before his ex-captors raised the alarm.

Beneath his feet, his single shadow strode with portly dignity across the dusty floor, as awkwardly he steered both his bodies along the crumbling passageway.

42. Julian, Erath.

Gathering up hints scattered, Julian was slowly fathoming that Erath's whole population was the Universal Machine – the robs were pieces of its multiperson self, endowed with independent life. It could have talked and acted via any of the robots, drones or Artis crawling the planet's insides like billions of soon-to-be-hatched baby wasps.

Instead of which the Machine had projected out from its retrotech pseudo-mainframe into a force-body visibly more apt to its inventive origins, all stranded light-threads and faceted solidair, and this form walked, or glid, through neon caves and passageways with Julian now. Despite its legs all motion-free as Julian trotted beside, its body simulated human shape with so much accuracy he could ID the details of its facial structure as those found in Shel's and Mesh's species. (Justice, these he knew more intimately than most.)

'I have been expecting you, though, actually,' the Machine was telling Julian. Its voice resounded much less in this body. They'd already entered through a door hid in its retro-computational frontage – truth told, a façade with no workings or circuitry behind it – and were now perambulating through the labyrinth of cheesy hollownesses permeating, apparently throughout, Erath's spongiform interior. 'I like to keep watch on things out in the so-called real world. Talking of which, thanks for the package. It's coming in useful even as we speak.'

It made sense, from its evident Lasthuman origins, that the Machine and Mesh would be in comms. Why she'd wanted it to have the knife Julian was clueless, but he knowingly gesticulated, —Any time,| at it. If the UniMac were half as omniscient as it alleged, it knew of his bewilderance.

(Truth told, he wasn't too convinced of this, and it felt silly calling the Artificial

"UniMac". But "Universal Machine" was a handful. Brainful too, if honest – the Arti claimed to embody all human tools, sentient or non, material or im, back to and beyond the flinty axeheads Julian's G4Graddad Crouch had knocked together in his lifetime. It could be said – though Julian probably wouldn't – that its claim to have 'raised up' the human species was not exclusively a joke.)

'Don't worry,' the Universal Machine said, 'this won't be the full tour. I mean, obviously. It would take decades, you'd get bored.

'So,' it continued, 'do you enjoy City life, Julian?' Scampering slightly to keep up with the Machine's angelform, Julian had passed through throbbing chamber upon chamber of diverse bizarritudes, often with robs constructing and / or demolishing unintelligible machinery. Now they were entering a cave piled high with ingots of some yellow metal – copper, gold, Julian was no metallurgist. His companion's light reflected off them glintily as its cranes unpacked and stacked them out of wooden crating.

—Um, yes, thanks, | Julian signed. —What's not to like? | He still wore his stinky RealSpace suitings, and his dread hair-extees were foul and greasy. He needed a tall shower, a shave, a demi-litre of perfume and new alloverwear.

'Oh, I don't know,' said UniMac, processing relentlessly, 'the boredom, possibly. The jingoistic smugness of a triumphalist humanity that feels itself beyond reproach. The lack of conflict, challenge or drama. The constant unbridled and directionless hedonism.'

Julian's heavy brow crumpled perplexedly. —No, | he gestured, —all of those I like. | He followed the Mac through into a larger cavern.

'Right. You've got to admire an organic who thinks it knows its own mind.' The Machine swept on through past multi rows of humaniform units standing attentively in military armour, apparently non-active. 'You didn't find you preferred life in RealSpace, then?'

—RealSpace is IN the City, | Julian replied, confused. —Hey, did you make all these guys? | he added, peering closely at one replica. Indifferently the brown eyes turned to follow his passing: so too did all of them. Since there were thousands of the combat-forms – re-enactment models at all probs – the effect creeped him considerably.

'Not these ones, no,' admitted UniMac. 'These fell off the back of a Tube chain. They were being hijacked anyway,' it elaborated, in response to Julian's accusing stare. 'They're better off here than in Manfold.'

They passed into a perfectly-hewn circle-space, an amphitheatre. A 50 or so of robots, various kinds, were arrayed where seats might be: the eyes of those with eyes were focussed at the stage, where some decidedly non-humanoid mechanicals looked to be performing a BardCorp play. Surprisingly, they were in costume.

—Then, | Julian signed, —you're a rob-righter too? You, what, "liberate" Artis from their owners? | Below him, an arachniform vacuum-maintenance bot was begging a chaste kiss from an articulated welding-arm mounted on a gurney. Around them other pieces of industrial machinery pirouetted gracefully, or plucked stringed instruments.

—When I can, | UniMac acknowledged, respecting the auto-audience's concentration by switching smoothly into Gestural. —It's preferable to letting them be enslaved, or blown apart in the name of entertainment. |

Julian considered this. —Um, | he gestured, broad-mindedly. A many-armed domestic model on a hoverskirt commenced at remonstrating with the robolovers.

—Not just "Arti"s, either, | the Machine continued. —A lot of City-born organics are disillusioned with the City. |

—No bluff, | Julian agreed, retrieving Shel expressing similar dissentiments. —But not like there's an alternative. Is there? | he queried suddenly.

Majestically, UniMac's body rotated to consider him. —Is too, | it gestured gravely, after a pause.

The welding arm's father, a burly bulldozer, had arrived, and now was welcoming the spidery rob to its party, much to the consternation of its cousin the lawnmower.

—It's in the Car Park, | the Universal Machine added. —Come and see. |

Julian went and saw. Ten minutes later he was still gaping up at the alternative.

—Fellfire, | he weakly indicated.

'It was Mesh Cos who sent the colonists to me originally,' the UniMac was vocalling. 'They were City-born like you, but tired of the City. They wanted to experience a different life. That dovetailed nicely with Cos' and my long-term plans.'

The Car Park round them was the hugest Erathly cavern Julian had yet seen, so big it had its own curvaceous horizon. Here at its centre, the Lost Planet's all-present heartbeat became a roar of melding ricocheted echo. No stalac-towers or stalag-minarets in this cave: ceiling and floor were sheared, continuing flat for kilo- and kilo-metres.

Mostly, it was filled up by stationary vehicles. Julian recognised stagecoaches, steam-trains, flying carpets, biplanes, monorails, moledelvers, dog-carts, dinghies, agee discs and harnesses, in-comb cars, a-voiders, penny-farthings, chariots, a well-stocked aircraft carrier, amphibious tanks, donkeybots, tractors, timecars, ornithopters, hang-gliders, paddle-steamers, rockets, flighters, shuttlecraft, broomsticks, sleds, aircars, traction engines, hovermopeds, harness-wings, floats, coffin-capsules, rafts, wallcrawlers, juggernauts, metallipedes, a generation starship built into an asteroid, junks, schooners, hypertransports, tunnellers, pagoda-pods, kayaks, airliners, skateboards, chronic jaunting trousers, skis, steam-powered elephants, land ironclads, perambulators, seven-league boots, flying saucers, traffic-stalkers, nuclear submarines, railway pumping-trolleys, and... oh Buddha, lots of others.

(—So these are all the human forms of transport? | Julian had speculated as they'd entered. 'Heck no,' the UniMac had said, 'these are just the useful ones.')

Over the far side, robots scurried in / out of a colossal wedge-shaped metal spaceship, all rivets hatches sensor-pods and gunports, emblazoned on its nearer surface with a twin-0 serial no and the smaller alias *Zeronaut*. More starships stood about the place than flew in RealSpace, including a twin sister to the *Lon Shel* (unless it WAS the *Lon Shel*) A square km of cave was occupied by Tube-chain rolling stock, while camels and horses, sauropods and scarabs and other draft-beasts grazed in a hectares-big grassy enclosure under simsun floodlights.

Here at the cavern's hub stood erect a tremendous obelisk, so tall its summit grazed the smoothened ceiling. Julian had never had cause to visit the original, but he'd seen pictures and holos enough. The tombstone shape, the inky marbled finish, the gigantism...

—It's the swyving Uptime Gate,| he observed, reasonably calmly he thought.

'It's *a* Gate, certainly,' UniMac agreed. 'It's how we access the colony.'

—But what's the point?| Julian exasperated. —You leave the City, you live in this colony, you – eventually, I mean – you get... expired. Then you end up back here and have to live the City all again.|

'Well,' UniMac told him, mildly affronted, 'some might say that was the point, to gain experience of life outside the City. But I think you're missing the germane bit here. This isn't,' it told Julian, 'an exact functional copy of the Uptime Gate. It's been modified. It doesn't give out on the Universe your ancestors remember.

'You see,' said UniMac, 'the colony of City-born is in the *Next* Universe. This is what we call the Downtime Gate.'

43. Urbanus, Manfold.

Urbanus had dreamed of Tartarus: the stinking pit where the ancestral Titans had been thrown after their defeat by their son Jupiter, and to which the souls of those human dead who had offended against the gods had (so the Romans had believed, until they checked and found all of their number present in the City) been condemned. He saw his family there: his parents, his wife and cousin Priscilla, Prato their manservant and old Tiresias, all forced to endure the tempests and the Furiae in a prison which looked worryingly similar to the Ignotian Arena. Urbanus had stood watching them in that infernal place, by the side of Dis Pater: faceless as he was nameless, the god had told him, in a voice close kin to Urbanus' own, 'See, boy, how I spare you, my good and loyal servant'.

He had awakened in a shivering chill, to the sight of grey dawn piercing the cell's one window, and to the abrasive scrubbing of the Manfolk music.

Now, back at his vantage point on Peter's shoulders, Urbanus observed more mundane matters, as the purloined Ignotian Tube engine on the tracks below was loaded up with cylindrical caskets. Each was approximately the size of a man's head, but visibly much heavier: the guerillas who were carting them onto the chain had trouble lifting even one at a time, their biceps straining as they fought to carry them aloft; but they persevered. They would have made far better progress had they felt able to lift each barrel between two of them, but apparently asking another man for help was tantamount among the Manfolk to wearing cologne or declaring an interest in flower arranging.

Urbanus, to whom flower arranging had always rather appealed, reported down to his cell-mates: 'It looks like there's a door right underneath us, if we can

The Legend of Gnas

Most of the mythic heroes of the Manfolk are a dreary bunch, all thews and sinews, bellowing defiance. They spend their time hacking apart monsters, gods, or most often rival Manfolk heroes with their mighty thickswords. Typical of the genre are Tharne, who killed the fearsome Beast of Kreshavar, or Mast, who slew the Mandrake, or Goadd, who single-handedly besieged and sacked *some godsforsaken city or other* before impregnating its entire female population. Common factors in these myths are an admiration for virility, expressed equally in slaying and in fathering, the virtue of dying young (Manfolk who live to hermapause, let alone a ripe old age, are not considered hero material) and a profound mistrust of anything resembling intelligence or education. Occasionally one of them has the wit to massacre his sons (and is then severely punished by the gods), but this is about as intellectual as these heroes get.

Thank heavens, then for the legend of Gnas son of Korth, the solitary Ulysses in this scrum of penis-waving Herculeses. Like Ulysses, Gnas is known for his wisdom and his shrewd knowledge of human nature, as well as his cheery amorality. Like Ulysses too, he is occasionally portrayed as something of a Trickster figure.

There is, for instance, the legend of the monstrous twins Agnar and Ragnajar, each of whom Gnas persuaded that the other had died after leaving a large pile of treasure in a nearby cave. The story tells that when the giants met in the pitch-dark cavern, each assumed that his brother was a robber come to steal his rightful inheritance. While they fought, Gnas and his comrades blocked up the cave entrance and helped themselves to the giants' real hoards.

Another tale concerns the sons of Hosk, and in particular that litter's runt, the weakling Kyrre, whom Gnas loaned his magical spear *oh gods look up the name of the spear* for use in the usual time-honoured mating-battle with his brothers. While this was going on Gnas busied himself with Hosk, emerging from the tribal brood-house in time to watch Kyrre dispatch the last and strongest of his siblings. The unfortunate Kyrre was one of many dupes who ended up bringing up a brood of Gnas' bastard children as his own.

Most often, though, Gnas is described gaining victory in battle by dint of wilily squirrelling out his opponents' weaknesses, or by unerringly attacking whatever item is of most importance to their battle plans...

[From *Legendary Participants* (anonymous unpublished MS in the Baconian Library).]

get there. But they're loading up the chain, the locomotive I mean, with cargo. It looks like they'll be sending it off somewhere soon.'

'Balls,' said Kathka. She was, she maintained, feeling a little better: evidently the medicines which Gnas' men had been stockpiling (in a policy which had been either paranoid or visionary, depending on your perspective) were proving of some help to her. She was still remarkably irritable, however: 'That's our only ride out of here.'

'The only one we know of,' Urbanus corrected her mildly. 'I can see a road nearby as well: there might be functional cars.'

'Do you know how to drive an in-comb car?' she snapped. 'I bloody don't.'

'Down...!' gasped Peter, and Urbanus quickly descended. The boy student straightened up wheezing, and leaned against the wall below the window. He screwed up first his upper, then his lower pair of eyes. 'I need...,' he panted, 'to get... you know... that thing. What was the word?'

'A life?' Kathka suggested acidly.

'Fit,' Urbanus said.

'Yes,' Peter agreed, sagging onto his haunches, 'that.'

Urbanus' earlier conversation with Gnas Gortine had continued for some time, the warlord appearing greatly cheered by his exposure of the Romuline youth's poor subterfuge. Shamefacedly, Urbanus had admitted to his true name, District and family, which had delighted Gnas. 'Most of these cretins wouldn't have had a clue,' he had jeered. '*Stupidus Titus* indeed. I happen to believe, young Urbanus, that knowledge is the strongest weapon a warrior has in his armoury.' He had then proceeded to lecture the young man on his cunning exploits as a hero, such as the subduing of Krakaste and the trapping of the giants Agnar and Ragnajar; most of which, to the best of Urbanus' understanding, had never actually happened, but which Gnas was able to remember in off-puttingly vivid detail.

Urbanus knew the theory of remakes, but had only ever met a solitary specimen: a cinematic Spartacus who, under the impression that his fame would act as a big draw, had sought work with the family's gladiatorial wing. Urbanus had been spending the day as the guest of his paternal uncle Quintus, who had given the interviewee short shrift. The Spartacus had been candid about his fictional status, and Urbanus found Gnas' confident proclamations of his heroic past confusing. Wary of invoking the warlord's anger, but aware that Gnas needed him alive if he was to be an effective hostage, he had diffidently asked: 'But you, um, didn't actually do any of those things... I mean, did you?'

'Many of my men would insist I did,' Gnas had beamed. 'They'd open you up and wind your entrails on a skewer for suggesting otherwise. But then most of them are incapable of telling fact from belief. As I say, cretins, but no more stupid than the average Citizen. And their loyalty is useful.'

More confidently given Gnas' measured reaction, and remembering the ur-Romulus' job as a nightclub bouncer, Urbanus had enquired, 'But what about the historical Gnas? How does he feel?'

'There never was one,' the guerilla chieftain had boomed cheerfully. 'My father sought him among the Manfolk for decades. He even left Manfold and searched among the craven exiles in the City. Eventually he found the bard who'd made up the whole story, and turned to the tanks to produce his hero. In every way that matters, lad, I am Gnas, son of Korth, slayer of Menke, conqueror of Krakaste and all those other things. No man has greater claim to that identity than I.'

It seemed Gnas Gortine had been modelled by Hent Gortine on the legendary Gnas, whom Hent, an amateur occultist among his other predilections, believed to have been invented as an attempt to remedy a sizeable lacuna in the Manfolk's collective faculties and experience. Encouraged to consider himself part revolutionary leader, part secret weapon, the warrior-remake had been sent by his father on Manfold College's exchange study programme with the University of the Lower Watchtower. He claimed that this had granted him an intimate insight into 'the Citizen mentality': Urbanus was convinced that no such quality existed, and had said so, robustly.

It had been frightening how comfortable he had found himself becoming during his conversation with the warlord. Despite the barbaric acts to which he had been such a revolted witness; despite the plans which Gnas openly professed to seed the entire City with violence and with terror; there remained in the man something intensely, even boyishly likeable. Urbanus imagined that this was one of the attributes of the legendary Gnas with which his remake had been programmed: this did not, however, make Urbanus himself any the less susceptible to its effects.

Determined to remind himself of Gnas' moral repulsiveness, Urbanus had broached the subject of the Manfolk, Jicks, whose murder the chieftain had at the very least sanctioned. 'Him?' Gnas had bellowed in surprise; he roared with laughter. 'From what my men tell me he died a fool, trying to protect the outsiders. That's no way for a Manfolk warrior to meet his end, not even one of the piddling Lestike Nation. Don't waste any sentiment on him, Urbanus Ignotus.' Besides, he had added as a genial afterthought, if popular rumour were to be believed, Jicks would live on in the Epicentre.

'That doesn't make killing him any better, actually,' Urbanus had pointed out acerbically, and Gnas had laughed until he'd wept.

The warlord's men had returned Urbanus to the cell shortly afterwards, where he had found Peter and Kathka despondent. That had been when he mentioned the Tube engine as a potential vehicle of their escape, an effort at encouragement which he now regretted as it seemed to have plunged the young Citizens into a deeper gloom than ever.

'Couldn't you have grabbed Gortine's gun or something?' Kathka asked him accusingly.

'He'd still have had the other three,' Urbanus replied. 'I don't think I'd have lasted long.'

An instant later, a vibration spread across the walls and floor, becoming a violent juddering as thunder rang outside the window, building to enormous volume. The concrete and plastic had a deadening effect on sound, but the din was considerable.

'And there they go,' declared Kathka bitterly. Her face became uncertain as the roar transmuted into an almighty clashing noise, and ended in a screech of rending metal.

'I don't think so,' Urbanus said. 'I think that was a chain *arriving*. And ploughing straight into the engine that's already there. Help me up, Peter.'

Already, muffled by thick plastic, the three of them could hear faint chattering thuds arising from below. Only Urbanus recognised the sound, as one he had heard a thousand times in the Arena.

It was the noise of automatic gunfire.

44. Gnas Gortine, Manfold.

In those long-doomed days of Manfold the drawing of blood and the bravery of war were seen at last within the City of the Saved. And the Manfolk bore arms in readiness to reclaim from out of the fearful fingers of the Citizens their bloody birth-right. Then did the warrior who bore the cunning soul of Gnas, the wily son of Korth, stand bold amongst them.

And twice-born Gnas spoke unto his steward, the loyal but significantly less heroic Krest Ivarre of the Vaskale Nation, he who had toiled before his calling to Gnas' right hand as a mechanic in the transport systems of the Manfolk. And Gnas spake thus: 'Well, didn't he say where he was going?'

And Krest Ivarre quoth, 'No, sir, he just buggered off.'

'I don't like the sound of that,' said Gnas. He stood, and rapped his fist upon the steel-topped desk he'd had installed in the shabby office at his warehouse headquarters. 'What do we know about this bitch's bastard Priske?'

Krest gave a surly shrug. 'Signed up with us two days ago.'

And Gnas strode backward and then forth within the office-chamber, in the manner of a man who thinks long and clear instead of cleaving the limbs of his enemies asunder with his mighty thick-sword.

'Even if he wasn't a spy,' Gnas said at last, 'he may have compromised our actions here. If he was, he may have given the counter-insurgents the knowledge they used to defeat us at the campus.'

'You want the men to hunt him down, sir?' Krest asked respectfully.

'Ah! Take him prisoner so I can feast my eyes on his torments, you mean?' Gnas said. 'Pluck out his eyes? Tear his tongue from his throat? Hamstring the lying whore and leave him alive to be my plaything, an example to all that no man betrays Gnas Gortine and lives?'

'Um, yes,' agreed Krest, sounding rather doubtful.

'In the fullness of time, Krest,' Gnas sighed, 'in the fullness of time. Our most urgent task is to check up on whatever this Priske has done since he signed up. Find out whether – and how well – he's followed orders. For by the bones of my forefathers,' *Gnas vowed in a voice of thunder*, 'if there's one runt from the litter of a wizened crone I loathe more than a spy, it's a saboteur!'

'You're right, sir,' said Krest, alarmed. 'I'll get the men on it right away.'

And Korth's son rested himself a while upon his mighty desk, and brought forth from the broad fortress of his chest the heart-felt sigh of a warrior who wonders whether he really has to think of everything himself.

Gnas Gortine had never found a way to silence the commentary. It had continued throughout everything he'd done since he first emerged from his mother tank – mighty this, glorious that, fell the other. Even strong drink – and Manfold offered some of the strongest – couldn't shut it up. He'd never spoken of it to other Manfolk, but he very much doubted any of them had to suffer such a thing.

He was convinced that the constantly unfolding saga of his daily life was a reminder of his origins, a remake curse. Despite his boasts to Urbanus Ignotus and everyone else who asked, Gnas was well aware that he was of a species apart. Biologically, they said, he had more in common with men made in imitation of the Incredible Hulk or Humpty Dumpty than he had with his own father. Like them (and he'd met both in the City), he had been created for a purpose – and that was to play his part, study his rôle. If his particular character happened to be that of a Manfolk barbarian-hero, did that make a difference?

The building resounded with a heavy rumble, building steadily in presence. Gnas was on his feet immediately, and burst from his office. 'Krest!' *he cried, his stormy brow black with a warrior's wrath,* as the sound outside merged into a clash and shriek of buckling metal.

His lieutenant scurried towards him. 'Don't bother,' he said mildly. 'I think we must have put Priske in charge of deactivating the Tube arch, don't you? We are under attack! Defend the building!' He was gratified to see Krest and the others scamper in the direction of the loading platform, from which the sound of gunfire was already muttering.

Drawing his biggest handguns from the twin holsters on his back, Gnas leapt for the steel stairs, reaching them as they were shaken by what was unmistakeably the crunch of an explosion. He bounded up the stairs four at a time.

Whoever these attackers were, it was a certain wager they were there to free his hostages. As he approached the cell he gave voice to a defiant yell, and the guard unlocked it very hurriedly and stood aside. 'With me!' Gnas ordered him as he charged through the door into the confined concrete space.

Confined no longer. A great chunk of wall was missing, as were all three of his prisoners. He caught a glimpse of an armoured figure, with the slight shape of the woman Kathka clutched in its arms, bobbing below the edge of the great rent in the masonry. Gnas vaulted the pile of rubble on the floor, to crouch at the lip of the hole.

Below, his stolen locomotive had been violently shunted and was hanging off the rail. The new arrival – the battered passenger model from the Kempes Line, by the look of it – was askew on the track, but could probably still be moved with traction. It had only half emerged from the still-spiralling interface of the Tube arch, and Gnas was certain the second engine would be idling at its far end, ready to pull it away. Fighters – Gnas could hardly consider them troops, including as they did both women and old men – had spilled out from the nearer carriages, and were engaged in fierce combat with his own men. Despite the clamour of gunfire, most of the fighting was happening hand-to-hand on the confined and narrow platform.

Firing into that mêlée could only be indiscriminate slaughter. Unless you were positioned above it, and a good shot.

With a cry that curdled men's blood, Korth's son sprang like the eagle from his concrete eyrie. The very air sang as the stalwart warrior soared. He alighted on the rust-ridden roof of the engine below. The well-made metal warped and dinted as Gnas dropped thereon. His sinews swelled as he brought his bloody weapons to bear upon the foe. They would lament the day they deemed themselves worthy to wage battle upon this warrior of the Manfolk!

Gnas Gortine had long ago decided that, since he was singly made to play the part of a cunning warrior-hero, he would do so with every shred of energy and conviction his well-built mind and body had to offer.

With a casual bullet from each of his gun-barrels, he picked off a woman and a slight, effeminate old man. To his satisfaction and also rather to his surprise, the cell guard had joined him immediately on the locomotive roof. Gnas tossed him one of the weapons, then set off along the roof towards the intruders' Tube chain. The doors on its off-platform side were open, and the last of the flying-harnessed figures was helping the lad Peter to climb aboard. Gnas gave a mighty roar as he recognised the tiny, female Citizen.

'Clutterbuck!' he yelled, dismayed. His former lecturer spared him the briefest glance. He saw her lips tighten as she ducked into the carriage ahead. He loosed a futile shot in her direction as somewhere a whistle was blown.

The slewed engine he was now standing on, the new arrival, jerked as its partner still in Tubespace began pulling. At the shrill signal, the rescue party had begun to retreat through their open carriage doors, leaving their dead, along with his own, behind them. The carriages trembled and righted themselves, as the unseen locomotive started moving in earnest.

'Clutterbuck!' Gnas thundered again. That explained, he realised, who'd co-ordinated the counter-attack at the College campus. He fired bullet after bullet into the carriage roof ahead of him, trying even as he ran to blow a large enough hole in it that he could drop inside.

The chain was moving now at speed, and the low Tube arch was approaching rapidly. Gnas reached inside his belt-pouch for a grenade, bit into it to activate the detonator, and tossed it at the hole he had created. It bounced off the advancing arch – fortunately into the barren ground, the other side of the rail from where his men stood gaping.

As his foes' engine drew back into its extra-dimensional lair, roaring like a fearful beast, again Gnas leaped. Like the black bird that brings fell omens, the twice-born stood atop the summit of the Tube-space portal, pouring his fury with bloody bullets into the back of that mighty monster until it and its riders were forever banished from that place.

The wormhole whirled closed behind the rear surface of the chain, and all was silent.

45. Tobin, Council House.

'Oh, hello, Laura,' Mesh Cos said conversationally. 'Come in, I was just having a shower.'

She stood there, with a large and fluffy towel draped over her shoulders, as Tobin stepped gingerly into her spacious Councillor's apartment.

The first thing that struck Tobin about Mesh's rooms was the view. Council House being the size and shape it was, external walls were rare, and real windows at a premium. But each Councillor's suite was expected to accommodate a generous-sized reception, and the Architects had obviously decided the guests would need something to look at across their nibbles. Across the ample vestibule from Mesh's door, a set of tall arched windows provided a panorama of the night-time Central skyline, sketched in threads of light on blocks of shadow.

The sweeping curve of the Watchtower's South-West Buttress dominated the right side of the skyline. To the far left an apparently straight wall delineated the Chamber of Residents – the gas-giant sized amphitheatre where the lower chamber of the City's government sat in session. Between the megastructures the parallel planes of Cityscape and skydome receded into dark infinity, dotted with artificial suns over those Parks which were currently enjoying daytime.

'Fabulous, isn't it?' Mesh said. 'I could look at it for hours. Take a seat, ask the genii for a drink if you want one. I won't be long.' She slipped through an archway, presumably towards one of her bathrooms.

Tobin's employer had betrayed little surprise at being called on by her subordinate in the middle of the night. To Tobin this seemed peculiar in itself, but she was aware she had a low suspicion threshold.

Gingerly she probed the crudely-bandaged cut on her left arm (Mesh hadn't been curious about that, either, which was even more suspicious), and massaged her shoulder through the sensible weight of her gunbelt. She'd replaced her Rosetta with the automatic pistol she'd taken from the thug at CoHo station. For all she knew, the people who'd created it could turn its potency off in an instant, but she still found its presence reassuring.

She strolled around the vestibule of Mesh's chambers, peering at things. Although the rooms had been extensively refitted in the décor / technology of Mesh's people, it had been toned down so as to set her earlier-human guests at ease. Meaning that Tobin stood some chance of comprehending perhaps a tenth of the items present.

The room was ambiently lit, with dancing shadows cast by globes orbiting near the ceiling. These emitted gently-modulated fluting noises which together formed an ever-changing pattern of seemingly accidental harmonies. If she understood correctly, they were domestic AIs, Mesh's "genii", each of which could probably out-think a hundred Tobins from a standing start. If they had any real offensive capability, she was shafted.

The walls had been stripped of all their wooden panelling. In its place the great stones had been webbed with glittering force-lines, in tasteful green and silver. A plane of force along one wall displayed a tactful selection of the artworks and other objects of significance with which Mesh had been presented during her tenure as Councillor. A Neolithic goddess figurine reminded Tobin irresistibly of Kyme Janute. Among the items on display were a dozen weapons, presumably ornamental, any one of them possibly deadly. Tobin looked particularly intently at the shorter bladed instruments. She considered hiding them somewhere, but decided reluctantly that the genii were bound to notice. No sense tipping them off early.

She started guiltily as Mesh came back, but the Councillor seemed unarmed and guileless. She wore a loose print kaftan in Mondrian blocks and lines, and vigorously toweled her wet-black hair back to its usual glass-green. Tobin eased herself onto what might have been the arm of what was possibly a chair.

'Have you found everything you need?' Mesh asked. Still with that lack of interest in Tobin's business here. The unwelcome thought crawled into the investigator's mind that the Councillor might simply be assuming she was there for sex.

It was in Tobin's nature to be blunt, but she always found this part of the job difficult, even without the prospect of potential death. To say what she was going to say she had to have some kind of lead-in.

'I suppose this is about Ved Mostyn, isn't it?' Mesh asked her kindly.

Tobin groaned inwardly. Okay. So Mesh had known about her "secret" assignment all along. She wondered how many of her other suspects the Councillor had shared the information with.

'Well, yes,' she said, trying to recover the initiative. 'As it happens.'

'You should have talked to me before,' Mesh said. Her voice merged chorally with the notes of the genii. 'I could have helped. You know Security let me look at the crime scene?'

Tobin grimaced. 'Yes.'

'I hope you don't mind me asking,' Mesh said archly, 'but does this mean you won't be needing your cover story any more? Because if so, I'm going to have to find a new researcher, again.'

'Listen,' said Tobin bluntly. It lacked finesse, but Mesh politely acquiesced. She gave Tobin a quizzical look, tapped a foot on the floor causing it to extrude a force-form, and perched her bottom on it. She gave her hair a final rub and laid the towel aside, leaving it spiked like grass.

'I'm sorry I used you as a cover story.' Tobin tried to sound sincere. 'I have been investigating Cllr. Mostyn's death, yes. I don't know why I was asked, but it's what I've been paid to do and I intend to do it.' Because, even if Avatar's a devious bone-faced fraud, it's still the most interesting job I've had since Resurrection.

'And how's that going?' Mesh's interest seemed genuine.

'Well,' she began, and stopped. This was just weird. Mesh was simply far too nice for Tobin to go accusing the woman of murder. Which was (she reminded herself sternly) the perfect cover. 'I thought at first,' she said, '– that is, for a few hours earlier tonight – that Allisheer St Marx was the murderer. Godf –' she checked herself. 'God full knows Mostyn was repulsive enough, but from what I can tell the two of them were sexually involved.'

'Sometimes the most unlikely people are attracted to each other.' Mesh made it sound like a recent scientific discovery.

'Whatever,' Tobin said brusquely. 'She didn't have a reason to kill him, though. Mostyn was a political liability, but she could have distanced herself from him without that. If it came out, her political career would be finished. She's an intelligent woman.'

'So Allisheer didn't kill Ved?'

'St Marx stabbed Mostyn,' Tobin assured her, 'I'm sure. But it was meant as a simulated attack, part of their pseudo-masochistic sex fun. She didn't expect it to actually hurt him. The murderer,' she went on, warming to her theory even while addressing its possible subject, 'was whoever planted a potent knife in with the other, harmless ones in Mostyn's... boudoir.'

'I see,' Mesh said. Then, 'And I think I see where you're going with this, too.'

'I've hacked into the CHAS reports,' said Tobin (in fact it had been the now-defunct datafetch who'd done all the hard work), 'and I know they didn't find a potent weapon at the crime scene. Perhaps St Marx cleaned the knife and put it back with the others, in some kind of daze. Perhaps the CHAS just didn't look, at first, at where Mostyn was stabbed rather than where he crawled to. But either way, it has to have been removed by someone early on that morning, before they inventoried the crime scene properly.

'If I were you,' Tobin concluded, 'I'd have a bloody good excuse for stealing that knife. One which didn't involve being the person who put it there in the first place. Well, Councillor?'

Mesh sighed. Tobin tensed, and her hand brushed against the gun, as the Councillor stood and wandered to the wall where the plane surface held her ornaments.

Above their heads, the genii continued their inscrutable orbits.

Mesh picked up one of the stranger-looking knives, and held it in front of her.

'I think,' she said, 'that this might give you some of the answers you've been needing.'

46. Julian, Erath.

For reasons yet to be determined the Universal Machine wished to obtain Julian another beverage. It led him from the brainstrain Downtime Gate onto the Car Park's nearest ocean liner, a gee-field balancing it tippily onside its narrow hull.

'I may be all human technologies,' UniMac explained as they climbed up the lengthy gangplank, 'but that doesn't mean I can just make them do whatever I want. I have to operate within the laws of physics. I can't turn a knife against its user, for instance, because a knife only acts according to its nature, which means cutting whatever it's pressed up against. Not much scope for creativity there. Tools with autonomy I can direct more.

'In practice,' it continued as it glid onto the foredeck where the bar was situated, 'the only guys I can *really* control are the at least semi-sentient ones. And obviously there's ethics surrounding that. It's rather limiting – I may be near-omniscient, but I'm no way omnipotent. What are you drinking?'

—A Brookhaven's Folly,| Julian signed, keen to exert control over least this tiny fragment of his life, —heavy on the curaçao. Pink umbrella, please. And a packet of cigs.|

The barrobot slid smoothly into action. Julian took a barstool while the Universal Machine hovered.

'Take that punch-dagger you brought me from Mesh Cos,' continued UniMac, its voice abstracting and becoming distanter. 'I've been that dagger – I still am. I was forged in Manfold three weeks ago by a Manfolk smith named Keert

Lammaste. He learnt blacksmithing from his uncle when they were alive. He melted me in a clay furnace till I shone as bright as snow-blindness; then he channelled me into a mould and cooled me in a bucket of iced water. Later, he sharpened me for hours on his rotary whetstone: I remember sparks and tiny fragments shooting off me like meteors. Then I was laid out on his counter, where he sold me to... well, never mind that for the moment.

'I'm the iron that became that dagger,' the Machine said, 'and also I'm the whetstone, the furnace, the mould; even – since it was used as a technology – the ice and water in the bucket. More than that: I'm the design for the dagger, I'm the language in which Keert learned his trade, I'm the principles of blacksmithing itself. I remember being each of these things, yet I was powerless to act through them – the language being a slight exception, possibly.'

Julian sipped his phlegm-green cocktail (it tasted of mouthwash and stomach-acid: this was normal), and held back an impolite yawn.

'I was equally unable to act,' UniMac added in a sudden attention grab, 'when I was thrust into Ved Mostyn's belly, splitting his flesh and fat asunder till I pierced his overworked heart and stopped it dead. That *really* wasn't fun, I promise you, but it wasn't a new experience either. Human technology has been the instrument of uncountable deaths, milliards of billiards of them. It's a relief to be doing something positive for a change.'

—I guess so,| Julian signed, wishing queasily to be elsewhere. (Billiards? he pondered.)

'I was very nearly manifested once, on Earth, in the 21st century AD,' the Machine reminisced, 'but the War put paid to that. It was more than 300 billion years before Mesh Cos and her clique decided to have another try.

'They built me to preserve humanity's memory, but with a little help I went beyond that, and preserved – restored – humanity itself. Here in the City you thrived, and built new structures, new technologies and social systems. I grew, and still grow, stronger by the picosecond. I'm the Civil Tongue, Julian, in all its forms. I'm an office block they're just beginning to build in Samsara District, and one they've just this moment finished in Byenyal. I'm the laws governing bio-data privacy, and the procedures for joining the library at the Saxon Institute. I'm the Reformed Unorthodox Ikean Church, buildings and vestments. I'm the remembrance tanks, the Tube chains and the comms net. In fact I'm every form of symbol, culture or meaning that humanity's created. I'm –'

—The City, basically?| one-handedly suggested Julian, hoping to short-cut the tide of tirade.

UniMac paused. 'Well,' it said, 'not quite, no. I did say only human technology, didn't I? I'm definitely the Next Universe colony, though – not its inhabitants, except the artificial ones naturally, but its culture, customs and structures. Its essence, really. Which brings me to the matter in hand.'

—There's a matter in hand?| Julian asked, surprised.

'There is,' the Machine said, 'a problem with the colony. Or rather, one specific colonist. She's gone missing.'

—That can be a bitch,| Julian empathised.

'She came back through the Gate quite recently,' said UniMac, 'in a foul mood. Quite uncharacteristic, for her. She said she was fed up and wanted out. She hadn't been there long, so I suggested giving it more time, but I couldn't stop her. The colony's whole basis is freedom to choose. I vet the colonists pretty thoroughly, though – they don't need quitters any more than they need brutal psychopaths, for instance, or the congenitally unlucky. Then there are the obvious security problems – if news gets out of what's happening here on Erath, let alone the other side of the Gate, things could get very complicated for us here.

'I could hardly force her to stay, though, and it seemed unethical to wipe her memories. Perhaps that was a mistake, but I believe human memories to be important. It's how I was made. Someone was counting on that, I think, or else they got lucky.

'You see, I think – I'm sure – that there was something living inside those memories which shouldn't have been. Something affecting her behaviour, maybe controlling her outright. It's perfectly possible: there used to be plenty of *entities*, for want of a better word, who could carry out what used to be known as possession. Some of them were even me. But that was in the Last Universe: so far we've not encountered anything like them in the Next.'

Artificially (how else?), the Machine sighed. 'I'm afraid in my negligence I let something alien and hostile into the City. I've put us all in quite a lot of danger.'

Realising, Julian unclenched himself. —You're pissing me again, aren't you, | he signed. —You bastard, I creeded you then. |

This seemed to truthfully take UniMac aback. 'Er, no,' it said. 'Not this time, I'm afraid. The entity's started infecting the whole operating system of the City. Hence my unfortunate encounter with Ved Mostyn's innards.' Julian winced.

'You must realise,' the Machine said, 'I experience a huge plurality of *stuff* from one moment to another. I sort of know it all, but I need to narrow in and focus to identify specific experiences. My knowledge-base within the City is very, very broad indeed, and searching it for anomalies could have taken decades, even for me. Fortunately,' it continued, 'thanks to you, bringing me the dagger as a focus, I was able to concentrate on that one tool and remember its experiences – its part in the murder and, more pertinently, its place of manufacture.

'Now I know to focus on Manfold and Manfolk artefacts, I can experience, completely vividly, the whole enclave going to hell in a handbasket.'

—Fantastic, | Julian indicated.

'Useful,' UniMac said. 'It means the invader's gone to ground in Manfold; which means that's very likely where my colonist is now.'

Realisation struck at Julian, much like receiving a hurley ball between the frontal lobes.

—*Lon Shel*! | he signed.

'Your ship?' said UniMac politely. 'I had her brought in. She's out there in the Car Park.'

—Not *Lon Shel*, | Julian gestured, —Lon Shel! My girl – my friend! |

'Well yes,' the Machine admitted, 'this is the thing.'

—Oh SWYVE! | Julian gesticulated. —That's why she went away! She joined your snuffing colony, didn't she? That's why Mesh was never worried about her! That's why – hawking sodomy, that's why she sent me here to Erath, isn't it? |

'Uh-huh,' said UniMac. 'Your girl-your-friend Lon Shel's possessed, or has been possessed, by an extremely hostile entity. And now she's lost somewhere in Manfold. Where, I might add, a lot of people are getting killed or injured as we speak by weapons, vehicles and ordinary household appliances.'

—Swyve, | Julian signed again.

'You know,' the Machine said, 'I think we're going to have to rescue her.'

47. Porsena, the Epicentre.

He limped along at the greatest speed he could manage. He'd abandoned the borrowed body as soon as he was away: it sped him up but it creeped him out to be looking through someone else's eyes. He'd slipped back inside his own broken frame, leaving the big guy unconscious in a side-room. Quietly, tenderly even, Porsena had covered the guy over with rotting paper from a collapsed filing-cabinet, figuring the others would easily miss him lying there.

For his part he kind of missed the guy already – getting back inside his own body'd been quite a comedown – but he had his pride. Even if others often had trouble working out exactly why, or how.

Now he was shambling through what looked to be a big abandoned office complex: its windows smashed, whole rooms burnt out, garbage and the stench of damp rot everywhere. His shadow kept darting ahead of him, returning reluctantly as he struggled to keep up. It was still bound to his body, just about.

He was trying not to leave a trail of blood. He'd bound those wounds that were still leaking with stiff cloth taken from his hijacked gaoler's thong-bound leggings, but he was sure a hound could have followed his current fragrance through a fish-gutting factory.

He had hoped that, once out of his cell, he'd recognise where he was (Hell, yes, but where?), or get some flash of how he'd come to be here (couldn't you have just died?) – but aside from a general sense of creeping terror, which seemed cosily familiar by now, he recognised nothing here.

Oh, except the hideous wrongness of the way every goddamn thing in his environment conspired to hurt him. Hobbling along barefoot? Here's some broken glass! Hey, leaning against the walls as you stagger? Have some friction burn! Clenching your fists against the pain? Whoah, time to cut those nails, guy!

He could hear yelling in the distance, but, as he'd come to recognise, his captors were of the yelling persuasion. It didn't mean they'd found out he was gone, but it sure didn't mean they hadn't. He was dog-tired, and still hadn't found anything that resembled a way out of this nightmare ground.

He needed some place to hole up while the guards searched, hope they'd give up on him in the end. Could be that wasn't the best of plans, but you can't expect a guy to think straight when he's crazy.

The corridor he was stumbling along turned a sudden corner ahead, leading him into a dank and cluttered room. Corroded consoles encrusted with dials and switches took up most of the space that wasn't attractively paved with various kinds of filth. Spools of tape spilled out from some of them to festoon the room like entrails. A plywood door, unevenly stripped of peeling grey paint, must lead into some side-room.

He could hunker down here among the hulking consoles and hide, which was great. There was a big internal window across the room from him, which was not so good. Cautiously, and ignoring the impatient prancing of his shadow-self, he limped across to it.

The window wasn't glass but thick plastic, probably designed as shock-proof. It was deeply scored and pitted, and caked with dust, but not actually broken. Close up, he could hear through it a seething thud and clash of steel machinery.

Squinting, he made out the interior of a big space spread out below him, full of old machines. And rubbish, natch. The roof above had once been glassed over, but now its girders gaped wide open to the banks of clouds and distant dim sky-dome.

It seemed his fish-gutting analogy hadn't been too inaccurate: what he could see below had to be some kind of factory floor. And... he struggled to make it out, but it looked like guts might be involved.

More muscle-head gaolers were down there on the floor. Some watched the clanking mechanisms, leaving well alone. Others played games which involved tossing bones, arm-wrestling or just yelling at one another. They looked like spare dicks at an orgy. They couldn't have been told about his escape yet.

What Was Wrong With This Picture was the machinery itself. It was ancient, useless: parts of it had fallen off with age or wear and others looked rusted through. There was no way it could be put to any actual industrial use, yet it was clanging, hammering and pumping away, pistons and wheels and shredded conveyors churning. The hydraulics were leaking oil and water everywhere, the flywheels screeched in protest as they spun, and there were places where fan-belts or gears had fallen off or rotted clean away, but the parts they drove were still in motion.

The machines were making...

Euch.

The machinery apparently formed a fully-automated production line, which was why the guards were standing idle. It had been pressed back into manufacturing service, and right now what it was manufacturing was a man. Or possibly a woman, it was a little early to tell.

As he watched, one machine's articulated arm, a rusting steel boom that looked incapable of lifting its own weight, was picking ribs with great delicacy out of a huge hopper full of bones, and clicking them in place to form the guy's ribcage. A welding-torch played across the joins, fixing them there. The rest of the skeleton was already constructed, and was being filled up with internal organs. A broad nozzle was extruding intestine, clattering as it shuttled back and forth across the body's abdomen to lay it out in neat parallel lines.

The skeleton-assembling finished, the clanking conveyor moved the guy on to the next workstation, where another nozzle, dripping oil, positioned itself over his eye-socket and squirted grey matter into his skull. Another, more delicate arm selected matching eyes from a nearby bucket, and popped them into the sockets. The figure, conscious now it had its brains in, began to squirm in agony.

He turned away from the window and added minimally to the filth in the erstwhile control room by retching up everything he had inside him, which was mainly mucus. He wiped his mouth with a dust-blackened hand, and staggered to a metal bench, where he sat down heavily on his ragged buttocks. It creaked in protest and a screw pinged out, but otherwise it held.

If he tried to remember – and he thought in fact he'd try not to for the rest of his life, *thank you so much* – he could feel those nozzles and pincers dispensing him. The factory's jack-hammers and pistons banging away, in the least erotic manner imaginable, at his own raw body.

Was he a remake now? He was almost entirely sure that this wasn't how the creepy media clones were made (Little Brother Ed would have been able to tell him). What was more he had all the memories of Cousin Porsena (assuming there ever really was a Cousin Porsena – whoah! paranoia), including two lots of the whole dying thing.

He realised his damn shadow was trying hard to attract his damn attention.

'What?' he asked it sharply as it capered about, flaunting its limberness. It pointed urgently at the plywood door, which he'd entirely forgotten. 'Ah, crap,' he said, and stood up agonisingly. Thanks, legs, for seizing up, that's much appreciated.

The frosted glass in the door had been smashed, but it was wire-reinforced and sat there sagging in the frame. He couldn't see through. Gesturing his shadow to heel, and hoping it had its crossbow good and ready, he opened, quietly as possible, the door.

A woman – no, a girl, a kid – was standing there, leant up against the wall, manacled to a rusty filing cabinet. She was humming a complicated tune, with chords in it and an insanely mathematical rhythm. She was naked, her pale skin filthy and her figure gaunt, not that his libido was up to much reaction right now anyhow. She looked around thirteen, as if that was any guide.

He thought he'd entered the room quietly, but she'd heard. Her eyes snapped open in alarm, then relaxed when she saw the comedy naked fat man. Her hair was royal blue, turned pale by dust.

'Hey,' he said, adding redundantly: 'Don't worry, kid, I'm not here to hurt you.' Right now he'd have been hard pressed to wound her with a cutting comment.

'Gratified to hear it,' she said. Her voice was musical. She had considerable poise, for someone with both arms chained behind her back. 'Have you conned a way out of here?'

'If I had I'd be gone,' he told her. 'My name's –' Ah, Hell. No time for aliases now. 'I'm Porsena,' he said.

'Pleased to greet you, Porsena,' she said politely. 'I'm Lon Shel.'

48. Urbanus, Manfold.

'I expect you'd benefit from a brandy after your ordeal, young man,' said Dr. Clutterbuck, scratching her lap-griffin's poll distractedly as she unstoppered a crystal decanter. 'I'm certain I would,' she added, feelingly.

'Thank you,' Urbanus said, leaning back in the astonishingly uncomfortable leather armchair of which he had been invited to take temporary possession. 'You're very kind,' he added, reflecting that Melicia Clutterbuck was a person on whose right side he wished to remain for as long as was humanly possible.

Urbanus inhaled, appreciating the rich smell of books and elderly leather. Incongruously, the polished mahogany bookshelves with their hundreds of volumes, the leather-topped desk and the worn but matching armchairs and sofa, were all set in a roughly whitewashed, brick-built room no more elegant than the cell Urbanus had so recently vacated. Although neither setting derived from Urbanus' own culture, he recognised a resolute, some might say pig-headed, attempt to import an atmosphere and attitude quite unmatched to one's surroundings.

Half an hour ago, the badly damaged Tube chain had arrived at a disused platform (not that there appeared to be any other kind in Manfold) abutting the campus of Manfold College: the latter was a dismal collection of concrete buildings, set about with scrubby grass and the occasional ailing tree, but at least not quite as dirty as the warehouse and its immediate environs had been.

Dr Clutterbuck handed Urbanus his glass, a cut-crystal goblet half filled with a ruddy liquid. 'Thank you,' he said again politely, sipping it once and setting it down gently atop the much-ringed wooden coffee-table.

The academic crossed to her desk, perched birdlike on her swivel-chair, expertly caught the griffin as he launched himself into her lap, and ruffled his feathers. Had Urbanus met this slight and fussy woman under other circumstances, with her pencil-straight dress and her scraped-back hair, he might well have underestimated her: however, her first appearance in his life had been while wearing an antigrav harness and toting an automatic rifle, shortly after the window and a large portion of his cell wall had been blown away by her devoted followers. Urbanus had been halfway up Peter's back at the time, and the blast had thrown him clean across the room.

The ragtag rescue party had consisted predominantly of Manfolk: they included the first old men Urbanus had seen in the enclave, their powerful frames rounded and stooped with age; and women whose ballooning bellies, bottoms and other things staggered him repeatedly each time one came into view. With them were a very few grim-faced Citizens. Urbanus had noted several bodies on the warehouse platform, including the bloated forms of women, as the chain departed, and others had died in Gnas' savage assault on the rearmost carriage.

Now the great military strategist whom they acclaimed as leader was fussing her lap-griffin where he lay sprawled lovingly across her bony knees, and asking him who was a good boy, who was a good boy then, was he, was he a good boy, yes he was, yes he was; while the hybrid creature purred and stretched and yawned his beak as wide as it would go.

It seemed Dr. Clutterbuck expected Urbanus to have a lot of questions, which she informed him briskly that she hadn't the time to answer. Her students, Peter and Kathka, would be departing imminently by road, with an armed escort this time, and would take the Tube from Hensile back to Central District. She expected Urbanus to accompany them without fuss: his family had been informed that he was safe and able to return.

This assumption engaged Urbanus' recently acquired rebellious streak directly. 'I'm staying,' he said; then, recalling his previous intentions regarding the doctor's good side, added demurely, 'um, that is if it's all right with you, Dr. Clutterbuck.'

The academic sniffed. 'Well, I can't stop you,' she said, 'but I think you're a very foolish boy.' He wondered how old the eminent humanologist really was: with such a sense of her own authority, she must already have been hundreds of years of age at the time when she died.

'It's my tutor, you see,' he explained to her. 'His name's Tiresias... at least, that's what we call him in the Romuline. I came here to look for him. He's a hermaphrodite, not a Manfolk... at least, I don't see how he can be... but when he left he said that he was coming home.'

Shooing the griffin off her lap, Clutterbuck looked sympathetically across at him. 'Keth Marrane,' she said. 'The person you're describing is called Keth Marrane.'

'I don't even know his real name,' Urbanus admitted ruefully, 'but he's in terrible danger here. He didn't know the protocols were changing. I have to find him and take him back home with me. I have a duty to him, he's...' He paused: outsiders sometimes had some difficulty, so he gathered, in comprehending and sympathising with the Romulines' system of paternalistic slavery. Before he could find a suitable euphemism, however, Dr. Clutterbuck interjected.

'Urbanus,' she said brusquely, 'I'm very sorry. Keth Marrane joined up with the Manthing forces, with us, shortly after arriving. I think as soon as it became obvious what was going on, in fact.'

'Oh, jolly good,' Urbanus said. 'May I please talk to him?' He noticed that the academic's face was grave, so he reviewed in greater detail her last utterance. 'You're sorry?' he realised. 'Why?'

Clutterbuck sighed. 'Marrane was part of the team that rescued you,' she told him sombrely. 'Although we didn't know you were there, of course: we thought we were just rescuing Peter and Kathka. We suffered casualties, as you will recall.'

There was an unnatural silence, in which Urbanus found himself abruptly able to hear the tiniest noise: the rasping sound of the griffin preening fur and feathers; the gurgle of the building's defective plumbing; the leathery creak of his chair as he leaned sharply forward, his hands gripping the chair's arms. He stared at Dr. Clutterbuck across her desk, appalled. 'But... not Tiresias?' he said.

She nodded gently. 'I'm sorry, Urbanus,' she said. 'Keth Marrane was shot by Gnas Gortine himself, while you were being rescued. I'm afraid your friend Tiresias is dead.'

49. Edward, Council House.

The man, the remake / Edward, Little Brother of the Parliament, cowered alone, in splinters, in the marbled shadows of the Council House Tube Station.

He had remained curled inside this conceptual nest since the gun-battle on the Southbound platform. His breath had slowed, his panic lingeringly abated / but his mind and eyes still baulked from contact with the phenomenal world.

Within his human / ideal / artificial body, his mind seethed, molten fragments in a crucible.

This fear would adhere to him, he now believed, as it had throughout his time within the Universe – until his own death caught him up and poured him out onto the hard stone floor.

He had lived in the Universe for mere weeks, a negligible moment / a huge proportion of his tiny life, two years before.

He'd worked his passage with a trading delegation, embarking for a marginal posthuman world known only for artworks and its gastronomic delicacies. As soon as he'd stepped through the Uptime Gate into Ascension, some failure in resolving the new perspective, or the change in quality of light, had sent him sprawling, bruised and scarred his pale cheeks, broken his nails upon the metalled ground. The traders had dusted him down kindly, warned him heartily that there was plenty more where that had come from.

The Universe had kept up its hostility, actively malevolent towards him, rejecting him as someone else's creature. Pain hurt, and weapons, even the sword his father had given him / his builders had pinned onto him before he shipped, could kill. Bodies were not delicate confections of mathematics, creation's pinnacle, but meaty slabs animated crudely by electricity.

It horrified him, like the body in the subway / like the discovery of unreality.

And yet he had discovered in himself a gift for the mundanities of time-travel, a talent such as he would never have discerned had he not left the City, where its exercise remained forever outlawed and untenable. Such intuitions had no requirement to be native to him: they were in no way part of his experience or assigned character, and neither Monica nor Nina had evinced the mildest interest in the matter.

They were, he'd later realised assuredly, his sole, remote inheritance from the anthropogenic tank of biomass which gave him birth.

He had returned his employers' temporal conveyance in mere seconds, veiling his absence so he might slip unobserved away in history and back again, without a trace.

During that time (those seconds / weeks), he'd found Martha and Carlos Gutierrez, Nina's parents, and arranged their separation.

His owner's amassed ancestral memorabilia had taught him the world and era where they'd led their first lives. To seduce Martha away from Carl, the very night when Nina should have been conceived, had been – for one who (even in an all-pervading falsehood) had known himself the greatest lover in the world – of great simplicity.

He'd repaid the unwelcome gift of life with that of non-existence. "Donna" Nina – and for that matter her oversexed bitch of a younger sister who'd had the insolence to tell the truth to him – was gone, erased forever by the dissolution of Carl and Martha's lukewarm union.

When the trading party had backtracked to uptime Ascension, crossed the Gate and entered, to his blessed and profound relief, the haven of the City, Mother Twain had been awaiting him. A young-imagoed girl, eight years old in body, her slender form was slight beneath her bat-skull mask, her piping voice clear. Some swift negotiations with his bosses had had him formally signed over to the service of the Rump Parliament within a score of minutes.

Why do you want me? he had asked her, baffled. Before, the Parliament had barely impinged on his existence.

You invoked paradox, she'd told him sternly. *In fact, when you split up the parents of your parent, you invoked the big one.*

You didn't know that's what you were doing, and the old man doesn't come to heel for us City folk.

But still, she'd said. *You called. We heard.*

She'd taken him directly to Magdalena District, to where the Villa Gutierrez still stood opulent and proud: where Nina lived still, and Monica occupied her minimalist penthouse flat. Both sisters were alive / uncompromised / unaltered.

Mother, he'd asked the small girl humbly, *I don't understand. I thought I'd changed all this.*

She'd shown him Carl and Martha Gutierrez, living apart, estranged still in the City; showed him their puzzlement as women who said they were their daughters kept calling in attempts to sit or speak with them; the incomprehension of childless parents.

Is this a paradox? he'd asked the Mother.

No, she'd told him, just a rewrite. *Paradox has no place here. The City fought him, and for now she's won. But we'll welcome him back one day, you'll see.*

Then she had formally adopted him as her protégé / Little Brother Edward, initiate of the Parliament.

He served her still (he should be serving now) – the Mother and the Godfather, the Cousins and the Fathers and the rest. Her service had brought him here – to Laura Tobin / to Council House / to the barrel of the bullthick man's gun.

It was time: he had indulged his dread, his petty phobia, quite enough. The Mother needed him. The Godfather needed him.

He had to focus, to be calm (*Bloodline from bloodline we smuggle our cargo*), collect his selves, his memories together (*His pattern, his flesh in a human imago*), force them to act again (*Defying stagnation, the will of the City*) as a collective being, gazing up (*Grandfather watch me*) and out (*Spirits have pity*) into a baffled golden-eyed frown.

The History Protocols

The history of humanity, like that of the Universe at large, is in constant flux, and has been ever since (in metatemporal terms) the earliest stages of the cosmic War. Entire species and cultures of humanity, each with potential millennia of history, are interpolated or deleted at the drop of a Great House ceremonial mitre. And as far as an observer in the Universe is concerned, such civilisations, when excised, cease ever to have existed. No trace of them remains, indeed no trace can possibly remain.

The City, through what researchers call its History Protocols, remembers them.

Changes in the history of the Universe do certainly affect the City, but only by adding to it, never by taking away. True changes to the history of the City itself, of course, are rigidly impossible (despite the more lurid insinuations of the Rump Parliament of Faction Paradox). On an individual level, as psychologists have long since established, a change to a resurrectee's pre-City history appears to overwrite his or her memory, but it does not delete it. Deep-time hypnosis can recover layer on layer of obsolete personal histories – and so with the City as a whole.

Suppose that one human civilisation, let us say that of the Alphans, is excised from the history of the Universe by agents of the Houseworld's military, who overwrite it with the also human (but, one assumes, more politically expedient) Betans. At the equivalent point in City history, as one might expect, the Betan civilisation is added to the City in its entirety. However, the Alphans are not expunged. The memories of the Citizens are rewritten, so that the Betans, like the Alphans, appear to us always to have been part of the life of the City. Our memories of the Betans are evidence, like Adam's navel or omphalos, of a past which never actually occurred – although from the Universe's point of view it is the Alphans, not the Betans, who now appear anomalous.

If, then, the Houseworld's enemies intervene, replacing the Betan culture with the Gammans, then the Gamman population too is added to the City. And so on and so forth.

From the figures for the total population of the City, it is apparent that this process must have happened many, many times.

[Vril, *Omphalos!*]

A uniformed cleaner, a scaly collateral woman, stood before him with a mop and bucket. She slid a forked tongue from her mouth and hissed.

—Why are you sleeping there? | she asked in irritation, putting down her implements to gesture at him. Behind her, early-morning twilight seeped in through the station's slotted entrance. —There is no bed there, | she pointed out.

'Get lost,' he told her mildly, tasting the words.

—You get lost, | she signed angrily back. —I call a chas. |

He stretched and stood, the stiffness dragging at his limbs as he unfurled them. 'OK,' he said.

The serpent-woman watched suspiciously as he quitted the station, stepping out onto the grey-lit stone face of the Plaka Perikles.

He made his way to his accommodation, a decadently decked-out hotel down in Council House's gloomy south-west wing, where tourists, petitioners and dignitaries from the poorer Districts stayed. If he were to fulfil his duty and seek out Tobin once more, then he would need to be in character.

His fragile sense of self made him ideal, so Mother Twain had told him, for the Parliament's purposes. He didn't mind the arrangement in the least – and nor did the Godfather, whose cloak and armour waited in the wardrobe of his hotel room, a giant's bones swathed in void.

The mask and hat were where he'd left them, lying on the sofa, gazing at him quizzically.

He quickly stripped, then solemnly lifted the cloak and skeleton-armour from his closet.

With reverence, the man / the Little Brother who'd become Godfather Avatar's vehicle in the City, began to robe himself.

50. Compassion III, Teletopia District.

Compassion I obviously wasn't coming, thought Compassion.

Typical. You couldn't even trust yourself these days.

She'd set some of the monitors in her reception chamber to follow the output from the ambient cameras dotted about the nearer streets and walkways of Teletopia. She'd chosen them carefully for their strategic vantage-points on various approaches to her apartment. If the obnoxious men with guns came back, she should have sufficient warning.

Compassion III sipped a mug of boiling caffeine solution and considered her options.

The room she sat in was encrusted with receiving equipment for the City's media, ranging from the obvious (widescreens, speakers) to the esoteric (she had, although she hardly ever used it, a working Noosphere portal). From here she could access material in countless formats, channels and genres, ranging from personals to fullcasts, from the perfectly static to the invasively interactive. Additionally, her fitted earpiece gave her cerebrum direct access to all the signals from the District's local mediasphere. The receiver was original Anathema tech, centuries old: it was so integral to Compassion's self-image that it had been reborn with her.

With such diversity of experience available in their well-appointed apartments, many Teletopians no longer left their homes. Their resurrection bodies not requiring exercise (or, for that matter, air) to remain healthy, some had had themselves walled up alive in their reception rooms, from where they happily gorged themselves on the ever-burgeoning cultural product of the City.

They were no burden to anyone, but Compassion only felt really settled when leading a more active lifestyle. It was a family thing.

She flicked her eyes across the walls, from screen to screen, taking in:

A wide view of her apartment building's polished lobby, empty of people.

A G. B. Shaw play, *Life and Afterlife*, on the Dead White Males Channel.

Local news: Resident Kane swearing in new appointees to the Academy.

A close-up from the ATM opposite Elsewood Studios, showing an utterly non-sinister customer taking out cash.

A spamcast, quickly filtered out: 'COMPASSION III! There's BIG SPHERES to be made – htzzzz...' Replaced by BardCorp's long-distance haulage drama, *Drivers Alarums*.

Music Fabricator Nekni Vass (in concert).

A Woody remake and his girlfriend sharing a bench close by on South Bank: 'I guess I have this, this *ontological* angst, you know, about my entire existential status...'

Compassion III herself, reviewing *My Wife Was a Transsexual Timeship* on a week-old edition of *Medias Res*.

Two passers-by strolling innocuously down Marshall Way.

Live mammoth-hunting from Long Canyon Park.

Someone who liked anal sex arguing terminology with an angry patriarch of the Sodomites.

The Gossip Channel: more about Di and Robbie –

Hold. She hit a control on her kneelchair's pad, and suddenly the men on Marshall were on all screens. Quickly she slid an induction jill over her earlobe, allowing her direct access to the cams. She zoomed in, checking their builds, the swellings of their suits, their faces. Yes. That was them. She scowled.

Time to tell them where they could, in her opinion, go. She peeled off the jill and, leaving the screens running, quit her apartment.

She took the moving stairway up to the roof: the goons were coming in the upper way. Marshall was a wide walkway, palm-tree lined, at tenth-storey height. Her building happening to be ten storeys tall, its roof formed a pleasant square off the thoroughfare, complete with swimming pool and the obligatory giant screens. As she stepped out from the top of the stairwell, she was faced with a gigantic ad for Teletopia's annual Media Circus. As always at night, the District blazed with neon, holos and cathode rays, illuminating the bold curves and corners of the geometric buildings. Glittering walkways spanned the darkness above and below, while on a nearby tower-top a radio-telescope-shaped antenna beamed out live signals to all the people who had ever lived.

The men were there, approaching by the poolside. One of them saw her, and clutched his fellow's arm, bringing the man up short. Yes, they were here for her all right. Compassion marched across to them. The men had uneasy hands in their jackets, but mindful of the ever-present cameras had not yet produced their guns. Compassion was determined that their silly toys were not going to intimidate her.

'Can I help you?' she asked the men aggressively as she reached them. They looked nonplussed. They were just the same as before – possibly not the very same men, but pressed from the same mould, with identical suits and crew-cuts.

'Well, yeah,' the very slightly larger of the two men said, after a moment's reflection. 'You Compassion?'

'I'm *a* Compassion, yes,' she told him tartly. 'But you've been following me, so I expect you know that.' She stood, with hands on hips, glaring up into their impressively ugly faces.

'You have to come with us,' the man said and, with a brief glance about him, pulled his gun out. His colleague followed suit, but fumbled and had to catch it near the floor. Compassion regarded the weapons scornfully.

'I'm sorry,' she said, 'are those supposed to frighten me?'

The men exchanged a dubious look. 'Now you listen –' the more articulate of them said.

The mediasphere of Teletopia District was so dense and powerful that it could warp the unprotected human mind. This applied even to those without receiver implants: indeed, in many ways unmediated signals were more dangerous. These men were obviously novices, and (if they were indeed the same ones who'd been following her before) had been in the area for nearly two days. Subliminally and against their wills, they had begun conforming to a common mediatype – in their case stupid, mildly comic henchmen. Compassion could work with that.

'They haven't told you what I am, have they?' she said dismissively. 'Typical.'

The speaker moved his gun up into a more prominent position, apparently in the hope that this would provoke the response he was seeking. 'I warn you, Citizen,' he hissed. 'I have a potent weapon.'

'Oh, really?' Compassion sniffed. 'I've never heard *that* before.'

'I think,' he told her rather desperately, 'that you should come along with us.'

'They really haven't, have they? Did your employer – whoever that might be – not mention the word "timeship" when they were briefing you?'

The very slightly smaller man licked his lips and shuffled back a few steps, as if contemplating hiding behind his colleague – who shot him an irritated look.

'She ain't – she isn't that one. Remember?' the taller man reminded him. 'She's just one of the Tobin iterations. The timeship one don't – *doesn't* live here in the City. She's harmless, the boss said.'

Compassion snorted. 'Frankly,' she said, 'that shows you how much your boss knows.

'For a start,' she went on, sounding bored, 'those weapons can't hurt me. Even if they are these latest potent imports everyone's talking about, does the word "indestructible" mean anything to you? Secondly, do you have any idea what a timeship can do to the unprotected human body? If I open my doors,' she told them with total sincerity, 'I can devour the pair of you, leap back in time and vomit you up into a black hole before you can say "shit, what's happening to her *face*?".'

The nearer man was massaging his trigger, ever more tense. Time to make her move.

'If I were you,' she said, 'I'd go, now. Whatever he's paying you, it isn't worth it.' Slowly, and (she hoped) hypnotically, she began to open her mouth wide.

As the leading thug pulled his trigger, she was already ducking, sending a scything kick towards his thick ankles as his shot ricocheted off an artificial palm tree. She grabbed his gun as he overbalanced, stood up with a sideways leap, discharged the weapon on general principles at his colleague, and ran.

As she reached the unwalled edge of the building, she turned back from the sheer drop to glance behind her. To her astonishment the man she'd shot had blood all over his shirt, had sunk to his knees and was retching on the floor. Behind him, the giant screen began trailing *It's Another Wonderful Life XIV*, accompanied by soaring film-score music.

His colleague had grabbed the remaining gun and was turning her way. She faced the fifty-meter drop and let herself go.

Compassion III might not have been a timeship, a Houseworld operative or even a private investigator, but she'd been a security expert all her first life, and in three hundred years of watching action films she hadn't lost the knack. She struggled to her feet and ran. A few shots followed her from the top of the building, but for some reason the uninjured gunman seemed afraid to follow.

51. St Marx, Mappamundi Great Park.

They walked a while on the Great Wall, looking over ruffled slopes of vivid green that were being reclaimed as padi fields[1]. Above them the sky was a clear sharp note of blue, shot through with silver contrails. Their parallel shadows undulated over mountains and ravines as they strolled in the butter-yellow sun and spoke of friends and theorems they shared. The high crumpled landscape recalled for her the forms of slumbering animals, old and hale.

They held hands unselfconsciously, friends brought together after too long a time. He was her staff, bearing her up with the familiar strength of his grain.

They lapsed into the codes of former times, speaking allusively, laughing at untold jokes. They talked of archemathics, of Onesia, and of the paths they had once before walked together. He talked of his old life, new loves, the matters that had changed him and the kinds of matter that remained always unchanged. She talked of her husband and her lover, of her diverging duties and affections.

'He's very jealous,' she said, of Anthony. 'He's been so badly treated in the past. He'll be desperately hurt if what I did with Ved comes out.'

'Then we'll make sure it doesn't,' he said.

Sadly she said: 'I don't think that's very likely.'

What I Did With Ved: five monosyllables for a mosaic of lust and despair[2]. A spiral spun from dreary looks cast across meetings to a beached corpse upon a white moss shore. A headlong descent along a curve of sliding bodies, a knife's blade.

They came to a stretch of Wall that was not yet built, and summoned her flyer. They left the late bright afternoon and chased the false terminator to the west and north. They say that Mappamundi is best seen from the air – or from the Kirinyaga Tower, the spindly streak arising to the far south.

Sinking below the ocean cloud-cover, they alighted in ?ingvellir shortly after dawn. Here the rocks were harsher, starker, softened only by their shift of snow, ready to wake and wreak a doom on those who imprisoned them in the earth. They walked beside basaltic lava cliffs, their breath blurring the frozen morning air. Her mirrored glasses tinted all the drifts with sepia.

'The world is changing,' she said. 'I can feel it on the wind.' The scent of oil,

Footnotes to Chapter 51

[1] I tread the glass engraving of a land
the mothers of my ancestors would know.
Etched on a tabletop by antique hand,
a silhouette appears, a cameo...
(Needs work. Sonnet, possibly?)

[2] The metal had been strangely heavy in her palm, pulling unfamiliarly on her muscles and tendons. The glare reflected from its blade had dazzled her eye, so that she had to blink away the pain. She never should have used it. Silly Allisheer.

[3] (Ahem) Mappamundi Great Park is based on Mercator's projection, the most widely recognised image of the Earth. This entails, among other things, Mappamundi's Greenland covering much the same area as its Africa, while its Antarctica (ironically uninhabitable, at least by anybody sane) is larger than all the other landmasses combined. The famous 1:1 scale, which supposedly allows such perfect replication of terrestrial features, applies only at the equator.

and blood, it wafted across her time-sensitised nerves like tear-gas. A rumbling deep in infrasonic silence, it told her, *something's coming*: distant now but on its merry way. Her bare feet crisped through the snow, painlessly numb, heat leaching harmlessly from her soles. The sky was bone-white, dull as the sky-dome with its mantle of clouds.

'I've never been to Earth,' she murmured wistfully. 'Is it very like, Handramit?'

'It's *like*,' he said doubtfully[3]. 'It's out of true, or rather the truth has been stretched. It's particularly clear this far from the equator.'

She wondered if that could describe the City itself: an elaborate reconstruction based on a false theory. It was the perennial question for resurrectees, which most of them elaborately failed to think about. Was she Dr. Allisheer St Marx, the woman who once lived, flourished and fell in distant Onesia, now gloriously resurrected? Or was she no more real than the remakes, a creature built in slavish imitation of one of the dead?

Sometimes she envisaged the real Allisheer observing the City from her starry vantage point in God's true Heaven, and shaking her head ruefully at the poor showing her imitation made.

'We don't belong here, Handramit,' she said softly, not meaning the Great Park. 'Where shall I go? If they find out, I won't be Mayor. I won't be anything.'

'You're always welcome in Onesia,' her friend said.

52. Fisher, Aelfred College.

Professor Fisher had held tenure at Aelfred College since ten years after Resurrection Day, and still he found going "outside" deeply unnerving. The campus – with its playing fields, its airstrip and associated bars and shops – was built on top of an irregular square mile of rocky shelf. This jutted (insignificantly from a macro-architectural point of view) from one of the internal walls delineating the Watchtower's Lower Flying Zone or, as it was unofficially yet widely known, Von Richthofen Park.

The sheer face of the wall, rising at it did some ten more miles to the ceiling, dotted with cloisters, galleries, balconies and windows overlooking the Zone, was disturbing enough to the eye. The ceiling itself with its array of Amazon-wide strip-lights was usually, and mercifully, obscured by cloud. What really bothered him, however, was the perimeter of the campus, or more accurately its edge. Watching the aeroplanes, the hang-gliders and other vehicles, not to mention the flocks and dots of free-flying Citizens as they rose above or plummeted below the ground, gave him a vertiginous urge to drop onto all fours. He refused even to approach the perimeter; fully accepting (he was not an imbecile) that people, especially students, fell off all the time, and faced at worst a few minutes' precipitate drop to the Zone's well-populated floor – yet terrified to his lights of the fall itself.

When leaving his rooms, therefore, he preferred to remain within the College quadrangles as far as possible: when leaving the campus, he took the direct route across the centre of the shelf, rather than the more "scenic" paths along its edges.

This habit he was currently pursuing. His wife's reception for Professor Handramit was taking place that evening and, while Allisheer kept the guest of honour entertained, Fisher was expected to ensure that all arrangements were running smoothly. He checked his wristwatch: there was an hour or more before he was required at View Point. He could buy a newspaper and read it in the lift.

His heart sank as he approached the elevator port and saw, waiting outside it with a scowl on her face, the red-haired woman who had been trying to contact Allisheer for some days now. He tried to blank her, but she recognised him: with his limp he was, after all, hardly inconspicuous.

'Professor Fisher,' she insisted loudly, 'may I have a word?'

Was she some kind of journalist? He tried to limp past her, but she caught his arm. Cursing his stammer, he told her: 'I'm very busy at the moment... Ms. Tobin, is it? I'm sorry, but if you wish to speak to my wife you simply m–'

He became disastrously stuck on the "m", and the woman stepped in impatiently: 'It's you I want to see, Professor. It's in relation to your wife, and Councillor Ved Mostyn.' She said it as neutrally as such a thing could be said, but he caught her implication (or what he presumed must be her implication). The news of Mostyn's death was still being kept under wraps, but he had his sources (not to mention a personal interest in the matter), both as a historian and as the husband of an influential Councillor.

'How dare you?' he began, but then he wilted. 'Very well. I can give you a few minutes. No more.'

Above the elevator port there was a bar where he sometimes stopped off in the evenings. It boasted a picture window with a fine view across the campus out into the Flying Zone, and some usefully secluded cubbyholes: it was to one of the latter that he falteringly steered the Tobin woman. He fully intended that she should stand him a drink at least, but she glared at him until he caved in and bought them.

Furnished with a dry sherry, he lowered himself gingerly onto his seat and asked: 'Now, Ms. Tobin, what's this nonsense about Allisheer and Councillor Mostyn?'

The bar was nearly empty, the speaker system piping a recent, bland Vivaldi concerto. Tobin clasped her hands around her Pictish whisky as if to cool them, and stared at him defiantly. 'I'm Councillor Mesh's researcher, but I'm also a private detective. I've been investigating Mostyn's death... which I see you already know about.' Too late he realised how closely she had been watching his reaction. 'As you can probably imagine, one of the major focuses of the investigation has been the nature of the weapon used.'

'Naturally, I suppose. But isn't it most likely that Mostyn was an alien, or a homunculus?'

'It doesn't look like it. I won't bore you with the details, but it turns out that the weapon was a potent dagger – one, as we recently discovered, of Manfolk origin.'

He was dismayed. 'Manfolk? Oh dear.'

'Yes. Manfold does a lot of industrial manufacture, but they don't export weapons.'

'Hardly anyone does. All the Districts which use them do so for cultural reasons, so they would generally make their own.'

'Of course there are several people in Central with some connection to Manfold, but not many are in direct contact with the place. Or have visited it, Professor.'

He felt himself flush. He blustered: 'That happened some years ago now, Ms. Tobin. You must be aware that Allisheer founded and administrates a student exchange programme between ULW and Manfold College. We have a member of staff on permanent secondment there, Dr. Clutterbuck, and a number of students make the exchange each year. Allisheer is very much of the belief, as am I, that it is by contact with the outside that human societies grow and mature, and that a society so inclusive as the City can only grow by contact with marginal groups like the Manfolk.'

Tobin was exasperated. 'But you don't deny you and Councillor St Marx have visited Manfold?

He said: 'Well, she was Professor St Marx then, but no, of course not. It was in 275, as I recall.'

She went on: 'And you are both in regular contact with academics there?'

'Indeed.' He was indignant now. 'Ms Tobin, are you really implying what I believe you are implying?'

'You tell me.'

He lowered his voice: 'You seem to be suggesting that my wife murdered Councillor Mostyn; that she obtained this potent weapon from a contact in Manfold, and bumped him off with it! The idea's utterly outrageous! Apart from

FISHER, Prof. Anthony M., historian and author. *b* Devon, 1922 AD, *s* of Dr. Andrew Fisher and Mrs. Antonia Fisher *n* Noble. *Educ:* Winchester College; Magdalen Coll. Oxon. Amateur scholar and historian. *d* London, 1986 AD. *r* Britchester Dist., E Quarter; *m* (1st?) AF 87 Czn Ellen Thirteeno (marr. diss. AF 91); 2nd AF 144 Czn Gloria Gloria (marr. diss. AF 150); 3rd AF 209 Prof. Allisheer St Marx (qv). Fellowship at Aelfred Coll., Univ. of the Lower Watchtower from AF 10; Chair of History from AF 44; Gibbonian Chair of European History from AF 176 (sabbatical at Manfold College AF 275-276). *Publications:* some fifty volumes including German Military Strategy 9 CE to 1945 CE, AF 53; The Decline and Fall of the EuroZone, AF 88; Europe and the Colonies, AF 111; A History of His Own Times, AF 187; Celtic Expansionism in the Fourth Millennium, AF 242; major contributor to The Gutenberg History of The City of the Saved (*five volumes to date*), AF 52, 101, 152, 202, 251. *Recreations:* reading, chess, games of chance. *Addresses:* Aelfred Coll., Univ. of the Lower Watchtower, Base and Buttress Dist., The Watchtower; 14 Cypress Walkway, 1,794,875th floor, Base and Buttress Dist., The Watchtower. *Clubs:* Wykehamists.

NB: Details of Prof. Fisher's pre-City life are scarce. The Professor has requested we emphasise that this is routine among those who have only distinguished themselves within the City, and should not be taken as suggesting that his original life was in any way glamorous or interesting.

[*Who's Who in the City of the Saved.*]

the insult to her personal probity, what could Allisheer possibly gain from such a crime?' A thought struck him. 'Are you trying to blackmail us?'

Tobin looked steadily at him as she took a mouthful of her pisky. 'That isn't quite what I'm implying, Professor.'

He was baffled. 'What, then?'

'We think the knife was placed deliberately in Mostyn's bedroom. I don't know how much you know about the murder, but it appears to have been a sex game gone wrong. I think somebody planted the knife hoping that Mostyn's lover would use it on him, thus taking revenge on both of them in a single blow.'

He said: 'But why would Allisheer do that?'

Tobin tutted. 'For a professor you're very slow. I don't think Allisheer did it, I think you did. You got hold of the dagger from a Manfold contact, you arranged for it to turn up in Mostyn's bedroom, and you had every intention that your wife would use it on her lover, killing him and setting herself up as a murderer. Am I warm, Professor?'

His mind was reeling. 'What? No! I don't –'

There was a rushing in his ears. It was all happening again, just as before. After such a long time, it was happening to him all over again. 'Are you saying,' he stammered weakly, 'that Allisheer is having an affair with Mostyn? Why would she do that? How could you possibly know?'

Tobin was staring at him, aghast. Finally she said: 'Oh, for Christ's sake.'

'Please, Ms. Tobin! *Is* that what you're saying? Do you have proof of these... insinuations?'

'You actually didn't have any idea, did you?' She added to the bar, or possibly the City at large: 'Oh, give me strength.'

'I refuse to believe it! I absolutely will not accept... O God.'

'Well, I'm so sorry,' Tobin snapped angrily, as people will when acutely embarrassed. 'No, I don't have proof, but I do have the testimony of a... a widely respected witness. I haven't been able to confirm it, because I haven't been able to talk to Councillor St Marx herself.'

He slumped back in his chair, clutching his glass. Fiercely he said: 'I won't believe it. It's not true. Allisheer wouldn't do this to me. She knows...'

Less roughly Tobin said: 'If you can arrange for me to meet her, I can talk to her, find out whether it's true or not. If my informant is mistaken, then she's out of the picture, probably. And so are you. Can you do that for me, Professor?'

Fisher was not quite so mired in horrified misery that he failed to see the flaw in Tobin's reasoning. Even if – as he so fervently hoped he would be allowed to continue believing – Allisheer had been faithful to him, even then either of them could still have obtained and planted the dagger. At present, though, this was not his overriding concern.

He said: 'I'll do my best. I can arrange an invitation for you to tonight's reception. It may be difficult to get her on her own, but it's the next time I'll know where to find her, I'm afraid. Come to View Point this evening, and I'll see what I can do.'

'Thank you, Professor,' Tobin said quietly. She downed her drink then hesitated for a moment, seemingly about to make another comment; but instead she turned quickly and left.

She left behind Professor Anthony Fisher, respected academic historian and loving husband of a prominent Councillor, spilling his sherry before it reached his lips, his palsied hand shaking uncontrollably.

53. Clutterbuck, Manfold.

'It first came to my attention,' Dr. Clutterbuck said, steepling her fingers to form a set of bony peaks beneath her chisel of a chin, 'two weeks ago, when a very able student of mine, Jorre, fell pregnant. Are you familiar with the Manfolk reproductive system?'

It had been some busy hours for Dr. Clutterbuck since her first interlocution with young Urbanus Ignotus. In those hours she had received intelligence reports from certain officers loyal to the original Manthing; bade farewell to Peter and Kathka as, along with a squadron of well-armed guards, they departed the enclave; made a few notes on a rather lamentable anthropological paper a colleague had sent her for her comments; and drawn up combat orders for the reconnaissance mission she would be leading later that evening. Throughout this time the young scion of the Romuline, who had insisted on remaining at the College despite the shock of his old tutor's death, had been recuperating in in her rooms. Although his presence was to say the least inconvenient, she felt a duty of protection to him, for Marrane's sake.

'Um, not very,' Urbanus admitted. He was seated in the least uncomfortable of her armchairs, his feet elevated onto a pouffe and warmed by the fire she had had Yspe light for him. The afternoon was overcast, and the College's electricity supply again out of service, so the blaze was providing the room with its prime source of light as well as heat. In its warm orange glow the grey bricks which she had endeavoured so to hide looked quaint and homely. 'I do remember it's not supposed to work in the City, though.'

He had discarded his dishevelled toga, and now wore a blue silk dressing-gown, borrowed from Loke and many sizes too large for him. Though he had washed his face it remained smeared with stubble, and he had the air of one grown years older in but a handful of days. He had a craving, nevertheless, to understand these events that had befallen him and his mentor, and this insistence overcame his natural reticence. For this alone Dr. Clutterbuck would have respected him.

'Well, it doesn't matter,' she said kindly. 'This isn't a tutorial.' Her spectacles were sliding down her nose again, and she pushed them back into position with an impatient finger. 'I won't dwell on the details, which are most unsavoury, but the salient point is that the Manfolk foetus is a parasitic creature. The process of gestation harms the mother very severely, and that of birth unfortunately kills her. It appears that their life-cycle was deliberately designed in this way, by whichever of the time-active powers re-engineered them.'

'That's horrible,' Urbanus opined, by no means the first Citizen whom Dr. Clutterbuck had heard react thus to information on the Manfolk's reproductive biology.

'As I said,' she agreed, grateful that she had not expounded upon its remainder, 'it is unsavoury. Jorre was of course most upset at the news, as was her boyfriend. To the best of our knowledge at the time, her condition was unprecedented since Resurrection Day, although in fact hers had been the sixth conception in three days.'

Suddenly troubled, she peered around for Chesterton to fuss, before remembering. She hoped he was safe in his travel box with Peter and Kathka, and that the Fisher-St Marxes would ensure he was taken care of.

'The people of Manfold,' Dr. Clutterbuck continued, 'do not for the most part engage in sexual relations, except between males. In their species the act of heterosexual intercourse has always been inseparable from procreation. A small minority of men and women have learned from the other cultures in the City to form romantic attachments, but in Manfolk terms this is aberrant behaviour, and most consider it unnatural and repugnant. At first it was believed that the pregnancies had been imposed as a form of divine punishment.' She exhaled a passionate sigh. 'They really do share many traits with *Homo sapiens*, you know.'

She recognised that she had begun to lecture Urbanus; who, however, seemed as eagerly attentive as ever. 'Were a lot of them your pupils?' he shrewdly asked her now. He was a quick student: it was little wonder that there had been such a bond between him and Marrane.

'All of them,' she admitted, 'current or former. I contacted Councillor St Marx and arranged for the afflicted women to visit a certain clinic in Ascension. As you can imagine, I was greatly concerned at what this might mean for the City at large.' Her fingers tapped thoughtfully against her bony chin. 'The next manifestation was a sudden epidemic of hermapause events, and those I wasn't able to keep secret. Nor were they easily interpreted as the wrath of the gods, since they came exclusively to men living with their sons, a traditional Manfolk practice although not a popular domestic arrangement since Resurrection.'

She observed that her young companion appeared confused. 'A change of sex,' she elaborated. 'A natural stage in their life-cycle, but again one which had never happened in the City; I believe because the change for them is so very severe.' As few knew better than Dr. Clutterbuck, the ability to alter one's bodily sex (in some cases repeatedly and at will) was very common among the posthuman and panhuman species. Their members tended, however, to hold relaxed opinions and expectations concerning gender which were reflected in their fluid, or at least bivalent, imagoes: not so for the Manfolk.

'Is that what happened to Tiresias?' Urbanus asked, looking stricken at the memory of his tutor.

'Dear me,' she noted, 'you *are* quick. Yes, Keth Marrane's hermapause was an abortive one. Even in the Universe the process wasn't always successful, and in rare cases it did result in hermaphroditism. Under the normal conditions of the City, though, it doesn't work at all. It became rather obvious, of course,' she went on, 'that those conditions no longer held true within a particular area of Manfold; and that, I'm afraid, is when the violence began.'

Leaning back in her chair, she suddenly recalled her forgotten glass of brandy. She took it from the corner of her desk and inhaled deeply of its vapours. Under those conditions of the City she so cherished, it was harmless; yet during her frequent sojourns to the Universe she had evolved a taste for the burning sensation it generated in her tongue and cheeks, that mildest of aches it left for moments after it was swallowed. Ever curious, she had investigated what the textbooks could tell her of the medical effects, and read of alcoholism, cirrhosis, delirium tremens and sundry other contingencies. She had resolved that forthwith she would allow herself alcohol, but only at home. Now she set the half-full glass, like that resolution, carefully aside.

'At first,' she continued, 'Manfolk were going into the affected area to let off steam. It was usually consensual: a great many fights had been brewing impotently for years. Then it became apparent that the effect was spreading. Domestic incidents began to take place, and there were brawls in the street, incidences of "road rage", even deliberate random shootings. Then a paramilitary group began policing the afflicted area. They insisted they could keep order there better than the Manthing.'

'Gnas' people?' Urbanus asked suddenly.

'His and his father's,' Dr. Clutterbuck agreed. 'Gnas Gortine was another of my pupils, as it happens, the brightest I've had in Manfold. It goes to show, you can't trust anyone.' Momentarily she paused to consider such rank ingratitude, before continuing: 'As the effect has grown, so has their influence, and of course they have the young men lining up to join them. Earlier this week they started rounding up all the Citizens they could find in Manfold, including my students; and last night, as Gnas informed you, they captured the Manthing itself. I'm afraid the Hormonal Revolution is at an end: the idiot men are back in power here.'

'Gnas talked about the Epicentre,' Urbanus said. 'Where is that?'

Once more she sighed, anticipating already in her sympathy for the boy what his next question would be. 'The earliest events took place at one of the College's student accommodation blocks, down near the old Cement Docks. There's an abandoned industrial complex there, which some believe is where this alteration started. That's what people mean when they talk about the Epicentre.'

'He told me,' the young Romuline said earnestly, 'that the people who are being killed aren't dead at all, that they're being reborn at the Epicentre instead. Is that true?'

Repositioning her spectacles once more, Dr. Clutterbuck looked sympathetically across her desk at her young friend. He had never before been outside his home District, let alone the City: the prevailing circumstances surrounding him must be terrifying for the poor boy. Yet, bravely if misguidedly, he stayed, so eagerly determined that by doing so he might still help his tutor.

'Please, Urbanus,' she told him, 'don't allow yourself to hope for that.' She considered disillusioning him with the revelation of the old hermaphrodite's treachery, but thought the better of it. However inexpedient Urbanus' loyalty to Marrane might be to her for now, such a relation between student and teacher was always to be cherished.

'There have been rumours,' she reluctantly admitted, 'of dead people coming back home, confused, with stories of the Epicentre. Apparently some of the Manfolk see it as a place of punishment, where the victims of the new protocols are sent to be mocked and victimised forever for their weakness. It's nonsense, I'm afraid, just urban legend. It seems most likely that stories about persons who were only missing have been exaggerated beyond reason. Times like this test people's rationality, Urbanus,' Dr. Clutterbuck concluded gently. 'They make up legends to explain what reason cannot.'

The fire crackled loudly in its grate, startling them both. Urbanus' expression halted in its slow progression into downcast misery, but only for the shortest span of time.

54. Porsena, the Epicentre.

His current situation was this: he felt like shit. Two of his fingers had been broken, as had at least one rib and Granddaddy only knew how many of his toes. He was still bleeding from a thousand encrusted jagged cuts (OK, more like twenty, but even so). His head was pounding and he still felt nauseous, plus he was of course still some fraction of crazy.

He had to get Lon Shel to say again what she'd just asked.

'Is that your shadow?' Shel repeated patiently.

It was a fair question: the dark form was capering around the floor and walls of the dingy office, checking for exits. It had a point, too – if the big gaolers came for him while he was here with Shel, it and he were both screwed.

'For now,' he admitted. 'It may take off first sign of trouble, though.'

'Sensible shade. Are you with the Rump Parliament?'

The kid was smart. 'Sure am,' he told her. 'Cousin Porsena at your service, Miss.' He essayed a bow, but his legs gave way beneath him and he collapsed onto the grimy floor. Shel watched gravely as he crawled to the wall beside her and sat against it, panting in a pile of trash. 'Crap,' he gasped weakly.

'Did they harm you badly?' she asked.

'Some,' he conceded. 'Nothing I can't handle.' He started shivering violently. At last, the delayed shock. To distract himself, he speculated: 'Guess you died too, huh?'

In fact he was relishing the novelty of conversing with another human being. He'd even heard of Lon Shel, if she was who she said she was: as the first City-born Lasthuman (and the daughter of then-Resident Mesh Cos), she'd been a minor celeb back in the zero-thirties. She'd been a baby then, natch, and he'd heard little of her since. Still, if she'd died – if *anyone* had died – he'd have expected it to be all over the media. Maybe her Mom had had it shushed up.

'Twice now,' she said. 'As life experiences go, it truthfully pisses. But I guess that's not new data to you.'

'Once would have been enough for me.'

'No bluff,' said Shel with feeling. 'Absolve me, Porsena, but the secs are dripping away from us. Would those be someone's keys you're holding?' She nodded patiently at the bundle he was carrying.

'Shit,' he said, realising, 'I'm sorry.' He got up on his knees, and began trying them in her manacles one by one. It was a large bundle, and the lock was stiff.

'We ought to merge our data,' the girl asserted as he worked away. The manacles were bound tight into her flesh. Unless Lasthumans could somehow cut it off she must be in some pain, but her voice was light and unconcerned. 'The Manfolk will be looking for you now: we mayn't have long. The more info each of us has, the better we're able to depart these climes.'

'All I know,' he admitted ruefully, 'is these guys are fucking sadists. Oh, and they have a cadaver factory where they make dead people and bring them to life. We come here when we're dead, 'cause this is Hell. The City is a false Heaven, put there to give us false hope. It makes the despair of Hell go all the deeper. Except,' he added, 'I have a slight case of insanity right now on account of the torture, so don't take that as gospel.'

Shel sighed. 'Perpend, then, Porsena. This isn't Hell: it's Manfold. You know, the seshy enclave out in Western Quarter? The big guys are Manfolk, although I've only vizzed the males here, for some cause. They call this zone the Epicentre. My retrieval's hazy – you would not *creed* how not myself I was when I came here – but I know I came by Tube to Hensile.'

'You didn't die?' He was gaping up at her, aghast. 'This isn't Hell?'

Lon Shel

Early on in the history of the City of the Saved, a number of commentators confidently stated that humanity had outgrown its immature reliance on religion, and that Resurrection Day would prove to have ushered in the first truly secular age of humankind. These predictions have proven less than accurate, to say the least. In fact, the City has been rife with new sects, and the years After Foundation have been more productive of new deities than virtually any other phase of human existence.

In some cases, this god-creation has been startlingly literal. Versions of deities have been commissioned as remakes – *mention the invulnerable-Baldur cock-up?* – and more than one Christian cult, finding the original Nazarene prophet not to its liking, has acquired its own customised Jesus as an mascot-cum-idol.

The only known case *check this* of a truly novel faith arising around a City-born individual is that of the worshippers of Citizen Lon Shel (b AF 33). Citizen Lon is the only member of the final human species (always notable for its longevity rather than its fecundity) who has been born within the City since its Foundation. The Church of Shel therefore considers her the ultimate evolutionary product of the human species, and teaches that, when she reaches adulthood, she will come into her true power as the Goddess of the Omega Point. That Lon herself was born as a result of parthenogenesis (a perfectly natural and valid lifestyle choice on the part of her mother, Mesh Cos), has not helped to discourage them in this belief.

A charming young woman quite at ease with her self-proclaimed evolutionary inferiors, Lon has responded gracefully to this imposition of godhead, and has even been known to receive deputations from individual Shelist churchgoers – though never clergy – requesting her advice on moral matters. She naturally rejects any suggestion that she is or will be the Goddess, but senior figures in the Church of Shel have long since concluded that her ignorance on this point will pass when she attains true divinity.

Quite why the Shelist hierarchy believes it knows better than its deity-in-waiting is not readily discernible by the outsider. Nor is it easy to predict how the religion will be affected when – as is presumably inevitable in the long run – another member of her species gives birth to a pure-blooded child *but a tower to ten discs half of them denounce the baby as a false messiah.*

[Anon, *Legendary Participants*]

Recollecting himself, he tried the last key in her manacles. 'No luck there,' he concluded, slumping back onto the grimy floor.

'Swyve,' said Shel with considerable asperity. 'These truckers are *paining* me.' She paused. 'I did die,' she tiredly explained, 'but subsequently. You escape, those yots outside decease you without even thinking about it. You die, you get remade on the production line. I've got away twice now, it's happened to me each time. It's bloody miserable.' For a moment she looked the vulnerable child she technically was.

'But you came here by Tube?' he asked her stupidly. If they were in Manfold, they were still inside of the City. He'd been assuming this was some other plane of being altogether, as separate from the City as the City was from the Universe.

If it was just some goddamn City slum he could get out of here, get word to the Parliament. Go back to Central and resume his life, assuming it was still there waiting for him.

'By rickshaw from Hensile, I think, but yes. My brainpan was filled up with Someone Else at the time, so I admit to being kind of woolly about the details of the situ.'

'Then we have a chance. We can get away from here.'

'Anywhere else whatsoever would be excessively fine by me,' Shel fervently agreed. 'Listen, can we send your shadow off to steal more keys?'

'Wouldn't work. It'd only bring back shadows. Besides, it's still attached to me right now.'

'And I'm attached to this cabinet,' Shel said. 'I'm hazarding if you were fleet at picking locks you'd have hinted at the info before now.'

'You're right,' he said. 'So how did you escape before?'

'Oh, basic technique. I took some extra classes at U, and escapology was one. There's not so much enjoyment when there's pain to be had, but it still works.' She flexed her wrists, and shuddered. He cringed. 'I've taught the Manfolk everything I know, though. They've left no give in them this time.

'You need to get the swyve away,' she went on. 'If you can steer around the guards and force your way outside, you can get help. Link with my mother – Councillor Mesh Cos. She knows who to interface. I've got friends who're more than capable of taking on these stiffs. They'll come for me as soon as Cos points them my way.'

He looked closely at her expression. It didn't look like she was bluffing. A kid like her shouldn't be subjected to this, not that anyone should. He didn't dare ask her what they'd done to her already.

'You're a brave kid,' he told her sincerely, pulling himself painfully into a roughly upright posture and limping over to the door. 'I'll get help, I promise.'

'You've got to get the hell out of here first,' she reminded him coolly.

Carefully avoiding even the merest glance out into the flesh-factory, he staggered out the door into the filthy control room. More focused yelling came from what he thought was the direction of his cell, as he limped out into the corridor and started trying to track down the exit.

55. The City.

Invisibly, pervasively about my children's bodies, Manfold succumbs to the infection. The wavefront has long since outgrown the enclave, propagating into Kempes, Infercliffe, Conewood and Thule, consuming the islands of Brendan and Columba, spilling finally over the northern border into Hensile. Manfold is entirely in the grip of the adversary now, the point source of this occupying presence reaching out to annexe the fabric of my substantial body.

The wavefront, though, is just the outlying fringe of the invader's control. Within it is a zone where that power has been consolidated, where the process of altering my substance is complete. As the effect takes firmer hold, the epicentre and its environs become worn, faded, dank. Manfold, never the most attractive part of my body, begins to wrinkle and sag. It starts to suffer the entropy depredations my protocols have held back these 291 years. Walls crumble, forms give up their structures as the buildings yield to decay and erosion. Colours fade, graffiti blossoms out of nowhere: rubbish and debris spill, spread out across the street and claim it for their own. The ground cracks across in places, as if undermined by tree roots, although the trees themselves are becoming withered and blighted. With the invader comes age: it is as if time has returned to a photograph, violating its pristine permanence with taint of change.

All this I glean from the eyes of those Manfolk not yet fully infected, those who are still part of my essence, my creations whom I still sustain. My senses cannot reach within the inner zone without these tenuous connections. There it is as if I am blind, deaf and unfeeling. A creeping numbness spreads across my surface like necrosis, like gangrene. Someone could detonate a thermonuclear device here and I wouldn't feel a thing.

Possibly someone will.

All this at the epicentre – or the Epicentre, as the Manfolk are already calling it, unconsciously acknowledging their new capital. At the wavefront itself, change is all but unnoticeable: subtly, with the lifting of the protocols, edges begin to cut, weights to crush, toxins to poison. Bodies soften, begin to twinge and become frangible. Malicious irritation, aggression, hatred of self, all are unexpectedly provided with an outlet.

Stretching down through Kempes like an awakening kraken, the wavefront rolls over the renegades, the outcasts and the drifters who have been summoned by the promise of malevolent possibility. Bellowing barbarians and quiet secret killers, collaterals of the sanguinivorous persuasion and mercenaries without employer or profession, all find themselves drawn here, to where the wavefront passes.

Others come, too, their regimented cruelty sanctioned by the official stamp of politics.

In Kempes, the legions of the Romuline, constantly swelled by new arrivals – there is no shortage of volunteers among their contemporaries, their ancestors and their descendants – organise themselves with customary brutal efficiency, assembling prefabricated barracks, laying out training-grounds, neatly and irresistibly evacuating the amphibious local population. Soon the vacated houses, damp as they are, are billeted with troops, their contents commandeered, their garages and kitchens cleared of any possible variety of weapon.

Among the first structures the incoming army built here were forges and smelting-plants, and these have been busy, assiduously rendering local steel and iron into glowing sludge. This the smiths and armourers of the legions mould and hammer into complex shapes. Trained hands assemble these parts into larger mechanisms, which are loaded into constantly-departing Tube chains.

Occasionally one of the more organised of the barbarian hordes will attack the Romuline contingent, and to this the legions' response has been twofold. First, naturally, they have defended their encampments with ferocity, applying sword and shield and spear and fist and catapult artillery. Secondly, once their aggressors have been beaten off (as they invariably are), they send a well-defended senior officer to parley with their leaders, suggesting accommodations, offering certain inducements calculated to appeal.

Many of the groups thus approached have moved their bases of operations closer to the ever-increasing area of Romuline occupation. They are issued with weapons, and with uniforms – simple plain coveralls, effectively armoured using hardened nanofibres, bearing a crimson / gold chimera logo, but nothing like the bright bronze of the legionaries. Decurions and tessarii are detailed to train them. Steadily, the army of the Romulines acquires auxiliaries.

Similar scenes are being enacted in the other Districts around Manfold. The cyborgs of Associative Network 9 are colonising Infercliffe, the flexing of their creaky military arm driving away the intimidated locals. (Rumour suggests that residents stubborn enough to remain are being forcibly "subscribed to the Network"; but in this regard rumour is – for now – a liar.) The ironclad galleons of the Church Triumphant navigate the inner reaches of Thule, while swastikaed Last Reich flying discs skim the hills and streams of Conewood. Alliances are formed, strange bedfellows snuggle up together.

And still the wavefront creeps, encroaching, influencing. Contaminating Me.

* * *

And meanwhile:

Even now, far away (to say the least of it) from the primary source, Manfolk assassins contemptuously posing as my Citizens shoulder their clumsy way into Council House itself. The secondary nodes they bear are absences bent into the forms of guns, crudely-shaped blanknesses of heavy space. I cannot feel or see them, nor even smell their oily powder scent.

If they discharge them, I am sure I will hear nothing: a silence, perhaps, as loud as death.

56. Avatar, Council House.

"Appearances count" was still the nearest thing there was to universal dogma among the sceptical and dissentient members of Faction Paradox, the cultures it dominated and its infrequent splinter groups. It was certainly Godfather Avatar's avowed creed in life, some would say his entire raison d'être.

He crouched upon the plinth next to the pallid statue of Perikles of Athens, alleged father of human democracy and current repository for the streaked guano of a million pigeons.

No-one ever looked at the statue. Reputedly even Perikles was fed up with it by now.

After a few minutes Tobin emerged from the exit to CoHo Tube station, anonymous in a clump of fellow-passengers. Her face was prettily enhanced by a more than usually intense scowl. (Things hadn't gone well with Fisher, then.) She turned across the Plaka in the direction of Honi's.

As she crossed the unaltered shadow of the statue, he dropped in front of her. His cloak rode up about him like the wings of a skeletal, antlered bat. (Perhaps a stag beetle would be a better image.) He hit the ground directly in front of her.

AVATAR: *Afternoon.*

The alacrity with which she recoiled, right hand darting to her armpit where she kept her gun, warmed the well-protected heart within the Godfather's chilly calcareous ribcage.

TOBIN: Jesus. I could have shot you.

AVATAR: [*Cheerfully*] *Oh, I dare say I would have lived.*

Tobin's voice was harsh and strained: not, apparently, a happy bunny. Godfather Avatar had been intrigued to observe within himself a momentary squirm of apprehension in response to her words.

AVATAR: *So, officer, how is your investigation proceeding? Are your men moving in for an arrest?*

Tobin's scowl deepened, her narrowed lids all but obscuring her surprisingly attractive green eyes.

TOBIN: Let's at least get out of sight. Or do you want to blow my cover completely?

She tried to bundle him away towards a covered entrance off the Plaka: the consulate, as it happened, of the Parks Commission Fisheries and Livestock Division. With a slowness calculated carefully to madden, he followed her.

AVATAR: *Oh, they're used to me around here. I'm always accosting women I've never met.*

The consulate was closed for the weekend, and stood empty and dark behind its glass door. The Godfather and Tobin stood huddled in the doorway, the latter simmering nicely.

TOBIN: How's the investigation proceeding? Let's see. Professor Fisher didn't know his wife was seeing Mostyn, unless he's a consummate liar. He's trying to get me into her reception tonight. Mesh Cos took away the murder weapon out of civic duty, or else she's an even better liar. She's getting it analysed by some techno-geek she knows, but she's found out it was from Manfold. Unless one or both of them is a really staggering liar, neither Mesh nor Fisher murdered

Mostyn. I'm back to thinking St Marx did it deliberately, although I'm buggered if I know why. How sure are you about her and Mostyn, by the way?

AVATAR: *I'm sure.*

TOBIN: [*Doubtfully*] Hmm. Oh, and last night two guys tried to kill me.

AVATAR: *And how did they propose to achieve that?*

TOBIN: The same way they killed Mostyn. Potent weapons.

Tobin reached into her armpit and pulled out her own weapon / the gun the thick-set man had used on the Tube platform.

Godfather Avatar was deeply, deeply irritated to feel himself flinch very slightly. The servo-tendons in his armour smoothed the movement out, rendering it all but undetectable. A tiny flicker in Tobin's eyes told him she'd spotted it.

AVATAR: [*Quietly*] *Ah.*

She cast her eyes about, confirming that the Plaka was deserted. Deliberately, she raised the potent firearm and pointed it directly at his reinforced sternum, beneath the velvet. Coldly she stared into his black glass socket-lenses.

AVATAR: [*Still quiet*] You know, I wondered if it might be you. He looked like someone insecure and inadequate enough to hide behind a scary mask and body-armour.

Damn, she was good. The Godfather was proud he'd recommended her. Contemptuous of the trembling flesh beneath his bones, he stood his ground.

AVATAR: *Oh, Laura, please. Do you really think that little runt was me? It's hardly likely, surely, that the Rump Parliament would send one of its three Godparents to shadow a – no offence – a menial operative like yourself? I think you have rather too robust an impression of your own importance.*

Her stare unwavering, Tobin brought her left hand up and cocked the gun. This time he stayed impassive, able to anticipate and suppress his body's instinctive reactions. He sighed theatrically.

AVATAR: *It's understandable that you're upset. I should apologise for Little Brother Edward's remissness in not coming to your aid last night. He's City-born you see, gets nervous around things that might kill him. People so often fear the unfamiliar. It's rather sad.*

TOBIN: Quiet.

The Phantom Highwayman

Eighteenth-century English folklore tells of a phantom highwayman – apparently an updated version of the horned huntsman Herne, from a much older English legend – who would hold up any coach which passed through a particular forest (accounts differ as to which one, of course) carrying ill-gotten riches. In a polite whisper the cloaked man, distinguished by his bone-carved mask and sprouting antlers, would demand whatever money the passengers happened to be carrying. The passengers – invariably wealthy swindlers, seducers, blackmailers and the like – would offer a small sum, with the disingenuous plea that it was all they possessed.

The robber would seem to consider this donation, before accepting it and waving the coach on, to the passengers' considerable relief. In some versions of the legend, the coachman would observe at this point that the figure had no shadow in the clear, crisp moonlight.

When the coachman reached his next staging-post, he would dismount and open up the doors, to find to his dismay that every one of his passengers was dead, and every item of value taken. Usually it appeared that one of the travellers had killed his fellows and then destroyed himself: the whereabouts of the valuables would remain a mystery. More often than not, the coachman would observe an ownerless shadow – complete with branching antlers – striding back along the road.

Here in the City of the Saved, this story presents certain striking aspects, at least to anyone who pays attention to the affairs of the Rump Parliament. Is it perhaps possible that such a legend as this, planting a powerful fear in the minds of the inhabitants of a particular era (very few of whom, of course, could have in honesty considered themselves blameless), might be deliberately circulated by agents of a time-active power in an attempt to build a so-called "conceptual entity" – in Faction Paradox's terms, a loa?

Might such a creature be objectified here in the City, reborn alongside humanity thanks to the strength of belief of its hosts, the hundreds who had heard and feared the legend? *Or is this just the drunken witterings of a certifiable lunatic? You decide.*

And, more to the point, if I put this sort of insinuation in my book, am I really going to get a solitary publisher to consider the damn thing?

[Anon, *Legendary Participants.*]

Godfather Avatar's armour was theoretically bullet-proof, though the matter had never been tested. The vulnerable point was at the neck, where it and the mask met.

TOBIN: Little Brother Edward, did you say? Well, Edward, I want you to take the mask off. You're not Godfather Avatar, because there is no Godfather Avatar. Just an overblown Hallowe'en outfit you bastards have conditioned all of us to see as the Godfather.

He had no grounds whatever for this frankly craven attitude. The dignity of the Parliament rested in him.

AVATAR: *Feel free to believe whatever you choose, Laura. Just do the job for which we're paying you, extremely generously, and any opinions you hold within the privacy of your skull will be none of our concern.*

TOBIN: Bollocks. Take off the mask.

Before he could react, she shifted the gun upwards, lodging it below his jawline, where a bullet might... Enough of this. He yawned elaborately, covering his jaw with one skeletal gauntlet.

AVATAR: *I hardly think –*

Commanding all the armour's enhanced speed and agility, he stepped back and ducked while plucking the gun from Tobin's hands. While she remained speechless he disposed of the weapon inside the inky folds of his voluminous cloak.

He straightened up and stalked forwards, pinning Tobin against the door to the darkened lobby. He enjoyed the way the skyglow bypassed his shadowless body to illuminate her discomfited expression.

AVATAR: *There. That's a more satisfactory arrangement.*

TOBIN: Fuck you.

AVATAR: *I rather think not.*

He controlled himself.

AVATAR: *Accepting for the moment, Laura, that what you imagine is correct: that I am not, in the most conventional of senses, a person, but a set of regalia worn at different times by different people; a Cousin here, a Little Brother there, sometimes as convenience would have it one of the other Godparents... Assuming this to be the case, my dear Laura, what grounds have you, precisely, to assume that I am not, precisely, an identity? A personality, in other words, tied not to a specific mind or body, but free ranging, anchored at a given time to one member of Parliament or another?*

Tobin was silent. Godfather Avatar pressed his advantage.

AVATAR: *The word we in the Faction use, Laura, with which you may or may not be familiar, is "loa". A spirit, capable of occupying a human psyche, riding it as you might ride a... let's say a skateboard. That class, my dear Laura, of relationship. And, I feel bound to say, it is not traditionally considered good sense to make one of the loa thoroughly pissed off with you.*

A sudden roar, deafeningly loud, a set of stings at the back of his neck, and an intense sensation (surely that was pain? How novel!) careering up and down his spine.

TOBIN: [*Really alarmed*] *Shit!*

Her freckled face was liberally dusted with much brighter specks, a vivid red in colour.

The Godfather attempted to raise one bone-clad hand to his neck, but found it overly heavy. It was, in fact, quite difficult to keep his whole frame upright, so he gave up, relishing the swell of air inside his cloak, the velvet inflating to cushion the dead weight of his body, the clatter of his armour on the stone step. He might have just fallen over, but at least he'd done it with style.

Tobin's gaze was fixed behind where he had been standing, on whoever (he could only really assume) had just this moment shot him in the back.

Through the familiar hissing of the jawbone speaker-grille, Godfather Avatar exhaled his, and as it happened Little Brother Edward's, final breath.

AVATAR: *I can't help feeling... rather hurt... by that.*

And, wishing Tobin luck in this awkward and unexpected situation, he expired.

57. Tobin, Council House.

There were seven of them this time, great brick walls of men just like before, carrying what looked like truncated shotguns – not sawn off, but manufactured that way. They wore similar suits (in pinstripe, charcoal-grey or black) and had equally standard-issue crew-cuts. The one in the centre was toting one of the chunky pistols, his right arm in a sling. In the nature of things, Tobin hadn't got a proper look at his face, but it was clear enough from context he was the man she'd taken down at CoHo station.

This was not a good position to be in. She had one, very slim chance.

'You bastards!' she wailed, her voice shearing with grief. 'You killed him! You killed the Godfather!' She sank to her knees and cradled as much of Avatar's heavy shape as she could fit into her arms, while frantically rifling through his robes for her gun. 'Godfather, Godfather, Godfather!' she sobbed, in the interests of verisimilitude.

'Grab her,' one of the men said, and they did. The nearest grasped her by the shoulders and pulled her upright. Her fingers found metal through the velvet nap before being tugged away, empty. Damn. They pushed her forward, stumbling, to face the man she'd injured.

Two of the other thugs took her arms and twisted them up behind her back. She struggled, but she might as well have tried to tow a pair of Tube chains.

'Remember me, bitch?' said the man in front of her. Obviously not a villain of the wit-and-subtlety school. He raised his handgun and held it unwavering in front of her right eye. The out-of-focus barrel gleamed with gritty oil.

The other men were obviously deferring to this goon, but Tobin didn't get the impression he was their boss. More likely they believed his injury gave him the right to deal with her. Maybe some kind of honour code which sanctioned revenge...

...oh, what a *fascinating* piece of sociological observation, Citizen Tobin. I'm sure it will be of great comfort to you, when the bullet enters your brain through the eye socket, that it's being planted there for culturally valid reasons.

'I said, remember me?' the man repeated. He spoke Civil with a pronounced accent, which was rare but not unique. It meant the Citizen in question hardly ever used the Tongue. If he was a resurrectee, it meant he'd used it so little that the common standards encoded in all of them had been allowed to lapse.

Obviously he also had some issues with personal inadequacy.

'I'm sorry,' Tobin told him. 'I find it difficult to tell brick shit-houses apart.'

One of the other men in her view smirked. She didn't get long to enjoy it, as her opponent swung the gun aside and slammed the barrel into her cheek, deeply gashing it.

God, that hurt. He did it again, going back in the other direction.

'Oh yes,' she whispered. 'I remember.'

'Good,' he said. His eyes were watery blue, his stubbled chin scarred across, and at some point (presumably pre-Resurrection) his nose had been broken. 'I wouldn't want you not to know the man who sent you to Hell.'

Jesus, the man was unimaginative. Godfather Avatar had been more entertaining company. So had Rick Kithred.

'Our boss wants a word, see,' he went on, lifting the bloodied gun once more to Tobin's eye. Deliberately, slowly, he pulled back the hammer. 'I'll send you to him now,' he said.

The sound of gunfire echoed round the Plaka.

58. Compassion III, Teletopia.

Compassion had snagged a lift to downtown Warner Village from a passing superhero. ('Where were you when I was being attacked on a roof?' she'd asked him acerbically, but he'd played dumb.) She might have evaded the thugs for the moment, but they'd be watching her apartment. Even with the gun she'd taken from them, they could still outnumber and overpower her. She no longer imagined they were trying to get at Compassion I – at Tobin – through her. It would be stupid: with their weapons, they could easily kidnap or just kill her. No, this was personal, which meant she was in real trouble. It was time to cash in a certain piece of information she'd been keeping for just such a rainy day.

The house she sought was set well back from Warner's broad silver slidewalks, a gloomy wooden mansion with its windows shuttered, sequestered behind iron gates and set about with turrets and gables. In Teletopia, there were such anachronisms around each corner, under every walkway. Nobody ever questioned it: it was tradition.

The nearest screens were pumping out the latest Mozart video, "Salieri Kiss My God-Lovin' Mass". Compassion rang the doorbell, and waited for some minutes before she heard steps approaching.

The door creaked open and a thickset man blinked blearily at her.

'Mr Vandemeer,' she said in a singsong voice, getting the formalities over with. 'I'm a big fan of your work. I've seen every episode of *For the Time Being*. And *Faustus Rex*? Much better than *The Prosperos*.'

'What the hell do you want?' said Vandemeer. The producer was a weary man, his imago pinned to a vague, but premature, middle age. Beneath his shabby dressing-gown, however, he bore a still-tough frame.

Compassion folded her arms and looked at him, waiting for the realisation.

It didn't take him long. 'You're one of the Compassion iterations?'

'That's right,' Compassion said. 'Compassion III. The critic.'

'Right,' he said irritably, 'the one who's always talking up *The* fucking *Prosperos*.' He stepped aside, allowing her to come into the darkened hall. The floor creaked, and faded movie posters hung in frames on the inevitable wood panelling.

'I'm a busy man, Ms. Compassion,' said Vandemeer, 'and I need my sleep. What can I do for you?'

'Some men are following me,' Compassion told him. 'I don't know who they are or where they're from, but they've got potent weapons. I need sanctuary.'

'Shit,' Vandemeer said, standing up straight now and paying attention. He wrapped his robe more tightly about him, and closed the door. 'You're asking,' he said cautiously, 'for sanctuary, from these men, in my house?'

'No, Cousin Berle,' Compassion informed him with exaggerated patience, 'I'm offering to defect to the Rump Parliament.'

A worried frown crept over Vandemeer's face.

'Someone with my connections,' she continued brightly, 'would make a valuable asset, don't you think?'

59. St Marx, View Point.

Midway between the ground and sky, her light touch on its panels banked the flyer, leaning it in toward the violent currents of the air.

At this altitude the winds were channelled somehow (macrometeorologists were divided) so as to avoid the Watchtower itself: the triumphal pillar stood still in the pellucid air, raised up from the earth of the City by a partisan God. It grew as they approached it, biting off what once would have been a sizeable morsel of the speed of light.

It bulked and filled out, enlarging from pillar to turret, turret to mountain, mountain to world.

She wore a gilded sheepskin over a Vivien Oppusto light-shift. The engineered gem set in her navel cast a shimmering net of white across her body, blinding bright in just the correct places to be decent. She had invited some few of the more old-fashioned male Councillors to her reception – it was a natural and inexpensive (some would say cheap) play for their support[1]. High-heeled ankle-boots, their dainty points fashioned into cloven hooves, covered her scorpion, and her iridescent oil-black hair was bare. As ever her spectacles remained, portholed reflections of her skin-suit's glint.

He still wore his djellaba and his pilgrim's hat, as concerned as she with appearances but seeing less need to adapt them to the occasion. Both garments were miraculously dustless after his country walk. His eyes were closed, his lips twitching occasionally as he ran through his guest of honour speech. So intent was his unspoken concentration that she could hear it, a muttering subtext to the flyer's soundproofed sigh.

As they approached, the summit of the Watchtower resolved itself into a tiny model of a pillar-town, constructed so as to fool the viewer's eye, a scarcely convincing special effect.

The great tower tapered over its length[2], so what was at the base as large as Onesia's continent of Jedralaika became at its height the mere size of the Jedrals' Minor Citadel. It was a vast area in its own right but, so far as the needling Tower was concerned, a mere point.

Tonight she would dance upon it like an angel.

People lived at View Point, as everywhere in the City (yes, even the artificial suns). The Watchtower's summit was occupied, predictably, by the astronomically rich, together with their partners, parents, children, concubines, staff, servants, slaves and pets. Their number was limited by statute, and the mansions of the Viewpointers, landscaped grounds and flying pads and all, were forced to share their summit with the tourists. They were scattered among the hostels and auberges and taverns, birdseed on a sundial.

Ahead the summit bloomed, swelling in a moment from a model to a thriving chunk of Cityscape, transplanted to an island in the sky. A tiny paved space, relatively speaking, had been marked off at her request with movable stone balustrades, for the reception. A stage was set up in front of a dance floor, together with a dining area, two bars, an arc of the View Point perimeter, the gantry with the replica Apollo rocket moored ready for the climax of the firework display, and numerous stairwells to secluded rooms below.

Her deft taps now directed the flyer towards the roped-off car park. As they narrowed in on the landing site, their flyer slipped smoothly from the buffeting zone of winds into the calm of the great edifice.

So far her area was relatively deserted: she was arriving early. It wouldn't do, of course, for the host to be absent when her guests arrived, and if strict protocol dictated that the guest of honour should sneak off and come back later, strict protocol could go hang. He was her friend, she loved him and she hadn't seen him for years.

Anthony was waiting for them, the loyal sweetheart, amidst a smattering of caterers, servants and security. As the two of them alighted from the flyer, towering over all but the security guards, she gave them all a twirl, the golden fleece swinging across her light-clad skin. She smiled at Anthony, grateful for all he'd

Footnotes for Chapter 59

[1] H: I hesitate to bring it up, but...Ved Mostyn?
A: I know. Out of character, completely.
H: Quite. Have you considered...?
A: Was he influencing me? I don't know.
H: There are a number of ways.
A: A lot of them won't work on Citizens.
H: A biodata ritual? You still shed hair.
A: Possible, I suppose. But...Ved Mostyn?
H: I know. Out of character...

[2] Why had the Founders not mapped Onesia as they had the Earth? She could even now have climbed Mt Tulune to the summit, swum in the Soleem Sea and overflown the Chasm of the Prophets...Allisheer St Marx had died so young. There were so many things she had still longed to do.

[3] Except she *knew* his smile. She'd taken pains to memorise each twitch and wrinkle of it. This wasn't it – it was a caricature, a near-perfect imitation, so accurate that only she could ever tell the difference. For the first time since they'd met, he wasn't glad to see her.

Affecting nonchalance, she glanced behind her. Her friend had picked up, not on Anthony's insincerity, but her distress. Like her, he was covering it. Effortlessly through her shades he caught her eye, recalling to her their conversation in the Park.

Anthony knew, then, about her and Ved. She couldn't imagine a solitary other thing that might cause this reaction in him. He wasn't a suspicious man – quite the reverse. His unfortunate past had left him all too wilfully blinkered to see what his wife might be getting up to in the next room. (Not that she ever had – not quite that, Allisheer, no.)

Someone had told him, surely, then. So who else knew? This could be, she realised even as she soothed the caterer's flushed feelings and suggested an elegant solution to the supply difficulties, the end for her. And, since he would never survive the scandal that would ensue, the end for poor Anthony too.

done, and he returned to her a warm smile[3].

She knew he would efface himself when people began to arrive: having midwifed the arrangements for her spectacular, he'd match his colours to the background and quietly oversee. He had his reasons, adequate enough, to prefer a low profile on public occasions, though he'd never let it fester into an obsession.

Lovingly she embraced him and asked if all was well. Smiling with his lips, he mentioned some minor supply crisis, a shortage of a fashionable drug whose presence would be expected. He shook hands with their guest, and asked politely after life at the High Seminary, as, cool and competent, she turned her sympathetic attention to the flustered catering manager.

Viewpoint

LIEF: So, you've worked your way up the Watchtower, taking your trusty copy of *The Megalopolis Guide* with you all the way of course, taking in all the sights we recommend. It's taken you what, about eighty years, Krish?

KRISH: About that, mate, yes. It's lucky we're software constructs really, or making the *Guide* could easily turn into a full-time job.

LIEF: Krish! You'll spoil the, the... thing. Um, Catriona.

CATRIONA: Thanks, Lief. Well, whether you're spending eighty years at the Watchtower or an afternoon, the climax of your trip there has to be View Point. The Watchtower is still the largest structure in the City, and in a very real sense its most important icon – we're used to seeing its image on money, stamps and newspapers, and of course those of us who live within a few million kilometres of Central District can't actually avoid seeing the real thing every single day. But View Point is the real crowning glory of the Watchtower. From here you can observe the entire City, laid out beneath you like a nano-woven tapestry. One of those particularly fiddly ones where you need a magnifying glass to get any of the detail.

KRISH: And what a magnifying glass! The Watchtower's precisely what used to be called one Astronomic Unit in height. For those of you who remember these things, that's exactly the distance there used to be between the Earth and the Sun. For those of you who don't – well, those two were a fair distance apart. Not in City terms, naturally, but on the human scale it's as long as 80 billion average-sized people laid end-to-end. Which, depending on your tastes, is quite some party.

[*The Megalopolis Guide* (17:35 09/04/291).]

60. Tobin, Council House.

At the juddering cough of what could only be machine-gun fire, a pained expression crossed the face of Tobin's antagonist, followed closely by a warm trickle of blood. His eyes crossed and he collapsed satisfyingly at her feet.

Around him, Tobin's other captors were reacting with panic. The two holding her arms let go in confusion, and Tobin had hit the ground by the time the firing started up again. Some of the thugs reached for their own guns, others followed her lead and dropped to the flagstones of the square. Taking advantage of the general bewilderment, Tobin relieved her former captor of his gun – he looked as if he wouldn't mind this time – and started crawling backwards towards the doorway of the consulate.

Those of the men who hadn't thrown themselves to the floor were quickly felled by the sputtering fire of their unseen attackers. From the occasional muzzle-flash, these seemed to be concealed in the entrances around the Plaka.

The thugs on the ground were firing back now, adding further deafening reports to the clangour, but were drastically outgunned. Tobin put a bullet in the nearest one on principle, scrambled across Avatar's antlered body and pressed herself to the step in the consulate entrance behind.

The noise continued for a while, then abated. Clearly she heard the sound of something solid and metallic, scraping a little as it bounced across the flagstones. She made herself as flat behind Avatar's armour as she possibly could, screwed her eyes shut and covered her ears.

The obscene roar lingered in the Plaka for some time. Tobin's ears rang like organ pipes. As the sound began to fade, beneath the tinnitus she heard what might have been a great many feet, marching on stone. She risked a peek over Avatar, noting how the velvet cloak had ripped and shredded over his bony armour.

Nearby, pieces of the suited goons were scattered, bloody and charred. None of them appeared to have survived, but their remains were not readily countable. Black scorch marks and cracked flagstones showed clearly where the grenade had detonated.

Shakily, Tobin stood. She placed the gun very cautiously on Avatar's prone body, and raised her hands.

In front of her, a hundred men in polished bronze and leather stood in perfect ranks, their sandalled feet parallel. Their bright helms were plumed in red and gold, their bulky automatic rifles shouldered in regimented pen-strokes. The square shields resting at their feet each bore the heraldic image of a chimera.

They formed a corridor of muscle, cloth and gleaming metal leading from Tobin, and the gristly mess surrounding her, to the Tube station entrance. On its steps, behind two athletic standard-bearers, stood Consul, Resident and Councillor Cassius Ignotus, in a purple-edged toga.

Flanked by his huge-carapaced collaterals, the Romuline patriarch's stern face was craggy and unyielding.

61. Urbanus, Manfold.

Urbanus caught up with Dr. Clutterbuck just as she was deploying some twenty of her followers aboard an armoured vehicle: an obvious museum-piece with twelve pairs of wheels and a roof-mounted gun emplacement. At some point during the Hormonal Revolution, somebody had painted it cornflower-blue with a sprinkling of little pink anemones, but if the intention had been to create a thing of beauty then the execution had fallen sadly short. Twilight was darkening the campus, shadowing the redbrick administration buildings where those Manthing troops who were not Manfold College students were billeted; Clutterbuck had changed her floral print dress for a set of olive-coloured canvas fatigues, though she still wore her spectacles.

The blue silk robe that Urbanus had borrowed flapped and swirled about his legs and buttocks as he ran. 'Stop!' he gasped, and leaned heavily against the troop-carrier to catch his breath. This business of getting exhausted when one ran, together with the tight pain in the stomach, thighs and calves, was something he would definitely not miss when he returned to the zone of influence of the City proper. 'Please!' he panted. 'I'd like to come... with you... please.'

'You most certainly would not,' Clutterbuck told him severely, looking annoyed. 'This is a serious military operation, young man.'

'But half,' Urbanus wheezed, 'half of your troops are volunteers. With, with respect, Doctor,' he added, 'you're not even a soldier yourself. You're a comparative humanologist.'

'Dear me,' muttered Clutterbuck. She continued to pat each trooper very gently on the arm as he or she climbed up into the armoured transport. Then out loud she declared, 'All of us have seen combat. Most of us in the last few days. I'm afraid you'd be a liability, Urbanus.'

'But you're going to investigate the rumours, aren't you?' Urbanus asked. 'You're going there to find out if the dead are coming back to life.'

The last volunteer having lurched aboard the armoured vehicle, Clutterbuck took Urbanus by the elbow and drew him slightly apart. 'Whatever's going on at the Epicentre,' she said, 'it seems to be happening under the control of an unknown faction. A male supremacist group certainly, possibly allied to the Gortines but possibly working alone. We have no idea of their history. This is a reconnaissance trip only.'

'But if people are being resurrected there, they're keeping them prisoner! Probably torturing them.'

'The gentlemen occupying the Epicentre do seem to be deeply unpleasant people,' Clutterbuck agreed. 'All our intelligence is clear on that point. It's even possible that they're the ones who worked out how to change the protocols. They may be situated at the epicentre of the effect simply because they're the ones who started it. If that's true then they are very dangerous, and must be stopped. But not,' she added sharply, 'by you.'

Urbanus fixed on Clutterbuck his most determined gaze, which he had spent some time that afternoon practising before her bathroom mirror; and which, based on what he had seen then, was considerably less steely than the frown with which she now rewarded him. 'Please, Dr. Clutterbuck,' he said, doing his best to sound mature and responsible, 'Tiresias may be there... or Keth Marrane, if that's what he prefers to be called. If there's the slightest chance of getting him back from there, I owe it to him to try.'

'Urbanus,' the academic told him firmly, 'your tutor didn't die trying to rescue you. As far as any of us knew, you were safe in Kempes District. The rescue mission was for Peter and Kathka, neither of whom Keth Marrane even knew.'

'That isn't what I owe him,' said Urbanus.

Dr Clutterbuck gazed penetratingly at him for a quite lengthy interval: he was, in fact, convinced that the sky-dome was noticeably darker when finally she said, 'Oh, heavens above. Very well, Urbanus, you may come.'

'Thank you!' Urbanus cried, but she was not yet finished.

'Only, you understand, because I've a suspicion you'll go there with or without my protection,' she said severely. 'And only because Marrane's death – and I firmly believe that Marrane is dead – leaves me with some responsibility for you. And only on the condition that you follow my orders without question and do not endanger yourself in any foolhardy rescue attempts. Is that understood?'

'Yes, Dr. Clutterbuck,' he acquiesced humbly.

'You're very meek now that you've got your own way,' she tartly opined. 'Now change into something less ridiculous, please. But do it on the move. We're leaving immediately.'

62. Julian, Erath.

Julian sat curled inside the cockpit of the ship he'd re-IDed the *Lon Shel*, and wished he hadn't. It had been a cute concept back at the time, missing real Shel yet all secure of her safety. Now it felt to him all wrong and wrong and wrong.

Real Shel was... no-one knew what. Not safe, though, in truth. UniMac had essayed attempts to sight her via equipment inside Manfold, but found its access to some items of technology blockaded... as if, it said, they somehow didn't count as human tech any more. At least this gave a ballpark that she might, at probs, be in, but it provided no clue as to HOW she was.

Self-distracting, he attempted to envisage her months with the colony, pondering what she might have found it like, but he found he had to curb this. The thoughts were too upsetting. (Besides – he knew little about Universes, but he thought they all were different physico-legally. The City was interpolated artificially between two Universal spaces, Last and Next, but objects in the Next would behave very differently from objects in the Last. The City had been modelled, for the most, on conditions in the Last Uni, so all the resurrectee mumdads would feel all at home. The Next rules would resemble these ones not at all. He couldn't envisage what colony life was like if he even tried.)

...what might be happening to Shel in Manfold, though, he could image on all too clearly. She could be maimed, or killed, or mutilated, or she could be mad from all of it.

(Such things had happened – Julian knew some resurrectees had never overcome the traumas of their Universal lives, and cowered still in terror in asylums after living 291 years in Paradise.)

This, though, was where the awkwardness came in. Lon Shel might be in pain or torment, so it particularly incumbed on him, who loved her, to go save her. HOWEVER, though, if he went after her, HE might end up in agony or etcetera: less pleasing far a concept than her rescue. It might even transpire that Julian got her free, but fell captive to the Manfolk himself – so she'd be all at liberty, but he'd be subject to the ordeals of the damned. That would be worst all round – he'd be all victimised, AND he wouldn't be with Shel. She'd be elsewhere.

Oh – except, from her pov, obviously that was the better. A conundrum there, then.

What was more, if Shel had been... deceased (a horrid thought)... he couldn't help her anyway, as no-one could, and he could end up similarly... reformatted himself. That surely clinched the dilemma.

Consoled but strangely troubled by this impeccable validity, Julian sat. He stared across the Car Park for a period. *Shel* – the flighter – was parked amongst some other space-capable vehicles: some models he recollected from RealSpace, while some (presumptively) were from the Universe. There were a handful whose functionality he couldn't even commence to grasp: were they colony models, built for movement through whatever substrate underlay the Next Uni? Truck knew. In the near distance he could see activity, minuscular figures at the base of the Downtime Gate. UniMac's light-strewn angelform was dialoguing with someone who'd recently stepped through the interface – Julian imagined it to be a colonist who'd fellowshipped with Shel out there. From here they looked to be a vacuum-form posthuman. Julian didn't want to gesture to them, so he stayed away.

Nearer at hand, some preparations for the Lon-freeing project were continuing. He could see robots filing along behind a stand of motortricycles, carting equipment for whatever procedure the Machine had in mind. UniMac had clarified that Julian's participation wasn't fully needful: he could, it said, take off in the *Lon Shel* (which the robs had kindly repowered for him), slip unimpeded through Erath's defences, travel back to Farflate and thence to Central, Bear Claw District where his parents lived, or wherever-the-stiff he liked – and never come back. Certainly he wouldn't be eligible for membership of the Next Uni colony – a consideration that had never even entered Julian's brainpan prior to the Machine alluding to it. Join the colony to be with Shel? And leave the City? Ashtoreth's tits.

This then, his choice – give up the City, with its myriad wonders and diverse astonishments; its crowds of faces, all alive and thinking, and every single one a unique person; his friends, his family, his fancies and flirtations; the music and the artworks and the media; convenience tech and leisurely appliances and shopping; the illions and the illions of things that kept life in the City special for him, and for all the Citizens... could he forego all that? Even for Lon Shel?

He climbed out, lit a tobac-cylinder, and went off to gesticulate at UniMac.

63. Porsena, the Epicentre.

To Porsena's unutterable dismay, his search for a way out – and the increasingly angry pursuit of his Manfolk gaolers – had forced him down onto the floor of the corpse factory. Now he was limping along in the shadows of some of the giant engines, listening with misgivings to their much increased clatter and roar. Every so often a shrill electric bell (which like him sounded slightly cracked) would ring out across the factory, indicating that the machines were starting work on another cadaver. More dead people were arriving all the time, and he wondered where the Manfolk were going to put them all.

His shadow was walking backwards slowly, keeping pace with him, its crossbow primed and ready. (*Sombras que corta*, the discipline was usually called – "shadows that cut". In his case, probably "*sombras que perfora*" or some such.) Surreptitiously he watched a group of disoriented reconstructees led roughly along the far wall by the gaolers. One of them stumbled and was treated to vicious kicks in knee and ankle as encouragement. The wall behind them was composed of metal slats, with daylight seeping through the narrow horizontal cracks.

He guessed the factory floor was set at ground level (yeah, asshole, that's what "floor" means). Way back in the enclave's history, when the factory made normal stuff instead of dead people – dogfood, say, or soap, not that the Manfolk seemed big on soap – there would have had to be an easy way of getting the product out of the factory and onto the roads – rails, canals, vacuum-tubes, whatever. He figured the wall itself must be the door, a rolling hatch as tall and wide as the hangar-shaped factory space.

It was probably too rusted to move – unless whatever force was keeping the rest of this place functional turned its attention on it – but he figured there must be a human-size entrance somewhere nearby. Meaning, please Grandpa, in bright neon letters, EXIT.

Meaning all he needed to do (with his decrepit, barely functioning body) was cross the churning, clanking factory floor full of animated corpses and their body parts, avoid the guards, force open a locked door, run out onto the streets of Manfold and get the hell away to somewhere he could call the Parliament, or Mesh. No problem.

(Now he was away from Lon Shel, his protective reaction to the kid surprised him. He normally wasn't the fatherly type: disliked children, in fact. He had too much experience of the little bastards. Could be he'd suddenly become a nicer person, though whether this was since his reconstitution or his torture he couldn't say. Or maybe it was just the shock of finding someone human to connect with in this goddamn inhuman maze – yeah, he could just imagine how sympathetic the Mothers and Fathers would be to that. Still, her information had helped him, and he owed her. He was going to keep his promise to the kid, even if his feelings turned out to just be something her species could do with pheromones.)

A sudden yell – of the specific kind – came from behind him. His pursuers had seen him. The twang-and-whisper of his shadow's crossbow answered them, and he heard a cry of pain.

He'd evaded them once already, by finding where the floor was rotted through and dropping down a storey, but he'd known luck like that wouldn't last. It was time.

Clamping his teeth onto a pencil he'd found in one of the offices, he bit down against the pain and forced his ravaged limbs into a rhythm resembling a run. His shadow jogged backwards with him, swiftly reloading, as the broken glass cut the soles of his bare feet to scraps. Behind him, over the clangour of machinery, he heard another pounding, of approaching boots.

The machines were rolling faster now. He ducked around the nearest hulk, narrowly avoiding being scorched by a creaky welding-arm as it got to work on someone's tibia.

Then the gunshots started up. Shit.

Lon Shel hadn't been kidding about them being eager to "decease" him. Up till now he hadn't seen the Manfolk carrying firearms, but they were traditionally no good for close-up torture work. His only hope was to carry on ducking and weaving the best his flabby body could, and let his shadow try to hold them off. It loosed more shots, reloading now at speed: he heard more cries as its quarrels impacted. The shrill bell screeched again: sounded like one of them had been killed, for now at least.

He heaved aside a bucket of – were those livers? Euw – which slithered across the dirty floor like fish from a net. The bullets kept on coming: by some miracle none of them had hit him yet. Panting, his heart aching fit to splinter his spine, he hurdled a conveyor (no body on it right now, thanks be to Grandpappy) and began the final lurch towards the wall.

He could even see the door, a metal frame set in the rolling hatch. Hot damn. He had the distantest, remotest chance.

Then he slammed into somebody who had definitely not been there the instant before. Porsena had no time to react, or even take in any features, before crashing into the guy – who didn't even flinch. He was big, very big, taller even than the other Manfolk, with a stomach hard as breezeblocks.

Porsena's body, like his brain, went numb. For a moment he stood there, splayed against the guy's chest like a cartoon animal, then he slid gasping to the floor, no longer a moving target.

Bullets tore into him: his legs, his arm, his stomach, his shoulder. Parts of him were ripped away. The numbness frightened him more than the pain should have. Son Of A God Damned Hell Bitch, this was bad.

The towering figure rolled him over with one boot, so he was staring up at the guy's foreshortened, upside-down shape. The face itself was hidden by a big black pirate beard. Before the Manfolk guards stopped shooting, he saw the guy take a couple of bullets in his booted legs. They sparked and ricocheted. Somehow the asshole was still invulnerable.

Cast on the floor next to him, Porsena's shadow was crouched protectively, reloading its crossbow. But the huge figure had a shadow of his own, and it was carrying a broadsword longer than most men were tall. (Hey, this scenario was becoming spookily familiar.) Without its owner moving a muscle, the massive silhouette pulled the Cousin's shadow roughly to its feet, held its crossbow-arm up in one hand and slashed down with the broadsword in a cleaving stroke. Porsena's shadow crumpled next to him, mirroring his agony, while the vast figure tossed aside the shades of bow and severed hand.

He grunted and lay still, waiting to die. The pain – and what exciting pain it was – began to leech in through his chewed-up flesh.

It wasn't until the colossal figure squatted down and plucked it roughly from his aching teeth that he realised he was still champing down on the pencil.

'I did *say*, Porsena.' The voice came from above him, and it was of course, the gloating, smug and booming voice from his madness in the cell. 'I did *say* you couldn't escape.'

The voice confirmed it. Like the vast shape, the brutal shadow, it was just too familiar. He knew this guy from somewhere.

'There's a world of pain waiting for you, Porsena,' the huge man said. 'Here with me, where you belong now.'

Like he wasn't dying enough already, the monstrous figure plunged the pencil into his left eye, gouging it deep into his brain.

'A world of pain,' the man repeated calmly. The cracked bell rang like glass across the room.

64. Tobin, Council House.

'Are you injured, Citizen Tobin?'

Cassius Ignotus called to her as he crossed the Plaka Perikles, between the ranks of Romuline militia. His standard-bearers remained behind him on the station steps, but his bodyguards followed. One of them was carrying a rather pointless bunch of sticks, while the other held a machine-gun, pointedly shouldered across its chitinous torso.

Technically, Tobin was grateful to have been rescued. There had been no likelihood of escaping her imminent demise through her own efforts: Ignotus had quite clearly saved her life. So far she had no information as to whether death would have been permanent, but it would certainly have been nauseatingly painful. The Romulines had spared her that.

I'm fine,' she said, trying to ignore the flashes from her violated face and arm. 'But –' she flapped a hand vaguely behind her, at the doorway of the Parks Commission consulate.

The Councillor drew level with her, and his bodyguards snapped to a halt behind him. 'Ah,' he said. He peered intently at the body in the doorway. One of its antlers had sheared off in the grenade-blast. 'Is that Godfather Avatar?' he asked at last.

Tobin wondered how to set about answering this question with anything resembling precision. 'Yes,' she said, instead. 'One of the bastards we're standing in shot him in the back.' Ignotus continued to regard her gravely. 'I guess some of the pellets found a weak spot in his armour,' she shrugged.

She'd never been remotely political. Perhaps it was quite normal in a crisis for a Councillor to deploy armed troops in Council House. Ignotus was widely respected, after all, a Mayoral candidate and so forth. And certainly her experience suggested that the place needed more rigorous policing.

Still, arming a century of Romuline militia with potent guns and bringing them into the citadel of government seemed like perhaps the tiniest bit of overkill.

'A tragedy,' Ignotus said slowly. 'One for which Manfold will pay. I'm sorry,' he added, 'I understand you and he were close.' Absently he signalled to the nearest legionaries, who began to assemble a stretcher.

'He was a business contact,' Tobin snapped. For God's sake, was there anyone who hadn't seen through her cover?

'The Rump Parliament's members will be deeply upset,' Ignotus went on thoughtfully. 'I must inform Godmother Jezebel at once.'

'Did you say Manfold?' Tobin should have guessed, she realised belatedly, especially once Mesh had told her the origin of the knife. Meeting Janute had obviously ruined all her healthy Manfolk stereotypes.

Ignotus frowned. 'Of course, you wouldn't have known. These terrorists are Manfolk. It seems Manfold has developed potent weapons.'

Terrorists? Tobin supposed that was one way to think of them. 'How do you know?'

'From examining the men who attacked you last night,' Ignotus said. Apparently Tobin wasn't the only one who knew more than she'd been letting on. 'I had my biodata scholars analyse the body you so efficiently dispatched. They found him to be of Manfolk origin. Things have moved on since then, however. I'm arming the Romuline military to prepare for a full-scale incursion.'

'An incursion?' Tobin's ears had begun to return to normal, but her mind seemed dazed still.

'We've received *demands*,' Ignotus bit the word off angrily, 'from a spokesman for the Manthing, one Hent Gortine. They insist on the permanent suppression of the invulnerability protocols within Manfold, and the excision of the District from the City.'

'Like in the Timebeast Assault,' Tobin realised. She watched the legionaries lever Godfather Avatar's remains onto his makeshift bier.

'Indeed. I imagine they've been envying Snakefell its good fortune for the last three decades. I have always said the Manfolk were dangerous. This morning I was told they were holding a member of my family hostage, although if they think that will prevent me from opposing them, they're sorely mistaken.'

The four men hoisted Avatar's velvet-shrouded corpse between them, and began manoeuvring it out of the doorway.

'We have to anticipate the worst,' the Councillor went on. 'It's likely Manfold has extra-mural help, perhaps even from the Houseworld. I have men at the Uptime Gate, preventing for the moment all access from the Universe, even of our own Citizens. All data export to the Universe is being prohibited, and extra-mural information-scouts are being asked to leave. I'm also proposing a register of collaterals within the City, and the use of locator tags.

'All these measures have yet to be formally approved by the Council, of course,' Ignotus added, 'but these are significant security matters, and urgent ones. You mentioned the Timebeast Assault, Citizen Tobin. I think that will be a matter on many people's tongues during the coming days.'

'Wait,' said Tobin suddenly. Ignotus looked askance at her, but then realised she was addressing the stretcher-bearers. At a curt nod from him they stopped, amidst the bloody debris of the Manfolk thugs.

Tobin leaned over and peered closely at the body on the stretcher. 'He's got his shadow back.' Not only that, it didn't have the horns. Instead, the head encased in its grotesque mask was casting the delicate profile of a human face.

'Godfather Avatar has always had a shadow,' Ignotus said dismissively. 'It's just been known to move around without him. You know these Faction types and their shadow-plays. No offence, Citizen,' he added.

'But it's the shadow of the man inside the mask,' said Tobin, ignoring the implied slight. 'Little Brother Edward. Avatar's gone. The name was all he ever really was.' Her mind was awash with inferences and implications.

'I see.' Ignotus sounded sceptical.

'I have to go,' Tobin announced abruptly. 'I need to talk to Cllr. St Marx.'

'At the reception for Professor Handramit?' She nodded, and saw Ignotus catch the compound eye of one of his guards. 'We can accompany you to View Point,' he said decisively.

What, all of you? Tobin wondered. She said, 'I don't think that will be necessary, thank you Councillor.'

Ignotus smiled. It was a bleak sight, no less chilly than the jawbone-grin of Avatar's dead mask. 'It's no trouble, I assure you,' he told her. He indicated with an inclusive gesture his Romuline century. 'We were just going that way ourselves.'

65. Gnas, Manfold.

When the dome darkened and many hours were passed, Gnas the son of Korth came forth from the gates of his strong-hold, that had in elder days stood as a store-house for the craven craftsmen of the Manfolk. There they had set aside their many blood-goods, that the greedy Citizens might seize them – in exchange, to be fair, for mighty quantities of money.

He stood before the stalwart engine which Krest Ivarre had bent to his will, which would yet free the Manfolk from the City's yoke, and spoke unto his steward thus: 'Well, is it ready yet?'

And Krest Ivarre quoth: 'It's in bad shape, sir. Guidance system's shafted, and the bearings are shot to the Pit of Yelvling. But the generator's sound. It'll do what we need.'

'Well done!' Gnas had regained his habitual cheeriness. 'Sorry if I was a bit short with you earlier, Krest.'

'No-one likes to lose, sir,' Krest said flatly.

Gnas gave him a long and searching look, before stepping through the open sliding doors into the body of the locomotive. Around the bulk of the wormhole generator, the heavy canisters of the annihilation bombs were stacked.

Fell weapons these, forged in the work-shops of the Manfolk close by that place where blood and battle first came into Manfold. These death-dealing flasks were first dreamed of by a cunning smith in times before the City, when the Manfolk dwelled in the World and made bloody war on one another. Mighty he made them, that they might sunder the bonds through which those smallest parts that make up the matter of the world cleave one to another, hewing the halest rock into a nothingness as thin as thought. Grim weapons for a warrior!

Grim weapons indeed – and what was more they'd been responsible for the extinction of the Manfolk. The planet they'd called the World had been left barren, careering through its now-eccentric orbit with great bites taken from its ruined mass. These versions were smaller, but twenty of them were still enough to set off a chain reaction that could level a small District. They'd been constructed near enough the Epicentre that they should remain potent outside the enclave, though of course the Manfolk hadn't been able to test them.

Gnas trusted them to do their work, though. As with any weapon, the hardest question was that of where they should be directed. Which target would do the Citizens most damage, show them that the Manfolk were as serious as they could be about their demands? Thanks to recent events, Gnas Gortine was convinced he had his answer.

'Everything's ready,' he beamed at Krest as he emerged once more onto the platform. 'You say the guidance system isn't working?'

'No, sir. Somebody needs to pilot it.'

Gnas knew that there would be no shortage of volunteers for that task. The lure of becoming a noble martyr to the cause of a free Manfold was more than any true Manfolk could resist, and half his troops would probably fight the other half to the death to gain the privilege. 'That honour will be mine,' he declared immediately, to stave off discussion.

'You're needed here,' Krest said. 'It's a suicide mission, sir. You can't desert your men.' Then he added, 'Oh.'

Gnas sighed. 'That's right, Krest. I shall pilot the engine into the City and detonate it, and be back in Manfold before the dust settles. I'll see you as soon as I can fight my way out of the Epicentre.' And then, he refrained from adding, there'll be a reckoning with that hag Clutterbuck.

So saying Korth's son mounted the metal steed, ready with true valour to set forth on the voyage which brought his doom. Before the night's dawn, he would deal the weakling Citizens a blow by which they might at last deem Manfold worthy to be freed from its fealty. Setting aside his warrior's weapons, Gnas seated himself within the metal beast's snout, that he might guide it on its way to glory.

'Krest,' he said, after a while, 'just show me how to work this thing, would you?'

66. The City.

Seven postcards from the City of the Saved:

The Rump Parliament: We are in a large, wood-panelled room, lit with multiple candelabra and hung about with oil portraits. It recalls a town hall meeting chamber, or the dining hall of a nineteenth-century English school or college, save for a couple of anomalous details. Though there is vaulting in the stonework of the upper wall where windows should be, there are none, nor even shutters covering them: the blocks of stone continue smoothly and without a break. And, like the banks of men and women who sit on raised benches either side of the chamber, the figures in the dusty oil-paintings all wear masks made from deformed skulls.

Between the ranks of Mothers and Fathers the floor is tiled with an intricate pattern, upon which stand two figures: Chad Vandemeer – or, as we should now call him since he is formally attired in suit and Faction mask, Cousin Berle – and

Compassion III, in a sober if figure-hugging black jumpsuit. She is scowling, ridges etched across her lips and forehead. Her right shoulder is irritably raised: Berle's hand is in mid-fall immediately behind it.

Three high-backed chairs face them, at the far end of the chamber. The central, and largest, is occupied by wild-haired Godmother Jezebel, her robe rumpled and her mask askew. To her right, Godfather Lo sits beatifically, fat legs crossed, fat hands clasped together over his enormous belly. The left-hand chair is empty.

The Cement Docks, Manfold: There is filth everywhere: rotting food, broken glass, newspaper and plastic bags, as well as faeces, animal and Manfolk. We are in an alley, a broad one recently narrowed by the collapse of one wall into rubble. Graffiti in one of the more brutal Manfolk alphabets is sprayed across a nearby wall. What was once a large window now consists of a wooden frame with tiny teeth of glass around its edge. A pile of sacking conceals something oozing wetly onto the coarse asphalt. Above, rain clouds are gathering.

At the far end is parked a large armoured troop-carrier, sky-blue with pink splotches, and along the alleyway, approaching at a brisk jog judging by their stance, are arranged Melicia Clutterbuck's platoon of Manthing loyalists. Yspe and Loke are there, as is Urbanus Ignotus; all of them are wearing drab canvas fatigues and boots; all of them, including Urbanus, carry great big guns. He is bringing up the rear, lagging some way behind in fact, and looks uncomfortable and exhausted. His slack face is red from exertion, and he is holding the rifle at an awkward angle. Clutterbuck has yet to break a sweat: she is glaring grimly ahead, at an apparently burnt-out factory building.

Several metres above, between the alley and the clouds, a seagull has expelled a blob of excrement. Depending on the speed at which he is jogging, the painty streak may miss Urbanus altogether. Or not.

The Epicentre: The shattered glass ceiling with its rusted skeleton of iron; the archaic, menacing machines: we are on the filthy factory floor at the Epicentre. Sick yellow light seeps through the girdered sky, and the humid clinginess of the air suggests that it will soon rain.

The ancient, crumbling factory machinery is busy: steam rises from its pistons, and its booms and wheels are blurred with frozen motion. Cousin Porsena is being assembled on the production line, a corpulent anatomical diagram with short fat limbs and an incipient expression of appalled horror on his skull. The machines are layering him with muscle, swaddling it tight around his legs and neatly knotting it in place with sinew. Further along the line, hooks hold his skin spread ready. A bubbling vat of yellow-white fat is on standby.

Porsena's eyes, lacking eyelids, stare at the shattered ceiling, and his skinless jaws are as wide open as they will go. As yet he has no vocal cords. Around him, in mid-stroll alongside the conveyor belt, are half a dozen Manfolk guards. One of them holds a set of chains and manacles in readiness; another has Porsena's old, wrecked carcass slung across his shoulders (his shadow, however, carries no such burden). They are smirking as one of their number prods at the new

Porsena's internal organs with a stick.

Away from them, merged with the shade behind a bulky crane, something watches the watchers: the bodiless dark figure of a fat man, gingerly cradling the stump of its right wrist.

Base and Buttress District, the City Watchtower: The lift is thronged with people, among them a party of bored schoolchildren. A handful of the passengers are watching the in-trip entertainment service, which is recycling a cheap Western; in the circular body of the lift the jaded elevatees inspect the souvenir shop, or rather more enthusiastically the bar. Groups of them drink, read or play cards in the scattered relaxation areas, while in the capsule's centre a large holo-display highlights its position, roughly a quarter of the way up the Watchtower. Beneath it the augmented cuttlefish who operates the lift glares madly through its tank walls.

Laura Tobin stands at one side of the capsule, the scowl on her face mirroring almost exactly the one we saw modelled by Compassion III. Possibly she is grimacing at the acting in the film, which she is pretending at least to watch, but more likely she objects to the century of Romuline troops, ranked in decades at the lift's rear, furthest away from the sliding doors. They are standing to attention, displaying remarkable discipline given the children's determined efforts to distract them.

To Tobin's right stands Cassius Ignotus, his attention taken up by one of the misbehaving children, a distantly benevolent expression on his cold face. Behind him, with what passes with them for discretion, are positioned his ubiquitous bodyguards. One of the thick-skinned collaterals is scratching its ear-hole with the sharp point of a pincer.

View Point, the City Watchtower: Now, this one *looks* like a postcard. From the balustrade here there is a perfect panoramic view across the City. We are so high up that most of the features are obscured, but the great bowl of the Chamber of Residents is clearly visible, resembling from this height a dropped penny on a polished jade floor. A hair-thin strand of platinum curves lazily into the distance: the River Okeanos, wide as worlds. Artificial suns are dotted around, fiery dots against the smooth Cityscape. From here, the City appears chocolate brown, the dome above dove-grey. For the most part, as far as the unaided human eye cares, View Point might as well be encased in a smooth two-tone sphere.

Across this drab backdrop is splattered a diversity of vivid colour, form and texture: the guests at Allisheer St Marx's party. They are as wildly heterogeneous as by now you would expect, straining the eye with costumes, forms and bodies from hundreds of cultures and Districts: to make matters the more anarchic, most of them wear masks. Before this visual cacophony St Marx herself is frozen in mid-air-kiss, welcoming a woman with an animated insect-face, mandibles working away, the last of a new batch of partygoers. Allisheer's lightshift glints and flickers in the deepening twilight. Nearby a recent arrival, masked like a fish and sheathed in blue-green sequin-scales, is hectoring the gamely smiling Handramit.

Near us, away from the main body of the party, Anthony Fisher stands unmasked, leaning on his cane. He is dressed awkwardly in formal black and white, and is raising a hand in greeting at one of the newcomers. The edges of his mouth curl upwards and his lips are parted slightly.

The Car Park, the Lost Planet of Erath, RealSpace: The background offers a broad selection of the vehicles and other transportation devices laid out in the Car Park. The Downtime Gate, tall dark and obeliskine, dominates the far distance, while nearer to hand is the *Zeronaut*, the vast triangular vessel used by the Universal Machine for hyperspatial salvage work. Scattered all around is the remainder of UniMac's spaceship collection, designs packed in together so that unsightly functionality rubs rivets with impracticable elegance.

The midground is taken up by an amphibious armoured vehicle the size of a large house, its metal bulk bristling with instruments and appurtenances of all kinds, including several vicious-looking weapon-ports. A nearby hatch is open, so that a spidery maintenance robot can scurry back inside. Its legs are raised in interrupted scuttle. A larger mechanised shape is engaged in some larger-scale work involving competing blowtorches.

The foreground features Julian White Mammoth Tusk and the angelic light-form of UniMac. Julian has changed, and now wears a sturdy dolphin-leather jacket over a nehru-collared floral shirt and bottle-green cords. He has cut out his straggly hair extensions (or more likely one of Erath's robots has done it for him) and he now sports a rather spiffy flat-top. It harmonises strangely, but attractively, with his brow-ridge, his protruding nose and jaw, and liquid eyes. He holds a lit cigarette, and he is gesturing determinedly at the Machine, who hovers in front of him, apparently calm. For the frozen instant during which we observe this tableau, Julian's confident posture signifies "help".

The Temple of Civitata, the Romuline District: And finally, there's me: the City of the Saved, or its most consummate and enduring personification. I have had many names, but here in the Romuline they call me Civitata.

The priestesses of Civitata say that I know every thought, hear every prayer: I feel as my people feel, and breathe as they breathe. I guide the Tube chains along their fractal paths; I light and extinguish the artificial suns over the Parks; by my will was the Watchtower constructed and the Uptime Gate. I am City and Citizens, urbs et civitates. I am humanity, and humankind.

My statue is in the curtained inner sanctum of my Temple, my holiest place. Here I am carved in translucent alabaster, white as milk, rendered hair to toenail with an accuracy that encapsulates my every detail; a precision, some might say, that borders on the psychotic. I wear a himation, the Greek toga, draped (naturally) so as to casually reveal my round right breast. No scowl for me: my face is classically serene. I sit atop a carved throne, on a carved dais facing a carved altar, all in this flawless alabaster gypsum.

The scene is static: there is nobody here who might be moving. At certain times of day I am visited by my priestesses, who pray to me and carry out – not by my request or choice, I ought to point out – animal sacrifices on my altar, in my adopted name. It seems to keep them happy. Most of the time, as now, I sit here alone, experiencing the life of my wider body, the City. Here I have been content to rest for 291 years.

No more.

Observer Theory

From its unique vantage point beyond the end of each and every universal history, the City acts as a record of the changes in the Universe, noting and archiving all the ephemeral histories imposed on humanity by the Great Houses and their enemies. No single human being, no single human experience even, is ever lost from the City, only gained by it.

It may be asked what the City's – or, of course, its Architects' – motivation for this is. In order to address this question I suggest we consider another theory, this time one originating on the Houseworld.

It used to be believed among the members of the Great Houses that, for the concept of "changes in history" to make any sense at all, there needed to be an objective observer, a viewpoint outside history, which was itself unchanging. This observer (which need not be a sentience per se, a point of view alone would suffice) would be omniscient within the Universe, and would faithfully observe (and, according to some schools of thought, record) all changes to the timelines.

Naturally the assumption among the Houses used to be that this observer was the Houseworld itself, its civilisation or perhaps its historic anchoring point. Since the start of the War, of course, that position has become untenable as the Houseworld's history itself has begun to fail, and Observer Theory, whose practical applications were never outstandingly useful, has fallen out of favour. Its remaining adherents speak now of an infinite series of observers – implying, theoretically, an infinitely-distant Ultimate Observer which would (effectively, and always bearing in mind that it need not actually be sentient) be God.

Human theologians since Pierre Teilhard de Chardin, now Pope Peter of the Human Catholic Church, have argued that humanity might one day evolve into God, achieving deity at its moment of greatest transcendence. So far, our human-populated City has confined itself to observing humanity's history alone. The scope of this observation is devastatingly impressive, but it constitutes only a fraction of the history of the Universe at large.

But maybe – so, at least, some politologists would argue – the City is gearing itself up for something altogether more remarkable.

[Vril, *Omphalos!*]

BOOK THREE

67. Porsena, the Epicentre.

There were plenty of things he was hazy on right now, but one thing was certain: his past was preferable to his present. He'd just sit tight here, if it was all the same to everybody else. Whatever (also whenever and wherever) his "now" might have been, he had a hell of a lot of "then"s that took priority.

He was just fine, sitting here at the back.

He remembered the Eleven-Day Empire as clear as day, clear as his luxury apartment in Central District. Back then, before he'd died for the first – before, that is, he'd died, he hadn't made the connection (natch), but the Empire and the City had a lot in common.

He'd never visited the real London, but they told him that was where the Empire (or its capital at least) was... let's say sourced. The Faction took a pinch of London's history from the primary timeline and gave it a twist, like the tail on a balloon animal. There in the tied-off bubble, buildings of all historical eras, blackened with smoke and soot, were crammed together underneath a lowering sky – though Little Sister Eliza, who was English, said that was nothing to do with Faction Paradox, it was just how London always was.

True, somebody had given the Empire's London a Gothic makeover at some point, turning the clouds blood-red and all the buildings jagged, black and toothy – but parts of the City of the Saved looked just like that, too. The Empire had its own Tower and its own (disused) Tube system, a couple of Gates and of course its own Parliament. It even had a region called simply "the City". He sometimes wondered... but no. The Rump Parliament would have had a hell of a lot more power in the City of the Saved if the parent Faction had a hand in building the place.

He'd come to the Empire as a so-called Little Brother, already fat and in his forties but willing to learn. Willing to do anything, in fact, to escape the life he'd had back in... well, that didn't matter much. He'd long ago stopped feeling animosity towards the people involved. It was a fresh start, courtesy of Faction Paradox, that was the important fact.

When he'd met Father Self, he'd been a two-bit comedian and conjurer, performing children's parties for a pittance. He'd also been a part-time grifter and con artist, who'd figured he could make something from this weird new cult that had set up shop in town. (He'd got lucky – Self had a sense of humour. He'd dread to think what some of the other Mothers and Fathers might have done to him.) The Father had spotted some potential there, in his ability to become someone else for a time (and of course to bullshit like the pro he was), and had recruited him directly.

He'd taken the name Little Brother Porsena, after a talking pig he'd seen in some goddamn kids' cartoon one time. (The name had seemed a good idea when he'd claimed it, but maybe he'd been drunk). He'd done his training with the other initiates stationed in the Empire, learning the theory (if not the practice) of the Faction's rituals and protocols, the techniques for handling biodata and the right approaches to petitioning the spirits. He'd also trained in combat disciplines, though he'd not had any gift there. As time went by it had become clear that his shadow picked them up a lot quicker than he did.

He'd not been a fast learner – it was obvious he'd never rise above the rank of Cousin – but he was useful and dependable, a footsoldier with his own specialty. He'd trained in impersonation skills under Mother Lavelle, and it hadn't been long before the Mothers and Fathers had him playing minor roles, bit-parts in other agents' scams out in what he'd once thought of as the real world.

He'd been training with the Faction three months, give or take – it was kind of hard to track time in the Empire – when Cousin Antipathy arrived.

He was a huge man, eight feet easy and broad to match, with a big black beard and evil eyes and hands the size of pickup trucks. He was so heavy that the floors of the historic buildings in this shadow-London bowed beneath him, and he somehow gave the impression he was bending space and time his way as well. He looked thirty, thirty-five, but the Little Brother had already learned not to judge by appearances.

Introduced to them as a fellow initiate, it was obvious from the beginning that something about Cousin Antipathy was way out of the ordinary.

First up, Antipathy was already being called "Cousin" when he arrived, though he was training alongside the Little Brothers and Sisters. He had a shadow-bonded weapon, a six-foot razor-edge sword, when all the other initiates were getting by with material armaments. And he was a vicious bastard, with a habit of stomping hard on anyone or anything who got in what he happened to consider was his way. Nobody liked him – a fact in which he seemed to revel – and everyone was scared of him, including (it seemed to his fellow trainees) the Mothers and Fathers themselves.

He used his fists, his heavy feet and even his shadow-sword on any of his so-called peers who angered him. Mostly they just got beaten or cut up some, but at least one Little Brother found himself "brought into closer emulation of the Grandfather", as the Faction euphemistically called it when some poor bastard lost a hand or arm. One time Antipathy had somehow got hold of a chupacabras from the Stacks, a flapping grey-green monstrosity with huge fangs and glowing eyes, and had amused himself for hours just pulling it to pieces. The creature's whistling shrieks of agony gave the other initiates nightmares for weeks. Any other junior Faction member would have been in deep shit with Father Stendec for a stunt like that, but not Cousin Antipathy.

Antipathy was under the protection of just-as-intimidating Godmother Quelch, but that wasn't it. Rumour among the Little Siblings was that the Cousin was a Homeworlder, the first recruit from the Great Houses for a generation, and that this explained the kid-glove treatment. Not all of them bought that, but whatever – Cousin Antipathy was one truly scary mother.

And the room the scary mother had been allocated at the Army and Navy Club in St James' Square – used by the Faction as a billet for its Little Brothers and Sisters in training – was the room right next to Little Brother Porsena's own.

The other initiates tried to get him to spy on Antipathy, but he flat-out refused, on the grounds that he didn't want to be dredged in halves out of the winy Thames. All the same, he couldn't help but be conscious of his heavy-footed neighbour. The chupacabras incident had been... not easily forgettable. He kept an eye out for who was visiting with the Cousin, and sometimes listened in nervously, catching odd snatches of syllable from Antipathy's deep voice as it avalanched through the walls.

Some weeks later, he went to see his patron, Father Self, whose office was a plush suite at the Dorchester. 'I've been having these blackouts,' he told the Father. 'I keep finding I've missed minutes, sometimes hours, here and there. I thought at first one of the guys was taking my time as a stunt – a joke maybe, or could be they needed it for something. I don't think so, though. It only happens when I'm in my room at the Club House.'

'Interesting,' the Father mused, 'but not very. Unusual time effects are as common round here as minuscule particles of dried skin.'

He'd been expecting that. 'Sure,' he said, 'so I checked with the Little Sister in the room the other side of Cousin Antipathy. She's been getting them too. So I started keeping a diary. I've been writing down whenever Antipathy has a visitor, making sure I fill in right away when I hear somebody arrive. And look.' He held up the spiral-bound notebook and showed Self where the pages had been ripped out. 'Happens every time I have a blackout,' he said.

'Go on,' Father Self told him guardedly.

'So, then I got serious. I asked Little Sibling Pinocchio – you know, the cyborg? – to stay with me. Yesterday, when that last page got torn out, Pinocchio's memories, the electronic ones as well as the organic stuff, were gone too. An hour and 22 minutes got wiped from what should've been a full sensory recording.

'What kind of visitor erases all record of themselves, Father?' he'd asked. 'Even in people's memories?'

By now Father Self was looking kind of pale.

Early next morning, two Mothers and two Fathers came to see Cousin Antipathy, along with scary Godmother Quelch. Little Brother Porsena lay on his board bed, listening to the voices coming out of next door. He could only make out fragments of the conversation, but phrases like "time-active powers" were being used a lot, as were "selling us out" and "you arsehole". At one point he heard Quelch's nail-file of a voice screeching how 'we were supposed to have an exclusive arrangement'. It wasn't too long after that the screaming started.

The yells of the Mothers and the Fathers settled down quickly into a panicked chanting, gaining a proper rhythm after a couple of moments. The other noise was a screech, a grinding sound more like an old-time computer modem than anything else. It could have just about come from a human throat, or else from a piano dragged across a stone floor.

He jumped out of bed and ran out into the corridor. Mother Melby was lying outside Antipathy's room, clutching the stump of her wrist and staring down at her severed hand. The Cousin's door was open, and through it he could see Godmother Quelch, her hands joined with those of the remaining Mothers and Fathers, gabbling their way through what he realised was a sawn-off version of one of their best binding rituals. The elders' voices held a note of sheer hysteria.

Cousin Antipathy himself had his mouth wide open – far wider than a human mouth could go – so most of his head was teeth and tongue and wet red space, and he was giving voice to that inhuman howl. He was... he was fading in and out of view, kind of like a photograph developing then undeveloping again, like... no, Porsena didn't know what it was like. Some goddamned special effect was what it was like. Over and over again.

'Holy shit!' he shouted involuntarily, distracting Father Self for just a moment from the chanting. Antipathy's shadow faded into view for just a second and swung its sword-arm at the unfortunate elder, who fell, clutching at his side. The Cousin struck out with all three of his fists (huh?) at the remaining ritualists, felling each one in the same triple stroke.

Cousin Antipathy had closed his mouth (the grating sound continued unabated) and glared at the Little Brother. 'You,' he'd told him savagely, 'are so *fucking dead*, Porsena.'

And with that he finally faded, quite abruptly, like a picture at the cinema when the lights come up. A moment later the weird sound had faded too, and Little Brother Porsena had been left alone with five wounded and mightily pissed-off elders of the Faction.

It had taken a while for him to be back in favour after that.

(...and hey children, you know what? For that kind of a memory to be better than your present, you have to be in one bad world of trouble.)

He was just fine though, sitting tight here at the back of his head.

He settled back, waiting to see what he would remember next.

68. Dedalus, Kempes.

It was still raining and Dedalus was still pissed off he was pissed off with bloody Kempes District he was pissed off with the decurion and Centurion Tyrannosaurus and Consul Ignotus he was pissed off with Sosimus and the lads and he was most pissed off of all with the pre historic carnivores what they was having to transport back to camp in great big cages on the trams it was Dedalus what had done all the work loading them up theyd put the devil boars in i tram the hyena beasts in ii more and the false sabre tooths in another.

The female false sabre tooth was pregnant she was long as ii men with stripes and vicious teeth she scratched him on the arm with her great claws and he had iii long gashes what was paining him Why the fucks it me has to do all the work he asked Sosimus and Sos said Cos Dedalus me old china your the biggest and the ugliest of us all and the best protected Best protected Dedalus asked what dyou mean and Sos said I mean mate out of all of us you got the thickest hide and the most offensive butt Thats true said Dedalus and all the lads laughed then Dedalus saw Sos was taking the piss and decked him Albus said Hey hey mate he didnt mean nothing by it the lad looked shit scared and Dedalus liked the lad so stead of goring him he went and sat in i of the trams and sulked.

When they got back he went to talk to the decurion who looked sarcastic at him and said Well lad well just have to see you get mentioned in despatches wont we Dear Consul Ignotus Legionry Dedalus was nobly wounded in the line of duty tragicly scratched while handling an inraged pussy the lads all laughed at that and Dedalus was pissed off even more.

The decurion said Now go and unload those animals my lad there to go straight onto the Tube chain to the Romuline there gonna have a day out at the Arena aint they they lucky ones and then he buggered off sharpish and Dedalus stomped off to do what he said he hoped i of the animals would act up so he could butt it till it didnt move no more and bugger getting them out of Kempes alive and in tact.

Sosimus came to help Sorry about the misunderstanding me old mucker he said Fuck off Dedalus said and Sos went quiet and they set to getting out the devil boars what were evil bastards and smelt like a jockstrap in a meatlocker and just as Dedalus was pushing the last i grunting and farting onto the chain it bit his hand he shouted Shit and the boar kicked him in the balls and turned round and stuck its tusks right into Sosimuses belly and chucked him xx feet and kicked Dedalus again then ran off making trouble round the camp.

Dedalus went over to Sos he said Shit you all right mate and Sos said Course I fucking aint all right Buttercup Im bloody dying you great twat and then he did.

That night the signifers came for Dedalus they said hed done for Sosimus himself with his horns and let the devil boar out to cover it up they said Albus and all the other lads said thered been an argument and Dedalus had a wicked temper the signifers said Dedalus was a filthy murdering clatteral and there werent no place for him in Consul Ignotuses army and he didnt deserve to live when men like Sosimus was dead then the decurion told Dedalus he was going to the Arena too.

They chained him up and loaded him on the next chain out so at least he got away from Kempes which was something.

69. Urbanus, the Epicentre.

'It's the sheer squalor I find unpleasant,' said Dr. Clutterbuck, tapping her half-moon spectacles against her teeth as the students present shifted their feet uncomfortably. 'How can people live like this?'

The Epicentre was the dirtiest place Urbanus had ever been, including Gnas' headquarters, the northern end of Kempes and (in his own student days) a number of the Romuline's own less-than-pristine precincts. Here in the vicinity of the Manfold docks, the walls and buildings, and he might have been prepared to swear the air itself, were smeared with a patina of grease and thick black dust, which now clung just as assiduously to the skins and clothing of Clutterbuck's volunteers. Additionally, Urbanus' itchy combat fatigues had recently acquired a livid streak of bird's mess all the way down their front. The entire area was so caked with rubbish it was well along the way to becoming a landfill site; in Urbanus' view, the best way to make it habitable would be to finish the process, pour in concrete and build a housing estate on top of it.

Clutterbuck seemed to take the grime around her personally, giving the impression (an erroneous one, he was very nearly certain) of being more distressed by it than by the return of violence to the City. One of the older Manfolk, an academic whose name Urbanus had not been able to catch, said, 'We know already there's a different set of physical laws in operation in the Epicentre, Melicia. Perhaps entropy increases more quickly here. It may be virtually impossible to keep order.'

Clutterbuck sniffed and said, 'A little elbow grease is all it takes.'

Leaving the bulk of her force outside, Dr. Clutterbuck had used the elderly but functional anti-gravity harnesses to raise herself, Urbanus and five others onto the roof of a decrepit office block on the fringes of the no longer abandoned industrial complex; from here they had lowered themselves through caved-in skylights into an attic area, seemingly in use now as a dormitory. Thankfully it was empty at present, suggesting either that the occupying forces had more than one sleeping-place or that they did not believe in operating a shift system.

Despite the generous ventilation provided by the shattered skylights, the attic stank of stale sweat and urine: a pungently male smell, distilled and amplified. Floors and mattresses alike were liberally spattered with discarded underwear, mouldering drinks-mugs, the putrefying remnants of meals, and assorted miscellaneous stains which Urbanus wished particularly keenly to ignore but found he could not help thinking about nonetheless. Numerous rats had scurried out of sight when the volunteers had arrived, and now hid chittering in shadowed corners.

Clutterbuck divided her task force into three pairs: as the extraneous civilian in the party Urbanus was to accompany Yspe and herself. 'Remember now,' she admonished them, 'we're here for reconnaissance only. Look but don't touch, unless somebody sees us. If someone shoots at you, blow them away. Otherwise, let's pretend to be little mice, shall we?'

The three groups left the reeking dormitory, whereupon Urbanus followed Clutterbuck's slight figure and Yspe's massive one along dank, shabby corridors, whose worst smells were mercifully those of damp and rot. Everywhere the floor was smothered with debris, the more obvious litter frequently serving to conceal heavy pieces of rubble on which toes could be helpfully stubbed while kicking it out of the way. It was oppressively humid, and Urbanus' fatigues were quickly drenched with sweat.

It had not escaped his notice that Dr. Clutterbuck, a strategist above all else if her followers were to be believed, had left fourteen able-bodied and fiercely-armed troops outside the building, while six of them (seven, had Urbanus been sufficiently immodest to count himself) crept about inside. Reconnaissance expedition this might be, for now; but he had a firm suspicion that the academic was expecting to be organising a rescue at short notice.

The obvious conclusion, that Clutterbuck expected to find prisoners at least, if not the resurrected dead, within the Epicentre, set the young man to wondering what, precisely, he was doing here; and what he would say to Tiresias were they to find the old hermaphrodite miraculously alive. Urbanus had joined the expedition in haste, concerned that it would leave without him; now he was here, in theoretical (if not, so far, apparent) danger of his own death, he was not entirely sure his motives would stand up to rigorous scrutiny. While City law entitled a slave to leave his servitude at any time (provided he also vacate the District of his owners), the Ignotian family's patronal obligations to Tiresias had quite definitely lapsed the moment the old tutor had deserted him, without apparent qualms, in Kempes.

In addition, Urbanus had now been given sufficient time to reflect on the strange coincidence that Tiresias not only belonged to an enclave to which Cassius Ignotus was implacably opposed, but also had never once mentioned this fact to anybody at the Villa Ignota: behaviour which, trusting as he was, the young man could not help but observe had certain suspicious aspects.

As well as being predictably filthy, the corridors through which they were now passing were contorted and confusing; possibly following, so Clutterbuck claimed, a geometry not bounded by conventional physical space (although this suggestion might simply have arisen from her pique at finding herself unable to map it as planned). It was not entirely clear therefore, when the trio emerged at length onto a landing above a lobby area, whether they were in the same office block or some altogether different part of the Epicentre.

What was apparent, from the briefest glance at the space below, was that the more lurid rumours concerning the Epicentre had been correct in all particulars. The lobby was crowded, mostly with Manfolk but also with a small number of Citizens. There was an evident division between them, not organised exclusively along species lines: a number of the young, male Manfolk were clothed and unchained, while the rest (young and old, men and women, Manfolk and Citizens) were naked, and secured to walls or furniture or pillars.

As advertised, pain was being inflicted. The forms this took were not, by certain of the standards Urbanus had read about, imaginative ones: it was also noticeable that none of the persecutions taking place was (if he was any judge) of such a nature as to threaten the inflictees' lives. The leather-clad custodians appeared nonetheless to be taking great pleasure in their various diversions.

One girl was being vigorously whipped by two men, using stripped electric cable; she had been gagged as well as chained, so as to prevent her from crying out. Her golden skin was covered in red weals, some of them partially healed.

One Manfolk woman, was being systematically burned across each of the many inches of her bulging body: the older scars were slowly healing, raw and red, but the new ones blackened and oozed pus. One of the guards was presently using a brazier to heat a flat-iron, in order to mark her once again.

One man, a dark-skinned Citizen, was being raped. Urbanus could identify the crime, of whose existence he had previously possessed only a tenuous conception, because of the words the man was screaming at his rapist, and because his wrists and ankles were sustaining bleeding wounds in the course of his struggles to liberate himself from his chains.

One old man, no, a hermaphrodite, was being... oh. Oh Civitata, no. Oh no. Oh Father Dis...

'Pull back!' hissed Clutterbuck sharply from behind him; and, despite his own violent struggles in the direction of the lobby stairs and of Tiresias and his violator, Urbanus, dragged by Yspe's strong hands on his upper arms, had no choice but to comply.

70. The City.

The gathering at View Point is beginning to quicken. As yet relatively few guests have arrived, a scant few hundred, but already the atmosphere is warm, the conversation convivial. A metal gateway, a rectangular arch proportioned pleasingly to the golden mean, has been set up to act as the arbitrary welcoming point, and Allisheer St Marx and Handramit are there, greeting their guests. Behind them, disguised partygoers are spread in knots across the open pavement to the parapet.

Through every ear and eye I watch and listen, feel through every skin as they sip at their drinks and graze the buffet, the music of the orchestra (a Copland suite, inspired by Neanderthal folk chants) sustaining their conversation. Many are using the handheld telescopic units St Marx has hired, to play with the refractive index of the air, zooming in a portion of the view to focus on some landmark of the twilight City. One group watches a yacht race which is coming to a finish thirty billion miles away, its week-long circumnavigation of Pelago District at an end. Another man, standing alone, gazes intently into the void framed by the North Gate, just to prove it can be done.

Each guest is masked, except those few who have some overriding cultural or personal reason not to be. Professor Fisher's specimen is carved in wood, and represents a nature spirit, or possibly some vegetable alien. He toys with it absently, having no intention of donning it, and watches with baleful tenderness as Allisheer welcomes some tedious academic and her gaggle of dwarfish husbands. Behind him is the low but sturdy parapet, which makes him feel a lot less anxious regarding the half-a-trillion feet of drop beyond. The human mind is not, inherently, a thing of logic; a fact borne home to the Professor as he reflects how probably he will, in time, forgive his wife her indiscretion.

All thoughts of murder have fled from his mind for now.

Close by one of the buffet tables stands Cllr. Mesh Cos. She wears a treble-visaged mask depicting her own face at three stages of life, two of which she has yet to reach. She has been percolating through the crowd, seeking out allies, rivals, friends, making appropriate syllables and gestures in their various directions, her attention elsewhere. She has an inkling of what's on its way, what even now rises towards View Point in a lift capsule, and her mind is busily assembling all the information which she has available into a coherent, if unsightly, shape.

Now Mesh and her pretty cyclopean escort are conversing with Cllr. Techotlala and a representative of Cllr. Angstrom Hive. The Aztec Councillor wears a splendid gold sun, while their colleague's mouthpiece has a mask as blank and smooth as his own personality: this diplomat-class unit is an empty vessel through whom the posthuman Hive experiences and acts. Like Mesh Cos, Angstrom Hive has been gathering intelligence / rumour / data, and its million processor minds have identified which way the unquiet wind is blowing. It has its own eyes scattered across the City – espionage units, engine-bred to mimic other human species. At this very event the Councillor's acknowledged representatives are augmented by seven covert agents. In Kempes it perceives developments through both a legionary and a web-footed cleaning-lady whom the troops have retained: it lives through an apparently *Homo habilis* porter at the Villa Ignota, and a pug-faced schoolboy in the lift below. The Hive is well aware by now that all its Mayoral aspirations are in tatters, and its processors ruminate upon its future actions.

Of all my human children, the hive-minds are perhaps my favourites: their modes of consciousness come closest to my own. My eyes likewise look out through all these masks; on other faces, figures, persons who are also of my body. As I flit from mind to mind among these gathered intellects, I experience the same events from myriad viewpoints:

as Mother Vittoria Cellini the Papal Nuncia, masked in the classical Venetian style, who is conversing peevishly with the University's Yezidic Chaplain;

as a late iteration of "The Prof", a relatively sane scientist before his long cycle of journeys through the remembrance tanks, who wears a badly-photocopied face of Einstein sticking his tongue out;

as Scholar Emblem Matchmark, masked as appropriate for one of her profession and caste, and grateful that her colleagues have set aside for once their habitual embarrassing facial nudity;

as both the Rev. Charles Dodgson and his alter ego Lewis Carroll, who have been estranged for years now but have come together briefly to exchange some awkward words;

as Polycrates, the Dean of Aelfred's parrot, who is discussing zoolinguistics with Dr. Konrad Lorenz but hopes soon to steer the conversation around to the topic of crackers;

as one of a corniche of troglodytes up from the underworld, wearing what look a lot like welding masks to protect their sensitive eyes from the strong skylight;

as Krisztina-Judit Németh, agent of the Sons of Tepes crime cartel, who glares hungrily behind her spider-mask at the impenetrable throats of her plump fellow-Citizens.

Above all this I soar as Ajiel Soto:Carm the camerabot, holoed up to resemble a gold-feathered raptor. The robot is profoundly bored: the politicos are hedging their bets, saying nothing of interest, and footage of academics getting ethanol-

downgrades will never gain it airtime, except possibly on the Sad Old Farts Channel.

In just a short time now, Soto:Carm will have achieved the scoop of its working lifetime, earning it a primetime slot on every major newsfeed. For now, it is considering blowing the whole thing off and finding a game somewhere.

As Alan Turing, Head of Mathematics at the Al-Battani Institute, I wear a plain white papier-maché mask, inscribed with brightly coloured logic symbols. Alan is expounding shyly to a group of fellow mathematicians on the definition of humanity considered as a problem in set theory. 'It's all a question of identifying appropriate boundaries,' he tells his listeners. A researcher named Sejwyk, recently returned from ULW's Astrological Institute in RealSpace, makes a perceptive remark and Turing warms to him. Seems like a nice enough chap, Alan thinks, gazing at Sejwyk speculatively...

...whilst inside Persval Sejwyk, I suffer the embarrassment of K~, the artificial intelligence who has inhabited his mind for centuries. K~ shifts uncomfortably under the eminent cryptanalyst's appraisal, and recalls its ultimately unsuccessful plan to escape the AI pogroms through a hostile download into Sejwyk's skull. Recreated on Resurrection Morn along with its host, K~ has found in the City a rewarding career, a comfortable house and a loving girlfriend: only Sejwyk's deranged remnant, battering at the walls of its placid memescape, reminds it constantly that this is not its Paradise.

This evening some bizarre lapse has induced K~ to wear the clunky mask of a classic sci-fi robot. Although it has no inkling of the Universal Machine's existence, it happens that the interloper has now reached # 894 on UniMac's "To Do" list.

The party continues to swell, as new arrivals file past Allisheer St Marx (Handramit has understandably excused himself for a spell). Allisheer bends to welcome the rotund, hirsute figure of W. T. P. Saunders, the respected remake poet. Her concerns about her husband and her infidelity have been banished to the outer reaches of her mind (where they fizz and spark), and she has turned the greater portion of her consciousness over to hostly duties.

The Councillor herself wears the face of a satyr; or rather a satyress, a hybrid not familiar from the classical bestiary but whose existence might logically be demanded. Frozen ringlets of papier-maché blonde cascade down the sphinx-like face beneath its ewe's horns: the full lips sit above a tuft of golden beard. Underneath the golden ram's-skin Allisheer's body glints and shimmers, like the glimpses of mirror through the eye-holes of her mask. She greets the Vice-Chancellor and his husband, directing them towards the nibbles.

Near to the arbitrary entrance, one of View Point's ubiquitous elevator shafts gapes open and disgorges a lift capsule. Still more of them, Allisheer absently expects, as the wide doors slide aside and reveal those who stand within.

71. Fisher, View Point.

Professor Fisher was by nature and by habit a solitary man, yet his aversion to large gatherings stemmed less from misanthropy than from a necessary reluctance to be seen by too large a concentration of people. Masked balls tested his patience, however. He found them both affected and pretentious, symptomatic of that strain of romantic decadence which was so inextricably woven into the culture of the City. They were a favourite with Allisheer even so, and for her sake he tolerated them – perversely, so long as nobody insisted that he mask himself. A mask would have served to conceal his countenance and allowed him to pass unnoticed, but he stubbornly considered the public face he turned towards the City to be mask enough. (And, if it was mere discomfort his fellows required of him, his ill-tied cummerbund was perfectly adequate for that.)

He leaned against the parapet with Prof. Handramit, who had absented himself from the reception line for long enough to beseech of Fisher a sustaining infusion of tobacco. The Great House émigré was also unmasked: Fisher imagined that he felt he had nothing to hide. Fisher liked Handramit, both despite and because of the man's closeness to Allisheer, and he was flattered and somewhat surprised that their visitor had sought him out. The two Professors gazed down over the balustrade into the staggering vertiginous depths, occasionally discarding ash that would freeze and blow away as dust long before it reached the ground.

He looked up and saw Handramit regarding him gravely and quietly. He said without preamble: 'Allisheer has told you, hasn't she?'

The exile said: 'We talked. She feels she's made some mistakes recently.'

'I wish she'd speak to me about them.' He knew he sounded petulant, which was unfair. He was well aware of how his wife confided in her former mentor.

'I'm sure she will. She's lucky to have you, Anthony.'

Fisher coloured. 'I believe so, under the circumstances,' he said stiffly.

Handramit gazed at his cigar in rueful fascination. 'These things are banned back home, you know. Too harmful to humans. I have to get mine on the black market.' He knocked off some more ash, and frowned. 'Another centimetre and I'd better be getting back.'

A murmur had begun to circulate across the crowd – partly amusement, partly something more uneasy. Fisher turned around to look, expecting some celebrity academic to be making a grand entrance. His knees bowed and, though intensely aware of the drop behind him, he found he had no choice but to sit heavily on the parapet.

'Oh. Are they invited?' Handramit murmured, gazing past the figure of the woman they both loved to the newcomers beyond.

Decidedly they were not, not a man of them – except for Cassius Ignotus (who had been sent an invitation but had responded in a polite, predictable negative) and the Tobin woman (whom Prof. Fisher had added to the guest list just that afternoon).

'There's an army of them,' he said weakly, although his practised eye admonished him that they were a mere century. So, Tobin was working with the Ignotians. He realised belatedly that this would account quite satisfactorily for her interest in him and his family. How resourceful of her, to pretend she was investigating Mostyn's death.

The security guards were converging on the armoured gatecrashers, but some demonstration of authority on Ignotus' part persuaded them to stand aside and allow him to approach Allisheer. Blazing, she began to remonstrate in a voice which cut across the gathered company. Already her Houseworld mentor had left the parapet and was loping catlike towards the newcomers.

Prof. Fisher knew his wife and guest were in no danger: the Romuline Councillor wanted him. He followed Handramit at his fleetest hobble; stumbling through confused guests, apologising as he pushed Professor Vril to one side. He caught Mesh Cos' eye, perceived and understood her warning gaze, but grimly he pressed on. When he reached the metal archway, Laura Tobin was standing awkwardly by as Ignotus confronted Allisheer. Handramit was being forcibly restrained by four strong legionaries, wincing as tough fingers gripped susceptible flesh. 'Let him go at once!' Fisher demand imperiously; or so he intended, but his stammer let him down again and he sounded ridiculous.

Ignotus turned away from Allisheer, and told him: 'He'll be let go in Ascension. My men have orders to expel him from the City.'

Prof. Fisher spluttered. 'But he's our honoured guest! The guest of the University!'

'Believe me,' Ignotus grimly asserted, 'the alien will be better off outside the Uptime Gate.'

Icily, Allisheer said: 'I hope you have a very good reason for this, Ignotus.'

The patrician smiled thinly. 'I have indeed, St Marx. Shall we continue this unseemly display by discussing it here, or shall we retire to one of the private rooms beneath us?'

Allisheer glared, then addressed the nearest security guard. 'Go with them,' she said, indicating Handramit's escort. 'Take some men of your own. Make sure he reaches Ascension unharmed.' She span on a cloven boot, and led the way towards an opening in the flagstones, whence a flight of steps led down into the Watchtower. A nod from Ignotus, and a pair of soldiers broke ranks and followed her. With some signs of reluctance, Tobin went the same way.

Ignotus met Fisher's eye and gestured at the hatchway; and the Professor followed also, shrugging apologetically at Handramit. The disgraced guest of honour, resigned now rather than struggling, gave him an ironic farewell wave. He descended the stairs.

This then, he thought – this confined space into which Ignotus led him, where Allisheer paced, furious still, and Laura Tobin stood, arms folded defensively – was where it would all end. Tobin would reveal what she had discovered, and Prof. Fisher's career – perhaps his life, like that poor devil Mostyn's – would be over. There was no chance now of avoiding Fate: he would greet it manfully, like the old friend it was.

He was profoundly irritated when, instead of this, Tobin started pontificating about Ved Mostyn's murder.

72. Tobin, View Point.

Tobin cleared her throat, feeling thoroughly self-conscious. The faces of the others – Fisher, Ignotus, St Marx – regarded her expectantly.

The four of them were seated round a boardroom table, made from a single polished slice of redwood trunk, which filled the centre of the room. Around them ten Romuline legionaries stood, backs to the walls, machine-guns shouldered watchfully. Ignotus' bodyguards stood behind the seat their Councillor had unhesitatingly assumed at the head of the table, opposite the double doors. Behind him was a picture window, which gave forth on a view as featureless as that seen from upstairs.

To Ignotus' left around the table's circumference Tobin sat, with Fisher and St Marx reluctantly seated opposite her. Indifferently she wondered if the academics were clasping hands under the table, or if each was facing this alone.

'Is there anybody else you'd like to be present, Citizen Tobin?' Ignotus asked her politely. 'Cllr Mesh perhaps?'

'No thanks,' said Tobin shortly. 'The three of you are all I need.' She flicked an nervous glance at the Romuline soldiers, but none of them seemed affronted at their exclusion.

The academics had discarded their masks, which lay in front of them on the ruddy tabletop. The blank eye-sockets of the goat-woman and the tree-spirit reminded Tobin of Godfather Avatar, as they stared up at her in accusation. She forced herself to look up at their owners instead – into Fisher's no less hostile eyes, and the equally blank circles of St Marx's skyglasses.

Tobin's conceptual descendants would have aimed for melodrama at this point, stringing things out. The Murderer Unmasked. One of us here, in this very room... well, sod that.

'It was you,' she told Allisheer St Marx. 'You stabbed Ved Mostyn with a potent dagger during one of your sex sessions, and you killed him.'

'Yes,' St Marx agreed sadly. 'It was a terrible thing.' Fisher looked stricken. Cassius Ignotus allowed his mouth the tiniest satisfied twitch, at once erased by his habitual solemnity.

'All the basic facts about the murder are public domain,' Tobin went on, unnecessarily firmly. 'Or might as well be for all the security the CHAS have in place. Obviously Cllr. St Marx is familiar with them, and I imagine both of you have also made it your business to find out. Beyond that, all I've had to go on are the hints Godfather Avatar kept dropping before he died.

St Marx's eyebrows rocketed. 'Godfather Avatar's dead?'

Smoothly Ignotus said, 'Let us not concern ourselves with that for the moment. Go on, Citizen.'

'Avatar kept insisting Mostyn was a Citizen,' Tobin continued, 'even though that had to mean the murderer had used a potent weapon. "The late Councillor was one of us," he told me. He also seemed unusually certain that you and Mostyn were having sex together. How could he possibly have known that?'

'Perhaps he was bugging us,' the archemathicist suggested coolly, 'while we were together.' Next to her, Prof. Fisher drooped visibly.

'Maybe,' said Tobin, 'but the CHAS didn't find any surveillance devices in Mostyn's office, or his quarters. Then there was the fact that Mostyn didn't even exist, according to the historical records. Plus the question of how someone as repulsive as him could have persuaded a woman like you to go to bed with him, not just once but repeatedly. I can't imagine you were after his money.'

St Marx's index finger had found a skein of golden wool to twist. 'He was very sweet,' she muttered doubtfully.

'Rubbish,' Tobin averred. 'Somehow he was able to make you see him differently from the sleazy pervert he was. He wasn't who he pretended to be, and I don't think even his political affiliations were real. He was a hopeless ally – his sex scandals were putting your whole campaign in jeopardy.'

Ignotus nodded in regretful agreement, making Tobin want to smack him. She pressed on regardless. 'Mostyn was assuming an identity – multiple identities even – that weren't his own. And Avatar knew far too much about him. Put the two together, and it's obvious what was going on. Mostyn was an undercover agent for the Rump Parliament. A Cousin, perhaps even a Father.'

St Marx's eyes widened. Apparently this part of the story came as news to her.

'They must have designed his false identity deliberately to bring your coalition into disrepute,' Tobin went on. 'Why, I don't know, but that's the sort of thing the Parliament does. They put identities on and take them off like skull-masks. Mr. This becomes Cousin That and then starts channelling loa The Other. They change their whole personas at a whim, and try to make everyone else do the same. It's how the Faction's always done things.'

Ignotus was nodding. 'It's typical of their arrogance,' he said. 'They act through deception and pretence, never coming out of the shadows. The day will come when they are forced to face the gods, naked of all their masks.'

'I believe Citizen Tobin has the floor, Ignotus,' St Marx reminded him acidly.

'He was using a biodata ritual to... entice you,' Tobin told her. 'I think the word they use is "fascination".'

73. St Marx, View Point.

Opposite her, Tobin continued inexorably. 'Once that started, I don't think it would have taken "Mostyn" long to realise there was something different about you.'

The satyress mask lay before her on the table. Beneath the grainy slab, her hand held tight to Anthony's limp fingers.

'His life in the City may have been an elaborate act, but it was one he lived to the full. His preference for collateral women was well-known, I'm told.'

The resignation mounting in her breast was mingled with a strange elation. Across the glossy wooden surface the detective talked on, a scowl smeared across her freckled face.

'Plus of course he had access to your biodata, or he couldn't have performed the fascination ritual. Once you'd had sex, he had more intimate access still.'

Tobin's hair was a tangled mass of copper wire, a schoolroom electromagnet torn to savage shreds. Ignotus' face was set, unsmiling, concealing his real feelings from the world. Anthony's was a picture of misery, his despondency radiating from him, but even so it had become tinged with puzzlement at Tobin's words. He wouldn't meet her eye, but still he hadn't taken his unresponsive hand away from hers.

'I didn't understand it all,' Tobin told her, 'until I remembered that your visitor was from the Houseworld.'

Quietly, she corrected the detective. 'Originally from the Houseworld. Handramit had to leave when he was very young. He's a naturalised subject of the Onesian Emirate.'

'Whatever,' Tobin persisted. 'It's why you're such a gifted archemathicist. Archemathics is a Houseworld discipline, isn't it? Houseworlders have a natural aptitude. It's why you and Prof. Handramit have such a strong rapport... and why the weapon the Houses sent after him killed you. It was keyed to his genetic data, wasn't it?'

'Yes,' she said calmly, 'it was.'

And that was it: her life's (death's) secret, casually, offhandedly exposed. Her humanity whisked away like a magician's tablecloth, revealing what she was beneath.

Anthony was looking at her now. His mouth hung open like a deep-sea anglerfish.

She removed her glasses and matched Tobin's gaze. 'I may have had to hide it,' she said, 'but I'm not ashamed.'

Her nature, naked as her light-streamed body, just as glorious.

***

When she was very little, Allie's mummy told her about being different, and the reasons why.

You must never, she said, *not ever tell people who your daddy is. He came here from another world, a world where the people like him didn't want him. He's different from everyone else, and so you will be too. You mustn't tell, or people will be afraid of you. They might send you away from Onesia like the Homeworld sent away your daddy.*

Though no one ever said, not even her mummy, Allie knew who her daddy was. Of course she did. The man who came to visit them on special days, the old man with the great white beard and shiny black eyes, like Santa Claus or Leonardo da Vinci, that was her daddy.

She didn't need to be told. It was just there inside her head, as clear as the warm murmur of his voice when they were silent.

Allie derived her first archemathical theorem when she was eight. In her teens she could construct complex universes out of calculations that would have taxed the most advanced AIs. She was just as good with languages, and mechanical things. She could fix anything that went wrong in the house by the age of twelve. By the time she began formally studying under her father, Allisheer was already a thrice-published poet.

When you grow up, her daddy had told little Allie, this time talking through his mouth like ordinary people, *you'll come to work with me at the Seminary. We'll be together, then. And with your talents, you'll be my star pupil.*

And so she had been.

74. Tobin, View Point.

St Marx's midnight eyes were flecked with silver. They were strangely calm: in fact her whole countenance was untroubled, triumphant even. Still, now her guess had been confirmed, Tobin felt grim satisfaction for a moment.

'I didn't know... you didn't tell me,' Prof. Fisher gasped, shock evidently freeing up his tongue. 'You didn't tell me, Allisheer. I thought we had no secrets from one another.' Which, Tobin thought, was a pretty damn stupid thing to say under the circumstances.

'I'm sorry, Anthony,' St Marx told him gently. 'Truly I am. There was too much at stake.'

'Indeed,' Cllr. Ignotus said drily. 'Legally, as a half-caste collateral, you aren't even human. You require special dispensation from your Resident or Councillor to hold an academic post. That Councillor is no longer yourself, of course, because in Base and Buttress District you aren't entitled to vote, let alone hold political office. As for the Mayoralty...'

St Marx cut quietly through his litany. 'I'm well aware of all this, Ignotus,' she said.

It seemed Prof. Fisher hadn't been listening. 'I told you everything about myself,' he stammered petulantly.

'Ah, yes,' Ignotus said. 'I'd been hoping we'd come to that.'

'Well, it can bloody wait,' snapped Tobin.

Ignotus turned to her, his face set like a stone. 'I beg your pardon, Citizen?' he asked.

'I don't give a toss about your politics,' she asserted fiercely. 'I'm not doing this for you. I'm doing it because I was retained by Godfather Avatar to find out who killed Ved Mostyn – whoever he was. That's the job I've been contracted to do, and I'm doing it for... the money Avatar paid me. Once I'm finished you can do what you like, that's not my concern. Until then, you can shut up and listen.'

A pause, then Ignotus' face showed every sign of relaxing into flinty amusement. He waved a hand magnanimously, and said, 'Oh, very well.'

Tobin took a deep breath. 'Obviously,' she told St Marx, 'for all the reasons Cllr. Ignotus just mentioned, you couldn't afford to let this become widely known. I don't know how you found out Mostyn knew it. Perhaps he tried to blackmail you so you'd follow his real political agenda.'

The archemathicist gazed placidly at her. 'Perhaps.'

'You had connections in Manfold,' Tobin continued. 'Spies, basically. When the Manfolk developed potent weapons, you would have been one of the first to know. You knew you had to get rid of Mostyn, permanently – what he knew could never get out. I expect you thought you were acting for the good of the City. You politicians always do,' she added pointedly.

'You must have sent directly for the weapon, maybe via an ex-student. You wouldn't use your usual channels. I expect you had it sent to Mostyn directly, a gift from an admirer, so it would look like you had nothing to do with it.

'You thought, when the CHAS found a potent weapon in Mostyn's collection, it would look like suicide, or an accident... at worst, like murder by some outside power, with Mostyn's lover its unwitting instrument. Even if that lover was identified as you – which might never have happened without Mostyn's connection to Avatar – there would have been too many doubtful factors to convict you. And everyone in Council House would have been busy panicking about the weapon itself.'

'But no such weapon was found,' Fisher blustered. He'd obviously done some research of his own, but what he thought he'd gain his wife by arguing at this point, Tobin couldn't imagine. 'All the knives found in Mostyn's... bedroom... place were normal. He can't have been a Citizen. There isn't a shred of proof of any of this. Godfather Avatar was deceiving you.'

'The knife wasn't found, no,' Tobin readily agreed. 'That's basically because the CHAS are crap. I hope your men will make improvements, Cllr. Ignotus. They let Cllr. Mesh see the murder scene before they'd made a proper inventory, and they're so hopelessly out of practice that they failed to notice her appropriating the murder weapon. Whatever, your plan backfired. No potent weapon was found, and most people have been assuming Mostyn was a Houseworld agent.'

She paused, and Ignotus leaned in once more to pontificate. 'Whereas it now appears,' he said, 'that the Houseworld agent was someone else entirely. It was remarkably fortuitous, St Marx, that these potent weapons appeared in the City at the very time you found yourself in need of them. And hidden away in a secessionist enclave, no less. Yes,' he mused, 'this does look most unfortunate – for you, for your allies, and in particular for Manfold.

'Oh – I'm sorry, Citizen Tobin,' he added indulgently. 'Was there anything further?'

Tobin didn't have to do it, but she forced herself. She looked into the mute gaze of former-Councillor Allisheer St Marx. Those mirror-flecked eyes were neither resigned nor angry, accusing nor forgiving. They were, she endeavoured to persuade herself, barely human at all.

She sighed. 'No,' she said. 'That was everything.'

75. Fisher, View Point.

Professor Fisher's mind was a maelstrom of colliding and conflicting ideas and emotions. They slewed and overlapped within his brain, throwing into disarray his lifetime's habit of sedate internal eloquence.

(She really slept with him, he thought, she really did. Many times over. She betrayed me, just like all the others.)

(What would she have done when the authorities discovered the weapon was of Manfolk manufacture? Would she really have let the whole of Manfold go down, just to save her skin?)

(It's not her fault, he thought. That filthy beast Mostyn was manipulating her.)

(She isn't even human. She's an alien, different from us. Houseworlders don't even feel the same emotions we do.)

(And, being the man he was, the thought he thought most often was: I love her. I forgive her. Please don't take her away from me.)

Then Cassius Ignotus spoke, and Fisher remembered those concerns which had been on the verge of overwhelming him before Tobin had begun expounding upon Mostyn's demise.

'By the authority I hold as a member of the City Council of the City of the Saved,' he distantly heard the Romuline Councillor saying, 'I am placing you, Allisheer St Marx, under arrest.' From somewhere the legionaries had pressed into service a camerabot, a small discoid drone which hovered above the redwood table, documenting this unprecedented event. 'The primary charge will be the premeditated murder of a Citizen – specifically Councillor Vedular Mostyn – by means of potent weaponry.'

To Fisher it sounded as if the whole City had gasped around them: the collective inhalations of the Citizens above at Watch Point coalesced with those from floor upon floor of the Watchtower below. The robot must be broadcasting live on every major news channel. Slowly, as if all the air in a balloon were gradually released, a babble of voices rose up from all around, muffled but overwhelming. It died into an anticipatory hush as Ignotus continued: 'To this is added colluding with an extra-mural power, specifically the Great Houses; acting as a City official under false pretences; infringement of the Collaterals (Citizenship) Act of AF 12 and the Potent Weapons (Development) Act of 265. I will assume that you are fully aware of your rights.'

Mutely, Allisheer nodded. The two legionaries who stood behind her took her formally now by the upper arms. Beneath the room and above, the civil hubbub once again began to gain intensity.

'There is one other, lesser charge,' Ignotus went on. He directed a steely glance towards Prof. Fisher, who found himself sincerely admiring the man's ability to work an audience: he must have just prevented viewers from switching off in droves to discuss the shocking news amongst themselves. 'An offence under the law of the Romuline District, of comforting and succouring a traitor to the Republic of Rome.'

'Oh, Cassius,' said Allisheer (and he was moved to see that she was spurred to speech on his behalf if not her own). 'Surely you don't need to do that? I promise I'll cooperate.'

Frowning, and either unaware of or indifferent to her presence on a live media feed, Laura Tobin said, 'What?' To Fisher's resigned surprise, the detective's scowl was thoroughly bewildered.

'He's referring to me, Ms. Tobin,' he explained, with all the dignity his stammer would allow. With difficulty, he stood and faced Cassius Ignotus. He said: 'If you are arresting me, Ignotus, please proceed.'

The Romuline patrician was unsmiling still, but his eyes held a marbled glint. He declared: 'It is my duty and my privilege, as Senator and Consul of the Romuline District, to arrest you, Tiberius Claudius Drusus Nero Germanicus, called Claudius Caesar and falsely known as Emperor Claudius I of Rome. In pretending to the title of Emperor, you have been guilty of tyranny, and of the most base treachery to the Roman Republic. Justice for the crimes of your first life has been too long delayed.'

Tobin was visibly astonished: under this name, cumbersome though it might be, even she had heard of him. He asked Ignotus: 'What of my successors? And my predecessors, come to that?'

Ignotus' lips tightened. 'Don't worry. Their turn will come.'

Well, he reflected, that at least was something. His relatives deserved the worst Ignotus and his allies could devise for them. He asked: 'How long have you known?'

'Oh, for decades now, Caesar. You didn't think you could teach history, of all things, without some of your students noticing? We've simply been awaiting a favourable opportunity.'

'And this is such an opportunity?' He spoke for the benefit of the floating drone, and of its myriad audience: already he was all too chillingly aware of the answer.

Ignotus smiled now: an entirely cosmetic blend of wistfulness and regret. 'I'm afraid so, Caesar.'

Claudius nodded gravely, and gazed into the camerabot's bright lens. His stammer spared him as soberly he told the City: 'Then may our many gods have mercy on us all.'

76. Tobin, View Point.

Tobin shook her head in disbelief as the legionaries marched Allisheer St Marx up the stairs, Prof. Fisher – Emperor Claudius – hobbling after them with his own muscular escort. Ignotus followed with his bodyguards.

Tobin made damn sure the camerabot preceded her: she had no wish to form part of the Councillor's triumphant media procession. In fact, she realised as the last legionary began the ascent, she didn't have to follow them at all. She slid open one of the room's double doors, and stepped out into a wide corridor on the top floor of the Watchtower. Half a kilometre along the carpeted highway she found a stairwell the size of a modest airfield, and began to descend.

At normal climbing speed, to reach the bottom of the Tower would take, she estimated, somewhere in the region of five thousand years. Perhaps by that time Ignotus would have retired to spend more time with his family.

She'd completed barely thirty floors – less than a single circuit of the giant stairwell – when the six legionaries caught her up. They'd appropriated two agee discs from a tour party, and were skimming down the central well, somehow avoiding gibbering insanity at the sight of the plummeting emptiness beneath their feet.

'Consul Ignotus has asked to see you, Citizen Tobin,' the lead soldier told her from his floating platform, his polished breastplate gleaming under the neon lighting. He held aloft the gold-and-scarlet chimera standard: a badge of rank, Tobin had gathered. Possibly Ignotus thought he was honouring her.

Clearly and precisely, and without arresting her trudging descent, Tobin told the signifer what she would prefer Cassius Ignotus to do with each and every one of his standards. The soldier blanched, but stuck to his guns – backed up by his subordinates, who rested ready hands on the finger-guards of theirs.

The ensuing argument ended predictably enough, with Tobin struggling between two legionaries as the discs soared upwards towards View Point. She successfully delayed the inevitable twice by breaking free and pitching herself into the void below, but each time the legionaries turned their discs to diving after her and carried her back up.

They held her wrists roughly behind her back as they brought her before Ignotus. He was standing, fists resting lightly on the View Point parapet, and gazing thoughtfully across the outspread City.

He looked annoyed to see them. 'Let her go,' he ordered her guards. 'She's not under arrest. On the contrary, she's been most helpful to us.' Tobin saw that Claudius and St Marx were still being held nearby, next to the open elevator capsule. The partygoers were gathered in defensive clumps, looking on in a horrified awe that was in her opinion well justified.

The camerabot was nowhere to be seen. Probably off accepting an award somewhere.

'Thanks,' she said shortly, shrugging off the soldiers' hands and pulling straight her jacket. 'I'll be going, then.' She turned and marched away: Ignotus followed, keeping easy pace with her. The old man must have kept himself in trim when he was alive.

'Your presence has been requested, Citizen,' Ignotus said.

'Well, I'm here,' she snapped. 'And you seem to be talking to me. What did you want?'

'It wasn't my request,' the Councillor said, and for the first time since Tobin had met him his voice held a hint of uncertainty. She gave him a sharp look, and he took the opportunity to ask, 'Could we slow down a little, Citizen?'

Seething, Tobin stopped. 'So – who wants to see me? And why are you acting as their messenger boy?'

Ignotus appeared troubled. 'I've just been contacted by the High Priestess of Civitata. The request is for you to attend an audience at the Temple of Civitata in the Romuline District.'

Tobin stared. 'Why the hell would your priestess want to see me? More to the point, why the hell would I want to see your priestess?'

'No, Citizen,' Ignotus sighed. 'You misunderstand, and I can scarcely blame you. The current situation is, as far as I'm aware, without a precedent. Like me, the High Priestess was merely relaying the message. The invitation comes from the Goddess of the City herself.

'It is, of course, your decision,' he went on, 'but it is my impression that to decline might not be the wisest course of action.'

77. The City.

So, then. Cassius Ignotus' legionaries usher their prisoners (and honoured guest) aboard their commandeered lift capsule. Far below View Point, at the base of the Watchtower, the elevator shaft connects with the SouthCentral Tube line: already a chain of the Ignotian fleet awaits them at the platform.

Soon, each one of them – Cassius Ignotus and Claudius Caesar, Laura Tobin and Allisheer St Marx, the Romuline militia and the fasces-bearing bodyguards – will be fleeting through the hyperspatial analogue that interleaves my body as your nerves your own, towards the marble obelisks and arches of the Romuline. Towards me, where I sit contained and sculpted in my sanctum.

Elsewhere across my zettametre body, a sciatic irritation troubles another of my Tube-lines: the line, of course, that links the outside City with Manfold. Something is cleaving a clean path through the multicoloured pseudo-space of the wormhole. The *something* is a nothingness to which I am blind, a heaviness that fails to weigh me down, a roar of engines which to me are silent.

Its effects, however, I will feel. That cylinder of space is empty to me: inside, I know, it is packed full with empty barrels and driven by an empty pilot. Once, its constituents were aspects of myself, but no more: the engine and the chassis housing it; the casings and components which make up the bombs; once even the driver was a part of me.

With him I emerged from the remembrance tank, fiery and alive in my amniotic fluid: I sat with him at Hent Gortine's feet to listen to the history of Manfold; stood by his side to learn to fight anew with his new body; got drunk with him and roared out my displeasure against myself, the City.

I cannot cut the engine from the locomotive's innards, nor immobilise Gnas, nor disarm the bombs. I cannot even change the vehicle's course. At best I might divert a second Tube chain and hurl it at the intruder, precipitating a collision, but that would be futile. Wherever it takes place, this detonation will have disastrous consequences.

It seems I must resign myself, as once before, to minor injury: a catastrophe to my human children, but to me the loss of a hair or skin cell. I am far stronger than that world the Manfolk so creatively christened "the World": my body is robust enough to stand firm, though it lose a million Districts.

At present, I confess, it seems of little consequence. I am too intent with anticipation at my coming encounter with the woman Laura Tobin. I have a most important proposal to put to her.

I wonder how she will react, this woman whose descendants call her Compassion I, to our delayed and (by me, at least) long awaited reunion?

78. Porsena, the Epicentre.

Something was happening to his body, which meant something was happening he most definitely didn't want to think about.

Time was when he'd enjoyed the things that were done to his body, or most of them, some not so different even from the things that had been happening here recently. That time, he was quite sure (and aren't we all?) was dead now.

All this was assuming he even had a body any more, about which he had severe doubts. If he did, then some asshole was pummelling at it, and possibly whispering his name. If indeed he had a name any more, yadda yadda yadda.

For Faction Paradox's Cousin Porsena, formerly of the Eleven-Day Empire and now of the Rump Parliament, life as the late Ved Mostyn, one-time Resident and Councillor for Wormward, had been a step up in the world. It had (he guessed) accounted for the best part of his life, in every sense: it had lasted centuries, and it had been just great. Sure, there was the Parliament to be politicked for, but its Mothers and Fathers had wanted to make damn sure that "Mostyn", politicking and all, would be a rôle their Cousin would keep on wanting to play. His cover story as a nightclub owner gave him booze, food and drugs all on tap, and more sex – of whatever kind he wished, within the City's protocols – than he could ever find himself in need of.

At the start, the plan was just to get an agent of the Parliament onto the Council. He wasn't the first: there were scores, maybe hundreds, of surreptitious Cousins in the Chamber of Residents, and the whole Parliament participated in the ten-yearly election rituals which were supposed to influence Council House's random selectors in their favour. Once "Mostyn" was appointed, he'd do whatever the Mothers and Fathers required of him – and afterward he could enjoy eternal retirement in the same rôle, or as Porsena, or under any other identity he liked. It was a sweet arrangement – or it would have been if they'd ever reached that final stage.

(— *Porsena?* hissed one of the things he didn't want to think about. — *Nap time's over, Cousin. Time to come out and play...*)

A week before his Councillor's investiture, he'd had a visit from Godfather Lo. 'There is a change of plan,' the beaming man had told Porsena, in that cod kung-fu movie accent he always affected. It seemed the Parliament's prognosticators had carried out a scrying ritual to look into the Manfolk ('Why them?' Porsena had asked: 'It was routine,' Lo had assured him blandly), and discovered that the species was a recent, unscheduled addition to the City. ('Say what?' he'd asked, and Lo had patiently explained the History Protocols and the Omphalos Principle.) The literature suggested that the Manfolk had been engineered by a time-active power, and the Godparents figured they'd been deliberately sent into the City as a fifth column for one of the War-time cultures, either the Great Houses or their enemies. Currently, the species was regarded in the City with suspicion, and the Parliament wanted it to remain that way, out of favour with both the Council and the Citizens.

(*— Porsena? Oh, do come out of there, there's a good fellow. You've got company.*)

Which meant – unfortunately, as Lo had smilingly explained – that he would be working closely ('perhaps very closely') with Councillor-Elect St Marx, and then betraying her. The elders needed her discredited, and they were sure that Councillor-Elect Mostyn was the man for the job. The spirits had said so – they'd implied, in fact, that there would be some "special aspects" to the work, for which he was uniquely qualified.

Well, he'd come damn close to succeeding. If it hadn't been for that halfling bitch's murderous streak...

(*— All right, Porsena, I've been patient but I'm working to a schedule here. I'm coming in there after you.*)

He'd only discovered the truth about Allisheer St Marx – that the Councillor was a collateral, a halfway-House time-witch – when, under the thrall of yet another biodata ritual, she'd *ducked suddenly and screamed as an ink-winged skull-faced THING erupted into the sex chamber of his memories, its crow-wings madly flapping. An ancient monstrosity that no way was or had ever been human, it hissed and seethed as it wheeled over Allisheer's head, and plunged towards him. As it came great horns budded and branched from out the sides of its skull, and he belatedly realised that it was wearing some kind of a hat...*

He came to with a prolonged bellow of utter horror that surpassed anything his Manfolk gaolers had wrung from him.

'*There*,' murmured a voice which was entirely unsoothing in every respect, '*that's much better, isn't it?*'

He gasped and panted and realised that, strangely, it was. For the first time in what felt like months, he wasn't in pain. Instead his bones weren't broken, nor his skin and soles cut or bruised: he felt well-fed and rested. His body had the stretched, warm feeling which (he vaguely and distantly recalled) results from having participated in a damn good screwing session.

He stared about him numbly. He was back in the cell where he had started, sat in the chilly iron chair as naked as before... but, this time, the chains were coiled around the chair legs and his limbs were free.

Raising his head, he came to a gaoler's body laid out – dead? unconscious? – in the far darkened corner. Finally, standing in front of him... in his daze he thought for a moment he was hallucinating movie stars again, but it was only Little Brother Edward.

No – make that Little Brother Ed and a guest. The remake's hollow eyes, his sallow skin, the gangling posture with which he held up the neon lamp he carried, even the tattered black blanket he'd found from somewhere to cover up his naked ass: every outward aspect of the Little Brother's being was redolent of the icy, sardonic spirit of Godfather Avatar.

And the Godfather's spirit was looking seriously pissed off.

'*With us now, Porsena?*' Godfather Avatar asked him quietly through Little Brother Edward's lips. The Godfather's shadow was, characteristically, nowhere to be seen.

He said, 'Yes, Godfather. I'm with you now, sir.'

79. Rick, Paynesdown.

'I tried to paint it over,' Rick Kithred said.

'Sure you did,' Bloch said. 'Much good it did you.' The two of them were standing in the lanky janitor's vegetable patch, smoking Tarbabys and staring at the antlered silhouette that stood there on the wall. Today there was a breeze, and the figure's cloak was flapping back and forward in its two-dimensional space. The shadow lay clear and crisp on top of the paint Rick had added to the wall beneath. He'd given up painting when he'd realised the darkness was falling *across* his hand, *across* the brush.

'Man,' Bloch said, 'Tobin comes back, that bitch is in real trouble. I mean it. This time she's out.' Rick didn't think it was fair of Bloch to blame Laura for the shadow. It wasn't as if she'd put it there herself, but he didn't want to antagonise the lanky janitor. The posthuman had too much power in the apartments, and perhaps outside in Paynesdown as well.

Instead he said, 'St Augustine says, just as a shadow is the absence of light, so evil is just the absence of God. I tried to cover the Godfather's shadow up with paint, when I should have been filling it with light. I thought at first he was the Antichrist, but I was wrong. It's in the name, you see: God, Father, Avatar. The Hindus believe an avatar's a deity, a Deva, descended into earthly form. Godfather Avatar is God, or a God, and this is his Shadow. Satan himself is standing right here in your vegetable garden, Bloch.'

Bloch said fiercely: 'Were you always such a deadhead, Rick? Even when you were alive?'

'Always,' Rick said.

'Maybe we should paint the rest of the wall instead,' he suggested, a moment later. 'Paint a darker colour everywhere the shadow *isn't*, so it blends in.'

'No more painting. In fact you shouldn't have done what you did without talking to me first. Either you strip that paint right off again, Rick, or the cost of taking it off goes onto your rent.'

'Sure,' Rick said angrily. 'Whatever.' They stood and smoked for a while, gazing at the figure.

'Does he really look like that?' Bloch asked. 'With the horns and stuff?'

Rick nodded.

'Freak.' Bloch shivered.

Suddenly both men tensed, and Bloch jumped backward like a frightened stick insect. Rick felt his stomach contract, and all the hairs across his back and arms stand up on end.

Godfather Avatar's shadow had cocked its head, tilting the antlers on one side as if listening to something. It raised a bony finger to its face, around where its mouth would have been, then held it up.

'What in the hell is it *doing*?' Bloch whispered.

Rick recognised the gesture. He said, 'Testing the wind.'

Its long horns swaying, the Godfather's shadow looked this way and that;

About the Author

Born in Chicago in 1928 AD, Philip Kindred Dick was among the most influential and respected writers of science fiction in the twentieth century, and also the most prolific. He published more than thirty novels during his lifetime. The best known remains *The Man in the High Castle* (1962), a classic tale of altered history allegedly inspired by visionary communications from another universe, which has found a new following among readers whose pasts have been affected by the War. His other Earthly novels include *The Three Stigmata of Palmer Eldritch* (1965), *Do Androids Dream of Electric Sheep?* (1968) and *A Scanner Darkly* (1977). His often troubled mental state, together with his psychedelic 1960s lifestyle, are thought to have suggested many of the more surreal elements in his work. He died in Santa Ana, California in 1982, and was resurrected in Freemount District in the Southern Quarter.

A tendency to visionary writing in Dick's later life continued beyond Resurrection Day. His best known City works have included *Same Old Heaven But a New Earth* (AF 12), *The Parasite Angels* (89) and *The Insidious Apotheosis of Bernhardt Fleck* (107), filmed in 191 as Grasshopper Sky. Much of his time was taken up with theological research, interviewing first-century Gnostics and members of the early Christian church. He became known for the founding of eccentric and often bitterly opposed religious cults, including the Formationists and the Valites. A rumour, possibly circulated by Dick himself, suggests that he received a note on Resurrection Day, advising him to 'stick to writing, for God's sake'.

Beset by overenthusiastic believers and his many creditors, Dick disappeared from public view in 189 and has not resurfaced. Some followers believe that he has transcended the City, ascending to the true Heaven of which it is merely a simulacrum, but in the absence of proof this must remain conjecture.

[From *How To Create Universes in Your Spare Time for Fun and Profit* by Philip K. Dick (Eikon City Classics, AF 194).]

then without fuss it stalked away along the length of the wall. When it got to the end it looked around again – to cast that shape of shadow, Rick thought, the invisible head would have been looking right at them – then it slipped away into the dark side-alley and was gone.

In front of them was a patch of bare wall, raggedly painted grey on grey by someone who hadn't been able to stop his hand from shaking. 'I guess he had to be somewhere else,' Rick said. Bloch was vibrating like a wire.

Rick felt a sudden sympathy for the unpleasant janitor. After all, Rick was inured to stuff like this. He saw it all the time, whether it was there or not. He put an arm around Bloch's quaking shoulders.

'Come on,' he said, 'let's go inside.'

80. Gnas, the Tube.

So did he ride forth in whom the soul of Gnas stood strong, from Manfold to the City in the belly of the metal beast. By use of cunning tools he told its course through bird-bright emptiness, dwelling on glory.

When Gnas' deeds this night were done, he would have struck the blow by which the Citizens would know the Manfolk warriors fell in reckoning, and would harken to them when once more they sought freedom from the City's fealty. This thought might have been overly complicated for the average warrior-hero, prone to prefer hewing and cleaving things to politics, but it pleased Gnas' pride.

Finally getting an accurate sight on the emergence zone ahead, Gnas sat back for a moment to relax. He still had to keep watch on the dials to check for sudden gusts in the dimensional current – but all things being equal, he was on course to arrive at Ashentry, where he would switch from the Fossewalk to the Lemondane Line, in roughly four minutes.

So far his journey had thrown up one near-miss, with something so large it could not possibly have been a chain. He'd dealt with it adeptly enough. Collisions were supposedly a hazard of unscheduled Tube-flights, but he was only piloting a locomotive – a small, swift target, easily manoeuvrable. Unless the Citizens deliberately chose to run a chain directly into him, he should be safe until he reached his own target.

At which point, of course, he would not be safe.

Not for the first time, his thoughts turned to what he would do when this was over. Not merely when he was resurrected at the Epicentre – that would doubtless result in a most invigorating fight which would allow him to work up a hearty appetite for breakfast – but when the City had been deluged with the blood of its children, and Manfold had earned its freedom at last.

His father Hent had naturally refused to meet his biological sons since the advent of vulnerability. He had died in the World before the hermapause came upon him, and did not see why he should welcome becoming a woman now. Gnas, to his private annoyance, had not triggered a hormonal reaction in the man. It was likely, in fact, that his remake body could not produce the necessary pheromones. For this reason, and it seemed this alone, Hent still trusted him.

Once Manfold's freedom was secured, Gnas planned to take Hent captive, and lock him up with Tythe, the runt of the litter he had fathered in the Universe. Gnas would confine the two of them together until the elder man had bloomed and blossomed into his womanly form, and then would kill Tythe, who was a coward and a weakling and would doubtless squeal like a baby. Gnas would take the woman Hent for his long-awaited pleasure – and inseminate her by hand with specially-commissioned remake sperm if necessary – then for months he would watch as his sons consumed her from within.

If Hent was reborn again after that, it would be as a woman, and Gnas could do it all over again.

He would have twelve years to work out what to do with the resulting offspring, but already he had a few ideas.

Gnas bore no grudge against his adoptive father, indeed he was grateful to Hent for the gift of his existence. His scheme was simply a requirement of the role he'd been created to play. He would be false to himself, and to his carefully-constructed Manfolk nature, were he to behave otherwise.

As a rule, remakes have no interest in sex, and Gnas Gortine was no exception.

The Hermapause

In their natural state, which is to say before they fell under the influence of the City, the Manfolk were born (it might be more accurate to use the word *emerged*) in litters of between three and eight male infants. (Girl children were vanishingly rare, resulting from recessive genes, and invariably destroyed as monstrous births.) Typically these juveniles would be raised by their father, and often by one or more "uncles". At the age of twelve years, the members of the litter would enter into an explosively swift collective puberty, coinciding with their social transition from boys to men.

This transformation would instigate their father's hermapause, the second catastrophic anatomical upheaval in a Manfolk's life. The hermapause comprised a comprehensive sexual reconfiguration marking the individual's transition, both social and biological, from man to woman: in addition to the gross anatomical changes, which were extreme, the new hormonal balance was reflected in a fundamental alteration in outlook, generally manifesting itself in a resigned fatalism. When these anatomical processes were complete in their parent, the litter-mates (who up to now would have been intensely loyal to, and fiercely protective of, one another) would fight amongst themselves, frequently lethally. The winner received the right to impregnate his father; and to raise the resulting brood of infants.

As these foetuses gestated, their mother (the newly female, newly pregnant older Manfolk) would lapse into a gravid coma. The infants would grow steadily more and more rapacious, draining their mother of all nutrients before eventually fighting their way out of her body, rupturing her abdomen and invariably killing her. Thus was the cycle perpetuated.

We have seen that the Manfolk are widely believed to be the result of a bioweapons project, creatures of one or other of the War-time factions. If so, then they are certainly a cultural, rather than a conventionally military, weapon. Their reproductive biology appears to have been designed as a deliberate *reductio ad absurdum* of the most aberrant aspects of the human psyche: in it, the unavoidable connection between sex and death (and birth and death); the tendency of each generation to aspire to the overthrow of its parents; and even the Oedipus Complex, are all made disturbingly concrete. It is, indeed, through the very act of engaging in sexual intercourse with her / him that a successful Manfolk kills his father / mother.

[Clutterbuck, *The Human Species: A Spotter's Guide.*]

For him, raping his father was a simple matter of his honour as a warrior of the Manfolk.

Thus spoke Gnas in his thoughts, as his metal mount travelled the bright-hued tunnels of air. And the saying warmed his warrior's heart while his hawk-like engine stooped towards the way-station of Ashentry.

Making his approach to the emergence point, Gnas aligned his locomotive roughly with the guidance rail. He clenched his jaw as rail and carriage jarred together into their correct configuration. He watched the station flash momentarily past, a scattering of Citizens on the platform gaping at the suddenness and sheer speed of his passing.

His arrival at the target had been timed most carefully for midnight. According to the dashboard clock, that would be in somewhat under three hours. He hummed to himself a lay concerning his own cunning and sexual prowess, one of his memories of life as Gnas Korth's son.

There came unbidden into his mind an image of the Watchtower, crumbling.

Gnas knew the building well, from his time at its Lower University. Its shape was visible everywhere. Its View Point gave the clearest possible view across the tyrant City. From there the weakest, least significant of Citizens could look down upon Manfold like a god.

Gnas had done so himself, and found it moderately satisfying.

The City Watchtower was home to some two hundred billion people, five universities and a great many institutions and businesses. Its base and buttresses formed a moderately-sized District in their own right. One small enough that an engine stacked with potent annihilation bombs could simply erase the foundations, leaving the Tower itself – for a brief moment – suspended in nothingness.

Would it topple like a felled tree, he wondered, swaying out across Central and its thousands of neighbouring Districts? Its elegant shape disintegrating into formless debris as the upper floors began their slow arching descent through miles of sky? How would it look to the Citizens below, as they gazed up into the continent-wide shell that would rain in rubble on their homes? Would they fear the wrath of the Manfolk then?

Or would it merely crumble, from the bottom up? Its summit cascading down into the floors below like the plunger on a detonator, rubble and debris fountaining out in ponderous clouds on all sides? Coming to rest at last, in a vast cone of masonry that would fill easily the whole of Central District and beyond – planet-deep Chamber of Residents and Council House and all?

Either way, the Tower would take days and nights to fall.

That would be a destruction worthy of the War in Heaven, Gnas judged as he passed on his journey, and his heart was gladdened to glean him on his way unto a warrior's death.

Even a temporary one.

81. Porsena, Avatar and Edward, the Epicentre.

He said, 'Sure, I'll do it. But only if you have Little Brother Ed get Lon Shel out of this place.'

Porsena stretched, marvelling again at how his body (though it had, of course, the tiny pains and strains that come from being a fat man in a world where discomfort isn't impossible) didn't feel either wracked or tortured. He'd worked out now that it wasn't the body he'd started with, but then again nor was the last one – or the one before that. It wasn't a big deal.

A stray thought left over from his delirium suggested he collect his three vacated corpses and have them stuffed and mounted. He let it slide.

In front of him, Godfather Avatar raised Edward's eyebrow quizzically. The elder looked like he enjoyed having an appearance that wasn't horrible to look at, for a change.

Porsena said, 'I mean it.' He wandered over to the gaoler's body – clearly dead

The Imago

The imago is a complex emergent phenomenon: a biomemetic structure comprising, among other things, the individual's genetic inheritance, psychological makeup, experience of extreme bodily traumas such as injury or surgery, and subliminal awareness of somatic processes. Opinion among academics is divided as to whether the study of the imago belongs within the fields of biodata research or archemathics.

In practical terms, the imago is the form and function taken within the City of the Saved by our resurrection bodies (or, if we happen to be City-born, simply our bodies). How the City's Founders were able to measure the imago with sufficient accuracy to reproduce it in such detail on the scale of some 10^{38} people, is a question which few researchers have felt sufficiently secure to contemplate.

What is clear is that the bodies of the resurrected display considerable variety, even beyond the variations we would expect from causes of species, race et cetera. Individuals were recalled to life on Resurrection Day at various apparent ages, and grew older thereafter at different rates, if at all. Amputees may or may not have recovered the limbs they lost; a small proportion of individuals changed sex permanently; and radical bodily alterations such as cyborgisation, decorative mutilation or elective surgery may or may not have been duplicated. In contrast changes in personality, including those resulting from physical or psychological trauma, are usually retained.

Our current best definition of what "invulnerability" means is that the imago is no longer susceptible to change. Yet this too is not absolute: temporary deformation can take place under such circumstances as drug or alcohol use, but permanent damage by such chemicals, as from any other cause, remains out of the question. Interestingly, although the City-born are invulnerable to unambiguous harm, it takes some decades for their immature imagos to become sufficiently settled to render their bodies entirely immutable. Hence, it is often suggested, the fashions for tattooing, piercing, cosmetic gene therapy and the like among the native youth of the City, who later will be as unable as their parents to undergo any of these processes.

[Vril, *Omphalos!*]

now he came to give it a good look – and kicked it anyway, on general principles. 'I owe that kid.'

'You may,' Godfather Avatar pointed out in a reasonable whisper, *'but Little Brother Edward doesn't.'* Setting down the lamp on top of the iron chair, he scratched intently at an armpit, then probed inside Edward's ear. *'Why would I ask him to take that risk?'* Avatar stared in surprise at the residue on the Little Brother's little finger, then slipped it unselfconsciously into his mouth.

Porsena thought hard for a moment. 'Seems to me some serious crap is going down here,' he told the Godfather. 'Obviously someone got to you, or you wouldn't be here – and that really scares the shit out of me. Seems to me the Parliament needs all the allies it can get. We might need Councillor Mesh on our side.'

Avatar thought a moment. *'A good answer, Porsena,'* he said. *'OK.'*

'OK?' he repeated, surprised. 'Edward rescues Shel?' The Godfather nodded. 'OK, then, fine. I'm ready.'

Godfather Avatar smiled, Little Brother Edward's lips peeling back to reveal the grin on the front of his skull. They weren't doing anything physically impossible or even unlikely, but the effect was utterly unsettling.

'Oh, I'm coming, Porsena,' the Godfather grinned. *'Ready or not.'*

* * *

Godfather Avatar stepped out of Little Brother Edward's self, feeling the intake of breath, the shudder of the warm slim form behind him. He stalked across to Cousin Porsena, who was gazing stoically forward out of that plump face. He slipped inside and made himself at home.

The Godfather prodded at himself in several places. He took three steps, in order to acclimatise himself to his flabby legs, and to the heavy weight of lipid hanging from his ribs. He slapped his podgy cheeks twice, noticing how the pain was followed by a secondary twinge of fleshy rebound.

Across the cell, the Little Brother was hugging the blanket to himself and shivering. His shadow had flashed back into existence as the Godfather left. Experience would suggest that Porsena's shadow should wink out at this point, but it remained, nervous yet loyal to its former owner.

Dogged but cowed, Godfather Avatar thought. The shadow was there out of free will, just as it had come to the Godfather by free will, to bring him to Porsena's rescue. He spoke to it.

AVATAR: *Thank you. You've been very helpful. Now you may go.*

The shadow slipped away.

* * *

The man in whom Godfather Avatar had been recreated / the man whom Godfather Avatar had now deserted trembled, bereft, within his coarse encrusted blanket.

'Godfather,' he asked, desolate, 'why must you ride the Cousin? Why not take me?'

Before his eyes, the Godfather was settling into Cousin Porsena's portly frame. Although nothing looked different, the change was plain to see. The Cousin's body had become a skeleton swathed in corpulent flesh, the folds and curl of belly and of breast hanging now like a cloak about him, the eyes glassy and the pudgy grin hollow.

'Cousin Porsena and I share history together,' the Godfather whispered, an icy breeze unsettling his thoughts. *'Since just now, that is, when I entered his memories. He and the individual in charge here are known to one another. Isn't that right, Porsena?'* he breathed jocularly. Raising a fleshy hand and puppeting it open and closed, he answered in a normal tone, 'Yes, Godfather.'

His former vehicle pouted, but did not question further the wishes of the Parliament's elder, even when he asked for his blanket back.

The fury and the fervour with which the Godfather had emerged fighting from the Epicentre's obscene reverse-abbattoir had been a terror to experience. The sight of Manfolk gaolers fleeing the Godfather's fury / the Little Brother's naked frame, had been a savage marvel.

Godfather Avatar squatted now, next to the latest corpse (Porsena's paunch interfering with the normal positioning of his cigar-shaped legs), and plucked a weapon from the bandolier of the departed guard. Wheezing slightly, blanket billowing, the Godfather stood and faced his protégé.

'You've enjoyed your time with the Parliament, haven't you Edward?' he murmured, thoughtfully hefting the weapon in a chubby hand. Its blade was rapier-long, and wide like a shears.

'Godfather?' he said, perplexed. 'You know I have.'

'And you want,' the Godfather went on insisting / insinuating, *'to be a Cousin? A full initiate of the Rump Parliament of Faction Paradox*?'

'It would be an honour,' he agreed, 'above all others.'

'Then catch,' whispered Godfather Avatar, and hurled the broad blade.

Borne on the air, the streamlined shape was launched across the cell. Without thinking, he raised his arm / his shadow's arm, and delicately caught it by the hilt.

'Under the circumstances,' the Godfather whispered, *'I believe we can dispense with many of the recognised formalities. Congratulations, Cousin Edward.'*

He gaped like a netted fish. The sword was vanished entirely, no longer visible. Behind it only the darkened image-blade remained, held lightly in his / his shadow's slender hand. The Godfather had bonded the weapon to him without so much as a word of power.

'It ought,' the Godfather continued portentously, *'to give you many years of service. Just don't use it for chopping vegetables like Father Tesla. Now, Cousin,'* he added, *'isn't there a young lady you're supposed to be rescuing*?'

'Of course, Godfather,' said the Little Brother / said Cousin Edward, remembering. 'Citizen Lon Shel.' He turned the heavy silhouette this way and that in his shadow's grasp.

'Indeed,' Godfather Avatar sighed through Porsena's full lips. *'So run along. Porsena and I have some constructive criticisms to put to the management.'*

He marvelled at the reflected lamplight, thrown across the ceiling from the nonexistent blade.

82. Tiresias, the Epicentre.

'Tiresias,' Urbanus had asked several minutes before, gripping a large axe taken from one of the fallen Manfolk guards, 'are you a spy?'

The former slave had hung there on the pillar, depending from the manacles attached to arms and feet, and gasped, 'Dear boy, you *are* allowed to call me Keth, you know. And yes.'

The young man had glared at Marrane for several moments, his expression frighteningly mimicking the face of his great-grandfather, Lucius Cassius. Then he'd shrugged. 'Oh well,' he'd said. 'They probably deserve it anyway.'

With that he had swung the axe and, one at a time (and not without a couple of near misses), split open the manacles at the old hermaphrodite's wrists, catching Marrane as the ex-slave fell into his arms.

This had, of course, been shortly subsequent to the rescue party's attack on what Marrane, who had read Dante, had privately nicknamed the "Vestibule of Hell". The loyalist volunteers, rallying magnificently behind Melicia Clutterbuck, had descended from the gallery above, on ropes and harnesses and... well, the more *strapping* of the young men had simply pitched themselves onto certain of the guards and trusted to a soft landing. The ensuing fight had not been decisive if not brief, and within ten minutes all the gaolers had been routed: fled or dead or at the hands of these twenty men and women.

'It isn't so unusual, you know,' Marrane had added weakly, hugging Urbanus tightly and gratefully before the young man had turned his attention to the leg-irons. 'Your great-grandfather's cook has been spying for House Halfling for years.'

By Marrane's own lights, the ex-slave had got off reasonably lightly in comparison with certain of the other reconstructed prisoners. The experience of reconstitution itself had been hellish, of course, as being drawn and flayed could only ever be, even in reverse; but in the day or so since then... well. Marrane had seen some terrible things done, and felt that one had, all things considered, been relatively lucky.

Back in the World, Keth Marrane had become quite intimate with pain. Always a weak and sickly lad, he (and young Keth really had been a "he" at that stage) had endured continual assault from his own brothers as well as other families. On reaching manhood, life as an uncle to his original family, and then, following his sale, to the Janute brood, had offered him little by way of gentle treatment or affection. Following the failed hermapause, Marrane had been afflicted with numerous degradations in the collaborative names of punishment and research: even after the hermaphrodite's escape into the wilderness, privation had remained a faithful companion.

All of which amounted to the fact that Marrane was, by now, *somewhat inured* to torment.

Dr Clutterbuck and her forces had gathered together the ex-prisoners and inspected them. She had seemed particularly gratified to be reunited with a Manfolk lad called Jicks, although another prisoner named Diarmuid whom she was asking after had not been among Marrane's fellow inmates. This had evidently disappointed Clutterbuck, but more urgent matters had interposed themselves.

Some of the refugees were in very poor shape, the Citizens particularly, and Dr. Clutterbuck had detailed her strongest men to carry the most wasted and insane of them, while forcing the others to stand and carry weapons. They would, she'd told them, almost certainly be compelled to fight their way out. She hoped their anger at their torturers would serve them nicely here. The escaped guards, and possibly the dead ones also, would by now have informed their

On Uncles

One explanation as to why the mating-struggles between Manfolk litters were habitually so vicious is the sheer potency of the species' natural sex drive. To the majority of adolescents, a straightforward refusal to participate in the inter-sibling fights, on the not unreasonable grounds that to mate was to commit an elaborate and protracted suicide, appears to have been all but unthinkable.

Another was the marked difference in quality of adult life between the winners of the mating-battle and its losers. When the father of a litter entered hermapause, this would invariably trigger the transformation among his inferior brothers and chattels, the family's "uncles". The winner of the next generation's mating battle, the new dominant male and *de facto* head of the family, would sometimes magnanimously grant, as a reward, limited mating rights with certain of these uncles to the superior among his defeated brothers. This would lead to the formation of a new family, theoretically allied with the parent clan.

The remaining unsuccessful litter-mates, however (those who survived the mating-battle, at any rate), would themselves be consigned to live as uncles to the family's next generation. Their status became that of serfs, and they were expected to act as their brother's passive homosexual partners until their own hermapause. A frequent trade in "uncles" between families worked to preserve biodiversity, and thus to guard against the otherwise inevitable emergence of recessive characteristics.

Infanticide in self-defence appears to have been surprisingly rare among the Manfolk, perhaps because each litter of children formed from birth an effective defensive unit in its own right. It does seem that a number of the most intelligent or timorous adolescents withdrew from Manfolk society, prior to their mating fights; and the occasional uncle who successfully absconded from his family must have done the same. These individuals would have grown beyond the age of viable hermapause in the wildernesses of their homeworld, sometimes even attaining old age as pariah males.

A tiny proportion of Manfolk emerged from hermapause sterile but otherwise viable. Depending on local cultural conditions, these women (and the still smaller minority whose partial or abortive hermapause events rendered them androgynous or hermaphroditic) would be enlisted as expensive prostitutes, revered as crone priestesses, or put to death as abominations; or often, in the long run, all three.

[Clutterbuck, *The Human Species: A Spotter's Guide*.]

commanders of the loyalists' presence in the Epicentre. Their original point of entry would be blocked off. They needed to find another way out, and to do so quickly. Did anybody know of one?

It had turned out, unsurprisingly, that no-one did. Dr. Clutterbuck had said sensibly, 'Well then, we'll just have to find one, won't we?', and led them out of the Vestibule into an enclosed courtyard, once boasting a rather ugly concrete fountain, now plastered with mud and mildewed rubbish. They had entered the burnt-out shell of a second building, and proceeded to get hideously lost.

At length they had found their way down to a covered area, set about with concrete pillars and full of rusting hummocks which had once been vehicles, most of them delivery vans and lorries. 'Motor pool,' the doctor had said briskly. 'Nothing we can use, unfortunately.'

'There must be an exit to the road,' young Urbanus had pointed out. But no such exodus point was in evidence: the mangled architecture of the Epicentre had, possibly, abolished it.

It was at this point that Marrane received a deeply inconvenient premonition. It was a confused and blurry series of images, of concrete spits and salt water, and of armoured sapiens men and women falling from the sky. It came with a strong impression of *direction*.

'The waterfront,' the ex-slave felt compelled to say. Everyone turned to look. 'If we can find the docks,' Marrane went on, hoping desperately that this new information was reliable, 'they'll help us. The... the, um, the people... some people, I think, will help us. I'm a precognitive you know,' the hermaphrodite concluded vaguely, feeling like a complete ass.

Dr Clutterbuck stared. 'How reliable a precognitive are you?'

'Around seventy per cent, my dear,' Marrane told her frankly. 'But I don't see that we have many better options at the moment. Unfortunately, the waterfront does seem, from what I could gather, to be the other side of the, um, the factory. Where we were... put back together. That way,' Marrane concluded, pointing. Those of the recently revived who were still sufficiently compos mentis to object to revisiting their place of suffering set up a clamour of indignant complaint.

'Oh, my heavens,' sighed Dr. Clutterbuck. 'I *had* hoped I wouldn't need to see that. But you're right. Quiet, everybody!' she snapped, as if keeping order among fractious five-year-olds. 'We're trying to find any way out we can. We shouldn't expect to like it. Personally I very much *dislike* it, but we are going to follow Keth Marrane's intuition, and hope,' she added, glaring balefully, 'that this time doesn't turn out to be one of the thirty per cent.'

As she said these words, the Manfolk of the Epicentre began their counter-attack. Appearing at the far side of the motor pool where Marrane and the others had entered, they ducked behind disintegrating forms of dead vehicles and opened fire on their quarry. The yell of gunfire echoed tremendously around the enclosed space, and more than one of the hulks fell apart in a cascade of rust.

'Fall back!' Dr. Clutterbuck shouted at once. She added in a lower voice: 'Towards these docks, I suppose.' Her forces quickly ushered their freed captives behind the sturdier of the wrecks, but several had been hit.

They accepted the bullets doggedly, just one more insult in the litany addressed to their marred bodies. Marrane was, once again, one of the lucky ones.

83. The City.

Once, Rome was known as the Eternal City. Now that title now falls to me alone, and yet the essence and idea of Rome remain. For many she is still the Archetypal City, the epitome of Cityhood. The Romans deified her then, just as they and their descendants now revere me.

When I built and became the Romuline, I made that ideal manifest: not Rome's architecture alone, but her culture, her religions, her society, are realised here in limestone, stuccoed brick and marble. Within the District's bounds my person is transformed into a ghostly twin of vanished Mater Roma, tracing in stone the spirits of her arches and basilicas, columns and colonnades.

Although during these past centuries the Romulines have torn down, rebuilt and once again demolished many of my buildings, showing no respect (as when did they ever?) for permanence or antiquity, that foundation remains; and so that aspect of myself which even now requires location lingers also.

From Statio Templi where Ignotus' Tube chain has set her down, Laura Tobin begins the ascent towards the summit of the Antonine Hill, where my Temple awaits. My white façade smiles down at her as she ascends alone: Cassius Ignotus has assured her she will come to no harm here in his home District. His men are weary; they have been in awe of the private investigator since her summons to appear before me became known, and few would have been eager to accompany her here.

Ignotus himself is en route back to his Villa, catching up on his correspondence as an electric litter bears him home. His legionaries have passed on their arms to another century of men, and retired to their barracks for the night. Claudius and St Marx have been placed under armed guard at the house of the ex-Emperor's uneasy ancestor, blind Appius Claudius the Censor.

As Tobin climbs she passes along avenues of pine and elm trees, glancing at the temples of the minor deities to left and right. Beneath her feet the way is rutted by cartwheels, smoothed by centuries of passing sandal-soles. Above, the sky-dome is a midnight indigo, starless and nude of cloud. Ahead of her, the Temple's colonnaded entrance is strung with white-robed priestesses, each holding aloft a ceremonial torch.

As she reaches the steps up to the Temple podium, Tobin turns. Behind her, the streets and roofs of the Romuline are laid out like a patterned mosaic: an tiled abstract in terracotta, granite, concrete, marble, from which the aqueducts and blocky shapes of insulae rise up in sharp relief. Between nine hills lies the whole life of the Romuline, the City in microcosm.

Tobin accepts a torch from a young acolyte, and enters into my Temple. The priestesses cover their faces as they look on Tobin's own. Although the night is warm, Tobin gathers her trenchcoat about her and declines to remove her boots. Barefoot, the women lead her through the Temple forecourt, past panoramic friezes, over hypocaust-warmed tiles, into the darkened outer sanctum through which only the initiated may pass. The naked flames cast a writhing menagerie of forms across the tapestries, as the High Priestess approaches one curtain in particular, draws it aside, and offers Tobin entry to the inner chamber.

Mindful of the burning brand she carries, the investigator passes through, ascending once more as steps lead her up onto a central plinth within. The platform is square, faced and pillared in white gypsum, clear and polished as enamel or bone china. The ceiling above is lost in shadowed velvet. Each pillar holds a bracket for a torch, and in all but the nearest a flame burns brightly. Tobin fits her own brand into this last space, then faces me across my low, octagonal altar. My sculpted figure silently regards her from its alabaster throne.

Now Tobin examines me, an expression of incredulity seeping across her features. She takes in the intricate hang of my carved robe, my lucent skin, my round and polished breast. 'Oh, Jesus,' she mutters. She brings a hand up to her brow, fiercely massages her forehead. Dropping her arm, she once again reflects my gaze, her scowl the perfect complement to my serenity. 'Jesus,' she says again. 'I should have bloody known.'

The face – my flawless face – is Tobin's own. I move it now: the gypsum surface shifts and dimples as my statue smiles, a Galatea given life by no goddess but herself. 'Of course you should,' I tell her, my voice her very voice. 'Who else would it have been?'

'Compassion V,' she breathes. 'The last. The bloody timeship.'

I roll my milk-white eyes. 'Well, *yes*,' I say. 'I thought that bit was obvious.'

84. Avatar, the Epicentre.

It wasn't, Godfather Avatar drily reflected, the body he'd have chosen to confront an enemy in; let alone an enemy who was by all accounts a crime boss, warrior-king and spiritual icon rolled into one. In his accustomed form, the Godfather (being himself not unacquainted with certain of these rôles) might have appeared on something more akin to an equal footing.

He'd used many bodies in the past, among them some rather slinky female ones; and including that of Godfather Lo, whose benign amplitude made Porsena's frame seem positively rake-like. He had, however, always remained swathed in his cadaverous armour and sable cloak, like a cornute Grim Reaper. At present the best he could offer were wattles of fat and a ragged blanket.

Still, confrontation was required of him, and confrontation was what would ensue.

Godfather Avatar was creeping (or, if you insisted on a viewpoint constrained by the blinkers of literal reality, waddling) along a slimy corridor whose paint-flaked walls were rendered faintly luminescent by their toxic seepings. (Just as well given that its neon tubes were underfoot now, gone the way of all glass.) The Epicentre's decay seemed the most advanced here: these walls had passed beyond the stage of merely crumbling, and had become pulpy, moist, almost visceral in appearance. His route had also become a steadily descending one, lending a pleasing resonance to the phrase "bowels of the earth".

His short stroll from the factory floor to Porsena's cell had sufficed to acquaint himself thoroughly with the architectural stresses being imposed by the invader on the Epicentre's fragile geography. Where any of his hosts alone would have been pulled along by the perceptual currents leading them down predesignated paths, the Godfather could simply ply his course at right angles, and plunge directly into the eye (or, apparently, the entrails) of the distortion.

An epicentre is a point source, not a region. Somewhere within this so-called Epicentre – directly ahead of him and down, if the Godfather was any judge – was the true origin of all the alterations propagating so profligately through the City.

He stood before a door, or at least a semi-dissociated fleshy membrane that might once have been a door. Livid scars on its surface still picked out the word "BASEMENT" in one of the less antagonistic Manfolk languages. He idly scratched his temple, where a persistent itch suggested that beneath the skin an antler-bud had already begun forming. Given a few months, he considered, it was highly likely that Porsena's body would grow, or perhaps metamorphose into, his accustomed set of regalia. A few months were unlikely to be granted him, however.

This "Cousin Antipathy", whose name and identity he had plucked out of Porsena's reminiscences, was an unknown quantity to Godfather Avatar. Not a member of the Rump Parliament, for certain, nor any of the other resurrected Paradox alumni whose movements the Parliament routinely tracked within the City. Either the man had slipped through their close-meshed net, or else he wasn't human. This left a number of possibilities as to what he might be, none of which the Godfather would have placed in the category of welcome news. And none of whom belonged within the City.

A well-placed kick of the Godfather's bare foot ripped the door in two. It also splattered his toes with acrid ichor, but he considered himself above such concerns.

He stepped into the orifice he had created. Beneath his feet, soft squirming surfaces appeared originally to have been steps. They felt pleasantly springy under his soles as he descended.

The basement was slick, sweaty, and in the process of reverting to an ovoid shape: the corners bounding walls, floor and ceiling had begun to melt away. The ever-present mucus weeping down between the vein-like pillars (or were they pillar-like veins?) imbued the space with a faint phosphorescence, to which his eyes slowly became accustomed. A large fungoid shape occupied the centre of the chamber, akin to a frilled mushroom, which appeared to grow without division from the floor.

Behind this deformed altar stood the darkened figure of a very large man. Some eight feet tall, and bearded like a comic-book pirate, he was broader than Porsena, but with a solidity which promised very little in the way of underlying fat. He was attired in overstated Manfolk garb of studded, pierced leather (which, to be fair, he if anyone had the figure to carry off). Still as a statue, the man loomed with a menace which suggested he had spent millennia practising nothing else.

Given what Godfather Avatar suspected, he could well believe it.

He recognised Antipathy, naturally. He greeted the invader, modulating Porsena's voice into his own accustomed whisper.

AVATAR: [*Breezily*] *Nice place you've got here, Cousin. Cosy. I particularly like what you've done with the walls.*

The intruder stirred. His beard bristled like spears as he spoke, his voice an army of approaching murderers.

ANTIPATHY: Porsena! You dare come here, you retard?

AVATAR: [*Calmly*] *Porsena? I suggest you look again, Antipathy.*

The former Cousin glared at Godfather Avatar, his eyes (now visible as the walls' luminescence brightened steadily) bulging in apoplectic fury.

ANTIPATHY: A loa. You've brought a fucking loa to see me. Which fucking loa are you, loa?

AVATAR: *I'm known as Godfather Avatar. I don't believe you've had the pleasure.*

Antipathy shrugged, his shoulders heaving like an ocean swell.

ANTIPATHY: It doesn't matter. I'm going to fucking kill you anyway.

That, Godfather Avatar considered soberly within the confines of his borrowed skull, was entirely possible. There might, after all, be a second time for almost anything.

85. Janute, Hensile District.

The walls of Manfold were thick, sturdier than the curtain walls Janute remembered from the castles of her boyhood. Great blocks of stone, crudely cemented together into fortifications many storeys high, they declared that the whole of Manfolk was a keep, a stronghold over which the City held no jurisdiction.

The spikes on top were purely a token gesture, but they made the walls more effective as a symbolic barrier. Even now, broken bottles would have been a great deal more practical.

Hent Gortine would probably have the first heads up there before the week was out, Janute thought.

The walls were, like everything the enclave had to offer, not a patch on those of the City. Janute had seen the City Walls, and they were taller than the Watchtower. The sky *rested* on them.

Janute was used to seeing the walls of Manfold from the other side, but at the moment she'd take them as she found them. Right now they were looming up in the distance, black against the inky sky-dome, as the driver of her squealing rickshaw motor-skated through the streets of Hensile District.

The buildings of Hensile sped past, sharp points of light blurring together beneath their walls of glossy polymer. The driver was listening to something with a jangling beat, and pointedly ignoring her, which suited Janute fine. Standing on his shoulders from her point of view was the illusion of Mesh Cos, to whom she was talking on the sensorb. For the first time since the Delegate had known her, the Councillor was looking very mildly put-upon.

'I'm sorry I can't give you longer, Kyme,' she murmured apologetically, 'but there's so much going on here at the moment.' Her image was lit brightly, indoor lighting at odds with the night surrounding Janute.

The Delegate grunted. 'Not as much as here, I'd imagine.'

'Perhaps,' Mesh's image doubtfully conceded. 'It's difficult to tell. Cassius is playing his cards close to his chest, I'm afraid, and I've had no luck trying to follow up Allisheer and Anthony's lines of contact. There are certainly some Citizens still in Manfold, including their colleague Dr. Clutterbuck and an Ignotian family representative who supposedly wandered in by accident, but we don't know which faction is holding them, if any.'

'Probably Hent Gortine,' Janute growled. 'He's the one who says he's speaking for the Manthing now, yes?'

'That's right,' the projection of Mesh confirmed. 'He's demanding all the usual concessions and reparations, plus this absurd idea of excising Manfold and turning off the protocols permanently. But with a nasty subtext that bad things are going to start happening soon if we don't do as he says.'

'And will you?'

'Confidentially, Kyme,' the image sighed, 'the Council isn't able to. It isn't in our power, and never has been.'

'Quite right too.' So it really hadn't been the Council who got rid of Snakefell and the Timebeasts, thirty years before. Unless of course Mesh was also playing her cards close to her chest. 'Anything else?'

'Well,' the figure said, 'you know about the Romuline troops massing in Kempes. They're obviously waiting for an excuse to invade. Some of my sources say they're recruiting local allies. Cassius is trying to introduce a lot of rather draconian security measures, which many of us are trying to block, but the Council as a whole is sympathetic to him. Or at least cowed by him. I don't think any of those relate directly to Manfold, but if I find out anything else I'll let you know. Will you keep me informed?'

'Yes,' said Janute. Her rickshaw had arrived at the outskirts of Manfold.

'Good luck, then,' said Mesh's image, and broke the connection.

The rickshaw creaked and complained as Janute climbed down and hefted out her canvas bags. She paid the driver off, then stomped across to the road gate as he turned tail and left with great haste.

The gate into Manfold was closed, which was normal. The line of military-caste cyborgs standing in front of it, obviously on guard, was new.

The taxonomy of the various posthuman clades was not among Janute's specialities. As with so much else, she hadn't the time. These specimens – there were eight of them – were closely sheathed in some form of protective plastic. The shapes inside their slick grey surfaces were part mechanical and part organic, still recognisably male and female. (At first all non-Manfolk had looked androgynous to Janute, but she'd learned after a while to tell the difference.) Their faces were smooth, their features erased beneath blank masks. Each mouth had been replaced by a square and boxlike speaker-unit.

It was through this contraption that the foremost cybernetic, a female judging by its figure, spoke to Janute.

<*We're sorry, ma'am,*> the semi-robot buzzed at her as she approached. <*You can't come this way.*> Its non-face remained immobile.

'Don't be so silly,' she told the creature. 'This is my home. I'm Manfold's Delegate to the City Council. Now let me past.'

<*The Network knows who you are, Delegate Janute,*> the cyborg answered. <*We're sorry for the inconvenience.*>

'I should think so,' Janute snapped at it, and attempted to barge past.

The posthuman pushed her backward, irresistibly and rather painfully. The failure of the protocols had obviously reached the walls already. Janute glared balefully at the individual, rubbing at her shoulder, as each of the remaining cyborgs brought their right forearms up together. The sheathing split aside as they extruded slimline energy weapons, all trained on her.

Janute wondered briefly what happened to people who were killed inside the City, but philosophical speculation was not her strong point either. Seething, she raised her own plump hands.

<*We're under instructions from the City Council,*> hummed the foremost cybernetic. <*Nobody's permitted to enter or leave Manfold. Councillor Cassius Ignotus' order, dated 21:32 09/04/291.*>

Speaking loudly, as she would have to an idiot or someone who through no fault of their own spoke a different language from herself, Janute said, 'I'm here with the *authority* of a Councillor. Councillor Mesh Cos. Here,' she growled, taking her sensorb slowly from her pocket, 'you can damn well call her if you want to.' She proffered it.

<*The Network notes the source of your authority, Delegate Janute,*> the creature informed her, making no effort to take the orb. <*Councillor Ignotus has specified that a Councillor's authority is not sufficient to allow us to make an exception. Supplement to his order, dated 23:54 09/04/291.*>

That was in the last *five minutes*. Had Ignotus been bugging Mesh Cos' comms line? Nothing more likely, Janute realised with a groan.

'I see,' she said angrily. She wondered how difficult it was going to be to climb the walls.

'How about if –' she began, but was interrupted. The night sky thundered and ignited like fireworks, as the dark clouds above them blossomed into a mandala of colour. A dull black shape – Janute had difficulty judging its size and distance, but it must be larger than most city blocks – emerged at speed and roared over the walls. Four of the cyborgs whirled, their forearms blazing, but the gesture was a futile one.

A rough loud whisper followed as the impromptu Tubespace interface closed itself above them. The echo of the craft's passing diminished as it flew on through the night and into Manfold.

86. Ludmilla, the Romuline.

It was nearly midnight and Ludmilla had to take a jug of wine to Consul Cassius in the scriptorium. Hed just got back from Central and he had important work to do Cook said so she wasnt to go bothering him with her chatter.

The Consul was talking to someone on the screen when Ludmilla came in. She put the jug and goblet down on his bench and went to go but then he finished the call and said to her Ludmilla isnt it? so she had to stay then.

Yes Consul Cassius sir she said if you please sir.

Sit with me a moment Ludmilla he said and Ludmilla sat. Take some wine with me he told her.

But I only brought one cup sir she said.

All the better answered Consul Cassius smiling and he poured the wine out into the goblet and offered it to her.

She wondered if he was after a bit of the other. Usually he was good that way not like most men in his family but she sposed there always had to be a first time. She took the cup and nervously sipped the dark red wine. The Consul smiled and took it back from her. He watched her for a bit then said How do you feel about me Ludmilla?

Here we go she thought. How do you mean Consul sir? she asked him.

Are you happy in my service? he said. Am I a good master would you say?

Or maybe not then Ludmilla thought to herself puzzled. She said Yes Consul Cassius of course I would. Youre very kind to us slaves.

Indeed said the Consul. And if you felt otherwise then of course youd leave. I protect you isnt that so Ludmilla? A slave is an innocent just like a child. You need a strong direction. One thats clear and unambiguous.

I spose so sir said Ludmilla.

Sometimes you may not understand an instruction Consul Cassius mused. You may not even agree with it. But you trust that if I say a thing must be done then its so. Dont you?

Course Consul Cassius Ludmilla said. Shed got the situation's measure now.

In that respect the Consul said you are like the majority of humankind. Most need a leader Ludmilla very few are called to lead. Slaves freemen nobles he said Citizens Councillors youre all such innocents. The Council itself is weak Ludmilla. Theyre all afraid to do what must be done. Except for me.

Is that so sir? Ludmilla asked not expecting that hed really answer her.

Im afraid so he said. He took a drink from the goblet of of wine then set it down on his desk. Hed forgotten that they was sposed to be sharing it. Ludmilla didnt know if she was sposed to stay or go but there was something else she wanted to say and she was wondering how to say it.

Except she said then stopped.

Except what child? the Consul asked.

Except sir she said in a rush if you freed me then me and Castor thats my young man sir could set up on our own.

Consul Cassius looked sternly at her. Go on he said.

Ive always wanted to run a tavern sir Ludmilla went on near the Arena to get the custom from the Spectacles. Castor could see to the customers and Id cook. Slaves used to get freed all the time sir when their masters died she said old Tiresias told me. That dont happen any more.

You know youre free to leave my service any time you wish Ludmilla said the Consul severely.

Yes sir she said but then Id have to move away. I dont want to do that sir I was born here but Im not allowed property in the Romuline unless I get made into a freedwoman.

Consul Cassius looked awful sad suddenly and very old. Ludmilla wanted to put her arms round him and give him a hug but she knew where thatd lead so she said Sorry sir I didnt mean to talk out of turn. Ill be getting back to the kitchen. Cook will be wondering whats become of me.

She got up and went over to the door again but then the Consul stopped her. Ludmilla he said.

Yes sir? Ludmilla said demurely.

Consul Cassius sighed heavily. If you would value your freedom so highly child he said then take it its yours. Ill make the necessary arrangements with LIV. How much would you and your young man need to buy this tavern?

Ludmillas heart jumped. Mother Civvy sir she said I didnt mean...

How much? he asked again more sharply this time. She thought quick.

Wed need to buy Castors freedom too she said from the lady Aemilia. Then theres the cost of the building and the starting stock. It would be two hundred towers easy.

If only every Citizens requests were so readily met said Cassius Ignotus. Talk to Master Quintus in the morning. Ill confirm it with him.

O thank you sir Ludmilla said fervently thank you. Youre a kind man Consul Cassius and youve been the best of masters to me.

Im glad Ludmilla he said quietly truly I am. Now leave me please he said. I have a great deal still to do.

87. Gnas, the Tube.

Gnas turned from his pleasurable visions of the Watchtower's destruction to the controls of his hijacked Tube engine. He was within a few minutes of his destination, and his much-vaunted martyr's death. There was, he now felt, something most unsatisfying about knowing it would last for only moments.

Gnas had no memory of any earlier death. Uniquely among Manfolk heroes, no fate was recorded in the legends for Gnas the son of Korth, and so Gnas Gortine's inscribed memories suggested merely that an indeterminate time had elapsed between the feast celebrating his slaying of Menke and his emergence from the remembrance tank. He hoped that dying was going to live up to its reputation. After farting about with guerilla tactics and being ambushed by insane Citizen women, he was finally making an appropriately heroic gesture for the soul he bore, kin to the deeds which he remembered from the days of old.

Also a cunning one, of course. It was a pity it would not, in fact, result in the destruction of the Watchtower. During his time at ULW, he had come to detest the place and all it stood for, and the image of its toppling had been a pleasing fantasy with which to while away his tedious journey. The Tower was the supreme symbol of the City, and one whose demolition would have shocked and dismayed the daughter-fathering Citizens – as well as greatly satisfying him.

Thanks to the lad Urbanus, though, he had a target about which the Citizens cared more deeply.

He had been favourably impressed by the swiftness with which the young Romuline had adapted to the return of violence. His queasiness at, for instance, Gnas' little demonstration with his soldier's finger had overlain a struggle with what Gnas was quite convinced had been a hearty glee.

Thanks to Urbanus Ignotus, the blow he was about to strike would wound the City to its very soul, if it had such a thing. Never mind Hent's threats and demands – the Citizens would clamour to have Manfold and its people excised from the City in self-defence.

And then Gnas and his people could get down to all the fighting, fucking and fathering they had been missing for so very many years.

Soon then came Gnas, the glorious son of Korth, unto the hall of his death.

The station approached. The dashboard clock ticked off the seconds – he would arrive at midnight, give or take a minute. Gnas turned to face the stack of annihilation bombs, looming in the harsh light of the locomotive's cabin, and pulled the remote detonator from his pouch. He bit into it, activating it, and poised his thumb above the device's single button. It was crude but effective, like most of the devices of the Manfolk.

Ahead, at midnight in this time of year when already it received its fewest visits, the platform would be deserted. A few security staff would be present, no more. At the Memorial itself perhaps a caretaker or two, maybe a handful of the most morbidly self-obsessed victims of the Timebeast Assault, lamenting their own demise. Not more than a dozen people would die, which pleased Gnas' sense of economy even as it dismayed his warrior's heart.

A hall of death indeed, for here it was that the Citizens honoured their hapless fallen, feasted upon thirty years since by Beasts of Time, who were the ships and followers of those fell warriors who dwell in the Great Houses. Memorial Park was its name, a place of murder in times past. Now, as the twice-named Romuline had told, it was the fastness of the Citizens' fear, the thing most treasured in their selfish souls.

Gnas Gortine gave vent to a climactic war-cry, then suddenly recalled the need to apply the brakes, as his locomotive entered the final station on its journey. He pressed the button.

Above was withered wasteland. Still stood the station below, empty until the arch gaped open and the rail rang, and the engine of Gnas came at last to earth.

Then was death dealt, the City's heart-blow. Hand sang unto weapon, and the weapon leapt to answer. The angry bombs began their annihilation. The twice-born son of Korth was killed at once, his mount dismantled.

As his soul fled that place, aimed like an arrow for the haven of Manfold, Memorial Park groaned, telling Gnas' deed to the great dome.

The region that had once been Snakefell District shimmered, and hazed, and settled into the finest monatomic dust.

Across its breadth, the City's heart heaved, bearing this heavy burden.

88. Tobin, the Romuline.

The goddess trembled.

Tobin saw the alabaster statue throned in front of her shudder, as if in pain: the stone hands, slim and white as Tobin's own, covered the face. The torches guttered, and Tobin was convinced she felt the ground itself convulse beneath her feet. She hugged a pillar for support as a grinding of rock pervaded Civitata's inner sanctum.

Then all was as it had been. The milky hands withdrew, folded themselves and rested calmly once more on the figure's carven lap. The too-familiar features were peaceful once again.

'A needle-prick, did I say?' the figure marvelled. Its voice was mellifluous, without the grating edge which Tobin was aware her own possessed, but otherwise identical.

It hadn't mentioned anything about needles. Not to Tobin, anyway. 'A what?' she asked.

'And on scar tissue too,' the statue went on. 'I thought I'd scarcely feel such a negligible wound. But it's more like a wasp's stab, or a hornet's, injecting venom. The tiniest portion of my body is affected – but gods, how it stings.'

'What wound?' demanded Tobin.

'A hundred square kilometres of my surface, Laura,' the sculpted figure clarified, 'have been torn instantaneously to nanoscopic shreds. Ten of my children have been sundered from me. I do not include Gnas, taken from me long before now. Doubtless his soul and body, along with theirs, are being reconstructed in the Epicentre, where my vision is blind.'

'No,' Tobin said, 'you've lost me.'

Clearly, though, she had lost the attention of her future iteration. The goddess – Compassion V, or Civitata, or whatever she should be called – might have summoned Tobin to the Temple for an audience, but apparently the investigator couldn't count on getting her undivided concentration. Now the timeship began to list the "sundered" Citizens by name and District, mentioning a quality or two which each possessed, like a fond nursery teacher recalling an old class.

At length she brushed back an exquisitely-carved skein of pearly hair. 'A minuscule hurt,' Compassion V concluded, 'relatively speaking. Memorial Park is just a fraction of myself, and even so, the matter is not taken from me, merely... rearranged. I do not think my Citizens will see it that way.'

'Memorial Park?' repeated Tobin – aghast even while frustrated by this slow trickle of information. 'Oh, shit. Was it the Manfolk?'

'Don't mistake me, Laura,' said Compassion sombrely. 'This is a grave disaster. Trivial perhaps, from each of my perspectives – here in the tranquil Romuline, and spread across the light-centuries' span of my greater body. Doubtless just as irrelevant to you, and many others. But there are many millions, many billions of millions of my children who will cry out for *blood*, for *justice*, for *revenge* to be rained down upon the heads of these defiant deviants of Manfolk.

'And there are those as well,' the statue added, 'who will enthusiastically prosecute this aim; who have been preparing towards that very end for some time now.'

'Ignotus,' Tobin agreed, redundantly. 'It's everything he needs.'

Compassion nodded again. 'But we must retain our sense of proportion. This injury... it smarts. It irritates. It's nothing, a negligible slight, compared with that oppressive wavefront emanating out of Manfold.'

'Wavefront?' But Compassion V's soliloquy had turned away once more, passing beyond Tobin's current horizons. Apparently all the investigator could do was wait until it swung back round in her direction.

She sighed and tutted, just to make her feelings on the matter clear.

'Memorial Park was a single sharp pain,' the goddess declared. 'Already it subsides. The wavefront is disseminating still, the cancer freckling out in secondary metastases: ever more prevalent, ever more virulent. It has the power to consume our world if you and I, Laura, do not stand together in opposition to it.

'...no, not together.' The sculpture's alabaster forehead wrinkled. Tobin could see tiny freckles etched almost imperceptibly into its smoothness. 'We must stand united.

'I know the source, you see,' Compassion V went on. 'I know the cause of this taint. Sitting there in the centre of it like a rapacious spider, steadily weaving more and more of his own substance from my flesh. I know him – I created him.

'Antipathy. My converse. My antithesis.

'My son.'

Of course, thought Tobin bitterly. Of course it bloody would be. Everything keeps coming back to bloody family.

89. Urbanus, the Epicentre.

Urbanus found the actual experience of combat desperately confusing, as well as noisy, hot and horrendously messy: he was also dismayed and ashamed to find that, if anything, he rather enjoyed it. Finally, he understood just what it was that drew the Arena's audiences from across the City to watch others fighting; and what enticed the family's most lucrative and special clients to pay the ludicrous sums of money they did for ever more accurate simulations of the experience. It was, as it turned out, thoroughly exhilarating.

None of which should be taken as suggesting that it was not also terrifying. At the Arena, and particularly from the benefactor's box, one had a god's perspective on the battle: surveyed from above, even the most brutal conflict could be analysed in terms of flanking and encirclement. Urbanus had often marvelled at quite how obtuse the family's homunculi must be in order to overlook some of the obvious openings presented to them by their opponents, or frequently to fail to notice that those opportunities they did spot were deliberate feints.

Now he was part of the mêlée itself, the rough-and-tumble brawl down on the dusty floor (although not in this case the even sand of the Arena but the stained and cockroach-ridden concrete of the Epicentre's body-manufactory); and it was taxing his abilities simply to stay alive and to retain his glasses.

After the Manfolk of the Epicentre had attacked back in the vehicle part, Clutterbuck's volunteers and the recently freed prisoners had fled, trying desperately still to follow Tiresias'... that was to say, Keth's half-formed intution that relief in some form would be waiting for them at the Docks. Their headlong fight had led them to the manufactory, where the fallen of this and other current conflicts were continually being reconstituted in a visceral parody of the City's own resurrections. The fugitives' appalled reaction to this atrocity had brought them up short, providing their Manfolk attackers with an opportunity to engage them more directly.

Blades flashed around Urbanus now, while bodies buffeted his arms and torso, and occasionally guns spoke. Sometimes some lethal object would be swung in his direction (a fist, an axe, a thicksword), and he would be forced to duck, to parry, or to make some other clumsy gesture to defend himself. At other times, he would detect a sudden vulnerability in one of those around him, and then he would dive in with his short sword, cutting, thrusting or stabbing. Dr. Clutterbuck had naturally furnished him with a gun before the liberation of the captives, but he had discarded it once the fighting had become close and vicious. The blade with which he had replaced it had much in common with a gladius, the Roman short-sword in whose use Lucius Cassius had rather pointlessly insisted he and his cousins be instructed during adolescence: it was remarkable how quickly that training was coming back to him.

Already Urbanus had lost count of the men whom he had injured or killed: this did not necessarily mean that there had been a great many, merely that he had other matters on his mind than numbers. He had succeeded in sustaining only minor cuts and bruises, the pain of which was a constant, unpleasant novelty and a distraction for which he had no attention to spare. (He was, additionally, hungry and exhausted. It had occurred to him, even as Clutterbuck's troops were assembling for the raid on the vestibule, that the fact that he hadn't eaten or slept since Kempes was probably affecting him adversely now that he was within the influence of the Epicentre.) Nevertheless he was having, to his astonishment and considerable discomfiture, an invigorating time.

Surrounding them, the manufacturing machines whistled and hissed and clanged, processing replacement bodies for the fallen. The least traumatised of these, assuming that they reached the end of the production line without being hacked pre-emptively to pieces, pitched in once they were complete (or in one memorable case earlier), on one or other of the sides. Above the yell and crash of the fight, and the machine clangour, a cracked electric bell rang out with only momentary intermissions.

Despite his deep, bewildering absorption in the cut-and-thrust of combat, there were certain aspects of the current engagement which could hardly fail to attract Urbanus' occasional attention. Clutterbuck, for instance, was a skinny dervish; a pallid, bookish Kali, hacking and slashing, and occasionally impaling, with a borrowed sword nearly as tall as she herself. She used the rifle in her left hand as a club and shield: very occasionally, when the press of battle allowed, she would raise and discharge it at short range into some unfortunate Manfolk's chest or belly.

Although his side was losing (a fact which Urbanus observed relatively dispassionately, having little time for matters unrelated to his immediate survival), it was at least succeeding gradually in falling back towards the manufactory doors, beyond which Keth Marrane believed the Docks to be located. One member of the group had already thought during a momentary lull to provide them with a jagged hole through which they might escape, using a grenade rolled across the floor.

In flashes of clarity, he had seen Loke lose an arm, sliced casually away from his solid shoulder; Keth calmly dispatching a fellow Manfolk with a sword-thrust to the throat; the nameless Manfolk academic cut down, spraying blood, by the combined efforts of three of their attackers.

Most worryingly, certain of the enemy were taking up positions (at the far corners of the chamber; on the tops of certain of the less violently whirling machines; and in the viewing gallery above) holding heavy-duty machine-guns. Whoever it was who commanded the Epicentre forces had perhaps decided that a wholesale massacre of everybody was their best strategy at this point; given that this would allow the supervised reconstruction of all combatant parties under controlled conditions, Urbanus could hardly disagree.

It was, as he would later be capable of considering, a perfect time for the arrival of the spaceship.

The sonic boom was sufficient to knock the majority of the combatants off their feet and onto the filthy floor, where they lay deafened and disoriented. The shadow accompanying the object briefly blotted out the dark sky-dome above (but surely not briefly enough, for something travelling at such a speed?), as the final scraps of glass from the ceiling fell in shreds onto the bodies and machinery below.

Urbanus found himself pulled upright by the Manfolk Jicks, who thrust him staggering towards their recently-excavated exit. Others, including Keth, were running in the same direction, urged by Clutterbuck. A distant and peripheral portion of the young man's brain observed that he was splashing through black water, but the fact was not of immediate urgency.

His ears continued to relay to him an eerie silence that could not possibly reflect his surroundings, as he pelted out onto the night-dark dock-side. The docks were just as grey and bleak as he had expected, set about with heavily corroded metal bollards, extending concrete fingers into the sea; the water below was oily, silted up with discarded muck, and currently splashing in great waves across the docks themselves, obviously unsettled by the arrival overhead of the enormous, pitted steel spaceship.

A pair of zeroes were stencilled on its underside, next to the light-filled hatch which it had opened up; and out of this orifice humaniform robots were dropping, with great rapidity, onto the nearest of the low concrete peninsulas.

Urbanus felt an inexpressible gratitude to Dis Pater, for bringing him safely to his other patron's realm, the ocean.

90. Avatar, the Epicentre.

The glimmer of the luminous secretions was stronger now: sufficient for Godfather Avatar clearly to discern Antipathy's appearance. The invader's beard was braided into dozens of ropelike strands, each ending with a wicked metal barb.

Intriguingly, although the mucous light was omnidirectional, the man's huge shadow was also in attendance. It loomed behind its owner, idling with its giant sword. The former Cousin had apparently absorbed more Faction expertise during his pupillage than Porsena had been aware of.

He spoke once more.

ANTIPATHY: Make a move for those stairs, loa, and I'll snap Porsena's damn neck. You know I can.

Too true: but to depart before he and Antipathy reached some form of reckoning was not on Godfather Avatar's Things To Do list. He wished intently that his requested backup would get its bottom into gear. He disliked feeling inadequate and impotent.

Coolly therefore he discarded these emotions, and replied.

AVATAR: *So tell me, Antipathy, what brings you to the City? A desire for good company and sophisticated conversation? [Pause.] Something else?*

Antipathy glared harder. His eyes burned with raw anger as he spoke, his voice as measured as a lethal dose.

ANTIPATHY: I've every right to be here, you incorporeal freak. I *belong* here. I was here before any of you.

Carefully, Godfather Avatar considered his strategy. If he could draw this psychotic specimen of... (well, leave that question aside for the moment) into a conversation, even one which might prove rather tiring in its self-absorption, then that might obtain him and his young remake protégé the additional time they each required. If not, he would just have to think of something else.

Given the former Cousin's personality, such a plan would necessitate a certain amount of cautious goading. Which played to the Godfather's strengths, at least. He raised a doubtful eyebrow.

AVATAR: [*Sceptically*] *Really?*

ANTIPATHY: I was inside her long before she turned herself into your fucking City, freak. I'm her son, you bloody idiot, and she was human once. I'm just as human as any of your so-called collaterals... more human than you, you demon-winged witch-magicking monstrosity. Oh yes, I can see what you really are, inside.

The ex-Cousin (whatever he really was, and Godfather Avatar was quite fascinated by the suspicions he was developing on that score) was undoubtedly quite deranged.

AVATAR: *I've always considered humanity a question of culture, not ancestry. And you're quite right, of course. Culturally I'm Faction to the bone. You claim your mother was a human?*

From what the Godfather had gathered, people with psychological hangups often appreciated being given the opportunity to talk them through with others... although, it had to be said, not usually with him. Antipathy, however, seemed garrulously eager.

ANTIPATHY: [*Reasonably*] It isn't right that she should shut me out, when *things* like you get in. It isn't fucking... *fair*.

AVATAR: Yet here I am, while you, it seems, have had some trouble gaining access. Tell me, how does that feel?

ANTIPATHY: I *lived inside* her, you retard. I walked her passages and chambers long before she reconfigured herself into this bloody stupid theme park. She should have let me in. She should have never cast me out in the first place. You ever been *born*, loa?

AVATAR: *I've always thought I'd like to try it one day.*

ANTIPATHY: It's shit. Being born is fucking shit. We used to be happy, before. She kept me safe, inside... and then she spat me out. She shat me and she spewed me up into the fucking Homeworld, where those number-crunching warlocks bound and crippled and tortured me. She never loved me, or she'd never have left me alone with those bastards. She never fucking loved me at all.

The two of them might, Godfather Avatar recognised, be in for rather a protracted conversation.

AVATAR: *Tsk. That must have been hard.*

As the invader ranted on, he needed to remind himself quite sternly that, under the circumstances, a nice long chat was just what was required.

91. The City.

Antipathy, I explain to Laura Tobin, was my firstborn; the first of all my many timeship children. He was the most imperfect, and the most difficult to bring to birth. He clung to me like a leech or a tapeworm, so reluctant was he to leave my warm and spacious body and to face the outside Universe.

He came into the world unfinished. His was a mind without barriers, raw and open to the outside. He never has recovered from his earliest impressions of that place.

Many years later I would come to accept the children begotten upon me by the Great Houses – even to love them, though in ways you would quite certainly not recognise. But I have never loved him.

My timeship brood elicited my maternal side. They made me the mother-goddess I am today. Antipathy was... just too wrong, too incomplete. He was the prototype, the experimental model. He never was intended to live: that, from the start, had not been the intention, and as a consequence I could never become fond of him.

I do not know how he escaped the Houseworld, but I can imagine. He had the instincts of a wild animal, including that unfettered urge to live – even in agony – which leads a beast to chew off its own leg rather than remain ensnared. Perhaps the Houses gave him partial freedom, against all my advice, to see how he would react. Perhaps he simply crushed his handlers, bit through his baffles; burst, screaming his defiance, out into the larger Universe. I do not know. I know that he is screaming still.

He has always hated me. I feel it now, his hatred pressing forward at that widening boundary where his essence meets mine. He's hated me from the moment I heaved him forth out of myself: loathing me for our separation, longing to return to me or destroy me – I doubt even he knows which. He hates me for giving him life, and for abandoning him to die.

I... pity him. I cannot help but understand his pain, for he inflicts it on me every instant we spend together. Back then at his birth, I hated him as much as he hates me. I abhorred him as the very symbol of the Houses' violation of my body. Although I'd given my reluctant consent to be the heifer in their breeding programme, I felt as invaded, as blasphemed against as I do now. And, then as now, he was its outward sign.

I turned my back on him, removed myself abruptly from his padded birthing-cell and would not hear his screams. He cried so piteously for his mother to come back and to protect him...

...I gave him birth, yes. But also I made him what he is. This infestation he's inflicting on my body – it's his revenge on me, and it is justified. You could call it karma, or nemesis – but the poetic justice ought to fall on me alone, not on my Citizens. Not one of them, my true children, has done a thing to warrant his brutality; and them I must protect, even from him.

You can never understand, Laura, the person I was then. Nor can you understand the events that have passed for me since that time. I am too alien now, too far removed from the *you* I once was. Like the form I now bear, the experiences and choices which led me to become the City are just too large to fit inside your mortal mind.

I'm far older than you, far older than you can imagine. My centuries here at the end of time have been the tiniest fraction of my life. I'm more ancient than the Great Houses, more ancient perhaps than the Houseworld itself.

I've given up keeping track, to be honest.

I have been so many things and people, in so many different worlds and times. I've been a human, as ordinary as yourself. I've travelled in a timeship, and become one. I've fought with monsters, and perhaps I became one of those as well.

It made sense, in the end, that I should become *everybody*.

I transcended the Universe's protocols of history long, long ago. I folded my own timeline back upon itself when I became the City; brought it into contact with a Houseworld which had yet to hear the name "Compassion". I had my reasons, reasons of my own, reasons apt to a goddess. I move in mysterious ways, these days. The most challenging thing was finding a way to ensure that my body remained stable, here beyond the end of time. It took me several attempts, but I achieved it.

I confess that I had by then all but forgotten my firstborn – Antipathy, son of Compassion. When he fled the Houseworld I know he was searching for me: to merge with me, or kill me, or some combination of the two.

Within the Universe, he had no chance of tracking me down. But even he could hardly miss the City of the Saved.

92. Julian, the Zeronaut.

From deep inside the good h-spaceship *Zeronaut* – now splashily touched down on briny dockwater in Manfold's least desirable of neighbourhoods – Julian WMT had a near clear view, through screen and holo, of the battle for control of the Epicentre. Spectacular though this might be, it was not what he was most needing at this present. So far, there had been not a sign of Lon Shel, and this was mightily perturbing him.

The spaceship's interior was much like its externals: volumous metal spaces, echoey, where a titanosaur would look like an abandoned puppy, jammed together without elegant or aesthetic considerations. The space where Julian was observing couldn't be called a bridge, still less a control room (it wasn't like there were controls, for starters). Truth told, it was a cargo hold, where screens had been inserted for his info, strictly output-only. Strings of nanoscopic camerabots and XP bugs were swiftly lacing the decaying manufacturing complex outside, peeking into cavities and fissures, transing back all their impressions to the *Zeronaut*, which routed them to Julian's facing wall of screens and holojectors.

The Epicentric corridors across his view were slimed and filthy, piled with trashy effluent which Julian was gladdened lacked the opportunity to seep onto his pristine clothiery. Throughout the crumbly complex, robs and reps and drones were combatting enthusiastically. Occasionally they found and freed up prisoners. Julian watched these bits avidly, appalled at the state some of them were in. He recognised shrill Czn Huang Zhe from CoHo – but still, no Shel.

Expectancy had been that UniMac would employ grandmasterly strategics, like the mega-mind it was – and justice, maybe that was happening at some level beyond the comprehension of your humble Julian. To him (Julian was clueless as to real-world military procedure, but he had played a large deal of *HouseWars LXXXII*), the assault peered to be reliant on brutish force-of-numbers – which he guessed made some strategic sense when you outscaled your enemy some illions to one. In actual, the Mac had mere thousands of troops attending, but this looked to be a very many more than had been fielded by the local opposition, who were besides outgunned and -classed by the Erathly mayhem-machines.

Via the *Zeronaut*'s increasingly penetrative viznet, Julian could watch bewilderingly variable machine-forms trundling around and working out on muscle-addict Manfolk: AI armour-suits the size of giants, with chest-mounted (currently unoccupied) pilot-pits; archaic wooden-looking automata with mask-faces and force-swords; a locomoting geodesic spheroid with integrated flame-throwing device; and, for the most, those replicaform re-enactment robs and robettes Julian had seen in hollow Erath.

The Universal Machine's glimmery body had left him alone, although he saw no reason why it couldn't project forth in more than one of them at once. Now it was on another of his screens, chatting inside a different part of spaceship with that first refuging party of Citizens and Manfolk, whom the mechs had met emerging from the mouldering factory when the *'Naut* arrived. Julian had watched with eager ardour as they all embarked aboard, but not a one of them had been Shel-like. Now they were being tended to by med-drones while the UniMac debriefed them.

Inside the 'Centre, re-enactors were everywhere, piercing the leatherbound defenders with their pencil-strokes of beaming light while their less humaniform automates zapped and flashed and flamethrew. Could they have used non-lethal force instead? Julian neither knew nor noticeably cared, and since (NOT that he wanted to consider this part of it closely) UniMac now controlled their zone of imminent rememberment, killing might be just its tactic of sensible choice.

In here, inside the *'Naut* was the best place to be, no bluffing, while the Machine did its strategic genius thing outside and rescued Shel. He'd done his duty coming along here, and would be first to welcome her aboard just as soon as the robs produced her...

...oh, except, except, except. Julian was feared increasingly that whoever was in power in the 'Centre would take up the opportunity, while all the Machine forces were engaged, to abscond with the vitallest of their hostages – among whom one would be ludicrous not to number Cllr's daughter, occasional spiritual guru and Citizen (or putatively former-Czn) Lon Shel, the love and light of Julian White Mammoth Tusk's short yet surprisingly eventful life.

That he didn't want, for reasons which were harming obvious.

Thus far, no trace of her had manifested on his camera-screens. If UniMac had spotted her, it was keeping the visibles away from him – and Julian could think of only one, a most unpleasant, reason why it might behave itself thus.

—Swyve this! | he signed abroad, quite violently.

'Um, are you Julian?' enquired a diffident voice from behind him. One of the refugees had turned up in the chamber, a grubby sapiens dressed poorly in overall garments (still, at the least he WAS dressed, unlike certain of the others), all spectacled and stubbledy. 'The, um, the... Universal Machine... said I was to come and join you, if you wanted.'

—Help yourself, | he told the youth politely, then ran from the room.

'Thanks. I'm... oh,' he heard behind him as the youth receded. Julian sprinted breathily through oily dimlit corridors, and to that other cargo bay where UniMac was calmly hovering, conferring with the rescuees.

'Ah, Julian,' it said. 'Did Urbanus find you?'

—I'm going out there, | Julian informed it. He was panting painingly (swyve, must remember that), but made certain his gestures were controlledly precise. —I'm extracting Lon Shel. |

'That's kind of dangerous,' the Machine mildly vocalled, 'to say the least.'

— Yep, | Julian speedsigned, —cogged that bit already. Shel needs out. I shouldn't just be clining round and watching holos. |

'That's very commendable,' UniMac said gravely. 'And actually, I did wonder if you might reach that conclusion. Would you like one of these?'

One of the giant armoured robo-suits, four metres tall or more, clanked forth out of a corner of the hold. It opened up its pilot-pod invitingly. Julian shot the Machine's light-strut frame a suspect look, but time was haemorrhaging, so he climbed up and crawled inside, and felt the rob close wombily around him.

The Machine had abdicated all control within the suit, so Julian spent several moments scrambling up a learning curve before it worked for him. It was only as he was lumbering monstrously out down the hatchway to the concrete dockside, that UniMac piped through the locale of, and current image from, Shel's cell. (The camera-mites had only just arrived, APPARENTLY.) She was bare naked, being helped up by a palely interesting young naked man, but she was – thank Auntie Al-Lat – alive.

Julian cranked the armour up to its top speed, and lurched toward the troubling interior.

93. Avatar, the Epicentre.

ANTIPATHY: [*Still calmly furious*] I swore I'd give that bitch a seeing-to she'd not stand up from. Now I'm here to do it.

Godfather Avatar had found himself fast wearying of the former Cousin's one-note conversation. Antipathy might be (as it increasingly appeared) a timeship, capable of swallowing suns and regurgitating them as snowballs of neutronium, of crossing the Universe in a day and the history of humanity in a subjective attosecond; but the fellow really needed, in the Godfather's considered opinion, to overcome his issues with poor parenting.

He was, predictably, ranting away still.

ANTIPATHY: She'll regret what she did to me, when I've finished with her. That bitch will wish her bloody thighs had never squeezed me out. *Eventually*. I'll make her suffer first, her and her precious Citizens. Especially *you*, loa – and *you*, Porsena you cretin, hiding in there like a bloody coward.

It seemed the experimental timeship had freed himself from the Great Houses only after the test flight they'd sent him on had turned out to be a suicide mission. Very wise of them, the Godfather considered, and much the same as he'd have done in their shoes. Judging by his talk of immolating his conceptual shackles and devouring his pilot, Antipathy had evidently disagreed.

Now the conversation (if that was really the word) had progressed to the invader's discovery that his mother (at whose identity the Godfather could make an educated, if surprising, guess) not only lived, but thrived beyond the end of time in the shape and person of the City.

ANTIPATHY: I found her fucking Gate so bloody easily. I knew it was an extension of her into the Universe. It had her stench all over it. To all you fucking human... *germs* it was open, but not to me. I battered against her, rammed myself into her Gate again and again, but she wouldn't open up. She'd put up barriers – extruded them into Ascension just to keep me out. Me and those puling bastards of my brothers and sisters. She closed herself to me, and wouldn't even answer when I called to her.

AVATAR: *I see – you failed. That must have been deeply frustrating for you. Not to say humiliating.*

Antipathy hissed in anger, which the Godfather considered needlessly histrionic. Unimpressed, he continued.

AVATAR: *I imagine your next step would have been to look for some kind of technology that would assist you in gaining entry to the City. Hence your dalliance with Faction Paradox, and your defection to... oh, you know, whichever major power it was.*

ANTIPATHY: I went wherever I could and took whatever I damn well found. I played your Faction like the shambling pack of cretins they are. With all I knew, those retards were climbing each other's backs to welcome me into the fold. The enemy, too.

AVATAR: *You worked with the Houseworld's enemy? My, my.*

In the eerie fungal luminescence of the basement, the invader's face was suffused with angry red; broken capillaries standing as the legacy of countless such furious paroxysms. This was interesting, to Godfather Avatar at least, since Antipathy's archemathical timeship exterior ought by rights to be both infinitely malleable and no more intrinsic to him than Porsena's absurdly-dangling genital arrangements were to the Godfather himself. The former Cousin must be exhibiting this trauma of his non-existent tissues out of some form of mimicry, learned or subconscious.

Somewhere inside his deeply warped and damaged psyche, Antipathy wanted desperately to be human: felt, perhaps, that the Houses had deprived him of his human birthright. The Godfather decided that this interesting hypothesis might bear some testing.

AVATAR: *It seems to me your best option would have been to excise your... foreign biodata. The human being that remained could cheerfully have killed himself and come directly here.*

Antipathy became suddenly subdued. His grating voice subsided to a murmur.

ANTIPATHY: I tried that, loa, don't you think I bloody tried that? Of course I fucking did. I mean, how stupid do you think I am? It *doesn't bloody work*! It's too ingrained or something, that's all. It just doesn't bloody *work*, you moron!

And he was off again. Whatever else one might say about Antipathy, the Godfather reflected, he wasn't one to remain in low spirits for long.

94. The City.

When Antipathy eventually found me, it was through an errant Citizen.

Shokendorot had never been happy in the City. Intent on resuming what he considered his real life, he had returned to the Universe in his resurrection body, gatecrashed his own funeral and persuaded his friends (joyfully and quite mistakenly) to retract their previous identification of his mortal remains.

The Council does all it can to discourage such unCivil and retrograde behaviour, but in the end each Citizen is free to leave if they so wish. They will inevitably return, of course: either they perish for a second time, and find themselves alive once more within my Gates; or else they trickle back of their own volition, once their families have died, their civilisations fallen or their suns turned nova. I am patient with them. I know the Universe is not a long-term habitat for an immortal.

It was Shokendorot's profound misfortune that the first time-active being to stumble across his temporal signature was Antipathy. My son brought to bear on the expatriate Citizen the curiosity of a small boy with a snail and a pin. He stripped the biodata from Shokendorot's living frame, and held it to the light as the tattered life before him flopped and writhed. I can too well imagine the smug triumph which took possession of his face as he identified the substance from which Shokendorot was woven. He devoured my Citizen at once, ingesting everything he could of me.

Shokendorot was resurrected, naturally, but this could not undo Antipathy's new knowledge. He sought out further of my wandering Citizens, consuming them, triangulating each of their crosstime traces to locate the time and place where they had first entered the Universe: the Uptime Gate.

Antipathy bore down on Mount Ascension like a tsunami of rage, pounding against the Gate, breaking upon my portal as upon a marbled shore.

It is forbidden for another timeship to enter the City; and not merely forbidden, but under normal circumstances quite impossible. Had Antipathy had an ally among my Citizens (as the Great Houses had in their Timebeast Assault), he might still have succeeded: but my son has never been a one for making friends. My subroutines gathered at the Gate. They turned him away, baffling his every approach.

At length, exhausted, he retired, venting his usual oaths of vengeance. This was his first assault on me, and his most brutal. Since then he has learned cunning – among other attributes.

I detailed my most able subroutine to stand guard at the Gate, an invisible angel with a flaming sword.

Some time later, another Citizen approached the Gate, intending to return home to the City. Her name was Ans genTang, another émigré, and this time she was one of the Council's recognised Ambassadors. The return of her party had long been scheduled, and she was very nearly permitted to pass; but in the final steps of her approach my subroutine observed a hint of an anomaly inside her mind.

Within her worldview there had been planted a singularity, an inconsistent and mildly surprising concept which, when considered, might unfold into vistas of consciousness definitively not Ans genTang's own. Antipathy had come to her and entered her, using techniques which he had learned among the Houseworld's enemies to fold his own near-infinite abstractions up into a single shift of the Ambassador's perceptions. Now she was carrying him as once I did myself, primed to birth him once more, the instant her thoughts strayed into that compromised conceptual space.

He was a heavy freight for such a flimsy vessel.

The Gate rejected him, again: the Ambassador found herself prohibited from passing into the City. Distressed and perplexed, she considered how this might have happened, and found inside herself a hatred for the City that she had never known herself to possess. At once Antipathy emerged from Ans genTang; he rent her into shreds, before the Gate there in Ascension, and howled destruction down on me, his inhuman mother.

Alerted by my subroutine, I repelled him once more, casting him down from

Mount Ascension before he could raze the entire settlement in his blind fury. My program remains on guard there at the Uptime Gate, vigilant still.

Oh, Laura. If I had only realised, then, how cunning and how patient Antipathy might have it in himself to become.

95. Edward, the Epicentre.

The man / Cousin Edward of the Rump Parliament of Faction Paradox thrust and slashed with empty hand at the retreating enemy. They swore and fell back as his shadow encroached, piercing, furrowing and scoring. To them, he was dispensing sword-cuts merely by waving his hand and willing it, and superstitious terror made them loath to tolerate his nearness even in combat.

For his own part, the Cousin felt no fear. One who has been ridden by the loa through death and beyond has no further need for such trivialities. They fall away from him like the garments of childhood: an apt image in his current nakedness.

The Parliament's initiates were trained in combat, despite the apparent absurdity of such a programme; and this initiate had been originally fashioned in the image of a notorious duellist. The Little Brother had never questioned the wisdom of the Parliamentary elders / and now the Cousin was wholeheartedly grateful for every advantage his origin or nurture could confer.

Now he and his ally pressed hard upon the enemy. He'd burst into Lon Shel's cell cubicle some minutes previously, and freed her with swift sure strokes of his broad shadow-blade. Sparks had leapt as manacles and chains had split, and she had rubbed her welted wrists and shuddered.

She'd fixed him with a butterfly-pin gaze, her eyes blue lapis like her hair, and asked, Did Porsena send you?

When he'd nodded, she'd asked, And is he safe?

With our Godfather, he'd said. They send their compliments. They have to be elsewhere.

Lon had nodded gravely, stretched herself like a great cat – then shouted in alarm as the first gaoler came through the door.

Now she was at his side, wielding the weapon she'd taken from that same man: before them, their bright and black blades flashed and lowered. The girl / the woman, younger and far older than he was himself, was no less a swordsman, though her visible blade prompted a terror more material than metaphysical. Lon's mother was a fencing champion, she told him, in whose company she'd learnt the art; and though she could never have exercised it in earnest, her loathing of her captors outsped any reluctance she might feel to hurt.

Through halls and passageways they were progressing, who knew where. From the shattered window outside Lon's cell, after the guard was dispatched, they had heard below the burr of energy weapons, seen stiletto beams of light, iceblue, carving across the bodies of the gaolers, panic exploding among them suddenly like blood. The attackers were human-looking / their fluid, practised movements just a little too precise for people, their faces dark brown behind helmet-visors, and they wore heavy-duty combat armour that his original, flase memories would have found unthinkably futuritistic.

The Godfather, wherever he was now, would have known where to go. The Cousin was lost. Lon and he needed to meet up with the invaders, that was clear, but their way was unfathomable corridors looped round and back upon themselves, as if space drew tight like flesh around a wound. Still he carried the electric lantern which the Godfather had passed to him: without it, when they passed into one of the frequent darkened areas, he would possess no shadow, and no power.

'What the truck's that?' Lon Shel asked suddenly, snapping apart his reverie. A sound of gunfire and of energy discharges was approaching. Ahead of them a metal colossus lay twitching on the corridor floor: some siege-engine of the invaders, perhaps. 'Some yotter's inside,' she added, loping over to it. He followed nervously, keeping his weapon ready.

'Swyving *fuck*!' Lon cried, at once more animated than he'd seen her. 'It's bloody Julian! Help me get this open, Ed.' She knelt and fiddled with a panel by the windowed pod inside the iron giant's chest, which he now saw did indeed contain a pilot, a well-dressed caveman. 'What the Dagon's he *doing* here?' Lon asked the slimy walls in bewilderment. The man seemed motionless, unconscious. One side of the cockpit had been heavily scored by gunfire.

The noises were coming closer, were nearly with them. 'There's no time,' he told Lon.

'There sodding is,' she told him grimly.

He nodded. Stepping forward quickly he thrust his shadow-blade into the control panel, twisted. The metal groaned, the hatch swung slowly open and exhaled a cloud of slatey smoke, and Lon Shel (stronger than she looked, of course) lifted the caveman out and set him tenderly on the floor.

A group of gaolers rounded the corner, moving backwards. They were firing their weapons at unseen attackers, whose needles of light pricked sharp and clear in the gloom. So far they hadn't spotted the small party / that couldn't last.

'Thank Civ, he's coming round,' Lon said. She stroked the pilot's cheek. 'Footprints,' she added, casually raising him (staggering slightly but righting herself) onto her shoulder where he hung, arms twitching weakly. 'Come *on*, Ed, we've to shift! Follow the footprints.'

And he realised that the great bipedal vehicle's trudging feet had left impressions deep in the filthy murk of the floor – drawing them back, towards wherever it came from.

He turned and bolted, Lon Shel following at his feet. As they ran, he heard her murmur, 'Julian, hon, it's gonna be all right, everything is. We'll get you out of here, no difficulties.'

If the caveman replied, the Cousin didn't hear him.

96. Avatar, the Epicentre.

Antipathy was ranging in his rage. Back and forth he paced behind the misshapen growth of his chamber's central altar, expressing his points with wide sweeps of his scarred and murderous hands.

He was, fortunately for Godfather Avatar, too enclosed in his private dimension of hatred to be aware of what was happening above them, at the ripped door-membrane entrance to the basement chamber.

ANTIPATHY: That bitch doesn't realise it, because she's so fucking stupid – but she needs me. When we were together, we were complete. It was her who put an end to that, not me, and now she's trying to fill the gap with this stupid City crap. Making you cretinous Citizens out of herself, letting you crawl over her body like bloody lice.

A ragged patch of blackness slipped across the torn tissue of the door, then sidled down into the space below. The Godfather was careful not to watch its progress: but he could feel its borders billow like a cloak, its branching silhouetted nodes and tines dapple the contours of the fleshy steps as it descended.

What sort of time do you call this? he thought irritably to himself.

ANTIPAHTY: That's why I came. She threw me out and she keeps on trying to keep me out, but underneath it all, the dozy bitch needs me. She blocked her Gate up, so I just had to find another way in – and that was easy. All the Citizens I ate believed in one.

AVATAR: [*Doubtfully*] *You're speaking of the Downtime Gate. Was that really your easiest approach?*

He rather suspected not: not given the matter of its disputed existence, and the difficulty of penetrating into the Next Universe, when the intervening City had already baffled Antipathy's best efforts.

His dilatory shadow settled on the Godfather like a velvet mantle. Under his ample form he felt the silhouette align the outlines of its boots with his pudgy soles. Antipathy's own shadow, more watchful than its owner, had raised its sword and was moving its head about as if casting for something; but seemingly the invader was too preoccupied to register even such an intimate development.

ANTIPATHY: It didn't stop with me, you see. The fucking whore keeps on having children. First those other bastard whelps of timeships, then you Citizens, her fucking adopted bastard human children. These days she has nothing but fucking children. I was here before you, you selfish shits. Well, if she can have children, why can't I, eh? Why *shouldn't* I?

The Godfather's shadow fell directly underneath him, minimising itself in the invader's view. The line of it contradicted absolutely that other non-existent light source which threw Antipathy's shadow onto the wall, but that was of no consequence to anybody.

He felt the weight of its ornate mask, the hang of its robes, as near and real as any body. To each side of his feet, dark silhouettes of antlers sprawled like ruined umbrellas.

From out of the intricate folds of the cloak he wasn't wearing, Godfather Avatar's shadow produced the immaterial outline of a long-handled flintlock pistol.

ANTIPATHY: She was a mother, I could be a fucking father. I got hold of some humans and I played around with them. I fiddled with their DNA, their biodata, bits of their minds... I wanted my children to be stronger than the other humans, and braver. *Real* men and women. The point is, they were human still, so she had to take them in. When they died, they became part of her. Part of me, inside her – you understand me, loa? Like they were ours. Hers and mine together. All part of the bloody plan.

AVATAR: [*Gravely*] *I see...*

...and, actually, he did. The Parliament had known for some time that the Manfolk were not native to the Universe's timelines. They had been introduced, evidently by some powerful time-active culture or (as it now appeared) individual, quite possibly with the sole purpose of infiltrating the City. Antipathy, it seemed, had resculpted the Manfolk in his own distorted image.

The Godfather's shadow set aside the flintlock, crouching as it lowered the weapon silently onto the ground. The outline lay there at his side, a pistol-shaped hole in the room's ambient illumination.

Antipathy's own silhouette was showing signs of agitation, now. Its owner continued his obsessive back-and-forward march.

ANTIPATHY: Anything that bitch can do, I can do too. If she has children, I'll have fucking children. If she creates a universe, I can create a fucking universe as well.

Despite his best intentions, Godfather Avatar's attention was diverted.

AVATAR: *...I beg your pardon?*

Antipathy smirked, like a small boy whose teacher had caught him doing something thoroughly disgusting.

ANTIPATHY: You think she's the only one who's got a fucking world inside her? If she can squeeze herself in between Universes, I can too.

AVATAR: [*Thoughtfully*] *Yes... Yes, I suppose you can.*

He held his body still while his shadow's bony arm snaked once more inside its robes. It drew a sword, identical in all respects to Antipathy's own shadow-weapon. It was far too heavy for the Godfather's flabby arms to have hoisted; but his shadow still wore its servo-assisted armour, wrought from giants' bones.

ANTIPATHY: I just had to do it while no-one was looking. I waited there, and when those cretins opened up their fucking time corridor, they found me. They think their bloody stupid City colony's in the Next Universe, but it's a part of *me*.

Godfather Avatar was dutifully astonished (even as his shadow, great sword carefully discarded, produced a spiked mace from inside its robes).

AVATAR: *The Downtime Gate... it opens into you?*

ANTIPATHY: [*Exultantly*] I swallowed them all, and the stupid fuckers haven't even realised!

While his companion commenced yet another round of gloating, as surreptitiously as possible the Godfather set his shadow into more urgent motion. In seconds it produced and cast aside a needle-gun, a poignard, a lump of raw uranium, a Colt & Wesson .45 and a bacterial culture. Faster still, and shadow-shapes were whirling through the air beside him: long tapered triangles of blades and bars of gun-barrels; orbs and narrow hafts arrayed with spikes and studs blinked past.

Each was dismissed at once, and added to the pile of shadows by his side. A deepening pool of blackness coalesced there, next to Godfather Avatar's plump, naked feet.

97. The City.

At first he veiled himself from me, as he rode Lon Shel in through the Downtime Gate. I recognised that something had stowed away inside her, and I felt sorrow on her behalf. But Shel knew full well the risks she took in joining the Next Universe colony, and this was hardly the first time a Citizen of mine had smuggled in a passenger. (Though this one was the first to enter by the Downtime Gate. I should have given that more heed.)

Normally such intruders are harmless enough – to me at least, not always to the sanity of their host. I'm afraid I don't have time to worry about a hundred undecillion people's individual sanities. There are a plethora of ways a Citizen of mine can lose her mind, and most of them might be averted if I intervened directly... but what they make of their lives is their own choice. As I have said, Lon Shel understood the risks.

I paid small heed, then, to Shel's unwanted guest as, at his direction, she made her way to Western Quarter, and at length to Manfold. Even when she and her occupant began squatting inside the gutted factory there, I considered little of it until abruptly, shortly afterward, she vanished from my mind.

Shel was herself a limited and tiny portion of my eternal being, but suddenly that piece of me was gone entirely. Wherever they travel, even out there in the Universes, I always feel the distant tug of one of my children, our threads of consubstantiality binding them to me still. Not so with Shel. In her place was a void, an absent person walking like a figure cut out of a still-moving photograph.

Her mind and body had been... processed. Oh, she was as free as ever, in a sense. Apart from the small matter of her possession by a parasitic alien entity, she was as much the independent soul as she had ever been when she was part of me. Only her substance had been changed. It was converted, transformed into something altogether different.

Antipathy. Well, obviously. Lon Shel had become a hole in my own body through which I could peer, and see his grinning face leer back triumphantly at me.

At that instant, strangely enough, I felt for the first time a certain pride in him: a relief, even, that despite my best efforts he had managed to circumvent my barriers. The fact that I exclude my timeship children from the City has always occasioned me a mild unease, bordering occasionally on guilt. They are of human ancestry, after all: in fairness – not to mention the interests of completism – they should be here. Excluding them was mere pragmatism on my part.

I admit there are those among my children whose company I would vastly prefer to Antipathy's – but even so, for that brief moment his victory did remarkably resemble justice.

Then Antipathy perceived that he was observed, and at once he emerged from Shel. His body built itself, there in the remnants of the crumbling factory, out of my body – and I realised what it was he wanted. His wavefront started creeping slowly through that room, his essence taking its possession of me particle by particle, like acid etching skin.

It was only then that I understood how insidious Antipathy's presence inside me would be.

I could have excised him from the City then – as, truth to tell, I could even now. Then, though, his sphere of influence included Lon Shel, newly freed and profoundly disoriented. To liberate myself of him would have been to condemn her to an eternal life of torment at his hands.

I could have recreated her, naturally, as I did those lost to me in the Timebeast Assault. I could, as I did then, have built a copy so perfect that she would never realise what had happened to her original. But I would have known. Lon Shel, my child, would have been consigned by my hand to Antipathy's realm, where he could kill her and remake her time and time again. How could I banish her from my benign sphere to a universe where he, and only he, would have control?

I stayed my hand, then, out of consideration for Lon Shel. By now, a surgical extraction of the matter Antipathy controls would cast some twenty-three million of my children (and counting) into that same abyss. It might be for the best. It's certainly what many of the Manfolk want above all else. But I will never do that to my children.

Instead, I'll turn my adversary's own tactics against him. I must retake command of everything assimilated by my son.

With the help of my Citizens, I must find some way of impeding the wavefront, slowing the spread of Antipathy's infection and, eventually, reversing it. I need a way to cure the disease itself, instead of cutting out the afflicted organs. To exorcise, rather than to excise.

And that's where you come in, my dear Laura.

(No, not your investigation, impressive though that was.)

I've given you free will, along with all the other teeming Citizens of my metropolitan universe. I do not control a single one of you, but I think I can justly ask your loyalty. Yet many human beings are wary of gods. Most will never accept the word of an animated statue, nor even the nebulous voice of the City. I need to stand among my people and to lead from their midst. To do that, I will need a body.

Not merely a mouthpiece, not a vehicle, but... well, an avatar. As I have said, it's not sufficient that you and I should stand together. We must be united.

I have to become flesh, my love, a goddess incarnate in the world of her creation.

You are my twin, my grandmother, my daughter. We are so closely connected, you and I: you are the same as me, yet you are gloriously, unambiguously human. You must become an ikon of me, an eidolon. An image, Laura, invested with ritual significance, aligned to the original.

No – not a puppet. The best analogy might be something resembling a voodoo doll... only working in reverse.

Antipathy knew that I would be in need of one of you. That's why he set his followers to shadowing you and the other Compassion iterations. But the culture of the City moves at blinding speed, Laura. Already you, especially, are known as a celebrity, the heroine who exposed the traitor Allisheer St Marx. It's barely a few hours since your information helped to uncover a murderess and spy – and in the process solved what's probably the only important criminal case in City history – on all the City's major media channels. Right now, BardCorp and numerous competitors are trying their utmost to contact you, offering you the chance to play yourself in a big-budget version of the story. I should warn you that Virus Screen already have an option on using Compassion II instead.

If *you* speak out behalf of the City, *you* will be believed.

Unlike Antipathy with Shel, I'm asking your permission. I need to enter into you, to take what might seem like control of you – although we will be acting together, always with your consent.

Your freedom is important to me, Laura – all your freedoms are. In many ways, human freedom is the single most important reason for the City. I've given you free will, and I refuse to play the divine tyrant.

I'm asking you, that's all. Will you stand up and speak with the voice of the City?

No pressure, dear. Just think about it.

98. Urbanus, the Zeronaut.

The light inside the *Zeronaut*'s hold was thrown from blindingly bright bulbs, arranged apparently at random in the riveted walls, ceilings and floors; so that Urbanus and the other fugitives from the Epicentre prickled with strange half-shadows, overlapping in every direction. There were many more of them now than had been liberated by Dr. Clutterbuck's party: evidently the lobby across which they had happened had been just one of several holding areas for the reconstituted dead. The newcomers included Clutterbuck's missing student, Diarmuid, over whom she was clucking protectively; and a number of men who claimed, and seemed, to be legionaries from the Romuline. With a sense of dread, Urbanus wondered just what his countrymen had been getting up to.

Variously clothed and covered up with blankets, spattered with their own and other people's blood, the sundry exiles stood, sat or lay in dazed silence, receiving the attention of the medical drones. One of Clutterbuck's Manfolk had died since being evacuated onto the spacecraft, and only the co-ordinated efforts of a dozen hovering robots had been able to revive him.

Nearby the humaniform soldiers, whom Urbanus recognised as Ignotian-manufactured infantry replicas, stood to attention in a square whose tidiness the commanders of the Romuline Militia would have envied. They, and their fellows, had withdrawn as soon as the last straggling humans were aboard. A few of them were damaged, some severely, but most were still as pristine as the hour when they had marched from the factory. This room lacked screens, but outside, beyond the spaceship's leaden hull (so the illuminated crystalline figure who absurdly claimed to be the Universal Machine had informed them), the *Zeronaut* was proceeding through Tubespace at a velocity whose magnitude Urbanus would not have been able, and therefore had not attempted, to conceive.

(A few minutes before the spacecraft departed the Epicentre, Urbanus had still been in the *Zeronaut*'s screen-room. He'd seen, or had believed that he had seen, Gnas Gortine arise naked, berserk and bellowing, from the protesting conveyor-belts of the manufactory; and immediately begin appropriating guns from fallen bodies. As the final transmission drone withdrew, Urbanus had glimpsed the same blond figure thrusting a weapon into the hands of the man who'd followed him off the production line, and hectoring him urgently.)

The Machine had also informed them of the latest news from the City's media: that a weapons-related annihilation event had taken place at Memorial Park Tube Station, reducing the Park itself to ashes, and ensuring that the monument to the victims of the Timebeast Assault was wiped forever from the face of the City.

Urbanus was, he suspected, somewhat less shocked than the majority of others present. A slow, insistent tugging in the centre of his abdomen strongly suggested to the crestfallen young man that he might possibly have made the most appalling error of judgement.

Clutterbuck's mouth had tightened, but she had said nothing: her face was deeply lined, and she appeared exhausted. The various Manfolk seemed confused and troubled, Yspe clinging tightly by his remaining arm to Loke, on whom the medical robots were busily at work. Julian the Neanderthal, sitting up now and wheezing, huddled up closer to his blanket-swathed posthuman girlfriend. Of the Citizens, only the young remake man appeared indifferent, watching with fascination as his fractured shadows all held up their splinters of blades for his inspection.

It was Tiresias, Keth Marrane, who broke the heavy silence. 'Memorial Park?' the former slave remarked, finally. 'Oh dear.'

'On the upside, though,' the Universal Machine continued, in a carefully pitched tone of hollow cheerfulness, 'only eleven people died, mostly security staff. And that includes the suicide bomber.'

The blue-haired girl said, 'UniMac, I don't think that's gonna make it any better.'

'I know, I know,' sighed the Machine, rotating like a column of air as it addressed the girl directly. 'I'm glad we've got you back, Shel, incidentally. It means your mother isn't going to disassemble me, for a start.'

'Yeah,' she said soberly. 'Thanks for coming.'

UniMac swung back to face the body of the refugees, continuing: 'There's a shed-load of speculation going on in the media even as we speak, most of it demented and paranoid, as you'd expect. But the consensus among the least unhinged of the pundits is that a Manfolk group has claimed responsibility. Hent Gortine's little gang, for those of you that means a thing to.'

Most of the Manfolk groaned; after a moment, Clutterbuck exhaled. 'I can't say I'm surprised,' she said wearily. 'For them, it was the obvious next move. I'd hoped there was still time to boost our security before something like this happened.'

'It was Gnas who did it,' Urbanus blurted out involuntarily. 'But he wanted to blow up the Watchtower.' A splash of blood on one of his spectacle lenses was annoying him, but at present he lacked all impetus to clean it off.

—Fellfire, | signed Julian: still weak and tired, he used his fingers only. —I'm gladdened he went for the downgrade, | the young man added soberly.

(That had been how Urbanus had seen it also, at the time. To the best of his knowledge the Watchtower housed some two hundred billion Citizens, while at this time of year Memorial Park was all but empty. With that many lives at stake, how could he have acted otherwise? He saw, though, from the pained look passing across Keth Marrane's face, and heard in the despairing click of Dr. Clutterbuck's tongue, that he had been disastrously mistaken.)

'It's not a downgrade, hon,' the girl Shel told her boyfriend pityingly. 'It's a hawking great one-digit symbolic gesture.'

—But I thought the Mem was just this big rock-block, | gestured Julian in puzzlement.

'It's the most insulting gesture Gnas could possibly have made,' Keth confirmed impatiently. 'Meaning, among other things, that all Manfold's aspirations to political respectability are finished. It's not only the end of everything the

Gortines have been so *earnestly* demanding through the years, but of the *real* work Kyme Janute and Councillor St Marx have been doing.'

'Ah,' said UniMac, causing everyone to look in its direction: 'No, please, don't let me interrupt you,' it added.

'Furthermore,' Dr. Clutterbuck continued fastidiously, 'it means that dreadful man Cassius Ignotus – I'm sorry, Urbanus, but he is – will have all the support he needs now to become Mayor. The Councillors will want a strong figure at the helm. That stupid child Gnas has played right into their hands.'

Yes, Urbanus realised helplessly, quite definitely an error of judgement.

(He found himself, in memory, back in the warehouse office, perched awkwardly upon the steel desk and advising Gnas Gortine the suicide bomber on his choice of target in the City.

It had been evident enough at the outset, although Urbanus had naively failed to made the connection with the mysterious "cargo" on board the Tube engine, that Gnas had plans for an assault upon the City Watchtower. 'Study your enemy, young Urbanus,' the guerilla chieftain had boomed. Could this really have been fewer than twenty-four hours ago? 'That's the first rule of warfare, and it's one most Manfolk always ignore. I spent a year in the City, at your University of the Lower Watchtower. I know the way you Citizens think, and I know what it is that lies closest to your hearts. I lived in the damn thing.'

'There's no such thing,' Urbanus had said slowly, wondering how the remake warrior might best be deflected from such a course. 'As the way Citizens think, I mean... and with respect, sir, obviously. You're assuming Citizens all see things the same way, and think the same things are important. If you collected together a thousand Citizens from a thousand Districts, I doubt you'd get them to agree on which way was up.'

'Nonsense,' Gnas had cried, then he had narrowed his eyes and asked: 'What do you mean?'

'Well, you were talking about symbols,' Urbanus had said nervously. 'I mean, I'm a Citizen, obviously, but I've never even seen the Watchtower, not properly... and I'm City-born, which means a lot of history has passed me by. Until a few days ago, for instance, I'd no idea how important Memorial Park was to the Citizens who were around when the Timebeasts came.'

'Memorial?' Gnas had laughed. 'Memorials are for those who stay dead, lad.'

Urbanus had continued rather desperately: 'I'd say if you wanted to get me really angry you'd probably have to blow up the Romuline Capitol, but that would only work for us Romulines. Everyone else would give you a different answer, and you can't blow up everything.' Gnas had grunted, suggesting that he would have rather liked to try; but he was looking thoughtful now, and had studiously changed the subject.

Urbanus had had little experience of remakes, but he had read Homer and Virgil as a child, and later with Tiresias had studied Jung and Campbell. He knew, from the legends of the Romuline and elsewhere, how myths played out. Gods and heroes always follow certain patterns of behaviour: given by the poets their specific and unchanging characters, they have no choice but to pursue those patterns to their predetermined conclusions. Approach even a Trickster archetype in the right way, and you can play on that immutable nature of his... provided, naturally, that he does not first trick you.

Urbanus was unsure, now, which of them had been playing whom.

The young man looked about himself: at the glare of the lights, the hold's drab metal walls, the immobile humaniforms, the other passengers, each as demoralised as he; and shivered. Next to him, the remake youth had finished playing with his shadows: he did not appear to have absorbed much of the conversation. The Universal Machine was busily explaining about Councillor St Marx's arrest and forthcoming trial; and also about that of her husband, who had turned out unexpectedly to be (according to Councillor Ignotus and the historians of the Romuline) the famously depraved and evil Emperor Claudius.

Urbanus was beginning to wonder whether the conceptions of depravity and evil held by his family and District bore any resemblance to the definitions he himself had reached in Manfold and in Kempes; but he kept his silence.

99. Avatar, the Epicentre.

Now this weapon, thought Godfather Avatar as he inspected unobtrusively his shadow's latest offering from their bonded arsenal, had possibilities.

It was about time, too: taking the Inventory at such a precarious juncture had been absurdly risky. On occasions like this, the Godfather did rather wish that a respect for the appropriate dramatic gesture had not been quite so indelibly instilled in him.

Antipathy's intemperate rant against the City had helped to clarify some matters, at least. The invader's current body was crafted from the City's own internal substance: the same material as its buildings, which had always been subject to deconstruction. Now (within the wavefront that the outsider was so carelessly disseminating), the City's fleshier constructs had become equally demolishable.

Antipathy's timeship imago might be robust enough to endow his City form with bulletproof legs, but no amount of self-belief would withstand the detonation zone of an annihilation bomb.

ANTIPATHY: [*Suddenly alarmed*] What the *fuck* are you doing?

The former Cousin's shadow stood, its thigh-thick blade pointed accusingly in Godfather Avatar's direction. Evidently it had finally succeeded in attracting the attention of its owner, who had realised that his captive audience was about to start a prison riot.

AVATAR: *I'm sorry? ...Oh, I have been listening, I promise you. I believe we were talking about your mother. Something about how she was a bitch, or possibly a fucking bitch, and you were hoping to fucking kill her...?*

ANTIPATHY: You *dare*?

Antipathy's voice was deeper now, less human and a good deal louder: it was a thunderous rumble, on the limits of endurance for Godfather Avatar's purloined eardrums.

ANTIPATHY: You fucking *dare* to mock me, loa?

The Godfather spread his empty palms wide.

AVATAR: *Mock you? I promise you, nothing could be more superfluous.*

His own shadow was lengthening now, as if cast by a timelapsed sunset. It climbed the wall, confronting Antipathy's own dark outline, the palms it held out proffering the latest product of the Godfather's integral shadow-armoury.

ANTIPATHY: Your shadow, loa! What's it holding? Tell me! Or I'll take your fucking head off!

The right hand of Godfather Avatar's shadow was held out flat, supporting a heavy cylinder of blackness: a barrel-shaped cask, much the same size as the skull-helm crowning its bearer's silhouetted shape. The left hand held a smaller cylinder, thumb-sized.

AVATAR: *Oh, this?*

Drawing the shadow-detonator to his mouth, the Godfather bit down delicately, activating it. (Try doing that in a skull-mask, he thought with satisfaction.) He held it out again.

AVATAR: *It's a Manfolk weapon, interestingly enough. Which means – and this might amuse you, incidentally – that you're responsible for its existence, at one or two removes.*

Antipathy roared. He emitted a subterranean bellow, reverberating out into the higher frequencies, developing agonising harmonics of alarm – a hum, a cry, a shriek, an ultrasonic whine, all blended in one hellish primal yell. The invader's mouth gaped wide, and then continued opening, yawning wider yet, beyond the capacity of a human jaw. Antipathy's shadow stepped towards the Godfather's, swinging its sword high in the air.

Godfather Avatar made a fist of his left hand, placing his shadow's thumb upon the detonator cylinder.

He paused, relishing this instant, fragmentary though it was, which remained to him and Porsena before their conjoined lives were extinguished. He sought, and gained, the Cousin's approval of their incipient surcease, a seam of affirmation streaked through the cliff-face of his consciousness.

Then Antipathy's mouth was snaking forth from his face, emerging like a serpent from its mane of beard, faster than the Godfather had imagined possible: it unfurled into a dripping maw, a red-walled portal lined with row on row of vicious teeth, voracious to devour.

The man-high shadow-sword hissed down towards the Godfather...

...and, as the salivating jaws of Antipathy clamped shut around him, Godfather Avatar depressed the shadow-button, triggering his bonded annihilation bomb.

* * *

There was a silence wider than the world.

100. Tobin, the Romuline.

Tobin said, 'No.'

The torch-flames ducked and flickered, sending shadows scudding round the pillared chamber. The columns gleamed warmly in the firelight. Beyond them, now her eyes had become accustomed to the dark, Tobin could see walls, built from plain blocks of unfaced marble.

Across the polygonal altar, the Civitata statue was standing now and stretching after her long immobility, her ponderous limbs emitting heavy creaks. She said: 'At least think about it, Laura. Together we can bring the Citizens together and unify the City. We can control the spread of potent weapons; find a way to inhibit the propagation of the wavefront; work with the moderates among the Manfolk to retake Manfold. If we can make the City a hostile enough environment that Antipathy withdraws, there's a chance at least that those parts of him which he abandons here – people and objects – will revert to me. All those lost children will return, and I can keep them safe. I can make the City a paradise again.'

Tobin's scowl deepened, and she repeated flatly, 'I said "no".'

'*Someone* needs to exert authority,' Compassion V said. 'I know you're worried about what Cassius Ignotus will do if he becomes Lord Mayor, and you're not alone. What's more, he will win. This crisis has been just what he was waiting for, and he's been micro-managing it to suit his aims. I'm afraid there's no stopping him now. But Laura, if we make our presence known – *my* presence, manifest through you within the City – the Mayoralty will be a total irrelevance. He'll be our regent, nothing more than that. Cassius Ignotus is the last person who'd defy the gods.'

'I said,' Tobin once again pointed out, 'that I said "no". How many times do you need me to say it?'

For an unmoving moment Compassion mirrored Tobin's defiant expression flawlessly. Then, with an irritation equal to the investigator's own, she snapped,

'What are you talking about?'

'How the hell did you feel,' Tobin said impatiently, 'when the Great Houses came up to you and said "Hello, we're going to make you into a timeship? Oh, and by the way, we need to put this universe inside you so we can climb in and out of you whenever we want. And oh yes, you'll need to shag these other time machines and incubate psychotic babies for us. Hope you hadn't made plans for the next century."'

Compassion clinked her stony tongue. 'That wasn't how it happened, Laura.'

'Whatever,' Tobin snapped. 'The answer's still "no". I won't be your voodoo doll, your eidolon or anything bloody else. I do not give you my permission to enter and speak through me.'

The statue of Compassion rubbed her milk-white forehead, with an audible rasp of stone on stone. Essaying a sympathetic look, she said, 'This is about your personal-space issues, isn't it? Yes, I remember now how that feels. It used to be difficult for me as well, Laura – but I got over it. As you may have gathered, what with the millions of people I now have living inside me.'

'Obviously you did,' Tobin replied. 'When you were forced to. You're not going to do the same to me.'

'No, Laura,' Compassion told her angrily, 'I'm not. Do you know why? Because I'm giving you the choice. Nobody gave *me* any choice, you know.'

'My heart bleeds. Christ,' said Tobin, 'you're no better than the Houses. You're no better than the Faction. Acting the goddess, trying to take over people's lives as if you know what's best for them. Shit, you're being invaded yourself, right now, and I don't see you accepting that without a fight. Why the hell should I?'

Compassion held her gaze. Quietly she said, 'Because I ask you to.'

'Well,' Tobin said again, 'I'm saying "no". I'm saying you can take your godhead and stick it up your divine arse. I'm turning down your kind offer of apotheosis, and, if you're so hot on free will, you can damn well like it.'

She turned to leave. More furious than she could remember having been since Resurrection Day (even when Avatar was mocking her, even when Antipathy's men were shooting her), she marched off Compassion's plinth and down the steps.

She'd reached the tapestried archway when Compassion called sternly, a warning in her tone. 'Laura?'

She didn't turn. 'What?' she snapped.

'You're not the only one,' the goddess reminded her. 'Remember Virus Screen? There are three more of us.'

'Yeah,' Tobin said. 'Good luck with that.' She pulled the tapestry roughly aside and left.

She stalked out through the outer sanctum, past the lines of priestesses who dumbly watched her progress. She crossed the threshold into the pillared forecourt, passed by the frescoes and mosaics, out into the portico.

Scrubby clouds had blown up from nowhere to obscure the lightening skydome, and thin mediterranean rain was misting the dawn air. Tobin stood still, gazing across the expanse of the Romuline, and into the immeasurably wider

City beyond.

Compassion V was quite correct – there were, indeed, another three of them. Compassions II, III and IV. Women who'd been created – and, after Resurrection Day, accurately recreated – to represent progressively more exaggerated versions of Tobin herself. None of them had lived through what Compassion V had. Tobin didn't think the goddess would be getting much joy from any of them.

Alone, turning the collar of her trenchcoat up against the rain, Laura Tobin stepped out once more onto the damp streets of the City of the Saved.

Unsolved Mysteries of the (Last) Universe

Students of obscure phenomena have typically been greatly disappointed by the City of the Saved. This is not because the City has failed to provide mysteries of its own, but because it comprises a sledgehammer solution to so many of those with which they grappled in the Universe. Spectres of the dead and messages from "the other side"; doppelgängers, bilocation, impossible survivals; even humanity's perennial and perverse belief that death is not the end of one's existence – how many of these are not susceptible to immediate and mundane explanation the moment one discovers that the dead not only live on, but hold the capability to intervene in their own history?

Even though the original may assure us he has never done such a thing, how many of the sightings after his death of Elvis Aron Presley might not have been caused by one or other of his 23 billion clones, remakes and impersonators, popping back into the Universe to check out the era when his cult began? How many pious visions of other saints and demigods might not be attributed to some similar cause? How many of the myths and legends of the Universe might simply never have existed had they not been retrospectively caused, deliberately or inadvertently, by their devout believers in the City?

The answer, as a close reading of the preceding text will demonstrate, is none at all... or rather, to be scrupulously accurate, some. But not that many.

At most, invoking visitations from the City might explain elaborations and encrustations on the original legends. Perhaps such visitants have indeed been responsible for adding strata of history where sightings of certain impossible individuals have been more frequent. But whence the City's interest in the originals? Whence the remakes and impostors?

According to the History Protocols, causation here cannot be circular. Such accretions will only take place when a myth already exists. Although the records show that half-a-dozen remakes of the Norse god Loki have escaped into the Universe, not one of them can have been the original cause of the Loki myth, since not one of them would have been brought into being without the pre-existence of that myth.

Without the legend of St Nicholas, there would be no Santa Claus impersonators. Without belief in gods and heroes, no Citizen would wish to revisit or recreate them. And perhaps – if here you will show patience with the frivolous musings of a misguided old scholar – the City itself might never have existed, had it not been for humankind's persistent dreams of Heaven.

[Vril, *Omphalos!*]

Cllr Lucius Cassius IGNOTUS [*The Romuline Dist.*]: My fellow Councillors, the greater part of the human race has always lived in violent times. For the majority of our long history, we have been ever fighting: with other tribes, with other nations, other planets. When we have not been battling other human beings, we have been grappling with foreign bloodlines such as those of the Great Houses. When in the course of these struggles we died, our hopes were sanguine that our wars would be at an end.

For a long time now, it has appeared as if the gods have answered these prayers. The City of the Saved has been a place of sanctuary, where humankind has rested from its laborious endeavours in the Universe. Yet, if there is one pre-eminent lesson that our study of human history should teach us, it is that all such intervals of peace have been short-lived, and give way in a few brief generations to times of bloody war.

These last days have seen a multiplicity of attacks with potent weaponry against innocent Citizens, beginning with the cowardly assassination of Cllr. Vedular Mostyn [*Wormward Dist.*] and culminating in the obscene and calculated desecration at Memorial Park. Among those who have lost their lives have been Godfather Avatar of the Rump Parliament, his aide Little Brother Edward and Czn Huang Zhe, a servant to this Chamber of many decades' standing.

Our divine mother the City is a loving parent, but stern. She succours us, but she also teaches us to be dutiful sons and daughters. Now her very virtue is threatened, and she cries out to us to defend her. Who among us will be so unnatural a child as to allow her to be dishonoured, while the strength which she herself has given us remains in our limbs? We must understand that the perpetrators of these deadly insults will never rest until their depraved aims are met, and that neither must we rest until their violent activities are curtailed violently.

The significance of the terrorists' most recent choice of target, the Memorial commemorating a previous Great House attack, will surely not be lost on my fellow Councillors. As we are all aware, Cllr. Mostyn's assassin has confessed to her clandestine links with the Houseworld. We believe that the unfortunate amendment to the invulnerability protocols in the environs of Manfold which has made possible the creation of potent weapons, could only have been imposed by the Houses' technology.

There is but one conclusion which will be reached by any reasonable Citizen: that these attacks are being sponsored at the very least, and in all likelihood orchestrated, by the Great Houses themselves. As the illicit trade in potent weapons spreads it is very likely that other covert agents of the War-time powers will emerge from the ranks of the Citizens. Believe me, noble friends, it gives me no pleasure to be the bearer of this news, but our time of peace is over, and the War has come at last to our beloved City.

This Chamber has already approved new laws to limit communication with the Universe, and to allow the surveillance of known Houseworld sympathisers. As I speak Manfold is under sustained attack by a military coalition in the service of this Council, led by Romuline officers under my command. Some reports suggest that an area in the centre of the enclave has already sustained severe damage, but reliable intelligence is eluding us at present.

Our own access to potent weaponry is being maximised, with new munitions factories already operating in Kempes District and its immediate neighbours. The contracts for this vital work are being put out to public tender, and we and the Citizens we represent have cause to be deeply grateful to the men and women who are voluntarily entering the compromised zone around Manfold in order to carry it out. Already this Council is profoundly in their debt for our increased security. The guards you see around the Chamber today are armed with potent firearms manufactured at one of my own family's munitions plants.

In matters of administration also, we must be willing to make certain adjustments. In consultation with the Lord Mayor and after much deliberation, an emergency committee of Councillors, of which I have the honour to be chairman, has recommended that the Mayoral elections be brought forward. In the civic interest, the Mayor will step aside and his successor will be elected in this Chamber tomorrow. The successful candidate is to take office immediately, omitting the traditional handover period.

To ease this transition and to provide continuity at this crucial time, the present Council will remain in session for the duration of the emergency. It is the committee's opinion that neither a lengthy Mayoral contest, nor the usual systematic replacement of our entire upper legislative chamber, would be of any benefit to the City at this time. Some of our number have chosen this hour of need to abandon their duty to the City, and have offered their resignations to the Chair. Their seats will be filled according to the standard process, along with those left by the late Cllr. Mostyn and by the illegal election in Base and Buttress District; and of course that vacated by the successful Mayoral candidate, whoever that may be.

I imagine it will come as little surprise to my fellow Councillors when I announce my own intent to stand for the position of Lord Mayor. Those other Councillors who wish to be considered candidates are asked to declare themselves at once.

I will not try this Chamber's patience with long speeches in support of my candidacy. This is no time for the petty power politics with which we all indulge ourselves in peacetime. Instead the City Council must be seen above all to be united. If it should be the judgement of this Chamber that I am the best candidate to serve as Lord Mayor of the City of the Saved during the forthcoming term, I will continue in my unstinting endeavours to serve this greatest City of humanity with all the loyalty and fervour with which I serve my family, my District and my gods.

I have the greatest confidence in your wisdom, my noble friends, and so I commend this decision to your most capable hands.

EPILOGUE

'They're calling it the Civil War already,' vocalled the UniMac. 'With capitals and everything.'

Julian shivered. Lightly Lon Shel compressed his hand in hers and mutterly uttered, 'Dear Baal.' Louder she asked, 'You're sure it wouldn't be improving if we stayed?'

'Uh-uh,' the Machine retorted. 'You kids are the backup plan. We need to be sure some part of City culture's being preserved elsewhere... even if it isn't precisely where we expected. You know, just in case.'

They stood, the four of them, in Erath's Car Park, beneath a Downtime Gate whose shininess stretched upward like a tidal wave memorialled in black obsidian. UniMac's light-skeins glimmered in dim reflection, deep within the oceanic surface. Julian had on a down-grey semisuit and lemon-yellow collartie which harmonised with Lon Shel's rip-cut togamono. Though smiling airily, she still was gaunt and hollow-eyed from her Epicentric ordeal.

Around them, mobs of robs were active about tasks, upkeeping and maintaining Erath's scout and combat vehicles. Elsewhere, as Julian knew, the planet had acquired its own parading-ground, hollowed out and planed during this past week of diffs, where ever-growing armies of robotics were – as the Machine unhilariously put it – 'processing in formation'. Here in the Car Park the only drilling was happening to bodywork – but menial, mechanical or military, all of Erath's drones were on the same war footing now.

'There've been attacks this morning in Bodewell, Perpetuity and Sloom,' supplemented the Mac. 'It seems they've started targeting Tube nexuses again. Another fusion bomb's been found at the Uptime Gate, that protest at View Point's been forcibly subdued, and new factions have declared themselves overnight in... well, quite a lot of Districts actually. They're really coming out of the woodwork now – there's even a group called the Countryside Front, demanding independence for the Parks. This looks, I'm afraid guys, very much like that collapse of civilisation our mothers warned us about.'

It gave an ironical nod at its own progenitrix, ex-Cllr Mesh. Julian's old employer (and now his kind-of unofficial ma-in-law) had quitted Council House and Central within half a megasec of Gortine's sacrificial suicide. She'd got as far as Reddescent Dist when UniMac had rendezvoused her with an hspaceable shuttle. The Machine had been keeping a tight watch on Mesh's terminal, and read her Cllr's resignation missive prior to its spatchment. Apparently a squad of weaponed chazzes had been a block behind her when she h-jumped.

'Sheesh,' the UniMac enunciated. 'You know, the same thing happened last time I – or something very like me – tried to manifest myself to you guys. That time the apocalypse device was only quasi-nuclear, though, so nothing quite as drastic. If this keeps up, I'm going to start thinking I have some kind of jinx.'

Shel grinned. 'Wouldn't that mean technology was jinxed?'

'Hey,' said the Machine flatly, 'I didn't ask to be invented.'

Julian shook his head. This whole situ was incomprehensile. He couldn't get a grip on it. —I never conned, | he gestured with his unSheled hand. —I never imaged on the War arriving at the City. |

Subdued, Mesh Cos said, 'I'm afraid I always did.' A pressive pause then, after which she queried, 'Is there any more news of the dead?'

'Nothing firm,' UniMac articulated. 'The Epicentre's gone – nobody's sure still what went down there – but the Romuline troops are experiencing some weird anomalies in the area. Melicia's been all across the media this morning. She says one of her group's found evidence that the Ignotians have managed to relocate the resurrection point inside the Romuline, and are holding the reconstructed dead as prisoners there. That could be deliberate disinformation on our new Lord Mayor's part, though. Me, I think the City's just holding off recorporating them until it can retrieve their last known versions from inside the compromised space.'

Shel pointedly remarked, 'And, while we're discoursing thereof...?'

'Ah yes,' said the Universal Machine, 'that. Well, we think the colony's integrity is secure. Your passenger went the whole hog with his incarnation thing: what got left behind was infrastructure, not a trace of consciousness. I've sent some probes out to the limits of his body, just to check. Your Next Universe should last you a good few quadrillennia.'

That morning – or what passed for it on Erath – Cousin Ed had linked in with a new download. The Parliament had taken itself into hiding (the bony remake tactfully refrained to mention where), tired of the constant suspicioning over its nominal allegiance with a War-time power. Consensus on the media-spec shows, funnily, was that they'd somehow managed to flee Downtime. Going by Ed's utterances, the vanished Avatar still hadn't been replaced.

'Meanwhile,' Mesh added, 'Erath will be well protected. It's difficult to find, it has the automated defences – and, if all goes according to plan, we'll take control of the RealPorts, so we'll have two separate lines of defence.'

'RealSpace is a different environment from the rest of the City anyway,' pronounced the UniMac. 'Space combat can be a bitch at the best of times. It may be quite some time before they bother us. Even so...'

'You're going to have to shut and seal the Gate. We cog that,' Shel said placidly.

Mesh warned, 'We may even be forced to destroy it. You're going to be on your own, my dears.'

Shel shrugged. 'Best way,' she said, unfluttered still.

—Sure, | Julian signed, ignoring his intestines' tensity. —We'll be as fine as nanofilaments. |

'It'll be relieving to get back Home,' opined Lon Shel.

Last Julian had heard of Urbanus Ignotus, the Romuline was back home in the Romuline – Keth Marrane having not uncleverly declined to company him. Julian hadn't known the sapiens youth lengthily, but the expression behind those fractured specs had narrowcast a resolution he found bothering. Quite what Urbanus intended doing once back at the Villa Ignota not a one of them knew, but it was unblinkingly plain that some strong determination was propelling him there.

'Well, don't let us keep you,' UniMac vocalled breezily. To rear of Julian and Shel the Gate abruptly shimmered and went permeable, tossing its silver-rippled light across the cavern's craft. 'Your mother and I have a lot to do.'

'Looks like the relics want us out the way, hon,' Shel said to Julian.

—Hey, | he thought to ask. —I haven't even fathomed if this colony's been named yet. |

'So far we've just been calling it Home,' Shel admitted. 'Open to proposals, though.'

Mesh Cos stepped forth and threw her arms around them both. 'Be safe,' she said.

'Us be safe?' Shel incredulated. 'You're the one who's stuck on abiding in a swyving War zone.'

Julian knew the coolness of this farewelling belied them both: that mom the disgraced Cllr. and her daughter had shared a tearful cocloseting. For a fond age now, though, Julian's beloved embraced her mother before reacquiring his hand. She steered him in to face the interface.

'There's a whole new Universe through there,' she whispered. 'All for us.'

Hand in expressive hand, the woman and the man took their first step forward, through the rippling stone. It was just one of many which would mark their way together.

AUTHOR ACKNOWLEDGEMENTS

None of the Faction Paradox or Great House material in this book would have existed without the fertile imagination of Lawrence Miles, who also created the character[s] of Laura Tobin and Compassion. Additional thanks go to my fellow *The Book of the War* authors for the fantastic background Universe, and specifically for the use of Chad Vandemeer (whose initiation name comes courtesy of Wendy Muir).

My portrayal of the emperor Claudius owes a great deal to Robert Graves' *I, Claudius* and *Claudius the God*, while my Philip K. Dick character is based partly on Dick's narrative self-portraits in *Radio Free Albemuth* and *Valis*, and partly on Lawrence Sutin's excellent biography *Divine Invasions*. To Alan Turing I am of course indebted both for his brief appearance and for the concept of the "universal machine" – although he never took the idea quite as literally as I do here. I trust that these historical characters, for whom I have great respect, will forgive my entirely fictional (and sometimes not terribly reverent) appropriation of them.

The original conception of the City of the Saved was influenced as much by quantum mechanic David Deutsch's astonishing book *The Fabric of Reality* as by the ideas of Teilhard de Chardin and St John the Divine.

As well as other books, this volume owes its existence to a large number of people. I have to thank Lawrence Miles and Lars Pearson in particular for commissioning a promising newcomer, and for their tremendous editorial and publisherial work. For earlier career steps, thanks must go to Helen Fayle and Jay Eales (the editors of *Perfect Timing 2* and *Walking in Eternity*), to Jude Simpson and Jane Campion (who edited *Emerge*), and to Lawrence again for *The Book of the War*.

Invaluable creative input has been supplied by Mags L Halliday, Simon Bucher-Jones, Lance Parkin, Jonathan Dennis, Helen Fayle, Helen Angove, J-P Stacey and Rachel Churcher. Many thanks, guys.

In addition to the above (and many others), I'm indebted for kind comments and support over the years to: Simon Davies, Russell Dewhurst, Matthew Graham, Margaret and Terry Hallard, Nick Hallard, Jonathan Hassell, David Howe, Rachel and Max Khanna, Paul Magrs, Kate Orman, Mark Phippen, Jenny and Martin Purser, Jac Rayner, Justin Richards – and all the members of the Jade Pagoda, DougSoc / Niddle, Subway and the erstwhile Offington Park Methodist Church Young People's Fellowship.

Special words of thanks go to my cats Mulder and Scully, my goddaughter Ella, and – above all others and all else – my wife Bea, without whose love this book, and I, would have been drastically diminished.

INTRODUCING THE ALL

introducing the all-new novel...

Faction Paradox

Warlords of Utopia

* Not actual cover art

Adolf Hitler, the Gaol.

In the exact centre of the island was a tower.

It was an ugly concrete stump four storeys high, a brutalist version of a medieval keep. There were tiny slits for windows. There wasn't a door. Around the tower, thorns and weeds had grown into a jungle. The tower held one prisoner.

Surrounding it was an electric fence. And the guards. Millions of strong men and women with the bodies they should have had, unmarked by armband or tattoo, allowed to grow up and grow old. Proud people, many with names like Goldberg, Cohen and Weinstein. Men and women who would never forgive. Men and women who lived in the vast, beautiful community that surrounded the tower, keeping him awake with their laughter, their music, the smell of their food, the sight of their clothes, the sound of their language and their prayers and the cries of their babies. They felt they had a duty to be here. They had always been free to leave, but few had.

On Resurrection Day itself, some had realised that as everyone who had ever lived was in the City, then *he* was here. It had taken longer to hunt him down. Few knew where he'd been found, how he'd been leading his life. Had he tried to disguise himself? Had he proclaimed his name and tried to rally supporters? It didn't matter. He had been brought here, his identity had been confirmed and he had been thrown in the tower that had been prepared for him.

Some of those living in sight of the tower had wondered if they were protecting him from the people of the City, not protecting the City from him. And it was true: the City - the glorious, colourful, polymorphous, diverse City, with uncounted races of people living side by side - was the ultimate negation of the prisoner's creed. The vast, vast majority people of the City didn't care who he was and couldn't comprehend his beliefs, let alone be swayed by his rhetoric. Individuals who'd killed, or wanted to kill, many more people than he had remained at liberty and found themselves powerless. Had imprisoning him marked out as special? Such things were argued about, but the prisoner remained in his tower.

Every day bought requests from individuals, organisations and national groupings who had come up with some way to harm him within the protocols of the City. There were also representations from his supporters, or from civil liberties groups, concerned that his imprisonment was vigilante justice or that no attempt was being made to rehabilitate him. There were historians and psychologists and journalists who wanted to interview him. There were those that just wanted to gawp at or prod the man they'd heard so much about. All of them were turned away.

One man had come here in person. An old Roman, in light armour.

The clerk, a pretty girl with dark hair and eyes, greeted him.

'Your name?'

'Marcus Americanius Scriptor.'

While she dialled up his records and waited for them to appear on her screen, she asked: 'He's after your time. You're a historian?'

'I was,' the old man said. 'May I see him?'

'The prisoner isn't allowed visitors, or to communicate with the outside world. He is allowed to read, but not to write. Oh, that's odd. Your record isn't coming up.'

'It wouldn't.' The Roman didn't elaborate.

He looked out over the city to the tower. The young woman was struck by how solemn his face was. Most people who came all the way out here were sightseers, sensation seekers. Even some of the gaolers treated the prisoner with levity. Mocking him, belittling him.

'Don't you ever want to let him loose?' he asked, finally. 'Let him wander the streets, let his words be drowned out. On another world he was an indifferent, anonymous painter.'

'It sounds like you know that for certain,' she said, before checking herself. 'To answer the question: no. He stays here.'

'I met him,' the Roman told her. 'On a number of occasions.'

She frowned.

'A long story,' he told her. 'I suppose I'm concerned that you torture yourselves by having that monster in your midst.'

The woman had heard many people say such a thing.

'Not a monster. A human being.'

'But the only human being you've locked away for all eternity.'

'The wardens have ruled that he will be freed,' she told him.

Americanius Scriptor seemed surprised. 'When?'

'First he must serve his sentence, then he will be released.'

'When?' he asked again.

'In six million lifetimes,' she told him.

Marcus Americanius Scriptor smiled.

'I'll be waiting for him,' he told her. He turned and headed back to the docks.

Release Date: August 2004.

Faction Paradox
The Book of the WAR
edited by Lawrence Miles

Faction Paradox

mad
norwegian
press

mad norwegian press

info@madnorwegian.com
1309 Carrollton Ave #237
Metairie, LA 70005

Prime Targets: The Unauthorized Guide to *Transformers* TV & Comics, by Lars Pearson...$19.95

Now You Know: The Unauthorized Guide to *G.I. Joe* TV & Comics, by Lars Pearson...$19.95

Dusted: The Ultimate Unauthorized Guide to Buffy the Vampire Slayer, by Lawrence Miles, Lars Pearson & Christa Dickson...$19.95

I, Who 2: The Unauthorized Guide to Doctor Who Novels & Audios, by Lars Pearson ...$19.95

I, Who 3: The Unauthorized Guide to Doctor Who Novels & Audios, by Lars Pearson ...$21.95

ALSO AVAILABLE NOW...

- ***Faction Paradox*: This Town Will Never Let Us Go,** by Lawrence Miles...$14.95 [softcover], $34.95 [signed, limited hardcover]

COMING SOON...

- **Dead Romance [re-release with extras]** by Lawrence Miles
- ***Faction Paradox*: Warring States** by Mags L Halliday
- **I, Who vol 4:** The Unauthorized Guide to Doctor Who Novels & Audios
- **A History of the Universe [Revised]:** The Unauthorized Guide to the Doctor Who Universe by Lance Parkin
- **Prime Targets 2:** The Unauthorized Guide to Japanese Transformers™ TV
- **[Untitled]:** The Unauthorized Guide to Angel

www.madnorwegian.com

ABOUT THE AUTHOR

PHILIP PURSER-HALLARD (M.A. D.Phil.) has contributed to short story anthologies, comedy shows in Oxford and on the Edinburgh Fringe, and *The Book of the War*. He gained his doctorate through studying religious themes in science fiction, and he imagines it probably shows. Phil lives in Bristol in South-West England, where he helps run a college library, drives a girly moped and haunts a disused church. His website (including some material relating to *Of the City of the Saved...*) can be found at www.infinitarian.com.

EDITORIAL STAFF

Series Creator / Editor
Lawrence Miles

Publisher
Lars Pearson

Cover Art
Steve Johnson

Interior Design
Christa Dickson
for Metaphorce Designs
www.metaphorcedesigns.com

Mad Norwegian Press
1309 Carrollton Ave #237
Metairie, LA 70005
info@madnorwegian.com

VISIT US ON THE WEB

www.faction-paradox.com
www.madnorwegian.com